The Amber Spyglass

Philip Pullman

THE GUARDIAN

"If anything *The Amber Spyglass* is more intense than its predecessors. The climaxes are bigger; there is fresh fire in the writing; and there is a wonderful new cast of characters … an exhilarating and poetic mixture of adventure, philosophy, myth and religion enriched by a heady brew of quantum physics."

Julia Eccleshare

◆

THE DAILY TELEGRAPH

"*His Dark Materials* stands revealed as one of the most important children's books of our time."

SF Said

Point

The Amber Spyglass

Philip Pullman

SCHOLASTIC

Scholastic Children's Books,
Euston House, 24 Eversholt Street,
London, NW1 1DB, UK
A division of Scholastic Ltd
London ~ New York ~ Toronto ~ Sydney ~ Auckland
Mexico City ~ New Delhi ~ Hong Kong

First published in the UK by David Fickling Books
An imprint of Scholastic Ltd, 2000

This edition published in Point, 2001

10 digit ISBN 0 439 99358 X
13 digit ISBN 978 0439 99358 6

The lines from *The Third Duino Elegy* by Rainer Maria Rilke are reproduced from
The Selected Poetry of Rainer Maria Rilke, translated by Stephen Mitchell. Copyright
© 1982 by Stephen Mitchell. Reprinted by permission of Random House, Inc.

The lines from *The Ecclesiat* by John Ashbery are reproduced from *River and
Mountains* (New York: Rinehart & Winston, 1967). Copyright © 1962, 1963,
1964, 1966 by John Ashbery. Reprinted by permission of Georges Borchardt, Inc.,
for the author.

Typeset by TW Typesetting, Midsomer Norton, Somerset
Printed and bound in Great Britain by Bookmarque Ltd, Croydon

40 39

O tell of his might, O sing of his grace,
Whose robe is the light, whose canopy space;
His chariots of wrath the deep thunder clouds form,
And dark is his path on the wings of the storm.

Robert Grant, from *Hymns Ancient and Modern*.

O stars,
isn't it from you that the lover's desire for the face
of his beloved arises? Doesn't his secret insight
into her pure features come from the pure constellations?

Rainer Maria Rilke, *The Third Duino Elegy*.
From *The Selected Poetry of Rainer Maria Rilke* (transl. Stephen Mitchell).

Fine vapors escape from whatever is doing the living.
The night is cold and delicate and full of angels
Pounding down the living. The factories are all lit up,
The chime goes unheard.
We are together at last, though far apart.

John Ashbery, *The Ecclesiast*.
From *River and Mountains*.

THE AMBER SPYGLASS is the third and final part of the HIS DARK MATERIALS trilogy, one story in three volumes which was begun in NORTHERN LIGHTS and continued in THE SUBTLE KNIFE. This final volume moves between our own universe and several others.

Contents

1

The Enchanted Sleeper

··· **WHILE**
THE BEASTS OF
PREY, COME FROM
CAVERNS DEEP,
VIEWED THE MAID
ASLEEP ···
WILLIAM BLAKE

*I*n a valley shaded with rhododendrons, close to the snow line, where
a stream milky with melt-water splashed
and where doves and linnets flew among
the immense pines, lay a cave, half-
hidden by the crag above and the stiff
heavy leaves that clustered below.

The woods were full of sound: the stream between the
rocks, the wind among the needles of the pine branches, the
chitter of insects and the cries of small arboreal mammals, as
well as the bird-song; and from time to time a stronger gust
of wind would make one of the branches of a cedar or a fir
move against another and groan like a cello.

It was a place of brilliant sunlight, never undappled; shafts
of lemon-gold brilliance lanced down to the forest floor
between bars and pools of brown-green shade; and the light
was never still, never constant, because drifting mist would
often float among the tree-tops, filtering all the sunlight to a
pearly sheen and brushing every pine-cone with moisture
that glistened when the mist lifted. Sometimes the wetness in
the clouds condensed into tiny drops half-mist and half-rain,
that floated downwards rather than fell, making a soft
rustling patter among the millions of needles.

There was a narrow path beside the stream, which led from a village – little more than a cluster of herdsmen's dwellings – at the foot of the valley, to a half-ruined shrine near the glacier at its head, a place where faded silken flags streamed out in the perpetual winds from the high mountains, and offerings of barley-cakes and dried tea were placed by pious villagers. An odd effect of the light, and the ice, and the vapour enveloped the head of the valley in perpetual rainbows.

The cave lay some way above the path. Many years before, a holy man had lived there, meditating and fasting and praying, and the place was venerated for the sake of his memory. It was thirty feet or so deep, with a dry floor: an ideal den for a bear or a wolf, but the only creatures living in it for years had been birds and bats.

But the form that was crouching inside the entrance, his black eyes watching this way and that, his sharp ears pricked, was neither bird nor bat. The sunlight lay heavy and rich on his lustrous golden fur, and his monkey-hands turned a pine-cone this way and that, snapping off the scales with sharp fingers and scratching out the sweet nuts.

Behind him, just beyond the point where the sunlight reached, Mrs Coulter was heating some water in a small pan over a naphtha stove. Her dæmon uttered a warning murmur, and Mrs Coulter looked up.

Coming along the forest path was a young village girl. Mrs Coulter knew who she was: Ama had been bringing her food for some days now. Mrs Coulter had let it be known when she first arrived that she was a holy woman engaged in meditation and prayer, and under a vow never to speak to a man. Ama was the only person whose visits she accepted.

This time, though, the girl wasn't alone. Her father was

with her, and while Ama climbed up to the cave, he waited a little way off.

Ama came to the cave entrance and bowed.

"My father sends me with prayers for your goodwill," she said.

"Greetings, child," said Mrs Coulter.

The girl was carrying a bundle wrapped in faded cotton, which she laid at Mrs Coulter's feet. Then she held out a little bunch of flowers, a dozen or so anemones bound with a cotton thread, and began to speak in a rapid, nervous voice. Mrs Coulter understood some of the language of these mountain people, but it would never do to let them know how much. So she smiled and motioned to the girl to close her lips, and to watch their two dæmons. The golden monkey was holding out his little black hand, and Ama's butterfly-dæmon was fluttering closer and closer until he settled on a horny forefinger.

The monkey brought him slowly to his ear, and Mrs Coulter felt a tiny stream of understanding flow into her mind, clarifying the girl's words. The villagers were happy for a holy woman, such as herself, to take refuge in the cave, but it was rumoured that she had a companion with her, who was in some way dangerous and powerful.

It was that which made the villagers afraid. Was this other being Mrs Coulter's master, or her servant? Did she mean harm? Why was she there in the first place? Were they going to stay long? Ama conveyed these questions with a thousand misgivings.

A novel answer occurred to Mrs Coulter as the dæmon's understanding filtered into hers. She could tell the truth. Not all of it, naturally, but some. She felt a little quiver of laughter at the idea, but kept it out of her voice as she explained:

"Yes, there is someone else with me. But there is nothing to be afraid of. She is my daughter, and she is under a spell that made her fall asleep. We have come here to hide from the enchanter who put the spell on her, while I try to cure her and keep her from harm. Come and see her, if you like."

Ama was half-soothed by Mrs Coulter's soft voice, and half-afraid still; and the talk of enchanters and spells added to the awe she felt. But the golden monkey was holding her dæmon so gently, and she was curious, besides, so she followed Mrs Coulter into the cave.

Her father on the path below took a step forward, and his crow-dæmon raised her wings once or twice, but he stayed where he was.

Mrs Coulter lit a candle, because the light was fading rapidly, and led Ama to the back of the cave. The little girl's eyes glittered widely in the gloom, and her hands were moving together in a repetitive gesture of finger on thumb, finger on thumb, to ward off danger by confusing the evil spirits.

"You see?" said Mrs Coulter. "She can do no harm. There's nothing to be afraid of."

Ama looked at the figure in the sleeping-bag. It was a girl older than she was, by three or four years, perhaps; and she had hair of a colour Ama had never seen before – a tawny fairness like a lion's. Her lips were pressed tightly together, and she was deeply asleep, there was no doubt about that, for her dæmon lay coiled and unconscious at her throat. He had the form of some creature like a mongoose, but red-gold in colour, and smaller. The golden monkey was tenderly smoothing the fur between the sleeping dæmon's ears, and as Ama looked, the mongoose-creature stirred uneasily and uttered a hoarse little mew. Ama's dæmon, mouse-formed, pressed himself close to Ama's neck and peered fearfully through her hair.

"So you can tell your father what you've seen," Mrs Coulter went on. "No evil spirit. Just my daughter, asleep under a spell, and in my care. But please, Ama, tell your father that this must be a secret. No one but you two must know Lyra is here. If the enchanter knew where she was, he would seek her out and destroy her, and me, and everything nearby. So hush! Tell your father, and no one else."

She knelt beside Lyra and smoothed the damp hair back from the sleeping face before bending low to kiss her daughter's cheek. Then she looked up with sad and loving eyes, and smiled at Ama with such brave compassion that the little girl felt tears fill her gaze.

Mrs Coulter took Ama's hand as they went back to the cave entrance, and saw the girl's father watching anxiously from below. The woman put her hands together and bowed to him, and he responded with relief as his daughter, having bowed both to Mrs Coulter and to the enchanted sleeper, turned and scampered down the slope in the twilight. Father and daughter bowed once more to the cave, and then set off, to vanish among the gloom of the heavy rhododendrons.

Mrs Coulter turned back to the water on her stove, which was nearly at the boil.

Crouching down, she crumbled some dried leaves into it, two pinches from this bag, one from that, and added three drops of a pale yellow oil. She stirred it briskly, counting in her head till five minutes had gone by. Then she took the pan off the stove, and sat down to wait for the liquid to cool.

Around her there lay some of the equipment from the camp by the blue lake where Sir Charles Latrom had died: a sleeping-bag, a rucksack with changes of clothes and washing equipment, and so on. There was also a case of canvas with a tough wooden frame, lined with kapok, containing various instruments; and there was a pistol in a holster.

The decoction cooled rapidly in the thin air, and as soon as it was at blood-heat she poured it carefully into a metal beaker and carried it to the rear of the cave. The monkey-dæmon dropped his pine-cone and came with her.

Mrs Coulter placed the beaker carefully on a low rock, and knelt beside the sleeping Lyra. The golden monkey crouched on her other side, ready to seize Pantalaimon if he woke up.

Lyra's hair was damp, and her eyes moved behind their closed lids. She was beginning to stir: Mrs Coulter had felt her eyelashes flutter when she'd kissed her, and knew she didn't have long before Lyra woke up altogether.

She slipped a hand under the girl's head, and with the other lifted the damp strands of hair off her forehead. Lyra's lips parted, and she moaned softly; Pantalaimon moved a little closer to her breast. The golden monkey's eyes never left Lyra's dæmon, and his little black fingers twitched at the edge of the sleeping-bag.

A look from Mrs Coulter, and he let go and moved back a hand's breadth. The woman gently lifted her daughter so that her shoulders were off the ground and her head lolled, and then Lyra caught her breath and her eyes half-opened, fluttering, heavy.

"Roger," she murmured. "Roger ... where are you ... I can't see..."

"Ssh," her mother whispered, "ssh, my darling, drink this."

Holding the beaker in Lyra's mouth, she tilted it to let a drop moisten the girl's lips. Lyra's tongue sensed it and moved to lick them, and then Mrs Coulter let a little more of the liquid trickle into her mouth, very carefully, letting her swallow each sip before allowing her more.

It took several minutes, but eventually the beaker was empty, and Mrs Coulter laid her daughter down again. As soon as Lyra's head lay on the ground, Pantalaimon moved back around her throat. His red-gold fur was as damp as her hair. They were deeply asleep again.

The golden monkey picked his way lightly to the mouth of the cave and sat once more watching the path. Mrs Coulter dipped a flannel in a basin of cold water and mopped Lyra's face, and then unfastened the sleeping-bag and washed her arms and neck and shoulders, because Lyra was hot. Then her mother took a comb and gently teased out the tangles in Lyra's hair, smoothing it back from her forehead, parting it neatly.

She left the sleeping-bag open so the girl could cool down, and unfolded the bundle that Ama had brought: some flat loaves of bread, a cake of compressed tea, some sticky rice wrapped in a large leaf. It was time to build the fire. The chill of the mountains was fierce at night. Working methodically, she shaved some dry tinder, set the fire and struck a match. That was something else to think of: the matches were running out, and so was the naphtha for the stove; she must keep the fire alight day and night from now on.

Her dæmon was discontented. He didn't like what she was doing here in the cave, and when he tried to express his concern she brushed him away. He turned his back, contempt in every line of his body as he flicked the scales from his pine-cone out into the dark. She took no notice, but worked steadily and skilfully to build up the fire and set the pan to heat some water for tea.

Nevertheless, his scepticism affected her, and as she

crumbled the dark grey tea-brick into the water, she wondered what in the world she thought she was doing, and whether she had gone mad, and over and over again, what would happen when the church found out. The golden monkey was right. She wasn't only hiding Lyra: she was hiding her own eyes.

Out of the dark the little boy came, hopeful and frightened, whispering over and over:

"Lyra – Lyra – Lyra..."

Behind him there were other figures, even more shadowy than he was, even more silent. They seemed to be of the same company and of the same kind, but they had no faces that were visible and no voices that spoke; and his voice never rose above a whisper, and his face was shaded and blurred like something half-forgotten.

"Lyra ... Lyra..."

Where were they?

On a great plain where no light shone from the iron-dark sky, and where a mist obscured the horizon on every side. The ground was bare earth, beaten flat by the pressure of millions of feet, even though those feet had less weight than feathers; so it must have been time that pressed it flat, even though time had been stilled in this place; so it must have been the way things were. This was the end of all places and the last of all worlds.

"Lyra..."

Why were they there?

They were imprisoned. Someone had committed a crime, though no one knew what it was, or who had done it, or what authority sat in judgement.

Why did the little boy keep calling Lyra's name?

Hope.

Who were they?

Ghosts.

And Lyra couldn't touch them, no matter how she tried. Her baffled hands moved through and through, and still the little boy stood there pleading.

"Roger," she said, but her voice came out in a whisper, "oh, Roger, where are you? What is this place?"

He said, "It's the world of the dead, Lyra — I dunno what to do — I dunno if I'm here for ever, and I dunno if I done bad things or what, because I tried to be good, but I hate it, I'm scared of it all, I hate it —"

And Lyra said, "I

2
Balthamos and Baruch

THEN A SPIRIT
PASSED BEFORE
MY FACE;
THE HAIR OF
MY FLESH
STOOD UP.
THE BOOK OF JOB

"*B*e quiet," said Will. "Just be quiet. Don't disturb me."

It was just after Lyra had been taken, just after Will had come down from the mountaintop, just after the witch had killed his father. Will lit the little tin lantern he'd taken from his father's pack, using the dry matches that he'd found with it, and crouched in the lee of the rock to open Lyra's rucksack.

He felt inside with his good hand, and found the heavy velvet-wrapped alethiometer. It glittered in the lantern-light, and he held it out to the two shapes that stood beside him, the shapes who called themselves angels.

"Can you read this?" he said.

"No," said a voice. "Come with us. You must come. Come now to Lord Asriel."

"Who made you follow my father? You said he didn't know you were following him. But he did," Will said fiercely. "He told me to expect you. He knew more than you thought. Who sent you?"

"No one sent us. Ourselves only," came the voice. "We want to serve Lord Asriel. And the dead man, what did *he* want you to do with the knife?"

Will had to hesitate.

"He said I should take it to Lord Asriel," he said.

"Then come with us."

"No. Not till I've found Lyra."

He folded the velvet over the alethiometer and put it into his rucksack. Securing it, he swung his father's heavy cloak around him against the rain and crouched where he was, looking steadily at the two shadows.

"Do you tell the truth?" he said.

"Yes."

"Then are you stronger than human beings, or weaker?"

"Weaker. You have true flesh, we have not. Still, you must come with us."

"No. If I'm stronger, you have to obey me. Besides, I have the knife. So I can command you: help me find Lyra. I don't care how long it takes, I'll find her first and *then* I'll go to Lord Asriel."

The two figures were silent for several seconds. Then they drifted away and spoke together, though Will could hear nothing of what they said.

Finally they came close again, and he heard:

"Very well. You are making a mistake, though you give us no choice. We shall help you find this child."

Will tried to pierce the darkness and see them more clearly, but the rain filled his eyes.

"Come closer so I can see you," he said.

They approached, but seemed to become even more obscure.

"Shall I see you better in daylight?"

"No, worse. We are not of a high order among angels."

"Well, if I can't see you, no one else will either, so you can stay hidden. Go and see if you can find out where Lyra's gone. She surely can't be far away. There was a woman – she'll be with her – the woman took her. Go and search, and come back and tell me what you see."

The angels rose up into the stormy air and vanished. Will felt a great sullen heaviness settle over him; he'd had little strength left before the fight with his father, and now he was nearly finished. All he wanted to do was close his eyes, which were so heavy and so sore with weeping.

He tugged the cloak over his head, clutched the rucksack to his breast, and fell asleep in a moment.

"Nowhere," said a voice.

Will heard it in the depths of sleep and struggled to wake. Eventually (and it took most of a minute, because he was so profoundly unconscious) he managed to open his eyes to the bright morning in front of him.

"Where are you?" he said.

"Beside you," said the angel. "This way."

The sun was newly risen, and the rocks and the lichens and mosses on them shone crisp and brilliant in the morning light, but nowhere could he see a figure.

"I said we would be harder to see in daylight," the voice went on. "You will see us best at half-light, at dusk or dawn; next best in darkness; least of all in the sunshine. My companion and I searched further down the mountain, and found neither woman nor child. But there is a lake of blue water where she must have camped. There is a dead man there, and a witch eaten by a Spectre."

"A dead man? What does he look like?"

"He was in his sixties. Fleshy and smooth-skinned. Silver-grey hair. Dressed in expensive clothes, and with traces of a heavy scent around him."

"Sir Charles," said Will. "That's who it is. Mrs Coulter must have killed him. Well, that's something good, at least."

"She left traces. My companion has followed them, and he will return when he's found out where she went. I shall stay with you."

Will got to his feet and looked around. The storm had cleared the air, and the morning was fresh and clean, which only made the scene around him more distressing; for nearby lay the bodies of several of the witches who had escorted him and Lyra towards the meeting with his father. Already a brutal-beaked carrion crow was tearing at the face of one of them, and Will could see a bigger bird circling above, as if choosing the richest feast.

Will looked at each of the bodies in turn, but none of them was Serafina Pekkala, the queen of the witch-clan, Lyra's particular friend. Then he remembered: hadn't she left suddenly on another errand not long before the evening?

So she might still be alive. The thought cheered him, and he scanned the horizon for any sign of her, but found nothing but the blue air and the sharp rock in every direction he looked.

"Where are you?" he said to the angel.

"Beside you," came the voice, "as always."

Will looked to his left, where the voice was, but saw nothing.

"So no one can see you. Could anyone else hear you as well as me?"

"Not if I whisper," said the angel, tartly.

"What is your name? Do you have names?"

"Yes, we do. My name is Balthamos. My companion is Baruch."

Will considered what to do. When you choose one way out

of many, all the ways you don't take are snuffed out like candles, as if they'd never existed. At the moment all Will's choices existed at once. But to keep them all in existence meant doing nothing. He had to choose, after all.

"We'll go back down the mountain," he said. "We'll go to that lake. There might be something there I can use. And I'm getting thirsty anyway. I'll take the way I think it is and you can guide me if I go wrong."

It was only when he'd been walking for several minutes down the pathless, rocky slope that Will realized his hand wasn't hurting. In fact he hadn't thought of his wound since he woke up.

He stopped and looked at the rough cloth that his father had bound around it after their fight. It was greasy with the ointment he'd spread on it, but there was not a sign of blood; and after the incessant bleeding he'd undergone since the fingers had been lost, this was so welcome that he felt his heart leap almost with joy.

He moved his fingers experimentally. True, the wounds still hurt, but with a different quality of pain: not the deep life-sapping ache of the day before, but a smaller, duller sensation. It felt as if it were healing. His father had done that. The witches' spell had failed, but his father had healed him.

He moved on down the slope, cheered.

It took three hours, and several words of guidance, before he came to the little blue lake. By the time he reached it he was parched with thirst, and in the baking sun the cloak was heavy and hot; though when he took it off he missed its cover, for his bare arms and neck were burning. He dropped cloak and rucksack and ran the last few yards to the water, to fall on his face and swallow mouthful after freezing mouthful. It was so cold that it made his teeth and skull ache.

Once he'd slaked the thirst he sat up and looked around. He'd been in no condition to notice things the day before, but now he saw more clearly the intense colour of the water, and heard the strident insect noises from all around.

"Balthamos?"

"Always here."

"Where is the dead man?"

"Beyond the high rock on your right."

"Are there any Spectres around?"

"No, none."

Will took up his rucksack and cloak and made his way along the edge of the lake and up on to the rock Balthamos had pointed out.

Beyond it a little camp had been set up, with five or six tents and the remains of cooking fires. Will moved down warily in case there was someone still alive and hiding.

But the silence was profound, with the insect-scrapings only scratching at the surface of it. The tents were still, the water was placid, with the ripples still drifting slowly out from where he'd been drinking. A flicker of green movement near his foot made him start briefly, but it was only a tiny lizard.

The tents were made of camouflage material, which only made them stand out more among the dull red rocks. He looked in the first and found it empty. So was the second, but in the third he found something valuable: a mess-tin and a box of matches. There was also a strip of some dark substance as long and as thick as his forearm. At first he thought it was leather, but in the sunlight he saw it clearly to be dried meat.

Well, he had a knife, after all. He cut a thin sliver and found it chewy and very slightly salty, but full of good flavour. He put the meat and the matches together with the mess-tin into his rucksack and searched the other tents, but found them empty.

He left the largest till last.

"Is that where the dead man is?" he said to the air.

"Yes," said Balthamos. "He has been poisoned."

Will walked carefully around to the entrance, which faced the lake. Sprawled beside an overturned canvas chair was the body of the man known in Will's world as Sir Charles Latrom, and in Lyra's as Lord Boreal, the man who stole her alethiometer, which theft in turn led Will to the subtle knife itself. Sir Charles had been smooth, dishonest, and powerful, and now he was dead. His face was distorted unpleasantly, and Will didn't want to look at it, but a glance inside the tent showed that there were plenty of things to steal, so he stepped over the body to look more closely.

His father, the soldier, the explorer, would have known exactly what to take. Will had to guess. He took a small magnifying glass in a steel case, because he could use it to light fires and save his matches; a reel of tough twine; an alloy canteen for water, much lighter than the goatskin flask he had been carrying, and a small tin cup; a small pair of binoculars; a roll of gold coins the size of a man's thumb, wrapped in paper; a first-aid kit; water purifying tablets; a packet of coffee; three packs of compressed dried fruit; a bag of oatmeal biscuits; six bars of Kendal Mint Cake; a packet of fish-hooks and nylon line; and finally, a notebook and a couple of pencils, and a small electric torch.

He packed it all in his rucksack, cut another sliver of meat, filled his belly and then his canteen from the lake, and said to Balthamos:

"Do you think I need anything else?"

"You could do with some sense," came the reply. "Some

faculty to enable you to recognize wisdom and incline you to respect and obey it."

"Are you wise?"

"Much more so than you."

"Well, you see, I can't tell. Are you a man? You sound like a man."

"Baruch was a man. I was not. Now he is angelic."

"So —" Will stopped what he was doing, which was arranging his rucksack so the heaviest objects were in the bottom, and tried to see the angel. There was nothing there to see. "So he was a man," he went on, "and then... Do people become angels when they die? Is that what happens?"

"Not always. Not in the vast majority of cases... Very rarely."

"When was he alive, then?"

"Four thousand years ago, more or less. I am much older."

"And did he live in my world? Or Lyra's? Or this one?"

"In yours. But there are myriads of worlds. You know that."

"But how do people become angels?"

"What is the point of this metaphysical speculation?"

"I just want to know."

"Better to stick to your task. You have plundered this dead man's property, you have all the toys you need to keep you alive; now may we move on?"

"When I know which way to go."

"Whichever way we go, Baruch will find us."

"Then he'll still find us if we stay here. I've got a couple more things to do."

Will sat down where he couldn't see Sir Charles's body and ate three squares of the Kendal Mint Cake. It was wonderful how refreshed and strengthened he felt as the food began to nourish him. Then he looked at the alethiometer again. The thirty-six little pictures painted on ivory were each perfectly clear: there was no doubt that this was a baby, that a puppet, this a loaf of bread, and so on. It was what they meant that was obscure.

"How did Lyra read this?" he said to Balthamos.

"Quite possibly she made it up. Those who use these instruments have studied for many years, and even then they can only understand them with the help of many books of reference."

"She wasn't making it up. She read it truly. She told me things she could never have known otherwise."

"Then it is as much of a mystery to me, I assure you," said the angel.

Looking at the alethiometer, Will remembered something Lyra had said about reading it: something about the state of mind she had to be in to make it work. It had helped him, in turn, to feel the subtleties of the silver blade.

Feeling curious, he took out the knife and cut a small window in front of where he was sitting. Through it he saw nothing but blue air, but below, far below, was a landscape of trees and fields: his own world, without a doubt.

So mountains in this world didn't correspond to mountains in his. He closed the window, using his left hand for the first time. The joy of being able to use it again!

Then an idea came to him so suddenly it felt like an electric shock.

If there were myriads of worlds, why did the knife only open windows between this one and his own?

Surely it should cut into any of them.

He held it up again, letting his mind flow along to the very tip of the blade as Giacomo Paradisi had told him, until his consciousness nestled among the atoms themselves, and he felt every tiny snag and ripple in the air.

Instead of cutting as soon as he felt the first little halt, as he usually did, he let the knife move on to another and another. It was like tracing a row of stitches while pressing so softly that none of them was harmed.

"What are you doing?" said the voice from the air, bringing him back.

"Exploring," said Will. "Be quiet and keep out of the way. If you come near this you'll get cut, and if I can't see you, I can't avoid you."

Balthamos made a sound of muted discontent. Will held out the knife again and felt for those tiny halts and hesitations. There were far more of them than he'd thought. And as he felt them without the need to cut through at once, he found that they each had a different quality: this one was hard and definite, that one cloudy; a third was slippery, a fourth brittle and frail...

But among them all there were some he felt more easily than others, and, already knowing the answer, he cut one through to be sure: his own world again.

He closed it up and felt with the knife-tip for a snag with a different quality. He found one that was elastic and resistant, and let the knife feel its way through.

And yes! The world he saw through that window was not his own: the ground was closer here, and the landscape was not green fields and hedges but a desert of rolling dunes.

He closed it and opened another: the smoke-laden air over an industrial city, with a line of chained and sullen workers trudging into a factory.

He closed that one too and came back to himself. He felt a little dizzy. For the first time he understood some of the true power of the knife, and laid it very carefully on the rock in front of him.

"Are you going to stay here all day?" said Balthamos.

"I'm thinking. You can only move easily from one world to another if the ground's in the same place. And maybe there are places where it is, and maybe that's where a lot of cutting-through happens... And you'd have to know what your own world felt like with the point or you might never get back. You'd be lost for ever."

"Indeed. But may we –"

"And you'd have to know which world had the ground in the same place or there wouldn't be any point in opening it," said Will, as much to himself as to the angel. "So it's not as easy as I thought. We were just lucky in Oxford and Cittàgazze, maybe. But I'll just..."

He picked up the knife again. As well as the clear and obvious feeling he got when he touched a point that would open to his own world, there had been another kind of sensation he'd touched more than once: a quality of resonance, like the feeling of striking a heavy wooden drum, except of course that it came, like every other one, in the tiniest movement through the empty air.

There it was. He moved away and felt somewhere else: there it was again.

He cut through, and found that his guess was right. The resonance meant that the ground in the world he'd opened was in the same place as this one. He found himself looking at a grassy upland meadow under an overcast sky, in which a herd of placid beasts was grazing – animals such as he'd never seen before – creatures the size of bison, with wide horns and shaggy blue fur and a crest of stiff hair along their backs.

He stepped through. The nearest animal looked up incuriously and then turned back to the grass. Leaving the window open, Will, in the other-world meadow, felt with the knife-point for the familiar snags, and tried them.

Yes, he could open his own world from this one, and he was still high above the farms and hedges; and yes, he could easily find the solid resonance that meant the Cittàgazze-world he'd just left.

With a deep sense of relief, Will went back to the camp by the lake, closing everything behind him. Now he could find his way home; now he would not get lost; now he could hide when he needed to, and move about safely.

With every increase in his knowledge came a gain in strength. He sheathed the knife at his waist and swung the rucksack over his shoulder.

"Well, are you ready now?" said that sarcastic voice.

"Yes. I'll explain if you like, but you don't seem very interested."

"Oh, I find whatever you do a source of perpetual fascination. But never mind me. What are you going to say to these people who are coming?"

Will looked around, startled. Further down the trail – a long way down – there was a line of travellers with packhorses, making their way steadily up towards the lake. They hadn't seen him yet, but if he stayed where he was, they would soon.

Will gathered up his father's cloak, which he'd laid over a rock in the sun. It weighed much less now it was dry. He looked around: there was nothing else he could carry.

"Let's go further on," he said.

He would have liked to re-tie the bandage, but it could wait. He set off along the edge of the lake, away from the travellers, and the angel followed him, invisible in the bright air.

Much later that day they came down from the bare mountains

on to a spur covered in grass and dwarf rhododendrons. Will was aching for rest, and soon, he decided, he'd stop.

He'd heard little from the angel. From time to time Balthamos had said, "Not that way," or, "There is an easier path to the left," and he'd accepted the advice; but really he was moving for the sake of moving, and to keep away from those travellers, because until the other angel came back with more news, he might as well have stayed where they were.

Now the sun was setting, he thought he could see his strange companion. The outline of a man seemed to quiver in the light, and the air was thicker inside it.

"Balthamos?" he said. "I want to find a stream. Is there one nearby?"

"There is a spring half-way down the slope," said the angel, "just above those trees."

"Thank you," said Will.

He found the spring and drank deeply, filling his canteen. But before he could go on down to the little wood, there came an exclamation from Balthamos, and Will turned to see his outline dart across the slope towards – what? The angel was visible only as a flicker of movement, and Will could see him better when he didn't look at him directly; but he seemed to pause, and listen, and then launch himself into the air to skim back swiftly to Will.

"Here!" he said, and his voice was free of disapproval and sarcasm for once. "Baruch came this way! And there is one of those windows, almost invisible. Come – come. Come now."

Will followed eagerly, his weariness forgotten. The window, he saw when he reached it, opened on to a dim tundra-like landscape that was flatter than the mountains in the Cittàgazze world, and colder, with an overcast sky. He went through, and Balthamos followed him at once.

"Which world is this?" Will said.

"The girl's own world. This is where they came through. Baruch has gone ahead to follow them."

"How do you know where he is? Do you read his mind?"

"Of course I read his mind. Wherever he goes, my heart goes with him; we feel as one, though we are two."

Will looked around. There was no sign of human life, and the chill in the air was increasing by the minute as the light failed.

"I don't want to sleep here," he said. "We'll stay in the Ci'gazze world for the night and come through in the morning. At least there's wood back there, and I can make a fire. And now I know what her world feels like, I can find it with the knife... Oh, Balthamos? Can you take any other shape?"

"Why would I wish to do that?"

"In this world, human beings have dæmons, and if I go about without one, they'll be suspicious. Lyra was frightened of me at first because of that. So if we're going to travel in her world, you'll have to pretend to be my dæmon, and take the shape of some animal. A bird, maybe. Then you could fly, at least."

"Oh, how tedious."

"Can you, though?"

"I *could*..."

"Do it now, then. Let me see."

The form of the angel seemed to condense and swirl into a little vortex in mid-air, and then a blackbird swooped down on to the grass at Will's feet.

"Fly to my shoulder," said Will.

The bird did so, and then spoke in the angel's familiar acid tone:

"I shall only do this when it's absolutely necessary. It's unspeakably humiliating."

"Too bad," said Will. "Whenever we see people, in this world, you become a bird. There's no point in fussing or arguing. Just do it."

The blackbird flew off his shoulder and vanished in mid-air, and there was the angel again, sulking in the half-light. Before they went back through, Will looked all around, sniffing the air, taking the measure of the world where Lyra was captive.

"Where is your companion now?" he said.

"Following the woman south."

"Then we shall go that way too, in the morning."

Next day, Will walked for hours, and saw no one. The country consisted for the most part of low hills covered in short dry grass, and whenever he found himself on any sort of high point he looked all round for signs of human habitation, but found none. The only variation in the dusty brown-green emptiness was a distant smudge of darker green, which he made for because Balthamos said it was a forest and there was a river there, which led south. When the sun was at its height, he tried and failed to sleep among some low bushes; and as the evening approached, he was footsore and weary.

"Slow progress," said Balthamos sourly.

"I can't help that," said Will. "If you can't say anything useful, don't speak at all."

By the time he reached the edge of the forest the sun was low and the air heavy with pollen, so much so that he sneezed several times, startling a bird that flew up shrieking from somewhere nearby.

"That was the first living thing I've seen today," Will said.

"Where are you going to camp?" said Balthamos.

The angel was occasionally visible now in the long shadows of the trees. What Will could see of his expression was petulant.

Will said, "I'll have to stop here somewhere. You could help look for a good spot. I can hear a stream – see if you can find it."

The angel disappeared. Will trudged on, through the low clumps of heather and bog myrtle, wishing there was such a thing as a path for his feet to follow, and eyeing the light with apprehension: he must choose where to stop soon, or the dark would force him to stop without a choice.

"Left," said Balthamos, an arm's length away. "A stream and a dead tree for firewood. This way…"

Will followed the angel's voice, and soon found the spot he described. A stream splashed swiftly between mossy rocks, and disappeared over a lip into a narrow little chasm, dark under the over-arching trees. Beside the stream, a grassy bank extended a little way back to bushes and undergrowth.

Before he let himself rest, he set about collecting wood, and soon came across a circle of charred stones in the grass, where someone else had made a fire long before. He gathered a pile of twigs and heavier branches and with the knife cut them to a useful length before trying to get them lit. He didn't know the best way to go about it, and wasted several matches before he managed to coax the flames into life.

The angel watched with a kind of weary patience.

Once the fire was going, Will ate two oatmeal biscuits, some dried meat, and some Kendal Mint Cake, washing it down with gulps of cold water. Balthamos sat nearby, silent, and finally Will said:

"Are you going to watch me all the time? I'm not going anywhere."

"I'm waiting for Baruch. He will come back soon, and then I shall ignore you, if you like."

"Would you like some food?"

Balthamos moved slightly: he was tempted.

"I mean, I don't know if you eat at all," Will said, "but if you'd like something, you're welcome."

"What is that..." said the angel fastidiously, indicating the Kendal Mint Cake.

"Mostly sugar, I think, and peppermint. Here."

Will broke off a square and held it out. Balthamos inclined his head and sniffed. Then he picked it up, his fingers light and cool against Will's palm.

"I think this will nourish me," he said. "One piece is quite enough, thank you."

He sat and nibbled quietly. Will found that if he looked at the fire, with the angel just at the edge of his vision, he had a much stronger impression of him.

"Where is Baruch?" he said. "Can he communicate with you?"

"I feel that he is close. He'll be here very soon. When he returns, we shall talk. Talking is best."

And barely ten minutes later the soft sound of wingbeats came to their ears, and Balthamos stood up eagerly. The next moment, the two angels were embracing, and Will, gazing into the flames, saw their mutual affection. More than affection: they loved each other with a passion.

Baruch sat down beside his companion, and Will stirred the fire, so that a cloud of smoke drifted past the two of them. It had the effect of outlining their bodies so that he could see them both clearly for the first time. Balthamos was slender; his narrow wings were folded elegantly behind his shoulders, and his face bore an expression that mingled haughty disdain with a tender, ardent sympathy, as if he would love all things if only his nature could let him forget their defects. But he saw no defects in Baruch, that was clear. Baruch seemed younger, as Balthamos had said he was, and was more powerfully built, his wings snow-white and massive. He had a simpler nature; he looked up to Balthamos as to the fount of all knowledge and joy. Will found himself intrigued and moved by their love for each other.

"Did you find out where Lyra is?" he said, impatient for news.

"Yes," said Baruch. "There is a Himalayan valley, very high up, near a glacier where the light is turned into rainbows by the ice. I shall draw you a map in the soil, so you don't mistake it. The girl is captive in a cave among the trees, kept asleep by the woman."

"Asleep? And the woman's alone? No soldiers with her?"

"Alone, yes. In hiding."

"And Lyra's not harmed?"

"No. Just asleep, and dreaming. Let me show you where they are."

With his pale finger, Baruch traced a map in the bare soil beside the fire. Will took his notebook and copied it exactly. It showed a glacier with a curious serpentine shape, flowing down between three almost identical mountain peaks.

"Now," said the angel, "we go closer. The valley with the cave runs down from the left side of the glacier, and a river of melt-water runs through it. The head of the valley is here…"

He drew another map, and Will copied that; and then a third, getting closer in each time, so that Will felt he could find his way there without difficulty – provided that he'd crossed the four or five thousand miles between the tundra and the mountains. The knife was good for cutting between worlds, but it couldn't abolish distance within them.

"There is a shrine near the glacier," Baruch ended by saying, "with red silk banners half-torn by the winds. And a young girl brings food to the cave. They think the woman is a saint who will bless them if they look after her needs."

"Do they," said Will. "And she's *hiding*... That's what I don't understand. Hiding from the church?"

"It seems so."

Will folded the maps carefully away. He had set the tin cup on the stones at the edge of the fire to heat some water, and now he trickled some powdered coffee into it, stirring it with a stick, and wrapped his hand in a handkerchief before picking it up to drink.

A burning stick settled in the fire; a night bird called.

Suddenly, for no reason Will could see, both angels looked up and in the same direction. He followed their gaze, but saw nothing. He had seen his cat do this once: look up alert from her half-sleep, and watch something or someone invisible come into the room and walk across. That had made his hair stand up, and so did this.

"Put out the fire," Balthamos whispered.

Will scooped up some earth with his good hand and doused the flames. At once the cold struck into his bones, and he began to shiver. He pulled the cloak around himself and looked up again.

And now there was something to see: above the clouds a shape was glowing, and it was not the moon.

He heard Baruch murmur, "The Chariot? Could it be?"

"What is it?" Will whispered.

Baruch leaned close and whispered back, "They know we're here. They've found us. Will, take your knife and —"

Before he could finish, something hurtled out of the sky and crashed into Balthamos. In a fraction of a second Baruch had leapt on it, and Balthamos was twisting to free his wings. The three beings fought this way and that in the dimness, like great wasps caught in a mighty spider's web, making no sound: all Will could hear was the breaking twigs and the brushing leaves as they struggled together.

He couldn't use the knife: they were all moving too quickly. Instead, he took the electric torch from the rucksack and switched it on.

None of them expected that. The attacker threw up his wings, Balthamos flung his arm across his eyes, and only Baruch had the presence of mind to hold on. But Will could see what it was, this enemy: another angel, much bigger and stronger than they were, and Baruch's hand was clamped over his mouth.

"Will!" cried Balthamos. "The knife – cut a way out –"

And at the same moment the attacker tore himself free of Baruch's hands, and cried:

"*Lord Regent! I have them!*"

His voice made Will's head ring; he had never heard such a cry. And a moment later the angel would have sprung into the air, but Will dropped his torch and leapt forward. He had killed a cliff-ghast, but using the knife on a being shaped like himself was much harder. Nevertheless, he gathered the great beating wings into his arms and slashed again and again at the feathers until the air was filled with whirling flakes of white, remembering even in the sweep of violent sensations the words of Balthamos: *You have true flesh, we have not.* Human beings were stronger than angels, and it was true: he was bearing the angel down to the ground.

The attacker was still shouting in that ear-splitting voice:

"*Lord Regent! To me, to me!*"

Will managed to glance upwards, and saw the clouds stirring and swirling, and that gleam – something immense – growing more powerful, as if the clouds themselves were becoming luminous with energy, like plasma.

Balthamos cried, "Will – come away and cut through, before he comes –"

But the angel was struggling hard, and now he had one wing free and he was forcing himself up from the ground, and Will had to hang on or lose him entirely. Baruch sprang to help him, and forced the attacker's head back and back.

"No!" cried Balthamos again. "No! No!"

He hurled himself at Will, shaking his arm, his shoulder, his hands, and the attacker was trying to shout again but Baruch's hand was over his mouth. From above there came a deep tremor, like a mighty dynamo, almost too low to hear, though it shook the very atoms of the air and jolted the marrow in Will's bones.

"He's coming –" Balthamos said, almost sobbing, and now Will did catch some of his fear. "Please, please, Will –"

Will looked up.

The clouds were parting, and through the dark gap a figure was speeding down: small at first, but as it came closer second by second the form became bigger and more imposing. He was making straight for them, with unmistakable malevolence; Will was sure he could even see his eyes.

"Will, you must," said Baruch urgently.

Will stood up, meaning to say, "Hold him tight," but even as the words came to his mind, the angel sagged against the ground, dissolving and spreading out like mist, and then he was gone. Will looked around, feeling foolish and sick.

"Did I kill him?" he said shakily.

"You had to," said Baruch. "But now –"

"I hate this," said Will passionately, "truly, truly, I hate this killing! When will it stop?"

"We must go," said Balthamos faintly. "Quickly, Will – quickly – please –"

They were both mortally afraid.

Will felt in the air with the tip of the knife: any world, out of this one. He cut swiftly, and looked up: that other angel from the sky was only seconds away, and his expression was terrifying. Even from that distance, and even in that urgent second or so, Will felt himself searched and scoured from one end of his being to the other by some vast, brutal, and merciless intellect.

And what was more, he had a spear – he was raising it to hurl –

And in the moment it took the angel to check his flight and turn upright and pull back his arm to fling the weapon, Will followed Baruch and Balthamos through and closed the window behind him. As his fingers pressed the last inch together, he felt a shock of air – but it was gone, he was safe: it was the spear that would have passed through him in that other world.

They were on a sandy beach under a brilliant moon. Giant fern-like trees grew some way inland; low dunes extended for miles along the shore. It was hot and humid.

"Who was that?" said Will, trembling, facing the two angels.

"That was Metatron," said Balthamos. "You should have –"

"Metatron? Who's he? Why did he attack? And don't lie to me."

"We must tell him," said Baruch to his companion. "You should have done already."

"Yes, I should," Balthamos agreed, "but I was cross with him, and anxious for you."

"Tell me now then," said Will. "And remember, it's no good telling me what I should do – none of it matters to me, none. Only Lyra matters, and my mother. And *that*," he added to Balthamos, "is the point of all this metaphysical speculation, as you called it."

Baruch said, "I think we should tell you our information. Will, this is why we two have been seeking you, and why we must take you to Lord Asriel. We discovered a secret of the kingdom – of the Authority's world – and we must share it with him. Are we safe here?" he added, looking around. "There is no way through?"

"This is a different world. A different universe."

The sand they stood on was soft, and the slope of the dune nearby was inviting. They could see for miles in the moonlight; they were utterly alone.

"Tell me, then," said Will. "Tell me about Metatron, and what this secret is. Why did that angel call him Regent? And what is the Authority? Is he God?"

He sat down, and the two angels, their forms clearer in the moonlight than he had ever seen them before, sat with him.

Balthamos said quietly, "The Authority, God, the Creator, the Lord, Yahweh, El, Adonai, the King, the Father, the Almighty – those were all names he gave himself. He was never the creator. He was an angel like ourselves – the first angel, true, the most powerful, but he was formed of Dust as we are, and Dust is only a name for what happens when matter begins to understand itself. Matter loves matter. It seeks to know more about itself, and Dust is formed. The first angels condensed out of Dust, and the Authority was the first of all. He told those who came after him that he had created them, but it was a lie. One of those who came later was wiser than he was, and she found out the truth, so he banished her. We serve her still. And the Authority still reigns in the kingdom, and Metatron is his Regent.

"But as for what we discovered in the Clouded Mountain, we can't tell you the heart of it. We swore to each other that the first to hear should be Lord Asriel himself."

"Then tell me what you can. Don't keep me in the dark."

"We found our way into the Clouded Mountain," said Baruch, and at once went on: "I'm sorry; we use these terms too easily. It's sometimes called the Chariot. It's not fixed, you see; it moves from place to place. Wherever it goes, there is the heart of the kingdom, his citadel, his palace. When the Authority was young, it wasn't surrounded by clouds, but as time passed, he gathered them around him more and more thickly. No one has seen the summit for thousands of years. So his citadel is known now as the Clouded Mountain."

"What did you find there?"

"The Authority himself dwells in a chamber at the heart of the mountain. We couldn't get close, although we saw him. His power –"

"He has delegated much of his power," Balthamos interrupted, "to Metatron, as I was saying. You've seen what he's like. We escaped from him before, and now he's seen us again, and what is more, he's seen you, and he's seen the knife. I did say –"

"Balthamos," said Baruch gently, "don't chide Will. We need his help, and he can't be blamed for not knowing what it took *us* so long to find out."

Balthamos looked away.

Will said, "So you're not going to tell me this secret of yours? All right. Tell me this instead: what happens when we die?"

Balthamos looked back, in surprise.

Baruch said, "Well, there is a world of the dead. Where it is, and what happens there, no one knows. My ghost, thanks to Balthamos, never went there; I am what was once the ghost of Baruch. The world of the dead is just dark to us."

"It is a prison camp," said Balthamos. "The Authority established it in the early ages. Why do you want to know? You will see it in time."

"My father has just died, that's why. He would have told me all he knew, if he hadn't been killed. You say it's a world – do you mean a world like this one, another universe?"

Balthamos looked at Baruch, who shrugged.

"And what happens in the world of the dead?" Will went on.

"It's impossible to say," said Baruch. "Everything about it is secret. Even the churches don't know; they tell their believers that they'll live in Heaven, but that's a lie. If people really knew…"

"And my father's ghost has gone there."

"Without a doubt, and so have the countless millions who died before him."

Will found his imagination trembling.

"And why didn't you go directly to Lord Asriel with your great secret, whatever it is," he said, "instead of looking for me?"

"We were not sure," said Balthamos, "that he would believe us, unless we brought him proof of our good intentions. Two angels of low rank, among all the powers he is dealing with – why should he take us seriously? But if we could bring him the knife and its bearer, he might listen. The knife is a potent weapon, and Lord Asriel would be glad to have you on his side."

"Well, I'm sorry," said Will, "but that sounds feeble to me. If you had any confidence in your secret, you wouldn't need an excuse to see Lord Asriel."

"There's another reason," said Baruch. "We knew that Metatron would be pursuing us, and we wanted to make sure the knife didn't fall into his hands. If we could persuade you to come to Lord Asriel first, then at least –"

"Oh, no, that's not going to happen," said Will. "You're making it *harder* for me to reach Lyra, not easier. She's the most important thing, and you're forgetting her completely. Well, I'm not. Why don't you just go to Lord Asriel and leave me alone? *Make* him listen. You could fly to him much more quickly than I can walk, and I'm going to find Lyra first, come what may. Just do that. Just go. Just leave me."

"But you need me," said Balthamos stiffly, "because I can pretend to be your dæmon, and in Lyra's world you'd stand out, otherwise."

Will was too angry to speak. He got up and walked twenty steps away through the soft deep sand, and then stopped, for the heat and humidity were stunning.

He turned around to see the two angels talking closely together, and then they came up to him, humble and awkward, but proud too.

Baruch said, "We are sorry. I shall go on my own to Lord Asriel, and give him our information, and ask him to send you help to find his daughter. It will be two days' flying time, if I navigate truly."

"And I shall stay with you, Will," said Balthamos.

"Well," said Will, "thank you."

The two angels embraced. Then Baruch folded his arms around Will and kissed him on both cheeks. The kiss was light and cool, like the hands of Balthamos.

"If we keep moving towards Lyra," Will said, "will you find us?"

"I shall never lose Balthamos," said Baruch, and stepped back.

Then he leapt into the air, soared swiftly into the sky, and vanished among the scattered stars. Balthamos was looking after him with desperate longing.

"Shall we sleep here, or should we move on?" he said finally, turning to Will.

"Sleep here," said Will.

"Then sleep, and I'll watch out for danger. Will, I have been short with you, and it was wrong of me. You have the greatest burden, and I should help you, not chide you. I shall try to be kinder from now on."

So Will lay down on the warm sand, and somewhere nearby, he thought, the angel was keeping watch; but that was little comfort.

'll get us out of here, Roger, I promise. And Will's coming, I'm sure he is!''

He didn't understand. He spread his pale hands and shook his head.

"I dunno who that is, and he won't come here," he said, "and if he does he won't know me."

"He's coming to me," she said, "and me and Will, oh, I don't know how, Roger, but I swear we'll help. And don't forget there's others on our side. There's Serafina and there's Iorek, and

3
Scavengers

Serafina Pekkala, the clan-queen of the witches of Lake Enara, wept as she flew through the turbid skies of the Arctic. She wept with rage and fear and remorse: rage against the woman Coulter, whom she had sworn to kill; fear of what was happening to her beloved land; and remorse... She would face the remorse later.

Meanwhile, she looked down at the melting ice-cap, the flooded lowland forests, the swollen sea, and felt heartsick.

But she didn't stop to visit her homeland, or to comfort and encourage her sisters. Instead she flew north and further north, into the fogs and gales around Svalbard, the kingdom of Iorek Byrnison, the armoured bear.

She hardly recognized the main island. The mountains lay bare and black, and only a few hidden valleys facing away from the sun had retained a little snow in their shaded corners; but what was the sun doing here anyway, at this time of year? The whole of nature was overturned.

It took her most of a day to find the bear-king. She saw him among the rocks off the northern edge of the island, swimming fast after a walrus. It was harder for bears to kill in the water: when the land was covered in ice and the great sea-mammals had to come up to breathe, the bears had the advantage of camouflage and their prey was out of its element. That was how things should be.

But Iorek Byrnison was hungry, and even the stabbing tusks of the mighty walrus couldn't keep him at bay. Serafina watched as the creatures fought, turning the white sea-spray red, and saw Iorek haul the carcass out of the waves and on to a broad shelf of rock, watched at a respectful distance by three ragged-furred foxes, waiting for their turn at the feast.

When the bear-king had finished eating, Serafina flew down to speak to him. Now was the time to face her remorse.

"King Iorek Byrnison," she said, "please may I speak with you? I lay my weapons down."

She placed her bow and arrows on the wet rock between them. Iorek looked at them briefly, and she knew that if his face could register any emotion, it would be surprise.

"Speak, Serafina Pekkala," he growled. "We have never fought, have we?"

"King Iorek, I have failed your comrade, Lee Scoresby."

The bear's small black eyes and bloodstained muzzle were very still. She could see the wind ruffling the tips of the creamy-white hairs along his back. He said nothing.

"Mr Scoresby is dead," Serafina went on. "Before I parted from him, I gave him a flower to summon me with, if he should need me. I heard his call and flew to him, but I arrived too late. He died fighting a force of Muscovites, but I know nothing of what brought them there, or why he was holding them off when he could easily have escaped. King Iorek, I am wretched with remorse."

"Where did this happen?" said Iorek Byrnison.

"In another world. This will take me some time to tell."

"Then begin."

She told him what Lee Scoresby had set out to do: to find the man who had been known as Stanislaus Grumman. She told him about how the barrier between the worlds had been breached by Lord Asriel, and about some of the consequences – the melting of the ice, for example. She told of the witch Ruta Skadi's flight after the angels, and she tried to describe those flying beings to the bear-king as Ruta had described them to her: the light that shone on them, the crystalline clarity of their appearance, the richness of their wisdom.

Then she described what she had found when she answered Lee's call.

"I put a spell on his body to preserve it from corruption," she told him. "It will last until you see him, if you wish to do that. But I am troubled by this, King Iorek. Troubled by everything, but mostly by this."

"Where is the child?"

"I left her with my sisters, because I had to answer Lee's call."

"In that same world?"

"Yes, the same."

"How can I get there from here?"

She explained. Iorek Byrnison listened expressionlessly, and then said, "I shall go to Lee Scoresby. And then I must go south."

"South?"

"The ice has gone from these lands. I have been thinking about this, Serafina Pekkala. I have chartered a ship."

The three little foxes had been waiting patiently. Two of them were lying down, heads on their paws, watching, and the other was still sitting up, following the conversation. The foxes of the Arctic, scavengers that they were, had picked up some language, but their brains were so formed that they could only understand statements in the present tense. Most of what Iorek and Serafina said was meaningless noise to them. Furthermore, when they spoke, much of what they said was lies, so it didn't matter if they repeated what they'd heard: no one could sort out which parts were true, though the credulous cliff-ghasts often believed most of it, and never learned from their disappointment. The bears and the witches alike were used to their conversations being scavenged, like the meat they'd finished with.

"And you, Serafina Pekkala?" Iorek went on. "What will you do now?"

"I'm going to find the gyptians," she said. "I think they will be needed."

"Lord Faa," said the bear, "yes. Good fighters. Go well."

He turned away and slipped into the water without a splash, and began to swim in his steady tireless paddle towards the new world.

And some time later, Iorek Byrnison stepped through the blackened undergrowth and the heat-split rocks at the edge of a burnt forest. The sun was glaring through the smoky haze, but he ignored the heat as he ignored the charcoal dust that blackened his white fur and the midges that searched in vain for skin to bite.

He had come a long way, and at one point in his journey, he had found himself swimming into that other world. He noticed the change in the taste of the water and the temperature of the air, but the air was still good to breathe, and the water still held his body up, so he swam on, and now he had left the sea behind, and he was nearly at the place Serafina Pekkala had described. He cast around, his black eyes gazing up at the sun-shimmering rocks of a wall of limestone crags above him.

Between the edge of the burnt forest and the mountains, a rocky slope of heavy boulders and scree was littered with scorched and twisted metal: girders and struts that had belonged to some complex machine. Iorek Byrnison looked at them as a smith as well as a warrior, but there was nothing in these fragments he could use. He scored a line with a mighty claw along a strut less damaged than most, and feeling a flimsiness in the quality of the metal, turned away at once and scanned the mountain wall again.

Then he saw what he was looking for: a narrow gully leading back between jagged walls, and at the entrance, a large low boulder.

He clambered steadily towards it. Beneath his huge feet, dry bones snapped loudly in the stillness, because many men had died here, to be picked clean by coyotes and vultures and lesser creatures; but the great bear ignored them and stepped up carefully towards the rock. The going was loose and he was heavy, and more than once the scree shifted under his feet and carried him down again in a scramble of dust and gravel. But as soon as he slid down he began to move up once more, relentlessly, patiently, until he reached the rock itself, where the footing was firmer.

The boulder was pitted and chipped with bullet-marks. Everything the witch had told him was true. And in confirmation, a little Arctic flower, a purple saxifrage, blossomed improbably where the witch had planted it as a signal in a cranny of the rock.

Iorek Byrnison moved around to the upper side. It was a good shelter from an enemy below, but not good enough; for among the hail of bullets that had chipped fragments off the rock had been a few that had found their target, and that lay where they had come to rest, in the body of the man lying stiff in the shadow.

He was a body, still, and not a skeleton, because the witch had laid a spell to preserve him from corruption. Iorek could see the face of his old comrade drawn and tight with the pain of his wounds, and see the jagged holes in his garments where the bullets had entered. The witch's spell did not cover the blood that must have spilled, and insects and the sun and the wind had dispersed it completely. Lee Scoresby looked not asleep, nor at peace; he looked as if he had died in battle; but he looked as if he knew that his fight had been successful.

And because the Texan aëronaut was one of the very few humans Iorek had ever esteemed, he accepted the man's last gift to him. With deft movements of his claws, he ripped aside the dead man's clothes, opened the body with one slash, and began to feast on the flesh and blood of his old friend. It was his first meal for days, and he was hungry.

But a complex web of thoughts was weaving itself in the bear king's mind, with more strands in it than hunger and satisfaction. There was the memory of the little girl Lyra, whom he had named Silvertongue, and whom he had last seen crossing the fragile snow-bridge across a crevasse in his own island of Svalbard. Then there was the agitation among the witches, the rumours of pacts and alliances and war; and then there was the surpassingly strange fact of this new world itself, and the witch's insistence that there were many more such worlds, and that the fate of them all hung somehow on the fate of the child.

And then there was the melting of the ice. He and his people lived on the ice; ice was their home; ice was their citadel. Since the vast disturbances in the Arctic, the ice had begun to disappear, and Iorek knew that he had to find an ice-bound fastness for his kin, or they would perish. Lee had told him that there were mountains in the south so high that even his balloon could not fly over them, and they were crowned with snow and ice all year round. Exploring those mountains was his next task.

But for now, something simpler possessed his heart, something bright and hard and unshakeable: vengeance. Lee Scoresby, who had rescued Iorek from danger in his balloon and fought beside him in the Arctic of his own world, had died. Iorek would avenge him. The good man's flesh and bone would both nourish him and keep him restless until blood was spilled enough to still his heart.

The sun was setting as Iorek finished his meal, and the air was cooling down. After gathering the remaining fragments into a single heap, the bear lifted the flower in his mouth and dropped it in the centre of them, as humans liked to do. The witch's spell was broken now; the rest of Lee's body was free to all who came. Soon it would be nourishing a dozen different kinds of life.

Then Iorek set off down the slope towards the sea again, towards the south.

Cliff-ghasts were fond of fox, when they could get it. The little creatures were cunning and hard to catch, but their meat was tender and rank.

Before he killed this one, the cliff-ghast let it talk, and laughed at its silly babble.

"Bear must go south! Swear! Witch is troubled! True! Swear! Promise!"

"Bears don't go south, lying filth!"

"True! King bear must go south! Show you walrus – fine fat good –"

"King bear go south?"

"And flying things got treasure! Flying things – angels – crystal treasure!"

"Flying things – like cliff-ghasts? Treasure?"

"Like light, not like cliff-ghast. Rich! Crystal! And witch troubled – witch sorry – Scoresby dead –"

"Dead? Balloon man dead?" The cliff-ghast's laugh echoed around the dry cliffs.

"Witch kill him – Scoresby dead, king bear go south –"

"Scoresby dead! Ha, ha, Scoresby dead!"

The cliff-ghast wrenched off the fox's head, and fought his brothers for the entrails.

they will come, they will!"

"But where are you, *Lyra?"*

*And that she couldn't answer. "I think I'm dreaming, Roger,"
was all she could find to say.*

*Behind the little boy she could see more ghosts, dozens,
hundreds, their heads crowded together, peering close and listening
to every word.*

*"And that woman?" said Roger. "I hope she en't dead. I hope
she stays alive as long as ever she can. Because if she comes down
here, then there'll be nowhere to hide, she'll have us for ever then.
That's the only good thing I can see about being dead, that she
en't. Except I know she will be one day..."*

Lyra was alarmed.

*"I think I'm dreaming, and I don't know where she is!" she
said. "She's somewhere near, and I can't*

4

Ama and the Bats

SHE LAY AS IF AT PLAY — HER LIFE HAD LEAPED AWAY ~ INTENDING TO RETURN ~ BUT NOT SO SOON~

EMILY DICKINSON

Ama, the herdsman's daughter, carried the image of the sleeping girl in her memory: she could not stop thinking about her. She didn't question for a moment the truth of what Mrs Coulter had told her. Sorcerers existed, beyond a doubt, and it was only too likely that they would cast sleeping-spells, and that a mother would care for her daughter in that fierce and tender way. Ama conceived an admiration amounting almost to worship for the beautiful woman in the cave and her enchanted daughter.

She went as often as she could to the little valley, to run errands for the woman or simply to chatter and listen, for the woman had wonderful tales to tell. Again and again she hoped for a glimpse of the sleeper, but it had only happened once, and she accepted that it would probably never be allowed again.

And during the time she spent milking the sheep, or carding and spinning their wool, or grinding barley to make bread, she thought incessantly about the spell that must have been cast, and about why it had happened. Mrs Coulter had never told her, so Ama was free to imagine.

One day she took some flat bread sweetened with honey

and walked the three-hour journey along the trail to Cho-Lung-Se, where there was a monastery. By wheedling and patience and by bribing the porter with some of the honey-bread, she managed to gain an audience with the great healer Pagdzin *tulku*, who had cured an outbreak of the white fever only the year before, and who was immensely wise.

Ama entered the great man's cell, bowing very low and offering her remaining honey-bread with all the humility she could muster. The monk's bat-dæmon swooped and darted around her, frightening her own dæmon Kulang, who crept into her hair to hide, but Ama tried to remain still and silent until Pagdzin *tulku* spoke.

"Yes, child? Be quick, be quick," he said, his long grey beard wagging with every word.

In the dimness, the beard and his brilliant eyes were most of what she could see of him. His dæmon settled on the beam above him, hanging still at last, so she said, "Please, Pagdzin *tulku*, I want to gain wisdom. I would like to know how to make spells and enchantments. Can you teach me?"

"No," he said.

She was expecting that. "Well, could you tell me just one remedy?" she asked humbly.

"Maybe. But I won't tell you what it is. I can give you the medicine, not tell you the secret."

"All right, thank you, that is a great blessing," she said, bowing several times.

"What is the disease, and who has it?" the old man said.

"It's a sleeping sickness," Ama explained. "It's come upon the son of my father's cousin."

She was being extra clever, she knew, changing the sex of the sufferer, just in case the healer had heard of the woman in the cave.

"And how old is this boy?"

"Three years older than me, Pagdzin *tulku*," she guessed, "so he is twelve years old. He sleeps and sleeps and can't wake up."

"Why haven't his parents come to me? Why did they send you?"

"Because they live far on the other side of my village and they are very poor, Pagdzin *tulku*. I only heard of my kinsman's illness yesterday and I came at once to seek your advice."

"I should see the patient and examine him thoroughly, and enquire into the positions of the planets at the hour when he fell asleep. These things can't be done in a hurry."

"Is there no medicine you can give me to take back?"

The bat-dæmon fell off her beam and fluttered blackly aside before she hit the floor, darting silently across the room again and again, too quickly for Ama to follow; but the bright eyes of the healer saw exactly where she went, and when she had hung once more upside down on her beam and folded her dark wings around herself, the old man got up and moved around from shelf to shelf and jar to jar and box to box, here tapping out a spoonful of powder, there adding a pinch of herbs, in the order in which the dæmon had visited them.

He tipped all the ingredients into a mortar and ground them up together, muttering a spell as he did so. Then he tapped the pestle on the ringing edge of the mortar, dislodging the final grains, and took a brush and ink and wrote some characters on a sheet of paper. When the ink had dried he tipped all the powder on to the inscription and folded the paper swiftly into a little square package.

"Let them brush this powder into the nostrils of the sleeping child a little at a time as he breathes in," he told her, "and he will wake up. It has to be done with great caution. Too much at once and he will choke. Use the softest of brushes."

"Thank you, Pagdzin *tulku*," said Ama, taking the package and placing it in the pocket of her innermost shirt. "I wish I had another honey-bread to give you."

"One is enough," said the healer. "Now go, and next time you come, tell me the whole truth, not part of it."

The girl was abashed, and bowed very low to hide her confusion. She hoped she hadn't given too much away.

Next evening she hurried to the valley as soon as she could, carrying some sweet rice wrapped in a heart-fruit leaf. She was bursting to tell the woman what she had done, and to give her the medicine and receive her praise and thanks, and eager most of all for the enchanted sleeper to wake and talk to her. They could be friends!

But as she turned the corner of the path and looked upwards, she saw no golden monkey, no patient woman seated at the cave-mouth. The place was empty. She ran the last few yards, afraid they had gone for ever – but there was the chair the woman sat in, and the cooking-equipment, and everything else.

Ama looked into the darkness further back in the cave, her heart beating fast. Surely the sleeper hadn't woken already: in the dimness Ama could make out the shape of the sleeping-bag, the lighter patch that was the girl's hair, and the white curve of her sleeping dæmon.

She crept a little closer. There was no doubt about it – they had gone out and left the enchanted girl alone.

A thought struck Ama like a musical note: suppose *she* woke her before the woman returned...

But she had hardly time to feel the thrill of that idea before she heard sounds on the path outside, and in a shiver of guilt she and her dæmon darted behind a ridge of rock at the side of the cave. She shouldn't be here. She was spying. It was wrong.

And now that golden monkey was squatting in the entrance, sniffing and turning his head this way and that. Ama saw him bare his sharp teeth, and felt her own dæmon burrow into her clothes, mouse-formed and trembling.

"What is it?" said the woman's voice, speaking to the monkey, and then the cave darkened as her form came into the entrance. "Has the girl been? Yes – there's the food she left. She shouldn't come in, though. We must arrange a spot on the path for her to leave the food at."

Without a glance at the sleeper, the woman stooped to bring the fire to life, and set a pan of water to heat while her dæmon crouched nearby watching over the path. From time to time he got up and looked around the cave, and Ama, getting cramped and uncomfortable in her narrow hiding-place, wished ardently that she'd waited outside and not gone in. How long was she going to be trapped?

The woman was mixing some herbs and powders into the heating water. Ama could smell the astringent flavours as they drifted out with the steam. Then came a sound from the back of the cave: the girl was murmuring and stirring. Ama turned her head: she could see the enchanted sleeper moving, tossing from side to side, throwing an arm across her eyes. She was waking!

And the woman took no notice!

She heard all right, because she looked up briefly, but she soon turned back to her herbs and the boiling water. She poured the decoction into a beaker and let it stand, and only then turned her full attention to the waking girl.

Ama could understand none of these words, but she heard them with increasing wonder and suspicion:

"Hush, dear," the woman said. "Don't worry yourself. You're safe."

"Roger –" the girl murmured, half-awake. "Serafina! Where's Roger gone... Where is he?"

"No one here but us," her mother said, in a sing-song voice, half-crooning. "Lift yourself and let Mama wash you... Up you come, my love..."

Ama watched as the girl, moaning, struggling into wakefulness, tried to push her mother away; and the woman dipped a sponge into the bowl of water and mopped at her daughter's face and body before patting her dry.

By this time the girl was nearly awake, and the woman had to move more quickly.

"Where's Serafina? And Will? Help me, help me! I don't want to sleep – No, no! I won't! No!"

The woman was holding the beaker in one steely-firm hand while her other was trying to lift Lyra's head.

"Be still, dear – be calm – hush now – drink your tea –"

But the girl lashed out and nearly spilled the drink, and cried louder:

"Leave me alone! I want to go! Let me go! Will, Will, help me – oh, help me –"

The woman was gripping her hair tightly, forcing her head back, cramming the beaker against her mouth.

"I won't! You dare touch me and Iorek will tear your head off! Oh, Iorek, where are you? Iorek Byrnison! Help me, Iorek! I won't – I won't –"

Then, at a word from the woman, the golden monkey sprang on Lyra's dæmon, gripping him with hard black fingers. The dæmon flicked from shape to shape more quickly than Ama had ever seen a dæmon change before: cat-snake-rat-fox-bird-wolf-cheetah-lizard-polecat –

But the monkey's grip never slackened; and then Pantalaimon became a porcupine.

The monkey screeched and let go. Three long quills were stuck shivering in his paw. Mrs Coulter snarled and with her free hand slapped Lyra hard across the face, a vicious backhand crack that threw her flat; and before Lyra could gather her wits, the beaker was at her mouth and she had to swallow or choke.

Ama wished she could shut her ears: the gulping, crying, coughing, sobbing, pleading, retching was almost too much to bear. But little by little it died away, and only a shaky sob or two came from the girl, who was now sinking once more into sleep – enchanted sleep? Poisoned sleep! Drugged, deceitful sleep! Ama saw a streak of white materialize at the girl's throat as her dæmon effortfully changed into a long, sinuous, snowy-furred creature with brilliant black eyes and black-tipped tail, and laid himself alongside her neck.

And the woman was singing softly, crooning baby-songs, smoothing the hair off the girl's brow, patting her hot face dry, humming songs to which even Ama could tell she didn't know the words, because all she could sing was a string of nonsense-syllables, la-la-la, ba-ba-boo-boo, her sweet voice mouthing gibberish.

Eventually that stopped, and then the woman did a curious thing: she took a pair of scissors and trimmed the girl's hair, holding her sleeping head this way and that to see the best effect. She took one dark blonde curl and put it in a little gold locket she had around her own neck. Ama could tell why: she was going to work some further magic with it. But the woman held it to her lips first... Oh, this was strange.

The golden monkey drew out the last of the porcupine quills, and said something to the woman, who reached up to snatch a roosting bat from the cave ceiling. The little black thing flapped and squealed in a needle-thin voice that pierced Ama from one ear to the other, and then she saw the woman hand the bat to her dæmon, and she saw the dæmon pull one of the black wings out and out and out till it snapped and broke and hung from a white string of sinew, while the dying bat screamed and its fellows flapped around in anguished puzzlement. Crack – crack – snap – as the golden monkey pulled the little thing apart limb by limb, and the woman lay moodily on her sleeping-bag by the fire and slowly ate a bar of chocolatl.

Time passed. Light faded and the moon rose, and the woman and her dæmon fell asleep.

Ama, stiff and painful, crept up from her hiding-place and tiptoed out past the sleepers, and didn't make a sound till she was half-way down the path.

With fear to give her speed, she ran along the narrow trail, her dæmon as an owl on silent wings beside her. The clean cold air, the constant motion of the tree-tops, the brilliance of the moon-painted clouds in the dark sky and the millions of stars all calmed her a little.

She stopped in sight of the little huddle of stone houses and her dæmon perched on her fist.

"She lied!" Ama said. "She *lied* to us! What can we do, Kulang? Can we tell Dada? What can we *do*?"

"Don't tell," said her dæmon. "More trouble. We've got the medicine. We can wake her. We can go there when the woman's away again, and wake the girl up, and take her away."

The thought filled them both with fear. But it had been said, and the little paper package was safe in Ama's pocket, and they knew how to use it.

wake up, I can't see her – I think she's close by – she's hurt me –"

"Oh, Lyra, don't be frightened! If you're frightened too, I'll go mad –"

They tried to hold each other tight, but their arms passed through the empty air. Lyra tried to say what she meant, whispering close to his little pale face in the darkness:

"I'm just trying to wake up – I'm so afraid of sleeping all my life and then dying – I want to wake up first! I wouldn't care if it was just for an hour, as long as I was properly alive and awake – I don't know if this is real or not, even – but I will help you, Roger! I swear I will!"

"But if you're dreaming, Lyra, you might not believe it when you wake up. That's what I'd do, I'd just think it was only a dream."

"No!" she said fiercely, and

5

The Adamant Tower

... WITH
AMBITIOUS
AIM AGAINST
THE THRONE AND
MONARCHY OF
GOD RAIS'D
IMPIOUS WAR
IN HEAV'N AND
BATTEL PROUD·
JOHN MILTON

A lake of molten sulphur extended the length of an immense canyon, releasing its mephitic vapours in sudden gusts and belches, and barring the way to the solitary winged figure who stood at its edge.

If he took to the sky, the enemy scouts who had spotted him, and lost him, would find him again at once; but if he stayed on the ground, it would take so long to get past this noxious pit that his message might arrive too late.

He would have to take the greater risk. He waited until a cloud of stinking smoke billowed off the yellow surface, and darted upwards into the thick of it.

Four pairs of eyes in different parts of the sky all saw the brief movement, and at once four pairs of wings beat hard against the smoke-fouled air, hurling the watchers forward to the cloud.

Then began a hunt in which the pursuers couldn't see the quarry, and the quarry could see nothing at all. The first to break out of the cloud on the far side of the lake would have the advantage, and that might mean survival, or it might mean a successful kill.

And unluckily for the single flier, he found the clear air a few seconds after one of his pursuers. At once they closed with each other, trailing streams of vapour, and dizzy, both of them, from the sickening fumes. The quarry had the best of it at first, but then another hunter flew free of the cloud, and in a swift and furious struggle all three of them, twisting in the air like scraps of flame, rose and fell and rose again, only to fall, finally, among the rocks on the far side. The other two hunters never emerged from the cloud.

At the western end of a range of saw-toothed mountains, on a peak that commanded wide views of the plain below and the valleys behind, a fortress of basalt seemed to grow out of the mountain as if some volcano had thrust it up a million years before.

In vast caverns beneath the rearing walls, provisions of every sort were stored and labelled; in the arsenals and magazines, engines of war were being calibrated, armed and tested; in the mills below the mountain, volcanic fires fed mighty forges where phosphor and titanium were being melted and combined in alloys never known or used before.

On the most exposed side of the fortress, at a point deep in the shadow of a buttress where the mighty walls rose sheer out of the ancient lava-flows, there was a small gate, a postern where a sentry watched day and night and challenged all who sought to enter.

While the watch was being changed on the ramparts above, the sentry stamped once or twice and slapped his gloved hands on his upper arms for warmth, for it was the coldest hour of the night, and the little naphtha flare in the bracket beside him gave no heat. His relief would come in another ten minutes, and he was looking forward to the mug of chocolatl, the smoke-leaf, and most of all his bed.

To hear a hammering at the little door was the last thing he expected.

However, he was alert, and he snapped open the spy-hole, at the same time opening the tap that allowed a flow of naphtha past the pilot-light in the buttress outside. In the glare it threw, he saw three hooded figures carrying between them a fourth whose shape was indistinct, and who seemed ill, or wounded.

The figure in front threw back his hood. He had a face the sentry knew, but he gave the password anyway, and said, "We found him at the sulphur lake. Says his name is Baruch. He's got an urgent message for Lord Asriel."

The sentry unbarred the door, and his terrier-dæmon quivered as the three figures manoeuvred their burden with difficulty through the narrow entrance. Then the dæmon gave a soft involuntary howl, quickly cut off, as the sentry saw that the figure being carried was an angel, wounded: an angel of low rank and little power, but an angel nevertheless.

"Lay him in the guardroom," the sentry told them, and as they did so he turned the crank of the telephone-bell, and reported what was happening to the officer of the watch.

On the highest rampart of the fortress was a tower of adamant: just one flight of steps up to a set of rooms whose windows looked out north, south, east and west. The largest room was furnished with a table and chairs and a map chest, another with a camp bed. A small bathroom completed the set.

Lord Asriel sat in the adamant tower facing his spy-captain across a mass of scattered papers. A naphtha lamp hung over the table, and a brazier held burning coals against the bitter chill of the night. Inside the door, a small blue hawk was perching on a bracket.

The spy-captain was called Lord Roke. He was striking to look at: he was no taller than Lord Asriel's hand-span, and as slender as a dragonfly, but the rest of Lord Asriel's captains treated him with profound respect, for he was armed with a poisonous sting in the spurs on his heels.

It was his custom to sit on the table, and his manner to repel anything but the greatest courtesy with a haughty and malevolent tongue. He and his kind, the Gallivespians, had few of the qualities of good spies except, of course, their exceptional smallness: they were so proud and touchy that they would never have remained inconspicuous if they had been of Lord Asriel's size.

"Yes," he said, his voice clear and sharp, his eyes glittering like droplets of ink, "your child, my Lord Asriel: I know about her. Evidently I know more than you do."

Lord Asriel looked at him directly, and the little man knew at once that he'd taken advantage of his commander's courtesy: the force of Lord Asriel's glance flicked him like a finger, so that he lost his balance and had to put out a hand to steady himself on Lord Asriel's wineglass. A moment later Lord Asriel's expression was bland and virtuous, just as his daughter's could be, and from then on Lord Roke was more careful.

"No doubt, Lord Roke," said Lord Asriel. "But for reasons I don't understand, the girl is the focus of the church's attention, and I need to know why. What are they saying about her?"

"The Magisterium is alive with speculation; one branch says one thing, another is investigating something else, and each of them is trying to keep its discoveries secret from the rest. The most active branches are the Consistorial Court of Discipline and the Society of the Work of the Holy Spirit, and," said Lord Roke, "I have spies in both of them."

"Have you turned a member of the Society, then?" said Lord Asriel. "I congratulate you. They used to be impregnable."

"My spy in the Society is the Lady Salmakia," said Lord Roke, "a very skilful agent. There is a priest whose dæmon, a mouse, she approached in their sleep. My agent suggested that the man perform a forbidden ritual designed to invoke the presence of Wisdom. At the critical moment, the Lady Salmakia appeared in front of him. The priest now thinks he can communicate with Wisdom whenever he pleases, and that she has the form of a Gallivespian and lives in his bookcase."

Lord Asriel smiled, and said, "And what has she learned?"

"The Society thinks that your daughter is the most important child who has ever lived. They think that a great crisis will come before very long, and that the fate of everything will depend on how she behaves at that point. As for the Consistorial Court of Discipline, it's holding an inquiry at the moment, with witnesses from Bolvangar and elsewhere. My spy in the Court, the Chevalier Tialys, is in touch with me every day by means of the lodestone resonator, and he is letting me know what they discover. In short, I would say that the Society of the Work of the Holy Spirit will find out very soon where the child is, but they will do nothing about it. It will take the Consistorial Court a little longer, but when they do they will act decisively, and at once."

"Let me know the moment you hear any more."

Lord Roke bowed and snapped his fingers, and the small blue hawk perching on the bracket beside the door spread her wings and glided to the table. She had a bridle, a saddle, and stirrups. Lord Roke sprang on her back in a second, and they flew out of the window which Lord Asriel held wide for them.

He left it open for a minute, in spite of the bitter air, and leant on the window-seat, playing with the ears of his snow-leopard dæmon.

"She came to me on Svalbard and I ignored her," he said. "You remember the shock... I needed a sacrifice, and the first child to arrive was my own daughter... But when I realized that there was another child with her, so she was safe, I relaxed. Was that a fatal mistake? I didn't consider her after that, not for a moment, but she is important, Stelmaria!"

"Let's think clearly," his dæmon replied. "What can she do?"

"*Do* – not much. Does she *know* something?"

"She can read the alethiometer; she has access to knowledge."

"That's nothing special. So have others. And where in hell's name can she be?"

There was a knock at the door behind him, and he turned at once.

"My lord," said the officer who came in, "an angel has just arrived at the western gate – wounded – he insists on speaking to you."

And a minute later, Baruch was lying on the camp bed, which had been brought through to the main room. A medical orderly had been summoned, but it was clear that there was little hope for the angel: he was wounded sorely, his wings torn and his eyes dimmed.

Lord Asriel sat close by and threw a handful of herbs on to the coals in the brazier. As Will had found with the smoke of his fire, that had the effect of defining the angel's body so he could see it more clearly.

"Well, sir," he said, "what have you come to tell me?"

"Three things. Please let me say them all before you speak.

My name is Baruch. My companion Balthamos and I are of the rebels' party, and so we were drawn to your standard as soon as you raised it. But we wanted to bring you something valuable, because our power is small, and not long ago we managed to find our way to the heart of the Clouded Mountain, the Authority's citadel in the kingdom. And there we learned..."

He had to stop for a moment to breathe in the smoke of the herbs, which seemed to steady him. He continued:

"We learned the truth about the Authority. We learned that he has retired to a chamber of crystal deep within the Clouded Mountain, and that he no longer runs the daily affairs of the kingdom. Instead he contemplates deeper mysteries. In his place, ruling on his behalf, there is an angel called Metatron. I have reason to know that angel well, though when I knew him..."

Baruch's voice faded. Lord Asriel's eyes were blazing, but he held his tongue and waited for Baruch to continue.

"Metatron is proud," Baruch went on when he had recovered a little strength, "and his ambition is limitless. The Authority chose him four thousand years ago to be his Regent, and they laid their plans together. They have a new plan, which my companion and I were able to discover. The Authority considers that conscious beings of every kind have become dangerously independent, so Metatron is going to intervene much more actively in human affairs. He intends to move the Authority secretly away from the Clouded Mountain, to a permanent citadel somewhere else, and turn the mountain into an engine of war. The churches in every world are corrupt and weak, he thinks, they compromise too readily... He wants to set up a permanent inquisition in every world, run directly from the kingdom. And his first campaign will be to destroy your republic…"

They were both trembling, the angel and the man, but one from weakness and the other from excitement.

Baruch gathered his remaining strength, and went on:

"The second thing is this. There is a knife which can cut openings between the worlds, as well as anything in them. Its power is unlimited, but only in the hands of the one who knows how to use it. And that person is a boy…"

Once again the angel had to stop and recover. He was frightened; he could feel himself drifting apart. Lord Asriel could see the effort he made to hold himself together, and sat tensely gripping the arms of his chair until Baruch found the strength to go on.

"My companion is with that boy now. We wanted to bring him directly to you, but he refused, because… This is the third thing I must tell you: he and your daughter are friends. And he will not agree to come to you until he has found her. She is –"

"Who is this boy?"

"He is the son of the shaman. Of Stanislaus Grumman."

Lord Asriel was so surprised he stood up involuntarily, sending billows of smoke swirling around the angel.

"Grumman had a *son*?" he said.

"Grumman was not born in your world. Nor was his real name Grumman. My companion and I were led to him by his own desire to find the knife. We followed him, knowing he would lead us to it and its bearer, intending to bring the bearer to you. But the boy refused to…"

Once again Baruch had to stop. Lord Asriel sat down again, cursing his own impatience, and sprinkled some more herbs on the fire. His dæmon lay nearby, her tail sweeping slowly across the oaken floor, her golden eyes never leaving the angel's pain-filled face. Baruch took several slow breaths, and Lord Asriel held his silence. The slap of the rope on the flagpole above was the only sound.

"Take your time, sir," Lord Asriel said gently. "Do you know where my daughter is?"

"Himalaya ... in her own world," whispered Baruch. "Great mountains. A cave near a valley full of rainbows..."

"A long way from here in both worlds. You flew quickly."

"It is the only gift I have," said Baruch, "except the love of Balthamos, whom I shall never see again."

"And if *you* found her so easily –"

"Then any other angel may too."

Lord Asriel seized a great atlas from the map-chest and flung it open, looking for the pages that showed the Himalaya.

"Can you be precise?" he said. "Can you show me exactly where?"

"With the knife..." Baruch tried to say, and Lord Asriel realized his mind was wandering: "With the knife he can enter and leave any world at will... Will is his name. But they are in danger, he and Balthamos... Metatron knows we have his secret. They pursued us... They caught me alone on the borders of your world... I was his brother... That was how we found our way to him in the Clouded Mountain. Metatron was once Enoch, the son of Jared, the son of Mahalalel... Enoch had many wives. He was a lover of the flesh... My brother Enoch cast me out, because I... Oh, my dear Balthamos..."

"Where is the girl?"

"Yes. Yes. A cave ... her mother ... valley full of winds and rainbows ... tattered flags on the shrine..."

He raised himself to look at the atlas.

Then the snow-leopard dæmon got to her feet in one swift movement, and leapt to the door, but it was too late: the orderly who knocked had opened without waiting. That was the way things were done; it was no one's fault; but seeing the expression on the soldier's face as he looked past him, Lord Asriel turned back to see Baruch straining and quivering to hold his wounded form together. The effort was too much. A draught from the open door sent an eddy of air across the bed, and the particles of the angel's form, loosened by the waning of his strength, swirled upwards into randomness, and vanished.

"Balthamos!" came a whisper from the air.

Lord Asriel put his hand on his dæmon's neck; she felt him tremble, and stilled him. He turned to the orderly.

"My lord, I beg your –"

"Not your fault. Take my compliments to King Ogunwe. I would be glad if he and my other commanders could step here at once. I would also like Mr Basilides to attend, with the alethiometer. Finally, I want No.2 Squadron of gyropters armed and fuelled, and a tanker zeppelin to take off at once and head south-west. I shall send further orders in the air."

The orderly saluted, and with one more swift uneasy glance at the empty bed, went out and shut the door.

Lord Asriel tapped the desk with a pair of brass dividers, and crossed to open the southern window. Far below, the deathless fires put out their glow and smoke on the darkling air, and even at this great height the clang of hammers could be heard in the snapping wind.

"Well, we've learned a lot, Stelmaria," he said quietly.

"But not enough."

There came another knock at the door, and the alethiometrist came in. He was a pale, thin man in early middle age; his name was Teukros Basilides, and his dæmon was a nightingale.

"Mr Basilides, good evening to you," said Lord Asriel. "This is our problem, and I would like you to put everything else aside while you deal with it..."

He told the man what Baruch had said, and showed him the atlas.

"Pinpoint that cave," he said. "Get me the co-ordinates as precisely as you can. This is the most important task you have ever undertaken. Begin at once, if you please."

stamped her foot so hard it even hurt her in the dream. "You don't believe I'd do that, Roger, so don't say it. I will wake up and I won't forget, so there."

She looked around, but all she could see were wide eyes and hopeless faces, pale faces, dark faces, old faces, young faces, all the dead cramming and crowding close and silent and sorrowful.

Roger's face was different. His expression was the only one that contained hope.

She said, "Why d'you look like that? Why en't you miserable, like them? Why en't you at the end of your hope?"

And he said, "Because

6
Pre-emptive Absolution

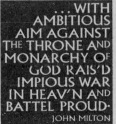

... WITH
AMBITIOUS
AIM AGAINST
THE THRONE AND
MONARCHY OF
GOD RAIS'D
IMPIOUS WAR
IN HEAV'N AND
BATTEL PROUD·
JOHN MILTON

"*N*ow, Fra Pavel," said the Inquirer of the Consistorial Court of Discipline: "I want you to recall exactly, if you can, the words you heard the witch speak on the ship."

The twelve members of the Court looked through the dim afternoon light at the cleric on the stand, their last witness. He was a scholarly-looking priest whose dæmon had the form of a frog. The Court had been hearing evidence in this case for eight days already, in the ancient high-towered College of St Jerome.

"I cannot call the witch's words exactly to mind," said Fra Pavel wearily. "I had not seen torture before, as I said to the court yesterday, and I found it made me feel faint and sick. So *exactly* what she said I cannot tell you, but I remember the meaning of it. The witch said that the child Lyra had been recognized by the clans of the north as the subject of a prophecy they had long known. She was to have the power to make a fateful choice, on which the future of all the worlds depended. And furthermore, there was a name that would bring to mind a parallel case, and which would make the church hate and fear her."

"And did the witch reveal that name?"

"No. Before she could utter it, another witch, who had been present under a spell of invisibility, managed to kill her and escape."

"So on that occasion, the woman Coulter will not have heard the name?"

"That is so."

"And shortly afterwards Mrs Coulter left?"

"Indeed."

"What did you discover after that?"

"I learned that the child had gone into another world through the rift opened by Lord Asriel, and that there she has acquired the help of a boy who owns, or has got the use of, a knife of extraordinary powers," said Fra Pavel. Then he cleared his throat nervously and went on: "I may speak entirely freely in this court?"

"With perfect freedom, Fra Pavel," came the harsh clear tones of the President. "You will not be punished for telling us what you in turn have been told. Please continue."

Reassured, the cleric went on:

"The knife in the possession of this boy is able to make openings between worlds. Furthermore, it has a power greater than that – please, once again, I am afraid of what I am saying… It is capable of killing the most high angels, and what is higher than them. There is nothing this knife cannot destroy."

He was sweating and trembling, and his frog-dæmon fell from the edge of the witness-stand to the floor in her agitation. Fra Pavel gasped in pain and scooped her up swiftly, letting her sip at the water in the glass in front of him.

"And did you ask further about the girl?" said the Inquirer. "Did you discover this name the witch spoke of?"

"Yes, I did. Once again I crave the assurance of the court that –"

"You have it," snapped the President. "Don't be afraid. You are not a heretic. Report what you have learned, and waste no more time."

"I beg your pardon, truly. The child, then, is in the position of Eve, the wife of Adam, the mother of us all, and the cause of all sin."

The stenographers taking down every word were nuns of the order of St Philomel, sworn to silence; but at Fra Pavel's words there came a smothered gasp from one of them, and there was a flurry of hands as they crossed themselves. Fra Pavel twitched, and went on:

"Please, remember – the alethiometer does not *forecast*; it says, '*If* certain things come about, *then* the consequences will be –' and so on. And it says that if it comes about that the child is tempted, as Eve was, then she is likely to fall. On the outcome will depend ... everything. And if this temptation does take place, and if the child gives in, then Dust and sin will triumph."

There was silence in the courtroom. The pale sunlight that filtered in through the great leaded windows held in its slanted beams a million golden motes, but these were dust, not Dust; though more than one member of the court had seen in them an image of that other invisible Dust that settled over every human being, no matter how dutifully they kept the laws.

"Finally, Fra Pavel," said the Inquirer, "tell us what you know of the child's present whereabouts."

"She is in the hands of Mrs Coulter," said Fra Pavel. "And they are in the Himalayas. So far, that is all I have been able to tell. I shall go at once and ask for a more precise location, and as soon as I have it I shall tell the court; but..."

He stopped, shrinking in fear, and held the glass to his lips with a trembling hand.

"Yes, Fra Pavel?" said Father MacPhail. "Hold nothing back."

"I believe, Father President, that the Society of the Work of the Holy Spirit knows more about this than I do."

Fra Pavel's voice was so faint it was almost a whisper.

"Is that so?" said the President, his eyes seeming to radiate his passion as they glared.

Fra Pavel's dæmon uttered a little frog-whimper. The cleric knew about the rivalry between the different branches of the Magisterium, and knew that to get caught in the crossfire between them would be very dangerous; but to hold back what he knew would be more dangerous still. ·

"I believe," he went on, trembling, "that they are much closer to finding out exactly where the child is. They have other sources of knowledge forbidden to me."

"Quite so," said the Inquirer. "And did the alethiometer tell you about this?"

"Yes, it did."

"Very well. Fra Pavel, you would do well to continue that line of investigation. Whatever you need in the way of clerical or secretarial help is yours to command. Please stand down."

Fra Pavel bowed, and with his frog-dæmon on his shoulder he gathered his notes and left the courtroom. The nuns flexed their fingers.

Father MacPhail tapped a pencil on the oak bench in front of him.

"Sister Agnes, Sister Monica," he said, "you may leave us now. Please have the transcription on my desk by the end of the day."

The two nuns bowed their heads and left.

"Gentlemen," said the President, for that was the mode of address in the Consistorial Court, "let's adjourn."

The twelve members, from the oldest (Father Makepwe, ancient and rheumy-eyed) to the youngest (Father Gomez, pale and trembling with zealotry), gathered their notes and followed the President through to the council chamber, where they could face one another across a table and talk in the utmost privacy.

The current President of the Consistorial Court was a Scot called Hugh MacPhail. He had been elected young: Presidents served for life, and he was only in his forties, so it was to be expected that Father MacPhail would mould the destiny of the Consistorial Court, and thus of the whole church, for many years to come. He was a dark-featured man, tall and imposing, with a shock of wiry grey hair, and he would have been fat were it not for the brutal discipline he imposed on his body: he drank only water and ate only bread and fruit, and he exercised for an hour daily under the supervision of a trainer of champion athletes. As a result, he was gaunt and lined and restless. His dæmon was a lizard.

Once they were seated, Father MacPhail said:

"This, then, is the state of things. There seem to be several points to bear in mind.

"Firstly, Lord Asriel. A witch friendly to the church reports that he is assembling a great army, including forces that may be angelic. His intentions, as far as the witch knows, are malevolent towards the church, and towards the Authority Himself.

"Secondly, the Oblation Board. Their actions in setting up the research programme at Bolvangar, and in funding Mrs Coulter's activities, suggest that they are hoping to replace the Consistorial Court of Discipline as the most powerful and effective arm of the Holy Church. We have been outpaced, gentlemen. They have acted ruthlessly and skilfully.

We should be chastised for our laxity in letting it happen. I shall return to what we might do about it shortly.

"Thirdly, the boy in Fra Pavel's testimony, with the knife that can do these extraordinary things. Clearly we must find him and gain possession of it as soon as possible.

"Fourthly, Dust. I have taken steps to find out what the Oblation Board has discovered about it. One of the experimental theologians working at Bolvangar has been persuaded to tell us what exactly they discovered. I shall talk to him this afternoon downstairs."

One or two of the priests shifted uncomfortably, for "downstairs" meant the cellars below the building: white-tiled rooms with points for anbaric current, sound-proofed and well-drained.

"Whatever we do learn about Dust, though," the President went on, "we must bear our purpose firmly in mind. The Oblation Board sought to understand the effects of Dust: we must destroy it altogether. Nothing less than that. If in order to destroy Dust we also have to destroy the Oblation Board, the College of Bishops, every single agency by which the Holy Church does the work of the Authority – then so be it. It may be, gentlemen, that the Holy Church itself was brought into being to perform this very task and to perish in the doing of it. But better a world with no church and no Dust than a world where every day we have to struggle under the hideous burden of sin. Better a world purged of all that!"

Blazing-eyed Father Gomez nodded passionately.

"And finally," said Father MacPhail, "the child. Still just a child, I think. This Eve, who is going to be tempted and who, if precedent is any guide, will fall, and whose fall will involve us all in ruin. Gentlemen, of all the ways of dealing with the problem she sets us, I am going to propose the most radical, and I have confidence in your agreement.

"I propose to send a man to find her and kill her before she *can* be tempted."

"Father President," said Father Gomez at once, "I have done pre-emptive penance every day of my adult life. I have studied, I have trained –"

The President held up his hand. Pre-emptive penance and absolution were doctrines researched and developed by the Consistorial Court, but not known to the wider church. They involved doing penance for a sin not yet committed, intense and fervent penance accompanied by scourging and flagellation, so as to build up, as it were, a store of credit. When the penance had reached the appropriate level for a particular sin, the penitent was granted absolution in advance, though he might never be called on to commit the sin. It was sometimes necessary to kill people, for example: and it was so much less troubling for the assassin if he could do so in a state of grace.

"I had you in mind," said Father MacPhail kindly. "I have the agreement of the Court? Yes. When Father Gomez leaves, with our blessing, he will be on his own, unable to be reached or recalled. Whatever happens to anything else, he will make his way like the arrow of God, straight to the child, and strike her down. He will be invisible; he will come in the night, like the angel that blasted the Assyrians; he will be silent. How much better for us all if there had been a Father Gomez in the garden of Eden! We would never have left paradise."

The young priest was nearly weeping with pride. The Court gave its blessing.

And in the darkest corner of the ceiling, hidden among the

dark oak beams, sat a man no larger than a hand-span. His heels were armed with spurs, and he heard every word they said.

In the cellars the man from Bolvangar, dressed only in a dirty white shirt and loose trousers with no belt, stood under the bare light bulb clutching the trousers with one hand and his rabbit-dæmon with the other. In front of him, in the only chair, sat Father MacPhail.

"Dr Cooper," the President began, "do sit down."

There was no furniture except the chair, the wooden bunk, and a bucket. The President's voice echoed unpleasantly off the white tiles that lined the wall and ceiling.

Dr Cooper sat on the bunk. He could not take his eyes off the gaunt and grey-haired President. He licked his dry lips and waited to see what new discomfort was coming.

"So you nearly succeeded in severing the child from her dæmon?" said Father MacPhail.

Dr Cooper said shakily, "We considered that it would serve no purpose to wait, since the experiment was due to take place anyway, and we put the child in the experimental chamber, but then Mrs Coulter herself intervened and took the child to her own quarters."

The rabbit-dæmon opened her round eyes and gazed fearfully at the President, and then shut them again and hid her face.

"That must have been distressing," said Father MacPhail.

"The whole programme was intensely difficult," said Dr Cooper, hastening to agree.

"I am surprised you did not seek the aid of the Consistorial Court, where we have strong nerves."

"We – I – we understood that the programme was licensed

by... It was an Oblation Board matter, but we were told it had the approval of the Consistorial Court of Discipline. We would never have taken part, otherwise. Never!"

"No, of course not. And now for another matter. Did you have any idea," said Father MacPhail, turning to the real subject of his visit to the cellars, "of the subject of Lord Asriel's researches? Of what might have been the source of the colossal energy he managed to release on Svalbard?"

Dr Cooper swallowed. In the intense silence a drop of sweat fell from his chin to the concrete floor, and both men heard it distinctly.

"Well..." he began, "there was one of our team who observed that in the process of severance there was a release of energy. Controlling it would involve enormous forces, but just as an atomic explosion is detonated by conventional explosives, this could be done by focusing a powerful anbaric current... However, he wasn't taken seriously. I paid no attention to his ideas," he added earnestly, "knowing that without authority they might well be heretical."

"Very wise. And that colleague now? Where is he?"

"He was one of those who died in the attack."

The President smiled. It was so kindly an expression that Dr Cooper's dæmon shivered and swooned against his breast.

"Courage, Dr Cooper," said Father MacPhail. "We need you to be strong and brave! There is a great work to be done, a great battle to be fought. You must earn the forgiveness of the Authority by co-operating fully with us, by holding nothing back, not even wild speculation, not even gossip. Now I want you to devote all your attention to what you remember your colleague saying. Did he make any experiments? Did he leave any notes? Did he take anyone else into his confidence? What equipment was he using? Think of *everything*, Dr Cooper. You'll have pen and paper and all the time you need.

"And this room is not very comfortable. We'll have you moved to somewhere more suitable. Is there anything you need in the way of furnishing, for example? Do you prefer to write at a table or a desk? Would you like a typewriting machine? Perhaps you would rather dictate to a stenographer?

"Let the guards know, and you shall have everything you need. But every moment, Dr Cooper, I want you to think back to your colleague and his theory. Your great task is to recall, and if necessary to rediscover, what he knew. Once you know what instruments you require, you shall have those as well. It is a great task, Dr Cooper! You are blessed to be entrusted with it! Give thanks to the Authority."

"I do, Father President! I do!"

Grasping the loose waistband of his trousers, the philosopher stood up and bowed almost without realizing it, again and again, as the President of the Consistorial Court of Discipline left his cell.

That evening, the Chevalier Tialys, the Gallivespian spy, made his way through the lanes and alleys of Geneva to meet his colleague, the Lady Salmakia. It was a dangerous journey for both of them: dangerous for anyone or anything that challenged them, too, but certainly full of peril for the small Gallivespians. More than one prowling cat had met its death at their spurs, but only the week before the chevalier had nearly lost an arm to the teeth of a mangy dog; only the lady's swift action had saved him.

They met at the seventh of their appointed meeting-places, among the roots of a plane tree in a shabby little square, and exchanged their news. The Lady Salmakia's contact in the Society had told her that earlier that evening, they had received a friendly invitation from the President of the Consistorial Court to come and discuss matters of mutual interest.

"Quick work," said the chevalier. "A hundred to one he doesn't tell them about his assassin, though."

He told her about the plan to kill Lyra. She was not surprised.

"It's the logical thing to do," she said. "Very logical people. Tialys, do you think we shall ever see this child?"

"I don't know, but I should like to. Go well, Salmakia. Tomorrow at the fountain."

Unspoken behind that brief exchange was the one thing they never spoke of: the shortness of their lives compared with those of humans. Gallivespians lived to nine years or ten, rarely more, and Tialys and Salmakia were both in their eighth year. They didn't fear old age; their people died in the full strength and vigour of their prime, suddenly, and their childhoods were very brief; but compared to them, the life of a child like Lyra would extend as far into the future as the lives of the witches extended past Lyra's own.

The chevalier returned to the College of St Jerome and began to compose the message he would send to Lord Roke on the lodestone resonator.

But while he was at the rendezvous talking to Salmakia, the President sent for Father Gomez. In his study, they prayed together for an hour, and then Father MacPhail granted the young priest the pre-emptive absolution which would make his murder of Lyra no murder at all. Father Gomez seemed transfigured; the certainty that ran through his veins seemed to make his very eyes incandescent.

They discussed practical arrangements, money, and so forth; and then the President said, "Once you leave here, Father Gomez, you will be completely cut off, for ever, from any help we can give. You can never come back; you will never hear from us. I can't offer you any better advice than this: *don't* look for the child. That would give you away. Instead, look for the tempter. Follow the tempter, and she will lead you to the child."

"She?" said Father Gomez, shocked.

"Yes, *she*," said Father MacPhail. "We have learned that much from the alethiometer. The world the tempter comes from is a strange one. You will see many things that will shock and startle you, Father Gomez. Don't let yourself be distracted by their oddness from the sacred task you have to do. I have faith," he added kindly, "in the power of *your* faith. This woman is travelling, guided by the powers of evil, to a place where she may, eventually, meet the child in time to tempt her. That is, of course, if we do not succeed in removing the girl from her present location. That remains our first plan. You, Father Gomez, are our ultimate guarantee that if that falls through, the infernal powers will still not prevail."

Father Gomez nodded. His dæmon, a large and iridescent green-backed beetle, clicked her wing-cases.

The President opened a drawer and handed the young priest a folded packet of papers.

"Here is all we know about the woman," he said, "and the world she comes from, and the place she was last seen. Read it well, my dear Luis, and go with my blessing."

He had never used the priest's given name before. Father Gomez felt tears of joy prick his eyes as he kissed the President farewell.

you're Lyra."

Then she realized what that meant. She felt dizzy, even in her dream; she felt a great burden settle on her shoulders. And to make it even heavier, sleep was closing in again, and Roger's face receding into shadow.

"Well, I ... I know... There's all kinds of people on our side, like Dr Malone... You know there's another Oxford, Roger, just like ours? Well, she... I found her in... She'd help... But there's only one person really who..."

It was almost impossible now to see the little boy, and her thoughts were spreading out and wandering away like sheep in a field.

"But we can trust him, Roger, I swear," she said with a final effort,

7

Mary, Alone

LAST ROSE AS
IN DANCE THE
STATELY TREES,
& SPRED THIR
BRANCHES
HUNG WITH CO
PIOUS FRUIT···

JOHN MILTON

Almost at the same time, the tempter whom Father Gomez was setting out to follow was being tempted herself.

"Thank you, no, no, that's all I need, no more, honestly, thank you," said Dr Mary Malone to the old couple in the olive grove, as they tried to give her more food than she could carry.

They lived here isolated and childless, and they had been afraid of the Spectres they'd seen among the silver-grey trees; but when Mary Malone came up the road with her rucksack the Spectres had taken fright and drifted away. The old couple had welcomed Mary into their little vine-sheltered farmhouse, plied her with wine and cheese and bread and olives, and now didn't want to let her go.

"I must go on," said Mary again, "thank you, you've been very kind – I can't carry – oh, all right, another little cheese – thank you –"

Evidently they saw her as a talisman against the Spectres. She wished she could be. In her week in the world of Cittàgazze she had seen enough devastation, enough Spectre-eaten adults and wild scavenging children, to have a horror of those ethereal vampires. All she knew was that they did drift away when she approached; but she couldn't stay with every-one who wanted her to, because she had to move on.

She found room for the last little goat's cheese wrapped in its vine leaf, smiled and bowed again, and took a last drink from the spring that bubbled up among the grey rocks. Then she clapped her hands gently together as the old couple were doing, and turned firmly away and left.

She looked more decisive than she felt. The last communi-cation with those entities she called Shadow-particles and Lyra called Dust had been on the screen of her computer, and at their instruction she had destroyed that. Now she was at a loss. They'd told her to go through the opening in the Oxford she had lived in, the Oxford of Will's world, which she'd done – to find herself dizzy and quaking with wonder in this extraordinary other world. Beyond that, her only task was to find the boy and the girl, and then play the serpent, whatever that meant.

So she'd walked and explored and enquired, and found nothing. But now, she thought, as she turned up the little track away from the olive grove, she would have to look for guidance.

Once she was far enough away from the little farmstead to be sure she wouldn't be disturbed, she sat under the pine trees and opened her rucksack. At the bottom, wrapped in a silk scarf, was a book she'd had for twenty years: a commen-tary on the Chinese method of divination, the I Ching.

She had taken it with her for two reasons. One was senti-mental: her grandfather had given it to her, and she had used it a lot as a schoolgirl. The other was that when Lyra had first found her way to Mary's laboratory, she had asked: "What's that?" and pointed to the poster on the door that showed the symbols from the I Ching; and shortly afterwards, in her spectacular reading of the computer, Lyra had learned (she claimed) that Dust had many other ways of speaking to human beings, and one of them was the method from China that used those symbols.

So in her swift packing to leave her own world, Mary Malone had taken with her the *Book of Changes*, as it was called, and the little yarrow stalks with which she read it. And now the time had come to use them.

She spread the silk on the ground and began the process of dividing and counting, dividing and counting and setting aside, which she'd done so often as a passionate curious teenager, and hardly ever since. She had almost forgotten how to do it, but she soon found the ritual coming back, and with it a sense of that calm and concentrated attention that played such an important part in talking to the Shadows.

Eventually she came to the numbers which indicated the hexagram she was being given, the group of six broken or unbroken lines, and then she looked up the meaning. This was the difficult part, because the Book expressed itself in such an enigmatic style.

She read:

Turning to the summit
For provision of nourishment
Brings good fortune.
Spying about with sharp eyes
Like a tiger with insatiable craving.

That seemed encouraging. She read on, following the commentary through the mazy paths it led her on, until she came to: *Keeping still is the mountain; it is a bypath; it means little stones, doors and openings.*

She had to guess. The mention of "openings" recalled the

mysterious window in the air through which she had entered
this world; and the first words seemed to say that she should
go upwards.

Both puzzled and encouraged, she packed the book and
the yarrow stalks away and set off up the path.

Four hours later she was very hot and tired. The sun was low
over the horizon. The rough track she was following had
petered out, and she was clambering with more and more
discomfort among tumbled boulders and smaller stones. To
her left the slope fell away towards a landscape of olive and
lemon groves, of poorly-tended vineyards and abandoned
windmills, lying hazy in the evening light. To her right a
scree of small rocks and gravel sloped up to a cliff of
crumbling limestone.

Wearily she hoisted her rucksack again and set her foot on
the next flat stone – but before she even transferred her
weight, she stopped. The light was catching something
curious, and she shaded her eyes against the glare from the
scree and tried to find it again.

And there it was: like a sheet of glass hanging unsupported
in the air, but glass with no attention-catching reflections
in it: just a square patch of difference. And then she
remembered what the I Ching had said: *a bypath, little stones,
doors and openings.*

It was a window like the one in Sunderland Avenue. She
could only see it because of the light: with the sun any higher
it probably wouldn't show up at all.

She approached the little patch of air with passionate
curiosity, because she hadn't had time to look at the first one:
she'd had to get away as quickly as possible. But she examined
this one in detail, touching the edge, moving around to see

how it became invisible from the other side, noting the absolute difference between *this* and *that*, and found her mind almost bursting with excitement that such things could be.

The knife-bearer who had made it, at about the time of the American Revolution, had been too careless to close it, but at least he'd cut through at a point very similar to the world on this side: next to a rockface. But the rock on the other side was different, not limestone but granite, and as Mary stepped through into the new world she found herself not at the foot of a towering cliff but almost at the top of a low outcrop overlooking a vast plain.

It was evening here, too, and she sat down to breathe the air and rest her limbs and taste the wonder without rushing.

Wide golden light, and an endless prairie or savannah, like nothing she had ever seen in her own world. To begin with, although most of it was covered in short grass in an infinite variety of buff-brown-green-ochre-yellow-golden shades, and undulating very gently in a way that the long evening light showed up clearly, the prairie seemed to be laced through and through with what looked like rivers of rock with a light grey surface.

And secondly, here and there on the plain were stands of the tallest trees Mary had ever seen. Attending a high-energy physics conference once in California she had taken time out to look at the great redwood trees, and marvelled: but whatever these trees were, they would have overtopped the redwoods by half again at least. Their foliage was dense and dark green, their vast trunks gold-red in the heavy evening light.

And finally, herds of creatures, too far off to see distinctly, grazed on the prairie. There was a strangeness about their movement which she couldn't quite work out.

She was desperately tired, and thirsty and hungry besides. Somewhere nearby, though, she heard the welcome trickle of a spring, and only a minute later she found it: just a seepage of clear water from a mossy fissure, and a tiny stream that led away down the slope. She drank long and gratefully, and filled her bottles, and then set about making herself comfortable, for night was falling rapidly.

Propped against the rock, wrapped in her sleeping-bag, she ate some of the rough bread and the goat's cheese, and then fell deeply asleep.

She awoke with the early sun full in her face. The air was cool, and the dew had settled in tiny beads on her hair and on the sleeping-bag. She lay for a few minutes lapped in freshness, feeling as if she were the first human being who had ever lived.

She sat up, yawned, stretched, shivered, and washed in the chilly spring before eating a couple of dried figs and taking stock of the place.

Behind the little rise she had found herself on, the land sloped gradually down and then up again; the fullest view lay in front, across that immense prairie. The long shadows of the trees lay towards her now, and she could see flocks of birds wheeling in front of them, so small against the towering green canopy that they looked like motes of dust.

Loading her rucksack again, she made her way down on to the coarse rich grass of the prairie, aiming for the nearest stand of trees, four or five miles away.

The grass was knee-high, and growing among it there were low-lying bushes, no higher than her ankles, of something like juniper; and there were flowers like poppies, like buttercups, like cornflowers, giving a haze of different tints to the landscape; and then she saw a large bee, the size of the top joint of her thumb, visiting a blue flower-head and making it bend and sway. But as it backed out of the petals and took to the air again, she saw that it was no insect, for a moment later it made for her hand and perched on her finger, dipping a long needle-like beak against her skin with the utmost delicacy and then taking flight again when it found no nectar. It was a minute humming-bird, its bronze-feathered wings moving too fast for her to see.

How every biologist on earth would envy her, if they could see what she was seeing!

She moved on, and found herself getting closer to a herd of those grazing creatures she had seen the previous evening, and whose movement had puzzled her without her knowing why. They were about the size of deer or antelopes, and similarly coloured, but what made her stop still and rub her eyes was the arrangement of their legs. They grew in a diamond formation: two in the centre, one at the front, and one under the tail, so that the animals moved with a curious rocking motion. Mary longed to examine a skeleton and see how the structure worked.

For their part, the grazing creatures regarded her with mild incurious eyes, showing no alarm. She would have loved to go closer and take time to look at them, but it was getting hot, and the shade of the great trees looked inviting; and there was plenty of time, after all.

Before long she found herself stepping out of the grass on to one of those rivers of stone she'd seen from the hill: something else to wonder at.

It might once have been some kind of lava-flow. The underlying colour was dark, almost black, but the surface was paler, as if it had been ground down or worn by crushing. It was as smooth as a stretch of well-laid road in Mary's own world, and certainly easier to walk on than the grass.

She followed the one she was on, which flowed in a wide curve towards the trees. The closer she got, the more astounded she was by the enormous size of the trunks, as wide, she estimated, as the house she lived in, and as tall – as tall as... She couldn't even make a guess.

When she came to the first trunk she rested her hands on the deeply-ridged red-gold bark. The ground was covered ankle-deep in brown leaf-skeletons as long as her foot, soft and fragrant to walk on. She was soon surrounded by a cloud of midge-like flying things, as well as a little flock of the tiny humming-birds, a yellow butterfly with a wingspread as broad as her hand, and too many crawling things for comfort. The air was full of humming and buzzing and scraping.

She walked along the floor of the grove feeling much as if she were in a cathedral: there was the same stillness, the same sense of upwardness in the structures, the same awe in herself.

It had taken her longer than she thought to walk here. It was getting on for midday, for the shafts of light coming down through the canopy were almost vertical. Drowsily, Mary wondered why the grazing creatures didn't move under the shade of the trees during this hottest part of the day.

She soon found out.

Feeling too hot to move any further, she lay down to rest between the roots of one of the giant trees, with her head on her rucksack, and fell into a doze.

Her eyes were closed for twenty minutes or so, and she was not quite asleep, when suddenly, from very close by, there came a resounding crash that shook the ground.

Then came another. Alarmed, Mary sat up and gathered her wits, and saw a movement which resolved itself into a round object, about a yard across, rolling along the ground, coming to a halt, and falling on its side.

And then another fell, further off; she saw the massive thing descend, and watched it crash into the buttress-like root of the nearest trunk and roll away.

The thought of one of those things falling on her was enough to make her take her rucksack and run out of the grove altogether. What were they? Seed-pods?

Watching carefully upwards, she ventured under the canopy again to look at the nearest of the fallen objects. She pulled it upright and rolled it out of the grove, and then laid it on the grass to look at it more closely.

It was perfectly circular, and as thick as the width of her palm. There was a depression in the centre, where it had been attached to the tree. It wasn't heavy, but it was immensely hard, and covered in fibrous hairs that lay along the circumference so that she could run her hand around it easily one way but not the other. She tried her knife on the surface: it made no impression at all.

Her fingers seemed smoother. She smelt them: there was a faint fragrance there, under the smell of dust. She looked at the seed-pod again. In the centre there was a slight glistening, and as she touched it again she felt it slide easily under her fingers. It was exuding a kind of oil.

Mary laid the thing down and thought about the way this world had evolved.

If her guess about these universes was right, and they were the multiple worlds predicted by quantum theory, then some of them would have split off from her own much earlier than others. And clearly in this world evolution had favoured enormous trees and large creatures with a diamond-framed skeleton.

She was beginning to see how narrow her scientific horizons were. No botany, no geology, no biology of any sort – she was as ignorant as a baby.

And then she heard a low thunder-like rumble, which was hard to locate until she saw a cloud of dust moving along one of the roads – towards the stand of trees, and towards her. It was about a mile away, but it wasn't moving slowly, and all of a sudden she felt afraid.

She darted back into the grove. She found a narrow space between two great roots and crammed herself into it, peering over the great buttress beside her and out towards the approaching dust-cloud.

What she saw made her head spin. At first it looked like a motorcycle gang. Then she thought it was a herd of *wheeled* animals. But that was impossible. No animal could have wheels. She wasn't seeing it. But she was.

There were a dozen or so. They were roughly the same size as the grazing creatures, but leaner and grey-coloured, with horned heads and short trunks like elephants'. They had the same diamond-shaped structure as the grazers, but somehow they had evolved, on their fore and rear single legs, a wheel.

But wheels did not exist in nature, her mind insisted; they couldn't; you needed a axle with a bearing that was completely separate from the rotating part, it couldn't happen, it was impossible –

Then, as they came to a halt not fifty yards away, and the dust settled, she suddenly made the connection, and she couldn't help laughing out loud with a little cough of delight.

The wheels were seed-pods. Perfectly round, immensely hard and light – they couldn't have been designed better. The creatures hooked a claw through the centre of the pods with their front and rear legs, and used their two lateral legs to push against the ground and move along. While she marvelled at this, she was also a little anxious, for their horns looked formidably sharp, and even at this distance she could see intelligence and curiosity in their gaze.

And they were looking for her.

One of them had spotted the seed-pod she had taken out of the grove, and he trundled off the road towards it. When he reached it, he lifted it on to an edge with his trunk and rolled it over to his companions.

They gathered around the pod and touched it delicately with those powerful, flexible trunks, and she found herself interpreting the soft chirrups and clicks and hoots they were making as expressions of disapproval. Someone had tampered with this: it was wrong.

Then she thought: I came here for a purpose, although I don't understand it yet. Be bold. Take the initiative.

So she stood up and called, very self-consciously:

"Over here. This is where I am. I looked at your seed-pod. I'm sorry. Please don't harm me."

Instantly their heads snapped round to look at her, trunks held out, glittering eyes facing forward. Their ears had all flicked upright.

She stepped out of the shelter of the roots and faced them directly. She held out her hands, realizing that such a gesture might mean nothing to creatures with no hands themselves. Still, it was all she could do. Picking up her rucksack, she walked across the grass and stepped on to the road.

Close up – not five steps away – she could see much more about their appearance, but her attention was held by something lively and aware in their gaze, by an intelligence. These creatures were as different from the grazing animals nearby as a human was from a cow.

Mary pointed to herself and said, "Mary."

The nearest creature reached forward with its trunk. She moved closer, and it touched her on the breast, where she had pointed, and she heard her voice coming back to her from the creature's throat: "Mèrry."

"What are you?" she said, and, "Watahyu?" the creature responded.

All she could do was respond. "I am a human," she said.

"Ayama yuman," said the creature, and then something even odder happened: the creatures laughed.

Their eyes wrinkled, their trunks waved, they tossed their heads – and from their throats came the unmistakable sound of merriment. She couldn't help it: she laughed too.

Then another creature moved forward and touched her hand with its trunk. Mary offered her other hand as well to its soft, bristled, questing touch.

"Ah," she said, "you're smelling the oil from the seed-pod..."

"Seepot," said the creature.

"If you can make the sounds of my language, we might be able to communicate, one day. God knows how. *Mary*," she said, pointing to herself again.

Nothing. They watched. She did it again: "Mary."

The nearest creature touched its own breast with its trunk and spoke. Was it three syllables, or two? The creature spoke again, and this time Mary tried hard to make the same sounds: "Mulefa," she said tentatively.

Others repeated "Mulefa" in her voice, laughing, and even seemed to be teasing the creature who had spoken. "Mulefa!" they said again, as if it was a fine joke.

"Well, if you can laugh, I don't suppose you'll eat me," Mary said. And from that moment, there was an ease and friendliness between her and them, and she felt nervous no more.

And the group itself relaxed: they had things to do, they weren't roaming at random. Mary saw that one of them had a saddle or pack on its back, and two others lifted the seed-pod on to it, making secure by tying straps around it, with deft and intricate movements of their trunks. When they stood still, they balanced with their lateral legs, and when they moved, they turned both front and back legs to steer. Their movements were full of grace and power.

One of them wheeled to the edge of the road and raised its trunk to utter a trumpeting call. The herd of grazers all looked up as one and began to trot towards them. When they arrived they stood patiently at the verge and let the wheeled creatures move slowly through them, checking, touching, counting.

Then Mary saw one reach beneath a grazer and milk it with her trunk; and then the wheeled one rolled over to her, and raised her trunk delicately to Mary's mouth.

At first she flinched, but there was an expectation in the creature's eye, so she came forward again and opened her lips. The creature expressed a little of the sweet thin milk into her mouth, watched her swallow, and gave her some more, again and again. The gesture was so clever and kindly that Mary impulsively put her arms around the creature's head and kissed her, smelling the hot dusty hide and feeling the hard bones underneath and the muscular power of the trunk.

Presently, the leader trumpeted softly and the grazers moved away. The *mulefa* were preparing to leave. She felt joy that they had welcomed her, and sadness that they were leaving; but then she felt surprise as well.

One of the creatures was lowering itself, kneeling down on

the road, and gesturing with its trunk, and the others were beckoning and inviting her... No doubt about it: they were offering to carry her, to take her with them.

Another took her rucksack and fastened it to the saddle of a third, and awkwardly Mary climbed on the back of the kneeling one, wondering where to put her legs – in front of the creature's, or behind? And what could she hold on to?

But before she could work it out, the creature had risen, and the group began to move away along the highway, with Mary riding among them.

because he's Will."

8
Vodka

 *B*althamos felt the death of Baruch the moment it happened. He cried aloud and soared into the night air over the tundra, flailing his wings and sobbing his anguish into the clouds; and it was some time before he could compose himself and go back to Will, who was wide awake, knife in hand, peering up into the damp and chilly murk. They were back in Lyra's world.

"What is it?" said Will, as the angel appeared trembling beside him. "Is it danger? Get behind me –"

"Baruch is dead," cried Balthamos, "my dear Baruch is dead –"

"When? Where?"

But Balthamos couldn't tell; he only knew that half his heart had been extinguished. He couldn't keep still: he flew up again, scouring the sky as if to seek out Baruch in this cloud or that, calling, crying, calling; and then he'd be overcome with guilt, and fly down to urge Will to hide and keep quiet, and promise to watch over him tirelessly; and then the pressure of his grief would crush him to the ground, and he'd remember every instance of kindness and courage that Baruch had ever shown, and there were thousands, and he'd forgotten none of them; and he'd cry that a nature so gracious could never be snuffed out, and he'd soar into the skies again, casting about in every direction, reckless and wild and stricken, cursing the very air, the clouds, the stars.

Finally Will said, "Balthamos, come here."

The angel came at his command, helpless. In the bitter cold gloom of the tundra, the boy shivering in his cloak said to him, "You must try to keep quiet now. You know there are things out there that'll attack if they hear a noise. I can protect you with the knife if you're nearby, but if they attack you up there, I won't be able to help. And if you die too, that'll be the end for me. Balthamos, I need you to help guide me to Lyra. Please don't forget that. Baruch was strong – be strong too. Be like him for me."

At first Balthamos didn't speak, but then he said, "Yes. Yes, of course I must. Sleep now, Will, and I shall stand guard, I shan't fail you."

Will trusted him; he had to. And presently he fell asleep again.

When he woke up, soaked with dew and cold to his bones, the angel was standing nearby. The sun was just rising, and the reeds and the marsh plants were all tipped with gold.

Before Will could move, Balthamos said, "I've decided what I must do. I shall stay with you day and night, and do it cheerfully and willingly, for the sake of Baruch. I shall guide you to Lyra, if I can, and then I shall guide you both to Lord Asriel. I have lived thousands of years, and unless I am killed I shall live many thousands of years more; but I never met a nature that made me so ardent to do good, or to be kind, as Baruch did. I failed so many times, but each time his goodness was there to redeem me. Now it's not, I shall have to try without it. Perhaps I shall fail from time to time, but I shall try all the same."

"Then Baruch would be proud of you," said Will, shivering.

"Shall I fly ahead now and see where we are?"

"Yes," said Will, "fly high, and tell me what the land's like further on. Walking on this marshland is going to take for ever."

Balthamos took to the air. He hadn't told Will everything he was anxious about, because he was trying to do his best and not worry him; but he knew that the angel Metatron, the Regent, from whom they'd escaped so narrowly, would have Will's face firmly imprinted on his mind. And not only his face, but everything about him which angels were able to see, including parts of which Will himself was not aware, such as that aspect of his nature Lyra would have called his dæmon. Will was in great danger from Metatron now, and at some time Balthamos would have to tell him; but not quite yet. It was too difficult.

Will, reckoning that it would be quicker to get warm by walking than by gathering fuel and waiting for a fire to catch, simply slung the rucksack over his shoulders, wrapped the cloak around everything, and set off towards the south. There was a path, muddy and rutted and pot-holed, so people did sometimes come this way; but the flat horizon was so far away on every side that he had little sense of making progress.

Some time later, when the light was brighter, Balthamos's voice spoke beside him.

"About half a day's walk ahead, there is a wide river and a town, where there's a wharf for boats to tie up. I flew high enough to see that the river goes a long way directly south and north. If you could get a passage, then you could move much more quickly."

"Good," said Will fervently. "And does this path go to the town?"

"It goes through a village, with a church and farms and orchards, and then on to the town."

"I wonder what language they speak. I hope they don't lock me up if I can't speak theirs."

"As your dæmon," said Balthamos, "I shall translate for you. I have learned many human languages; I can certainly understand the one they speak in this country."

Will walked on. The toil was dull and mechanical, but at least he was moving, and at least every step took him closer to Lyra.

The village was a shabby place: a huddle of wooden buildings, with paddocks containing reindeer, and dogs that barked as he approached. Smoke crept out of the tin chimneys and hung low over the shingled roofs. The ground was heavy and dragged at his feet, and there had obviously been a recent flood: walls were marked with mud to half-way up the doors, and broken beams of wood and loose-hanging sheets of corrugated iron showed where sheds and verandas and outbuildings had been swept away.

But that was not the most curious feature of the place. At first he thought he was losing his balance; it even made him stumble once or twice; for the buildings were two or three degrees out of the vertical, all leaning the same way. The dome of the little church had cracked badly. Had there been an earthquake?

Dogs were barking with hysterical fury, but not daring to come close. Balthamos, being a dæmon, had taken the form of a large snow-white dog with black eyes, thick fur, and tight-curled tail, and he snarled so fiercely that the real dogs kept their distance. They were thin and mangy, and the few reindeer he could see were scabby-coated and listless.

Will paused in the centre of the little village and looked around, wondering where to go, and as he stood there, two or three men appeared ahead and stood staring at him. They were the first people he had ever seen in Lyra's world. They wore heavy felt coats, muddy boots, fur hats, and they didn't look friendly.

The white dog changed into a sparrow, and flew to Will's shoulder. No one blinked an eye at this: each of the men had a dæmon, Will saw, dogs, most of them, and that was how things happened in this world. On his shoulder, Balthamos whispered: "Keep moving. Don't look them in the eye. Keep your head down. That is the respectful thing to do."

Will kept walking. He could make himself inconspicuous; it was his greatest talent. By the time he got to them, the men had already lost interest in him. But then a door opened in the biggest house in the road, and a voice called something loudly.

Balthamos said softly, "The priest. You will have to be polite to him. Turn and bow."

Will did so. The priest was an immense, grey-bearded man, wearing a black cassock, with a crow-dæmon on his shoulder. His restless eyes moved over Will's face and body, taking everything in. He beckoned.

Will went to the doorway and bowed again.

The priest said something, and Balthamos murmured, "He's asking where you come from. Say whatever you like."

"I speak English," Will said slowly and clearly. "I don't know any other languages."

"Ah, English!" cried the priest gleefully in the same

language. "My dear young man! Welcome to our village, our little no–longer-perpendicular Kholodnoye! What is your name, and where are you going?"

"My name is Will, and I'm going south. I have lost my family, and I'm trying to find them again."

"Then you must come inside and have some refreshment," said the priest, and put a heavy arm around Will's shoulders, pulling him in through the doorway.

The man's crow-dæmon was showing a vivid interest in Balthamos. But the angel was equal to that: he became a mouse, and crept into Will's shirt as if he was shy.

The priest led him into a parlour heavy with tobacco-smoke, where a cast-iron samovar steamed quietly on a side-table.

"What was your name?" said the priest. "Tell me again."

"Will Parry. But I don't know what to call you."

"Otyets Semyon," said the priest, stroking Will's arm as he guided him to a chair. "Otyets means Father. I am a priest of the Holy Church. My given name is Semyon, and the name of my father was Boris, so I am Semyon Borisovitch. What is your father's name?"

"John Parry."

"John is Ivan. So you are Will Ivanovitch, and I am Father Semyon Borisovitch. Where have you come from, Will Ivanovitch, and where are you going?"

"I'm lost," Will said. "I was travelling with my family to the south. My father is a soldier, but he was exploring in the Arctic, and then something happened and we got lost. So I'm travelling south because I know that's where we were going next."

The priest spread his hands and said, "A soldier? An explorer from England? No one so interesting as that has trodden the dirty roads of Kholodnoye for centuries, but in this time of upheaval, how can we know that he will not appear tomorrow? You yourself are a welcome visitor, Will Ivanovitch. You must stay the night in my house and we will talk and eat together. Lydia Alexandrovna!" he called.

An elderly woman came in silently. He spoke to her in Russian, and she nodded and took a glass and filled it with hot tea from the samovar. She brought the glass of tea to Will, together with a little saucer of jam with a silver spoon.

"Thank you," said Will.

"The conserve is to sweeten the tea," said the priest. "Lydia Alexandrovna made it from bilberries."

The result was that the tea was sickly as well as bitter, but Will sipped it nonetheless. The priest kept leaning forward to look closely at him, and felt his hands to see whether he was cold, and stroked his knee. In order to distract him, Will asked why the buildings in the village sloped.

"There has been a convulsion in the earth," the priest said. "It is all foretold in the Apocalypse of St John. Rivers flow backwards... The great river only a short way from here used to flow north into the Arctic Ocean. All the way from the mountains of central Asia it flowed north for thousands and thousands of years, ever since the Authority of God the Almighty Father created the earth. But when the earth shook and the fog and the floods came, everything changed, and then the great river flowed south for a week or more before it turned again and went north. The world is turned upside down. Where were you when the great convulsion came?"

"A long way from here," Will said. "I didn't know what was happening. When the fog cleared I had lost my family and I don't know where I am now. You've told me the name of this place, but where is it? Where are we?"

"Bring me that large book on the bottom shelf," said Semyon Borisovitch. "I will show you."

The priest drew his chair up to the table and licked his fingers before turning the pages of the great atlas.

"Here," he said, pointing with a dirty fingernail at a spot in central Siberia, a long way east of the Urals. The river nearby flowed as the priest had said, from the northern part of the mountains in Tibet all the way to the Arctic. He looked closely at the Himalayas, but he could see nothing like the map Baruch had sketched.

Semyon Borisovitch talked and talked, pressing Will for details of his life, his family, his home, and Will, a practised dissembler, answered him fully enough. Presently the housekeeper brought in some beetroot soup and dark bread, and after the priest had said a long grace they ate.

"Well, how shall we pass our day, Will Ivanovitch?" said Semyon Borisovitch. "Shall we play at cards, or would you prefer to talk?"

He drew another glass of tea from the samovar, and Will took it doubtfully.

"I can't play cards," he said, "and I'm anxious to get on and keep travelling. If I went to the river, for example, do you think I could find a passage on a steamer going south?"

The priest's huge face darkened, and he crossed himself with a delicate flick of the wrist.

"There is trouble in the town," he said. "Lydia Alexandrovna has a sister who came here and told her there is a boat carrying bears up the river. Armoured bears. They come from the Arctic. You did not see armoured bears when you were in the north?"

The priest was suspicious, and Balthamos whispered so quietly that only Will could hear: "Be careful." And Will knew at once why he'd said it: his heart had begun to pound when Semyon Borisovitch mentioned the bears, because of what Lyra had told him about them. He must try to contain his feelings.

He said, "We were a long way from Svalbard, and the bears were occupied with their own affairs."

"Yes, that is what I heard," said the priest, to Will's relief. "But now they are leaving their homeland and coming south. They have a boat, and the people of the town will not let them refuel. They are afraid of the bears. And so they should be – they are children of the devil. All things from the north are devilish. Like the witches – daughters of evil! The church should have put them all to death many years ago. Witches – have nothing to do with them, Will Ivanovitch, you hear me? You know what they will do when you come to the right age? They will try to seduce you. They will use all the soft cunning deceitful ways they have, their flesh, their soft skin, their sweet voices, and they will take your seed – you know what I mean by that – they will drain you and leave you hollow! They will take your future, your children that are to come, and leave you nothing. They should be put to death, every one."

The priest reached across to the shelf beside his chair and took down a bottle and two small glasses.

"Now I am going to offer you a little drink, Will Ivanovitch," he said. "You are young, so not very many glasses. But you are growing, and so you need to know some things, like the taste of vodka. Lydia Alexandrovna collected the berries last year, and I distilled the liquor, and here in the bottle is the result, the only place where Otyets Semyon Borisovitch and Lydia Alexandrovna lie together!"

He laughed and uncorked the bottle, filling each glass to the rim. This kind of talk made Will hideously uneasy. What should he do? How could he refuse to drink without discourtesy?

"Otyets Semyon," he said, standing, "you have been very kind, and I wish I could stay longer to taste your drink and to hear you talk, because what you tell me has been very interesting. But you understand I am unhappy about my family, and very anxious to find them again, so I think I must move on, much as I would like to stay."

The priest pushed out his lips, in the thicket of his beard, and frowned; but then he shrugged, and said, "Well, you shall go if you must. But before you leave, you must drink your vodka. Stand with me now! Take it, and down all in one, like this!"

He threw back the glass, swallowing it all at once, and then hauled his massive body up and stood very close to Will. In his fat dirty fingers the glass he held out seemed tiny; but it was brimming with the clear spirit, and Will could smell the heady tang of the drink and the stale sweat and the food-stains on the man's cassock, and he felt sick before he began.

"Drink, Will Ivanovitch!" the priest cried, with a threatening heartiness.

Will lifted the glass and unhesitatingly swallowed the fiery, oily liquid in one gulp. Now he would have to fight hard to avoid being sick.

There was one more ordeal to come. Semyon Borisovitch leaned forward from his great height, and took Will by both shoulders.

"My boy," he said, and then closed his eyes and began to intone a prayer or a psalm. Vapours of tobacco and alcohol and sweat came powerfully from him, and he was close enough for his thick beard, wagging up and down, to brush Will's face. Will held his breath.

The priest's hands moved behind Will's shoulders, and then Semyon Borisovitch was hugging him tightly and kissing his cheeks, right, left, right again. Will felt Balthamos dig tiny claws into his shoulder, and kept still. His head was swimming, his stomach lurching, but he didn't move.

Finally it was over, and the priest stepped back and pushed him away.

"Go then," he said, "go south, Will Ivanovitch. Go."

Will gathered his cloak and the rucksack, and tried to walk straight as he left the priest's house and took the road out of the village.

He walked for two hours, feeling the nausea gradually subside and a slow, pounding headache take its place. Balthamos made him stop at one point, and laid his cool hands on Will's neck and forehead, and the ache eased a little; but Will made himself a promise that he would never drink vodka again.

And in the late afternoon, the path widened and came out of the reeds, and Will saw the town ahead of him, and beyond it an expanse of water so broad it might have been a sea.

Even from some way off, Will could see that there was trouble. Puffs of smoke were erupting from beyond the roofs, followed a few seconds later by the boom of a gun.

"Balthamos," he said, "you'll have to be a dæmon again. Just keep near me and watch out for danger."

He walked into the outskirts of the scruffy little town, where the buildings leant even more perilously than the village, and where the flooding had left its mud-stains on the walls high above Will's head. The edge of the town was deserted, but as he made his way towards the river, the noise of shouting, of screams, and of the crackle of rifle fire got louder.

And here at last there were people: some watching from upper floor windows, some craning anxiously around the corners of buildings to look ahead at the waterfront, where the metal fingers of cranes and derricks and the masts of big vessels rose above the rooftops.

An explosion shook the walls, and glass fell out of a nearby window. People drew back and then peered round again, and more cries rose into the smoky air.

Will reached the corner of the street, and looked along the waterfront. When the smoke and dust cleared a little, he saw one rusting vessel standing off shore, keeping its place against the flow of the river, and on the wharf a mob of people armed with rifles or pistols surrounding a great gun, which, as he watched, boomed again. A flash of fire, a lurching recoil, and near the vessel, a mighty splash.

Will shaded his eyes. There were figures in the boat, but – he rubbed his eyes, even though he knew what to expect: they weren't human. They were huge beings of metal, or creatures in heavy armour, and on the foredeck of the vessel a bright flower of flame suddenly bloomed, and the people cried out in alarm. The flame sped into the air, rising higher and coming closer and shedding sparks and smoke, and then fell with a great splash of fire near the gun. Men cried and scattered, and some ran in flames to the water's edge and plunged in, to be swept along and out of sight in the current.

Will found a man close by who looked like a teacher, and said:

"Do you speak English?"

"Yes, yes, indeed –"

"What is happening?"

"The bears, they are attacking, and we try to fight them, but is difficult, we have only one gun, and –"

The fire-thrower on the boat hurled another gout of blazing pitch, and this time it landed even closer to the gun.

Three big explosions almost immediately afterwards showed that it had found the ammunition, and the gunners leapt away, letting the barrel swing down low.

"Ah," the man lamented, "it's no good, they can't fire –"

The commander of the boat brought its head round and moved in towards the shore. Many people cried out in alarm and despair, especially when another great bulb of flame burst into being on the foredeck, and some of those with rifles fired a shot or two and turned to flee; but this time the bears didn't launch the fire, and soon the vessel moved broadside on towards the wharf, engine beating hard to hold it against the current.

Two sailors (human, not bears) leapt down to throw ropes around the bollards, and a great hiss and cry of anger rose from the townsfolk at these human traitors. The sailors took no notice, but ran to lower a gangplank.

Then as they turned to go back on board, a shot was fired from somewhere near Will, and one of the sailors fell. His dæmon – a seagull – vanished as if she'd been pinched out of existence like a candle flame.

The reaction from the bears was pure fury. At once the fire-thrower was re-lit and hauled around to face the shore, and the mass of flame shot upwards and then cascaded in a hundred spilling gouts over the rooftops. And at the top of the gangway appeared a bear larger than any of the others, an apparition of iron-clad might, and the bullets that rained on him whined and clanged and thudded uselessly, unable to make the slightest dent in his massive armour.

Will said to the man beside him, "Why are they attacking the town?"

"They want fuel. But we have no dealings with bears. Now they are leaving their kingdom and sailing up the river, who knows what they will do? So we must fight them. Pirates – robbers –"

The great bear had come down the gangway, and massed behind him were several others, so heavy that the ship listed; and Will saw that the men on the wharf had gone back to the gun, and were loading a shell into the breech.

An idea came, and he ran out on to the quayside, right into the empty space between the gunners and the bear.

"Stop!" he shouted. "Stop fighting. Let me speak to the bear!"

There was a sudden lull, and everyone stood still, astonished at this crazy behaviour. The bear himself, who had been gathering his strength to charge the gunners, stayed where he was, but every line of his body trembled with ferocity. His great claws dug into the ground, and his black eyes glowed with rage under the iron helmet.

"What are you? What do you want?" he roared in English, since Will had spoken in that language.

The people watching looked at one another in bewilderment, and those who could understand translated for the others.

"I'll fight you, in single combat," cried Will, "and if you give way, then the fighting has to stop."

The bear didn't move. As for the people, as soon as they understood what Will was saying, they shouted and jeered and hooted with mocking laughter. But not for long, because Will turned to face the crowd, and stood cold-eyed, contained, and perfectly still, until the laughter stopped. He could feel the blackbird-Balthamos trembling on his shoulder.

When the people were silent, he called out, "If I make the bear give way, you must agree to sell them fuel. Then they'll go on along the river and leave you alone. You must agree. If you don't, they'll destroy all of you."

He knew that the huge bear was only a few yards behind him, but he didn't turn; he watched the townspeople talking, gesticulating, arguing, and after a minute, a voice called, "Boy! Make the bear agree!"

Will turned back. He swallowed hard and took a deep breath and called:

"Bear! You must agree. If you give way to me, the fighting has to stop, and you can buy fuel and go peacefully up the river."

"Impossible," roared the bear. "It would be shameful to fight you. You are as weak as an oyster out of its shell. I cannot fight you."

"I agree," said Will, and every scrap of his attention was now focused on this great ferocious being in front of him. "It's not a fair contest at all. You have all that armour, and I have none. You could take off my head with one sweep of your paw. Make it fairer, then. Give me one piece of your armour, any one you like. Your helmet, for example. Then we'll be better matched, and it'll be no shame to fight me."

With a snarl that expressed hatred, rage, scorn, the bear reached up with a great claw and unhooked the chain that held his helmet in place.

And now there was a deep hush over the whole waterfront. No one spoke – no one moved. They could tell that something was happening such as they'd never seen before, and they couldn't tell what it was. The only sound now was the splashing of the river against the wooden pilings, the beat of the ship's engine, and the restless crying of seagulls overhead; and then the great clang as the bear hurled his helmet down at Will's feet.

Will put his rucksack down, and hoisted the helmet up on its end. He could barely lift it. It consisted of a single sheet of iron, dark and dented, with eye-holes on top and a massive chain underneath. It was as long as Will's forearm, and as thick as his thumb.

"So this is your armour," he said. "Well, it doesn't look very strong to me. I don't know if I can trust it. Let me see."

And he took the knife from the rucksack and rested the edge against the front of the helmet, and sliced off a corner as if he were cutting butter.

"That's what I thought," he said, and cut another and another, reducing the massive thing to a pile of fragments in less than a minute. He stood up and held out a handful.

"That was your armour," he said, and dropped the pieces with a clatter on to the rest at his feet, "and this is my knife. And since your helmet was no good to me, I'll have to fight without it. Are you ready, bear? I think we're well matched. I could take off your head with one sweep of my knife, after all."

Utter stillness. The bear's black eyes glowed like pitch, and Will felt a drop of sweat trickle down his spine.

Then the bear's head moved. He shook it and took a step backwards.

"Too strong a weapon," he said. "I can't fight that. Boy, you win."

Will knew that a second later the people would cheer and hoot and whistle, so even before the bear had finished saying the word "win", Will had begun to turn and call out, to keep them quiet:

"Now you must keep the bargain. Look after the wounded people and start repairing the buildings. Then let the boat tie up and refuel."

He knew that it would take a minute to translate that and let the message spread out among the watching townsfolk, and he knew too that the delay would prevent their relief and anger from bursting out, as a net of sandbanks baffles and breaks up the flow of a river. The bear watched and saw what he was doing and why, and understood more fully than Will himself did what the boy had achieved.

Will put the knife back in the rucksack, and he and the bear exchanged another glance, but a different kind this time. They approached, and behind them the bears began to dismantle their fire-thrower; the other two ships manoeuvred their way to the quayside.

On shore, some of the people set about clearing up, but several more came crowding to see Will, curious about this boy and the power he had to command the bear. It was time for Will to become inconspicuous again, so he performed the magic that had deflected all kinds of curiosity away from his mother and kept them safe for years. Of course, it wasn't magic, but simply a way of behaving. He made himself quiet and dull-eyed and slow, and in under a minute he became less interesting, less attractive to human attention. The people simply became bored with this dull child, and forgot him and turned away.

But the bear's attention was not human, and he could see what was happening, and he knew it was yet another extraordinary power at Will's command. He came close and spoke quietly, in his voice that seemed to throb as deeply as the ship's engines.

"What is your name?" he said.

"Will Parry. Can you make another helmet?"

"Yes. What do you seek?"

"You're going up the river. I want to come with you. I'm

going to the mountains and this is the quickest way. Will you take me?"

"Yes. I want to see that knife."

"I will only show it to a bear I can trust. There is one bear I've heard of who's trustworthy. He is the king of the bears, a good friend of the girl I'm going to the mountains to find. Her name is Lyra Silvertongue. The bear is called Iorek Byrnison."

"I am Iorek Byrnison," said the bear.

"I know you are," said Will.

The boat was taking fuel on board; the rail trucks were hauled alongside and tilted sideways to let coal thunder down the chutes into the hold, and the black dust rose high above them. Unnoticed by the townspeople, who were busy sweeping up glass and haggling over the price of the fuel, Will followed the bear-king up the gangway and aboard the ship.

9

Up-river

"Let me see the knife," said Iorek Byrnison. "I understand metal. Nothing made of iron or steel is a mystery to a bear. But I have never seen a knife like yours, and I would be glad to look at it closely."

Will and the bear-king were on the foredeck of the river steamer, in the warm rays of the setting sun, and the vessel was making swift progress up-stream; there was plenty of fuel on board, there was food that Will could eat, and he and Iorek Byrnison were taking their second measure of each other. They had taken the first already.

Will held out the knife towards Iorek, handle first, and the bear took it from him delicately. His thumb-claw opposed the four finger-claws, letting him manipulate objects as skilfully as a human, and now he turned the knife this way and that, bringing it closely to his eyes, holding it to catch the light, testing the edge – the steel edge – on a piece of scrap iron.

"This edge is the one you cut my armour with," he said. "The other is very strange. I cannot tell what it is, what it will do, how it was made. But I want to understand it. How did you come to possess it?"

Will told him most of what had happened, leaving out only what concerned him alone: his mother, the man he killed, his father.

"You fought for this, and lost two fingers?" the bear said. "Show me the wound."

Will held out his hand. Thanks to his father's ointment, the raw surfaces were healing well, but they were still very tender. The bear sniffed at them.

"Bloodmoss," he said. "And something else I cannot identify. Who gave you that?"

"A man who told me what I should do with the knife. Then he died. He had some ointment in a horn box, and it cured my wound. The witches tried, but their spell didn't work."

"And what did he tell you to do with the knife?" said Iorek Byrnison, handing it carefully back to Will.

"To use it in a war on the side of Lord Asriel," Will replied. "But first I must rescue Lyra Silvertongue."

"Then we shall help," said the bear, and Will's heart leapt with pleasure.

Over the next few days Will learned why the bears were making this voyage into Central Asia, so far from their homeland.

Since the catastrophe which had burst the worlds open, all the Arctic ice had begun to melt, and new and strange currents appeared in the water. Since the bears depended on ice and on the creatures who lived in the cold sea, they could see that they would soon starve if they stayed where they were; and being rational, they decided how they should respond. They would have to migrate to where there was snow and ice in plenty: they would go to the highest mountains, to the range that touched the sky, half a world away but unshakeable, eternal, and deep in snow. From bears of the sea they would become bears of the mountains, for as long as it took the world to settle itself again.

"So you're not making war?" Will said.

"Our old enemies vanished with the seals and the walruses. If we meet new ones, we know how to fight."

"I thought there was a great war coming that would involve everyone. Which side would you fight for in that case?"

"The side that gave advantage to the bears. What else? But I have some regard for a few who are not bears. One was a man who flew a balloon. He is dead. Another is the witch Serafina Pekkala. The third is the child Lyra Silvertongue. So first, I would do whatever serves the bears, and then whatever serves the child, or the witch, or avenges my dead comrade Lee Scoresby. That is why I will help you rescue Lyra Silvertongue from the abominable woman Coulter."

He told Will of how he and a few of his subjects had swum to the river-mouth and paid for the charter of this vessel with gold, and hired the crew, and turned the draining of the Arctic to their own advantage by letting the river take them as far inland as it could – and as it had its source in the northern foothills of the very mountains they sought, and as Lyra was imprisoned there too, things had fallen out well so far.

So time went past.

During the day Will dozed on deck, resting, gathering strength, because he was exhausted in every part of his being. He watched as the scenery began to change, and the rolling steppe gave way to low grassy hills and then to higher land, with the occasional gorge or cataract; and still the boat steamed south.

He talked to the captain and the crew, out of politeness, but lacking Lyra's instant ease with strangers, he found it difficult to think of much to say; and in any case they were little interested in him. This was only a job, and when it was over they would leave without a backward glance, and besides, they didn't much like the bears, for all their gold. Will was a foreigner, and as long as he paid for his food, they cared little what he did. Besides, there was that strange dæmon of his, which seemed so like a witch's: sometimes it was there, and sometimes it seemed to have vanished. Superstitious, like many sailors, they were happy to leave him alone.

Balthamos, for his part, kept quiet too. Sometimes his grief would become too strong for him to put up with, and he'd leave the boat and fly high among the clouds, searching for any patch of light or taste of air, any shooting stars or pressure-ridges that might remind him of experiences he had shared with Baruch. When he talked, at night in the dark of the little cabin Will slept in, it was only to report on how far they had gone, and how much further ahead the cave and the valley lay. Perhaps he thought Will had little sympathy, though if he'd sought it, he would have found plenty. He became more and more curt and formal, though never sarcastic; he kept that promise, at least.

As for Iorek, he examined the knife obsessively. He looked at it for hours, testing both edges, flexing it, holding it up to the light, touching it with his tongue, sniffing it, and even listening to the sound the air made as it flowed over the surface. Will had no fear for the knife, because Iorek was clearly a craftsman of the highest accomplishment; nor for Iorek himself, because of the delicacy of movement in those mighty paws.

Finally Iorek came to Will and said, "This other edge. It does something you have not told me about. What is it, and how does it work?"

"I can't show you here," said Will, "because the boat is moving. As soon as we stop I'll show you."

"I can think of it," said the bear, "but not understand what I am thinking. It is the strangest thing I have ever seen."

And he gave it back to Will, with a disconcerting long unreadable stare out of his deep black eyes.

The river by this time had changed colour, because it was meeting the remains of the first flood-waters that had swept down out of the Arctic. The convulsions had affected the earth differently in different places, Will saw; village after village stood up to its roofs in water and hundreds of dispossessed people tried to salvage what they could with rowing boats and canoes. The earth must have sunk a little here, because the river broadened and slowed, and it was hard for the skipper to trace his true course through the wide and turbid streams. The air was hotter here, and the sun higher in the sky, and the bears found it hard to keep cool; some of them swam alongside as the steamer made its way, tasting their native waters in this foreign land.

But eventually the river narrowed and deepened again, and soon ahead of them began to rise the mountains of the great central Asian plateau. Will saw a rim of white on the horizon one day and watched as it grew and grew, separating itself into different peaks and ridges and passes between them, and so high that it seemed that they must be close at hand – only a few miles – but they were far off still; it was just that the mountains were immense, and with every hour that they came closer, they seemed yet more inconceivably high.

Most of the bears had never seen mountains, apart from

the cliffs on their own island of Svalbard, and fell silent as they looked up at the giant ramparts, still so far off.

"What will we hunt there, Iorek Byrnison?" said one. "Are there seals in the mountains? How shall we live?"

"There is snow and ice," was the king's reply. "We shall be comfortable. And there are wild creatures there in plenty. Our lives will be different for a while. But we shall survive, and when things return to what they should be, and the Arctic freezes once more, we shall still be alive to go back and claim it. If we had stayed there we would have starved. Be prepared for strangeness and for new ways, my bears."

Eventually the steamer could sail no further, because at this point the river-bed had narrowed and become shallow. The skipper brought the vessel to a halt in a valley bottom which normally would have been carpeted with grass and mountain flowers, where the river meandered over gravel beds; but the valley was now a lake, and the captain insisted that he dare not go past it, because beyond this point there would be not enough depth below the keel, even with the massive flood from the north.

So they drew up to the edge of the valley, where an outcrop of rock formed a sort of jetty, and disembarked.

"Where are we now?" said Will to the captain, whose English was limited.

The captain found a tattered old map and jabbed at it with his pipe, saying, "This valley here, we now. You take, go on."

"Thank you very much," Will said, and wondered if he ought to offer to pay; but the captain had turned away to supervise the unloading.

Before long all thirty or so bears and all their armour were on the narrow shore. The captain shouted an order, and the vessel began to turn ponderously against the current, manoeuvring out into mid-stream and giving a blast on the whistle that echoed for a long time around the valley.

Will sat on a rock, reading the map. If he was right, the valley where Lyra was captive, according to the angel, lay some way to the east and the south, and the best way there led through a pass called Sungchen.

"Bears, mark this place," said Iorek Byrnison to his subjects. "When the time comes for us to move back to the Arctic, we shall assemble here. Now go your ways, hunt, feed, and live. Do not make war. We are not here for war. If war threatens, I shall call for you."

The bears were solitary creatures for the most part, and they only came together in times of war or emergency. Now that they were at the edge of a land of snow, they were impatient to be off, each of them, exploring on their own.

"Come then, Will," said Iorek Byrnison, "and we shall find Lyra."

Will lifted his rucksack and they set off.

It was good walking for the first part of their journey. The sun was warm, but the pines and the rhododendrons kept the worst of the heat off their shoulders, and the air was fresh and clear. The ground was rocky, but the rocks were thick with moss and pine-needles, and the slopes they climbed were not precipitous. Will found himself relishing the exercise. The days he had spent on the boat, the enforced rest, had built up his strength. When he came across Iorek he had been at the very last of it. He didn't know that, but the bear did.

And as soon as they were alone, Will showed Iorek how the other edge of the knife worked. He opened a world where a tropical rainforest steamed and dripped, and where vapours laden with heavy scent drifted out into the thin mountain air.

Iorek watched closely, and touched the edge of the window with his paw, and sniffed at it, and stepped through into the hot moist air to look around in silence. The monkey-shrieks and bird-calls, the insect-scrapings and frog-croakings and the incessant drip-drip of condensing moisture sounded very loud to Will, outside it.

Then Iorek came back and watched Will close the window, and asked to see the knife again, peering so closely at the silver edge that Will thought he was in danger of cutting his eye. He examined it for a long time, and handed it back without a word except to say, "I was right: I could not have fought this."

They moved on, speaking little, which suited them both. Iorek Byrnison caught a gazelle and ate most of it, leaving the tender meat for Will to cook; and once they came to a village, and while Iorek waited in the forest, Will exchanged one of his gold coins for some flat coarse bread and some dried fruit, and for boots of yak leather and a waistcoat of a kind of sheepskin, for it was becoming cold at night.

He also managed to ask about the valley with the rainbows. Balthamos helped by assuming the form of a crow, like the dæmon of the man Will was speaking to; he made the passage of understanding easier between them, and Will got directions which were helpful and clear.

It was another three days' walk. Well, they were getting there.

And so were others.

Lord Asriel's force, the squadron of gyropters and the zeppelin fuel tanker, had reached the opening between the worlds: the breach in the sky above Svalbard. They had a very long way to go still, but they flew without pause except for essential maintenance, and the commander, the African King Ogunwe, kept in twice-daily touch with the basalt fortress. He had a Gallivespian lodestone operator aboard his gyropter, and through him he was able to learn as quickly as Lord Asriel himself about what was going on elsewhere.

The news was disconcerting. The little spy, the Lady Salmakia, had watched from the shadows as the two powerful arms of the church, the Consistorial Court of Discipline and the Society of the Work of the Holy Spirit, agreed to put their differences aside and pool their knowledge. The Society had a swifter and more skilful alethiometrist than Fra Pavel, and thanks to him, the Consistorial Court now knew exactly where Lyra was, and more: they knew that Lord Asriel had sent a force to rescue her. Wasting no time, the Court commandeered a flight of zeppelins, and that same day a battalion of the Swiss Guard began to embark aboard the zeppelins waiting in the still air beside the lake of Geneva.

So each side was aware that the other was also making its way towards the cave in the mountains. And they both knew that whoever got there first would have the advantage, but there wasn't much in it: Lord Asriel's gyropters were faster than the zeppelins of the Consistorial Court, but they had further to fly, and they were limited by the speed of their own zeppelin tanker.

And there was another consideration: whoever seized Lyra first would have to fight their way out against the other force. It would be easier for the Consistorial Court, because they didn't have to consider getting Lyra away safely. They were flying there to kill her.

The zeppelin carrying the President of the Consistorial Court was carrying other passengers as well, unknown to him. The Chevalier Tialys had received a message on his lodestone resonator, ordering him and the Lady Salmakia to smuggle themselves aboard. When the zeppelins arrived at the valley, he and the lady were to go ahead and make their way independently to the cave where Lyra was held, and protect her as well as they could until King Ogunwe's force arrived to rescue her. Her safety was to come above every other consideration.

Getting themselves aboard the zeppelin was hazardous for the spies, not least because of the equipment they had to carry. Apart from the lodestone resonator, the most important items were a pair of insect larvae, and their food. When the adult insects emerged, they would be more like dragonflies than anything else, but they were not like any kind of dragonfly that the humans of Will's world, or Lyra's, would have seen before. They were very much larger, for one thing. The Gallivespians bred these creatures carefully, and each clan's insects differed from the rest. The Chevalier Tialys's clan bred powerful red-and-yellow striped dragonflies with vigorous and brutal appetites, whereas the one the Lady Salmakia was nurturing would be a slender, fast-flying creature with an electric blue body and the power of glowing in the dark.

Every spy was equipped with a number of these larvae, which by feeding carefully regulated amounts of oil and honey they could either keep in suspended animation or bring rapidly to adulthood. Tialys and Salmakia had thirty-six hours, depending on the winds, to hatch these larvae now; because that was about the time the flight would take, and they needed the insects to emerge before the zeppelins landed.

The chevalier and his colleague found an over-looked

space behind a bulkhead, and made themselves as safe as they could while the vessel was loaded and fuelled; and then the engines began to roar, shaking the light structure from end to end as the ground crew cast off and the eight zeppelins rose into the night sky.

Their kind would have regarded the comparison as a mortal insult, but they were able to conceal themselves at least as well as rats. From their hiding place, the Gallivespians could overhear a good deal, and they kept in hourly touch with Lord Roke, who was aboard King Ogunwe's gyropter.

But there was one thing they couldn't learn any more about on the zeppelin, because the President never spoke of it: and that was the matter of the assassin, Father Gomez, who had been absolved already of the sin he was going to commit if the Consistorial Court failed in their mission. Father Gomez was somewhere else, and no one was tracking him at all.

10
Wheels

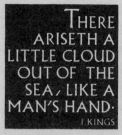

THERE ARISETH A LITTLE CLOUD OUT OF THE SEA, LIKE A MAN'S HAND·
I KINGS

"Yeah," said the red-haired girl, in the garden of the deserted Casino. "We seen her, me and Paolo both seen her. She come through here days ago."

Father Gomez said, "And do you remember what she looked like?"

"She look hot," said the little boy. "Sweaty in the face, all right."

"How old did she seem to be?"

"About..." said the girl, considering; "I suppose maybe forty or fifty. We didn't see her close. She could be thirty, maybe. But she was hot, like Paolo said, and she was carrying a big rucksack, much bigger than yours, *this* big..."

Paolo whispered something to her, screwing up his eyes to look at the priest as he did so. The sun was bright in his face.

"Yeah," said the girl impatiently, "I know. The Spectres," she said to Father Gomez, "she wasn' afraid of the Spectres at all. She just walked through the city and never worried a bit. I ain never seen a grown-up do that before, all right. She looked like she didn' know about them, even. Same as you," she added, looking at him with a challenge in her eyes.

"There's a lot I don't know," said Father Gomez mildly.

The little boy plucked at her sleeve and whispered again.

"Paolo says," she told the priest, "he thinks you're going to get the knife back."

Father Gomez felt his skin bristle. He remembered the testimony of Fra Pavel in the inquiry at the Consistorial Court: this must be the knife he meant.

"If I can," he said, "I shall. The knife comes from here, does it?"

"From the Torre degli Angeli," said the girl, pointing at the square stone tower over the red-brown rooftops. It shimmered in the midday glare. "And the boy who stole it, he kill our brother Tullio. The Spectres got him, all right. You want to kill that boy, that's OK. And the girl – she was a liar, she was as bad as him."

"There was a girl, too?" said the priest, trying not to seem too interested.

"Lying filth," spat the red-haired child. "We nearly killed them both, but then there came some women, flying women –"

"Witches," said Paolo.

"Witches, and we couldn' fight them. They took them away, the girl and boy. We don' know where they went. But the woman, she came later. We thought maybe *she* got some kind of knife, to keep the Spectres away, all right. And maybe *you* have, too," she added, lifting her chin to stare at him boldly.

"I have no knife," said Father Gomez. "But I have a sacred task. Maybe that is protecting me against these – Spectres."

"Yeah," said the girl, "maybe. Anyway, you want her, she went south, towards the mountains. We don' know where. But you ask anyone, they know if she go past, because there ain no one like her in Ci'gazze, not before and not now. She be *easy* to find."

"Thank you, Angelica," said the priest. "Bless you, my children."

He shouldered his pack, left the garden, and set off through the hot silent streets, satisfied.

After three days in the company of the wheeled creatures Mary Malone knew rather more about them, and they knew a great deal about her.

That first morning, they carried her for an hour or so along the basalt highway to a settlement by a river, and the journey was uncomfortable; she had nothing to hold on to, and the creature's back was hard. They sped along at a pace that frightened her, but the thunder of their wheels on the hard road and the beat of their scudding feet made her exhilarated enough to ignore the discomfort.

And in the course of the ride she became more aware of the creatures' physiology. Like the grazers, their skeletons had a diamond-shaped frame, with a limb at each of the corners. Some time in the distant past, a line of ancestral creatures must have developed this structure and found it worked, just as generations of long-ago crawling things in Mary's world had developed the central spine.

The basalt highway led gradually downwards, and after a while the slope increased, so the creatures could free-wheel. They tucked their side legs up and steered by leaning to one side or the other, and hurtled along at a speed Mary found terrifying; though she had to admit that the creature she was riding never gave her the slightest feeling of danger. If only she'd had something to hold on to, she would have enjoyed it.

At the foot of the mile-long slope there was a stand of the great trees, and nearby a river meandered on the level grassy ground. Some way off, Mary saw a gleam that looked like a wider expanse of water, but she didn't spend long looking at that, because the creatures were making for a settlement on the river bank, and she was burning with curiosity to see it.

There were twenty or thirty huts, roughly grouped in a circle, made of – she had to shade her eyes against the sun to see – wooden beams covered with a kind of wattle-and-daub mixture on the walls and thatch on the roofs. Other wheeled creatures were working: some repairing the roofs, others hauling a net out of the river, others bringing brushwood for a fire.

So they had language, and they had fire, and they had society. And about then she found an adjustment being made in her mind, as the word *creatures* became the word *people*. These beings weren't human, but they were *people*, she told herself; it's not *them*, they're *us*.

They were quite close now, and seeing what was coming, some of the villagers looked up and called to each other to look. The party from the road slowed to a halt, and Mary clambered stiffly down, knowing that she would ache later on.

"Thank you," she said to her … her what? Her steed? Her cycle? Both ideas were absurdly wrong for the bright-eyed amiability that stood beside her. She settled for – friend.

He raised his trunk and imitated her words:

"Anku," he said, and again they laughed, in high spirits.

She took her rucksack from the other creature (anku! anku!) and walked with them off the basalt and on to the hard-packed earth of the village.

And then her absorption truly began.

In the next few days she learned so much that she felt like a child again, bewildered by school. What was more, the wheeled people seemed to be just as wonderstruck by her. Her hands, to begin with. They couldn't get enough of them: their delicate trunks felt over every joint, searching out thumbs, knuckles and fingernails, flexing them gently, and they watched with amazement as she picked up her rucksack, conveyed food to her mouth, scratched, combed her hair, washed.

In return, they let her feel their trunks. They were infinitely flexible, and about as long as her arm, thicker where they joined the head, and quite powerful enough to crush her skull, she guessed. The two finger-like projections at the tip were capable of enormous force and great gentleness; the creatures seemed to be able to vary the tone of their skin on the inside, on their equivalent of fingertips, from a soft velvet to a solidity like wood. As a result, they could use them both for a delicate task like milking a grazer and for the rough business of tearing and shaping branches.

Little by little, Mary realized that their trunks were playing a part in communication, too. A movement of the trunk would modify the meaning of a sound, so the word that sounded like "chuh" meant water when it was accompanied by a sweep of the trunk from left to right, "rain" when the trunk curled up at the tip, "sadness" when it curled under, and "young shoots of grass" when it made a quick flick to the left. As soon as she saw this, Mary imitated it, moving her arm as best she could in the same way, and when the creatures realized that she was beginning to talk to them, their delight was radiant.

Once they had begun to talk (mostly in their language, although she managed to teach them a few words of English: they could say "anku" and "grass" and "tree" and "sky" and "river", and pronounce her name, with a little difficulty) they progressed much more quickly. Their word for themselves as a people was *mulefa*, but an individual was a *zalif*. Mary thought there was a difference between the sounds for *he-zalif* and *she-zalif*, but it was too subtle for her to make easily. She began to write it all down, and compile a dictionary.

But before she let herself become truly absorbed, she took out her battered paperback and the yarrow stalks, and asked the I Ching: should I be here doing this, or should I go on somewhere else and keep searching?

The reply came: *Keeping still, so that restlessness dissolves; then, beyond the tumult, one can perceive the great laws.*

It went on: *As a mountain keeps still within itself, thus a wise man does not permit his will to stray beyond his situation.*

That could hardly be clearer. She folded the stalks away and closed the book, and then realized that she'd drawn a circle of watching creatures around her.

One said, *Question? Permission? Curious.*

She said, *Please. Look.*

Very delicately their trunks moved, sorting through the stalks in the same counting movement she'd been making, or turning the pages of the book. One thing they were astonished by was the doubleness of her hands: by the fact that she could both hold the book and turn the pages at the same time. They loved to watch her lace her fingers together, or play the childhood game "This is the church, and this is the steeple," or make that over-and-over thumb-to-opposite-forefinger movement which was what Ama was using, at exactly the same moment in Lyra's world, as a charm to keep evil spirits away.

Once they had examined the yarrow stalks and the book, they folded the cloth over them carefully and put them with the book into her rucksack. She was happy and reassured by the message from ancient China, because it meant that what she wanted most to do was exactly, at that moment, what she should do.

So she set herself to learning more about the mulefa, with a cheerful heart.

She learnt that there were two sexes, and that they lived monogamously in couples. Their offspring had a long childhood: ten years at least, growing very slowly, as far as she could interpret their explanation. There were five young ones in this settlement, one almost grown and the others somewhere in between, and being smaller than the adults, they could not manage the seed-pod wheels. The children had to move as the grazers did, with all four feet on the ground, but for all their energy and adventurousness (skipping up to Mary and shying away, trying to clamber up tree-trunks, floundering in the shallow water, and so on) they seemed clumsy, as if they were in the wrong element. The speed and power and grace of the adults was startling by contrast, and Mary saw how much a growing youngster must long for the day when the wheels would fit. She watched the oldest child, one day, go quietly to the store-house where a number of seed-pods were kept, and try to fit his fore-claw into the central hole; but when he tried to stand up he fell over at once, trapping himself, and the sound attracted an adult. The child struggled to get free, squeaking with anxiety, and Mary couldn't help laughing at the sight, at the indignant parent and the guilty child, who pulled himself out at the last minute and scampered away.

The seed-pod wheels were clearly of the utmost importance, and soon Mary began to see just how valuable they were.

The mulefa spent much of their time, to begin with, in

maintaining their wheels. By deftly lifting and twisting the claw they could slip it out of the hole, and then they used their trunks to examine the wheel all over, cleaning the rim, checking for cracks. The claw was formidably strong: a spur of horn or bone at right angles to the leg, and slightly curved so that the highest part, in the middle, bore the weight as it rested on the inside of the hole. Mary watched one day as a zalif examined the hole in her front wheel, touching here and there, lifting her trunk up in the air and back again, as if sampling the scent.

Mary remembered the oil she'd found on her fingers when she had examined the first seed-pod. With the zalif's permission she looked at her claw, and found the surface more smooth and slick than anything she'd felt on her world. Her fingers simply would not stay on the surface. The whole of the claw seemed impregnated with the faintly fragrant oil, and after she had seen a number of the villagers sampling, testing, checking the state of their wheels and their claws she began to wonder which had come first: wheel or claw? Rider or tree?

Although of course there was a third element as well, and that was geology. Creatures could only use wheels on a world which provided them with natural highways. There must be some feature of the mineral content of these lava-flows that made them run in ribbon-like lines over the vast savannah, and be so resistant to weathering or cracking. Little by little Mary came to see the way everything was linked together, and all of it, seemingly, managed by the mulefa. They knew the location of every herd of grazers, every stand of wheel-trees, every clump of sweet-grass, and they knew every individual within the herds, and every separate tree, and they discussed their well-being and their fate. On one occasion she saw the mulefa cull a herd of grazers, selecting some individuals and herding them away from the rest, to dispatch them by breaking their necks with a wrench of a powerful trunk. Nothing was wasted. Holding flakes of razor-sharp stone in their trunks, the mulefa skinned and gutted the animals within minutes, and then began a skilful butchery, separating out the offal and the tender meat and the tougher joints, trimming the fat, removing the horns and the hooves, and working so efficiently that Mary watched with the pleasure she felt at seeing anything done well.

Soon strips of meat were hanging to dry in the sun, and others were packed in salt and wrapped in leaves; the skins were scraped clear of fat, which was set by for later use, and then laid to soak in pits of water filled with oak-bark to tan; and the oldest child was playing with a set of horns, pretending to be a grazer, making the other children laugh. That evening there was fresh meat to eat, and Mary feasted well.

In a similar way the mulefa knew where the best fish were to be had, and exactly when and where to lay their nets. Looking for something she could do, Mary went to the net-makers and offered to help. When she saw how they worked, not on their own but two by two, working their trunks together to tie a knot, she realized how astonished they'd been by her hands, because of course she could tie knots on her own. At first she felt that this gave her an advantage – she needed no one else; and then she realized how it cut her off from others. Perhaps all human beings were like that. And from that time on, she used one hand to knot the fibres, sharing the task with a female zalif who had become her particular friend, fingers and trunk moving in and out together.

But of all the living things the wheeled people managed, it was the seed-pod trees that they took most care with.

There were half a dozen groves within the area looked after by this group. There were others further away, but they were the responsibility of other groups. Each day a party went out to check on the well-being of the mighty trees, and to harvest any fallen seed-pods. It was clear what the mulefa gained; but how did the trees benefit from this interchange? One day she saw. As she was riding along with the group, suddenly there was a loud *crack*, and everyone came to a halt, surrounding one individual whose wheel had split. Every group carried a spare or two with it, so the zalif with the broken wheel was soon remounted; but the broken wheel itself was carefully wrapped in a cloth and taken back to the settlement.

There they prised it open and took out all the seeds – flat pale ovals as big as Mary's little fingernail – and examined each one carefully. They explained that the seed-pods needed the constant pounding they got on the hard roads if they were to crack at all, and also that the seeds were difficult to germinate. Without the mulefa's attention, the trees would all die. Each species depended on the other, and furthermore, it was the oil that made it possible. It was hard to understand, but they seemed to be saying that the oil was the centre of their thinking and feeling; that young ones didn't have the wisdom of their elders because they couldn't use the wheels, and thus could absorb no oil through their claws.

And that was when Mary began to see the connection between the mulefa and the question which had occupied the past few years of her life.

But before she could examine it any further (and conversations with the mulefa were long and complex, because they loved qualifying and explaining and illustrating their arguments with dozens of examples, as if they had forgotten nothing, and everything they had ever known was available immediately for reference) the settlement was attacked.

Mary was the first to see the attackers coming, though she didn't know what they were.

It happened in mid-afternoon, when she was helping repair the roof of a hut. The mulefa only built one storey high, because they were not climbers; but Mary was happy to clamber above the ground, and she could lay thatch and knot it in place with her two hands, once they had shown her the technique, much more quickly than they could.

So she was braced against the rafters of a house, catching the bundles of reeds thrown up to her, and enjoying the cool breeze from the water that was tempering the heat of the sun, when her eye was caught by a flash of white.

It came from that distant glitter she thought was the sea. She shaded her eyes, and saw one – two – more – a fleet of tall white sails, emerging out of the heat-haze, some way off but making with a silent grace for the river-mouth.

Mary! called the zalif from below. *What are you seeing?*

She didn't know the word for sail, or boat, so she said *tall, white, many*.

At once the zalif gave a call of alarm, and everyone in earshot stopped work and sped to the centre of the settlement, calling the young ones. Within a minute all the mulefa were ready to flee.

Atal, her friend, called: *Mary! Mary! Come! Tualapi! Tualapi!*

It had all happened so quickly that Mary had hardly moved. The white sails by this time had already entered the river, easily making headway against the current. Mary was impressed by the discipline of the sailors: they tacked so swiftly, the sails moving together like a flock of starlings, all changing direction simultaneously. And they were so beautiful, those snow-white slender sails, bending and dipping and filling –

There were forty of them, at least, and they were coming up-river much more swiftly than she'd thought. But she saw no crew on board, and then she realized that they weren't boats at all: they were gigantic birds, and the sails were their wings, one fore and one aft, held upright and flexed and trimmed by the power of their own muscles.

There was no time to stop and study them, because they had already reached the bank, and were climbing out. They had necks like swans, and beaks as long as her forearm. Their wings were twice as tall as she was, and – glancing back, frightened now, over her shoulder as she fled – they had powerful legs: no wonder they had moved so fast on the water.

She ran hard after the mulefa, who were calling her name as they streamed out of the settlement and on to the highway. She reached them just in time: her friend Atal was waiting, and as Mary scrambled on her back she beat the road with her feet, speeding away up the slope after her companions.

The birds, who couldn't move as fast on land, soon gave up the chase and turned back to the settlement.

They tore open the food-stores, snarling and growling and tossing their great cruel beaks high as they swallowed the dried meat and all the preserved fruit and grain. Everything edible was gone in under a minute.

And then the tualapi found the wheel-store, and tried to smash open the great seed-pods, but that was beyond them.

Mary felt her friends tense with alarm all around her as they watched from the crest of the low hill and saw pod after pod hurled to the ground, kicked, rasped by the claws on the mighty legs, but of course no harm came to them from that. What worried the mulefa was that several of them were pushed and shoved and nudged towards the water, where they floated heavily down-stream towards the sea.

Then the great snow-white birds set about demolishing everything they could see with brutal raking blows of their feet, and stabbing, smashing, shaking, tearing movements of their beaks. The mulefa around her were murmuring, almost crooning with sorrow.

I help, Mary said. *We make again.*

But the foul creatures hadn't finished yet; holding their beautiful wings high, they squatted among the devastation and voided their bowels. The smell drifted up the slope with the breeze; heaps and pools of green-black-brown-white dung lay among the broken beams, the scattered thatch. Then, their clumsy movement on land giving them a swaggering strut, the birds went back to the water, and sailed away down-stream towards the sea.

Only when the last white wing had vanished in the afternoon haze did the mulefa ride down the highway again. They were full of sorrow and anger, but mainly they were powerfully anxious about the seed-pod store.

Out of the fifteen pods that had been there, only two were left. The rest had been pushed into the water and lost. But there was a sandbank in the next bend of the river, and Mary thought she could spot a wheel that was caught there; so to the mulefa's surprise and alarm she took off her clothes, wound a length of cord around her waist, and swam across to it. On the sandbank she found not one but five of the precious wheels, and passing the cord through their softening centres she swam heavily back pulling them behind her.

The mulefa were full of gratitude. They never entered the water themselves, and only fished from the bank, taking care to keep their feet and wheels dry. Mary felt she had done something useful for them at last.

Later that night, after a scanty meal of sweet-roots, they told her why they had been so anxious about the wheels. There had once been a time when the seed-pods were plentiful, and when the world was rich and full of life, and the mulefa lived with their trees in perpetual joy. But something bad had happened many years ago; some virtue had gone out of the world; because despite every effort and all the love and attention the mulefa could give them, the wheel-pod trees were dying.

11

The Dragonflies

*A*ma climbed the path to the cave, bread and milk in the bag on her back, a heavy puzzlement in her heart. How in the world could she ever manage to reach the sleeping girl?

She came to the rock where the woman had told her to leave the food. She put it down, but she didn't go straight home; she climbed a little further, up past the cave and through the thick rhododendrons, and further up still to where the trees thinned out and the rainbows began.

There she and her dæmon played a game: they climbed up over the rock-shelves and around the little green-white cataracts, past the whirlpools and through the spectrum-tinted spray, until her hair and her eyelids and his squirrel-fur were beaded all over with a million tiny pearls of moisture. The game was to get to the top without wiping your eyes, despite the temptation, and soon the sunlight sparkled and fractured into red, yellow, green, blue, and all the colours in between, but she mustn't brush her hand across to see better until she got right to the top, or the game would be lost.

Kulang her dæmon sprang to the rock at the edge of the

topmost little waterfall, and she knew he'd turn at once to make sure she didn't brush the moisture off her eyelashes – except that he didn't.

Instead he clung there, gazing forward.

Ama wiped her eyes, because the game was cancelled by the surprise her dæmon was feeling. As she pulled herself up to look over the edge, she gasped and fell still, because looking down at her was the face of a creature she had never seen before: a bear, but immense, terrifying, four times the size of the brown bears in the forest, and ivory-white, with a black nose and black eyes and claws the length of daggers. He was only an arm's length away. She could see every separate hair on his head.

"Who's that?" said the voice of a boy, and while Ama couldn't understand the words, she caught the sense easily enough.

After a moment the boy appeared next to the bear: fierce-looking, with frowning eyes and a jutting jaw. And was that a dæmon beside him, bird-shaped? But such a strange bird: unlike any she'd seen before. It flew to Kulang and spoke briefly: *Friends. We shan't hurt you.*

The great white bear hadn't moved at all.

"Come up," said the boy, and again her dæmon made sense of it for her.

Watching the bear with superstitious awe, Ama scrambled up beside the little waterfall and stood shyly on the rocks. Kulang became a butterfly, and settled for a moment on her cheek, but left it to flutter around the other dæmon, who sat still on the boy's hand.

"Will," said the boy, pointing to himself, and she responded, "Ama". Now she could see him properly, she was frightened of the boy almost more than the bear: he had a horrible wound: two of his fingers were missing. She felt dizzy when she saw it.

The bear turned away along the milky stream and lay down in the water as if to cool himself. The boy's dæmon took to the air, and fluttered with Kulang among the rainbows, and slowly they began to understand each other.

And what should they turn out to be looking for but a cave, with a girl asleep?

The words tumbled out of her in response: "I know where it is! And she's being kept asleep by a woman who says she is her mother, but no mother would be so cruel, would she? She makes her drink something to keep her asleep, but I have some herbs to make her wake up, if only I could get to her!"

Will could only shake his head and wait for Balthamos to translate. It took more than a minute.

"Iorek," he called, and the bear lumbered along the bed of the stream, licking his chops, for he had just swallowed a fish. "Iorek," Will said, "this girl is saying she knows where Lyra is. I'll go with her to look, while you stay here and watch."

Iorek Byrnison, foursquare in the stream, nodded silently. Will hid his rucksack and buckled on the knife before clambering down through the rainbows with Ama. He had to brush his eyes and peer through the dazzle to see where it was safe to put his feet, and the mist that filled the air was icy.

When they reached the foot of the falls, Ama indicated that they should go carefully and make no noise, and Will walked behind her down the slope, between mossy rocks and great gnarled pine-trunks where the dappled light danced intensely green, and a billion tiny insects scraped and sang. Down they went, and further down, and still the sunlight followed them, deep into the valley, while overhead the branches tossed unceasingly in the bright sky.

Then Ama halted. Will drew himself behind the massive bole of a cedar, and looked where she was pointing. Through a tangle of leaves and branches he saw the side of a cliff, rising up to the right, and part-way up –

"Mrs Coulter," he whispered, and his heart was beating fast.

The woman appeared from behind the rock and shook out a thick-leafed branch before dropping it and brushing her hands together. Had she been sweeping the floor? Her sleeves were rolled, and her hair was bound up with a scarf. Will could never have imagined her looking so domestic.

But then there was a flash of gold, and that vicious monkey appeared, leaping up to her shoulder. As if they suspected something, they looked all around, and suddenly Mrs Coulter didn't look domestic at all.

Ama was whispering urgently: she was afraid of the golden monkey-dæmon; he liked to tear the wings off bats while they were still alive.

"Is there anyone else with her?" Will said. "No soldiers, or anyone like that?"

Ama didn't know. She had never seen soldiers, but people did talk about strange and frightening men, or they might be ghosts, seen on the mountainsides at night... But there had always been ghosts in the mountains, everyone knew that. So they might not have anything to do with the woman.

Well, thought Will, if Lyra's in the cave and Mrs Coulter doesn't leave it, I'll have to go and pay a call.

He said, "What is this drug you have? What do you have to do with it to wake her up?"

Ama explained.

"And where is it now?"

In her home, she said. Hidden away.

"All right. Wait here and don't come near. When you see her, you mustn't say that you know me. You've never seen me, or the bear. When do you next bring her food?"

Half an hour before sunset, Ama's dæmon said.

"Bring the medicine with you then," said Will. "I'll meet you here."

She watched with great unease as he set off along the path. Surely he didn't believe what she had just told him about the monkey-dæmon, or he wouldn't walk so recklessly up to the cave.

Actually, Will felt very nervous. All his senses seemed to be clarified, so that he was aware of the tiniest insects drifting in the sun-shafts and the rustle of every leaf and the movement of the clouds above, even though his eyes never left the cave-mouth.

"Balthamos," he whispered, and the angel-dæmon flew to his shoulder as a bright-eyed small bird with red wings. "Keep close to me, and watch that monkey."

"Then look to your right," said Balthamos tersely.

And Will saw a patch of golden light at the cave-mouth that had a face and eyes, and was watching them. They were no more than twenty paces away. He stood still, and the golden monkey turned his head to look in the cave, said something, and turned back.

Will felt for the knife-handle, and walked on.

When he reached the cave, the woman was waiting for him.

She was sitting at her ease in the little canvas chair, with a book on her lap, watching him calmly. She was wearing traveller's clothes of khaki, but so well were they cut and so graceful was her figure that they looked like the highest of high fashion, and the little spray of red blossom she'd pinned to her shirt-front looked like the most elegant of jewels. Her hair shone and her dark eyes glittered, and her bare legs gleamed golden in the sunlight.

She smiled. Will very nearly smiled in response, because he was so unused to the sweetness and gentleness a woman could put into a smile, and it unsettled him.

"You're Will," she said, in that low, intoxicating voice.

"How do you know my name?" he said harshly.

"Lyra says it in her sleep."

"Where is she?"

"Safe."

"I want to see her."

"Come on then," she said, and got to her feet, dropping the book on the chair.

For the first time since coming into her presence Will looked at the monkey-dæmon. His fur was long and lustrous, each hair seeming to be made of pure gold, much finer than a human's, and his little face and hands were black. Will had last seen that face, contorted with hate, on the evening when he and Lyra stole the alethiometer back from Sir Charles Latrom in the house in Oxford. The monkey had tried to tear at him with his teeth until Will had slashed left-right with the knife, forcing the dæmon backwards, so he could close the window and shut them away in a different world. Will thought that nothing on earth would make him turn his back on that monkey now.

But the bird-shaped Balthamos was watching closely, and Will stepped carefully over the floor of the cave and followed Mrs Coulter to the little figure lying still in the shadows.

And there she was, his dearest friend, asleep. So small she looked! He was amazed at how all the force and fire that was Lyra awake could look so gentle and mild when she was sleeping. At her neck Pantalaimon lay in his polecat-shape, his fur glistening, and Lyra's hair lay damp across her forehead.

He knelt down beside her and lifted the hair away. Her face was hot. Out of the corner of his eye Will saw the golden monkey crouching to spring, and set his hand on the knife; but Mrs Coulter shook her head very slightly, and the monkey relaxed.

Without seeming to, Will was memorizing the exact layout of the cave: the shape and size of every rock, the slope of the floor, the exact height of the ceiling above the sleeping girl. He would need to find his way through it in the dark, and this was the only chance he'd have to see it first.

"So you see, she's quite safe," said Mrs Coulter.

"Why are you keeping her here? And why don't you let her wake up?"

"Let's sit down."

She didn't take the chair, but sat with him on the moss-covered rocks at the entrance to the cave. She sounded so kindly, and there was such sad wisdom in her eyes, that Will's mistrust deepened. He felt that every word she said was a lie, every action concealed a threat, and every smile was a mask of deceit. Well, he would have to deceive her in turn: he'd have to make her think he was harmless. But he had successfully deceived every teacher and every police officer and every social worker and every neighbour who had ever taken an interest in him and his home; he'd been preparing for this all his life.

Right, he thought. I can deal with you.

"Would you like something to drink?" said Mrs Coulter. "I'll have some too... It's quite safe. Look."

She cut open some brownish wrinkled fruit and pressed the cloudy juice into two small beakers. She sipped one and offered the other to Will, who sipped as well, and found it fresh and sweet.

"How did you find your way here?" she said.

"It wasn't hard to follow you."

"Evidently. Have you got Lyra's alethiometer?"

"Yes," he said, and let her work out for herself whether or not he could read it.

"And you've got a knife, I understand."

"Sir Charles told you that, did he?"

"Sir Charles? Oh – Carlo, of course. Yes, he did. It sounds fascinating. May I see it?"

"No, of course not," he said. "Why are you keeping Lyra here?"

"Because I love her," she said. "I'm her mother. She's in appalling danger and I won't let anything happen to her."

"Danger from what?" said Will.

"Well…" she said, and set her beaker down on the ground, leaning forward so that her hair swung down on either side of her face. When she sat up again she tucked it back behind her ears with both hands, and Will smelt the fragrance of some scent she was wearing combined with the fresh smell of her body, and he felt disturbed.

If Mrs Coulter saw his reaction, she didn't show it. She went on: "Look, Will, I don't know how you came to meet my daughter, and I don't know what you know already, and I certainly don't know if I can trust you; but equally, I'm tired of having to lie. So here it is: the truth.

"I found out that my daughter is in danger from the very people I used to belong to – from the church. Frankly, I think they want to kill her. So I found myself in a dilemma, you see: obey the church, or save my daughter. And I was a faithful servant of the church, too. There was no one more zealous; I gave my life to it; I served it with a passion.

"But I had this daughter...

"I know I didn't look after her well when she was young. She was taken away from me and brought up by strangers. Perhaps that made it hard for her to trust me. But when she was growing up, I saw the danger that she was in, and three times now I've tried to save her from it. I've had to become a renegade and hide in this remote place, and I thought we were safe; but now to learn that you found us so easily – well, you can understand, that worries me. The church won't be far behind. And they want to kill her, Will. They will not let her live."

"Why? Why do they hate her so much?"

"Because of what they think she's going to do. I don't know what that is; I wish I did, because then I could keep her even more safe. But all I know is that they hate her, and they have no mercy, none."

She leaned forward, talking urgently and quietly and closely.

"Why am I telling you this?" she went on. "Can I trust you? I think I have to. I can't escape any more, there's nowhere else to go. And if you're a friend of Lyra's, you might be my friend too. And I do need friends, I do need help. Everything's against me now. The church will destroy me too, as well as Lyra, if they find us. I'm alone, Will, just me in a cave with my daughter, and all the forces of all the worlds are trying to track us down. And here you are, to show how easy it is to find us, apparently. What are you going to do, Will? What do you want?"

"Why are you keeping her asleep?" he said, stubbornly avoiding her questions.

"Because what would happen if I let her wake? She'd run away at once. And she wouldn't last five days."

"But why don't you explain it to her and give her the choice?"

"Do you think she'd listen? Do you think even if she listened she'd believe me? She doesn't trust me. She hates me, Will. You must know that. She despises me. I, well ... I don't know how to say it ... I love her so much I've given up everything I had – a great career, great happiness, position and wealth – everything, to come to this cave in the mountains and live on dry bread and sour fruit, just so I can keep my daughter alive. And if to do that I have to keep her asleep, then so be it. But I *must* keep her alive. Wouldn't your mother do as much for you?"

Will felt a jolt of shock and rage that Mrs Coulter had dared to bring his own mother in to support her argument. Then the first shock was complicated by the thought that his mother, after all, had not protected him; he had had to protect her. Did Mrs Coulter love Lyra more than Elaine Parry loved him? But that was unfair: his mother wasn't well.

Either Mrs Coulter did not know the boil of feelings that her simple words had lanced, or she was monstrously clever. Her beautiful eyes watched mildly as Will reddened and shifted uncomfortably; and for a moment Mrs Coulter looked uncannily like her daughter.

"But what are *you* going to do?" she said.

"Well, I've seen Lyra now," Will said, "and she's alive, that's clear, and she's safe, I suppose. That's all I was going to do. So now I've done it I can go and help Lord Asriel like I was supposed to."

That did surprise her a little, but she mastered it.

"You don't mean – I thought you might help us," she said quite calmly, not pleading but questioning. "With the knife. I saw what you did at Sir Charles's house. You could make it safe for us, couldn't you? You could help us get away?"

"I'm going to go now," Will said, standing up.

She held out her hand. A rueful smile, a shrug, and a nod as if to a skilful opponent who'd made a good move at the chessboard: that was what her body said. He found himself liking her, because she was brave, and because she seemed like a more complicated and richer and deeper Lyra. He couldn't help but like her.

So he shook her hand, finding it firm and cool and soft. She turned to the golden monkey, who had been sitting behind her all the time, and a look passed between them that Will couldn't interpret.

Then she turned back with a smile.

"Goodbye," he said, and she said quietly, "Goodbye, Will."

He left the cave, knowing her eyes were following, and he didn't look back once. Ama was nowhere in sight. He walked back the way he'd come, keeping to the path until he heard the sound of the waterfall ahead.

"She's lying," he said to Iorek Byrnison thirty minutes later. "Of course she's lying. She'd lie even if it made things worse for herself, because she just loves lying too much to stop."

"What is your plan, then?" said the bear, who was basking in the sunlight, his belly flat down in a patch of snow among the rocks.

Will walked up and down, wondering whether he could use the trick that had worked in Headington: use the knife to move into another world and then go to a spot right next to where Lyra lay, cut back through into this world, pull her through into safety and then close up again. That was the obvious thing to do: why did he hesitate?

Balthamos knew. In his own angel-shape, shimmering like

a heat-haze in the sunlight, he said, "You were foolish to go to her. All you want to do now is see her again."

Iorek uttered a deep quiet growl. At first Will thought he was warning Balthamos, but then with a little shock of embarrassment he realized that the bear was agreeing with the angel. The two of them had taken little notice of each other until now; their modes of being were so different; but they were of one mind about this, clearly.

And Will scowled, but it was true. He had been captivated by Mrs Coulter. All his thoughts referred to her: when he thought of Lyra, it was to wonder how like her mother she'd be when she grew up; if he thought of the church, it was to wonder how many of the priests and cardinals were under her spell; if he thought of his own dead father, it was to wonder whether he would have detested her or admired her; and if he thought of his own mother...

He felt his heart grimace. He walked away from the bear, and stood on a rock from which he could see across the whole valley. In the clear cold air he could hear the distant tok-tok of someone chopping wood, he could hear a dull iron bell around the neck of a sheep, he could hear the rustling of the tree-tops far below. The tiniest crevices in the mountains at the horizon were clear and sharp to his eyes, as were the vultures wheeling over some near-dead creature many miles away.

There was no doubt about it: Balthamos was right. The woman had cast a spell on him. It was pleasant and tempting to think about those beautiful eyes and the sweetness of that voice, and to recall the way her arms rose to push back that shining hair...

With an effort he came back to his senses and heard another sound altogether: a far-distant drone.

He turned this way and that to locate it, and found it in the north, the very direction he and Iorek had come from.

"Zeppelins," said the bear's voice, startling Will, for he hadn't heard the great creature come near. Iorek stood beside him looking in the same direction, and then reared up high, fully twice the height of Will, his gaze intent.

"How many?"

"Eight of them," said Iorek after a minute, and then Will saw them too: little specks in a line.

"Can you tell how long it will take them to get here?" Will said.

"They will be here not long after nightfall."

"So we won't have very much darkness. That's a pity."

"What is your plan?"

"To make an opening and take Lyra through into another world, and close it again before her mother follows. The girl has a drug to wake Lyra up, but she couldn't explain very clearly how to use it, so she'll have to come into the cave as well. I don't want to put her in danger, though. Maybe you could distract Mrs Coulter while we do that."

The bear grunted and closed his eyes. Will looked around for the angel, and saw his shape outlined in droplets of mist in the late afternoon light.

"Balthamos," he said, "I'm going back into the forest now, to find a safe place to make the first opening. I need you to keep watch for me, and tell me the moment she comes near – her or that dæmon of hers."

Balthamos nodded, and raised his wings to shake off the moisture. Then he soared up into the cold air and glided out over the valley as Will began to search for a world where Lyra would be safe.

* * *

In the creaking, thrumming double bulkhead of the leading zeppelin, the dragonflies were hatching. The Lady Salmakia bent over the splitting cocoon of the electric-blue one, easing the damp filmy wings clear, taking care to let her face be the first thing that imprinted itself on the many-faceted eyes, soothing the fine-stretched nerves, whispering its name to the brilliant creature, teaching it who it was.

In a few minutes, the Chevalier Tialys would do the same to his. But for now, he was sending a message on the lodestone resonator, and his attention was fully occupied with the movement of the bow and his fingers.

He transmitted:

"To Lord Roke:

"We are three hours from the estimated time of arrival at the valley. The Consistorial Court of Discipline intends to send a squad to the cave as soon as they land.

It will divide into two units. The first unit will fight its way into the cave and kill the child, removing her head so as to prove her death. If possible they will also capture the woman, though if that is impossible they are to kill her.

"The second unit is to capture the boy alive.

"The remainder of the force will engage the gyropters of King Ogunwe. They estimate that the gyropters will arrive shortly after the zeppelins. In accordance with your orders, the Lady Salmakia and I will shortly leave the zeppelin and fly directly to the cave, where we shall try to defend the girl against the first unit and hold them at bay until reinforcements arrive.

"We await your response."

The answer came almost immediately.

"To the Chevalier Tialys:

"In the light of your report, here is a change of plan.

"In order to prevent the enemy from killing the child, which

*would be the worst possible outcome, you and the Lady Salmakia
are to co-operate with the boy. While he has the knife, he has the
initiative, so if he opens another world and takes the girl into it,
let him do so, and follow them through. Stay by their side at all
times."*

The Chevalier Tialys replied:

"To Lord Roke:

*"Your message is heard and understood. The lady and I shall
leave at once."*

The little spy closed the resonator and gathered his
equipment together.

"Tialys," came a whisper from the dark, "it's hatching.
You should come now."

He leapt up to the strut where his dragonfly had been
struggling into the world, and eased it gently free of the broken
cocoon. Stroking its great fierce head, he lifted the heavy
antennae, still moist and curled, and let the creature taste the
flavour of his skin until it was entirely under his command.

Salmakia was fitting her dragonfly with the harness she
carried everywhere: spider-silk reins, stirrups of titanium, a
saddle of hummingbird-skin. It was almost weightless. Tialys
did the same with his, easing the straps around the insect's
body, tightening, adjusting. It would wear the harness till it
died.

Then he quickly slung the pack over his shoulder, and
sliced through the oiled fabric of the zeppelin's skin. Beside
him, the lady had mounted her dragonfly, and now she urged
it through the narrow gap into the hammering gusts. The
long frail wings trembled as she squeezed through, and then
the joy of flight took over the creature, and it plunged into
the wind. A few seconds later Tialys joined her in the wild
air, his mount eager to fight the swift-gathering dusk itself.

The two of them whirled upwards in the icy currents, took a few moments to get their bearings, and set their course for the valley.

12

The Break

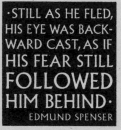

·STILL AS HE FLED, HIS EYE WAS BACKWARD CAST, AS IF HIS FEAR STILL FOLLOWED HIM BEHIND·
EDMUND SPENSER

As darkness fell, this was how things stood.·

In his adamant tower, Lord Asriel paced up and down. His attention was fixed on the little figure beside the lodestone resonator, and every other report had been diverted, every part of his mind was directed to the news that came to the small square block of stone under the lamplight.

King Ogunwe sat in the cabin of his gyropter, swiftly working out a plan to counter the intentions of the Consistorial Court, which he'd just learned about from the Gallivespian in his own aircraft. The navigator was scribbling some figures on a scrap of paper, which he handed to the pilot. The essential thing was speed: getting their troops on the ground first would make all the difference. The gyropters were faster than zeppelins, but they were still some way behind.

In the zeppelins of the Consistorial Court, the Swiss Guard were attending to their kit. Their cross-bows were deadly over five hundred yards, and an archer could load and fire fifteen bolts a minute. The spiral fins, made of horn, gave the bolt a spin and made the weapon as accurate as a rifle. It was also, of course, silent, which might be a great advantage.

Mrs Coulter lay awake in the entrance to the cave. The golden monkey was restless, and frustrated: the bats had left the cave with the coming of darkness, and there was nothing to torment. He prowled about by Mrs Coulter's sleeping-bag, scratching with a little horny finger at the occasional glow-flies that settled in the cave and smearing their luminescence over the rock.

Lyra lay hot and almost as restless, but deep, deep asleep, locked into oblivion by the draught her mother had forced down her only an hour before. There was a dream that had occupied her for a long time, and now it had returned, and little whimpers of pity and rage and Lyratic resolution shook her breast and her throat, making Pantalaimon grind his polecat-teeth in sympathy.

Not far away, under the wind-tossed pines on the forest path, Will and Ama were making their way towards the cave. Will had tried to explain to Ama what he was going to do, but her dæmon could make no sense of it, and when he cut a window and showed her, she was so terrified that she nearly fainted. He had to move calmly and speak quietly in order to keep her nearby, because she refused to let him take the powder from her, or even to tell him how it was to be used. In the end he had to say simply, "Keep very quiet and follow me," and hope that she would.

Iorek, in his armour, was somewhere close by, waiting to hold off the soldiers from the zeppelins so as to give Will enough time to work. What neither of them knew was that Lord Asriel's force was also closing in: the wind from time to time brought a far-distant clatter to Iorek's ears, but whereas he knew what zeppelin engines sounded like, he had never heard a gyropter, and he could make nothing of it.

Balthamos might have been able to tell them, but Will was

troubled about him. Now that they'd found Lyra, the angel had begun to withdraw back into his grief: he was silent, distracted, and sullen. And that in turn made it harder to talk to Ama.

As they paused on the path, Will said to the air, "Balthamos? Are you there?"

"Yes," said the angel tonelessly.

"Balthamos, please stay with me. Stay close and warn me of any danger. I need you."

"I haven't abandoned you yet," said the angel.

That was the best Will could get out of him.

Far above in the buffeting mid-air, Tialys and Salmakia soared over the valley, trying to see down to the cave. The dragonflies would do exactly as they were told, but their bodies couldn't easily cope with cold, and besides, they were tossed about dangerously in the wild wind. Their riders guided them low, among the shelter of the trees, and then flew from branch to branch, taking their bearings in the gathering dark.

Will and Ama crept up in the windy moonlight to the closest point they could reach that was still out of sight of the cave-mouth. It happened to be behind a heavy-leafed bush just off the path, and there he cut a window in the air.

The only world he could find with the same conformation of ground was a bare rocky place, where the moon glared down from a starry sky on to a bleached bone-white ground where little insects crawled and uttered their scraping, chittering sounds over a wide silence.

Ama followed him through, fingers and thumbs moving furiously to protect her from the devils that must be haunting this ghastly place; and her dæmon, adapting at once, became a lizard and scampered over the rocks with quick feet.

Will saw a problem. It was simply that the brilliant moon-light on the bone-coloured rocks would shine like a lantern once he opened the window in Mrs Coulter's cave. He'd have to open it quickly, pull Lyra through, and close it again at once. They could wake her up in this world, where it was safer.

He stopped on the dazzling slope and said to Ama: "We must be very quick and completely silent. No noise, not even a whisper."

She understood, though she was frightened. The little packet of powder was in her breast pocket: she'd checked it a dozen times, and she and her dæmon had rehearsed the task so often that she was sure they could do it in total darkness.

They climbed on up the bone-white rocks, Will measuring the distance carefully until he estimated that they would be well inside the cave.

Then he took the knife and cut the smallest possible window he could see through, no larger than the circle he could make with thumb and forefinger.

He put his eye to it quickly to keep the moonlight out, and looked through. There it all was: he'd calculated well. He could see the cave-mouth ahead, the rocks dark against the night sky; he could see the shape of Mrs Coulter, asleep, with her golden dæmon beside her; he could even see the monkey's tail, trailing negligently over the sleeping-bag.

Changing his angle and looking closer, he saw the rock behind which Lyra was lying. He couldn't see her, though. Was he too close? He shut that window, moved back a step or two, and opened again.

She wasn't there.

"Listen," he said to Ama and her dæmon, "the woman has moved her and I can't see where she is. I'm going to have to go through and look around the cave to find her, and cut through as soon as I've done that. So stand back – keep out of the way so I don't accidentally cut you when I come back. If I get stuck there for any reason, go back and wait by the other window, where we came in."

"We should both go through," Ama said, "because I know how to wake her, and you don't, and I know the cave better than you do, too."

Her face was stubborn, her lips pressed together, her fists clenched. Her lizard-dæmon acquired a ruff and raised it slowly around his neck.

Will said, "Oh, very well. But we go through quickly and in complete silence, and you do exactly what I say, at once, you understand?"

She nodded, and patted her pocket yet again to check the medicine.

Will made a small opening, low down, looked through, and enlarged it swiftly, getting through in a moment on hands and knees. Ama was right behind him, and altogether the window was open for less than ten seconds.

They crouched on the cave floor behind a large rock, with the bird-formed Balthamos beside them, their eyes taking some moments to adjust from the moon-drenched brilliance of the other world. Inside the cave it was much darker, and much more full of sound: mostly the wind in the trees, but below that was another sound, too. It was the roar of a zeppelin's engine, and it wasn't far away.

With the knife in his right hand, Will balanced himself carefully and looked around.

Ama was doing the same, and her owl-eyed dæmon was peering this way and that; but Lyra was not at this end of the cave. There was no doubt about it.

Will raised his head over the rock and took a long steady look down towards the entrance, where Mrs Coulter and her dæmon lay deep in sleep.

And then his heart sank. There lay Lyra, stretched out in the depths of her sleep, right next to Mrs Coulter. Their outlines had merged in the darkness; no wonder he hadn't seen her.

Will touched Ama's hand and pointed.

"We'll just have to do it very carefully," he whispered.

Something was happening outside. The roar of the zeppelins was now much louder than the wind in the trees, and lights were moving about, too, shining down through the branches from above. The quicker they got Lyra out the better, and that meant darting down there *now* before Mrs Coulter woke up, cutting through, pulling her to safety and closing again.

He whispered that to Ama. She nodded.

Then, as he was about to move, Mrs Coulter woke up.

She stirred and said something, and instantly the golden monkey sprang to his feet. Will could see his silhouette in the cave-mouth, crouching, attentive, and then Mrs Coulter herself sat up, shading her eyes against the light outside.

Will's left hand was tight around Ama's wrist. Mrs Coulter got up, fully dressed, lithe, alert, not at all as if she'd just been asleep. Perhaps she'd been awake all the time. She and the golden monkey were crouching inside the cave-mouth, watching and listening, as the light from the zeppelins swung from side to side above the tree-tops and the engines roared, and shouts, male voices warning or calling orders, made it clear that they should move fast, very fast.

Will squeezed Ama's wrist and darted forward, watching the ground in case he stumbled, running fast and low.

Then he was at Lyra's side, and she was deep asleep, Pantalaimon around her neck; and then Will held up the knife and felt carefully, and a second later there would have been an opening to pull Lyra through into safety –

But he looked up. He looked at Mrs Coulter. She had turned around silently, and the glare from the sky, reflected off the damp cave wall, lit her face, and for a moment it wasn't her face at all; it was his own mother's face, reproaching him, and his heart quailed from sorrow; and then as he thrust with the knife, his mind left the point, and with a wrench and a crack, the knife fell in pieces to the ground.

It was broken.

Now he couldn't cut his way out at all.

He said to Ama, "Wake her up. Do it now."

Then he stood up, ready to fight. He'd strangle that monkey first. He was tensed to meet its leap, and he found he still had the hilt of the knife in his hand: at least he could use it to hit with.

But there was no attack either from the golden monkey or from Mrs Coulter. She simply moved a little to let the light from outside show the pistol in her hand. In doing so she let some of the light shine on what Ama was doing: she was sprinkling a powder on Lyra's upper lip, and watching as Lyra breathed in, helping it into her nostrils by using her own dæmon's tail as a brush.

Will heard a change in the sounds from outside: there was another note now as well as the roar of the zeppelin. It sounded familiar, like an intrusion from his own world, and then he recognized the clatter of a helicopter. Then there was another and another, and more lights swept across the ever-moving trees outside, in a brilliant green scatter of radiance.

Mrs Coulter turned briefly as the new sound came to her, but too briefly for Will to jump and seize the gun. As for the monkey-dæmon, he glared at Will without blinking, crouched ready to spring.

Lyra was moving and murmuring. Will bent down and squeezed her hand, and the other dæmon nudged Pantalaimon, lifting his heavy head, whispering to him.

Outside there was a shout, and a man fell out of the sky, to land with a sickening crash not five yards from the entrance to the cave. Mrs Coulter didn't flinch; she looked at him coolly and turned back to Will. A moment later there came a crack of rifle fire from above, and a second after that a storm of shooting broke out, and the sky was full of explosions, of the crackle of flame, of bursts of gunfire.

Lyra was struggling up into consciousness, gasping, sighing, moaning, pushing herself up only to fall back weakly, and Pantalaimon was yawning, stretching, snapping at the other dæmon, flopping clumsily to one side as his muscles failed to act.

As for Will, he was searching the cave floor with the utmost care for the pieces of the broken knife. No time to wonder how it had happened, or whether it could be mended; but he was the knife-bearer, and he had to gather it up safely. As he found each piece he lifted it carefully, every nerve in his body aware of his missing fingers, and slipped it into the sheath. He could see the pieces quite easily, because the metal caught the gleam from outside: seven of them, the smallest being the point itself. He picked them all up, and then turned back to try and make sense of the fight outside.

Somewhere above the trees, the zeppelins were hovering, and men were sliding down ropes, but the wind made it difficult for the pilots to hold the aircraft steady. Meanwhile, the first gyropters had arrived above the cliff. There was only room for them to land one at a time, and then the African riflemen had to make their way down the rock-face. It was one of them who had been picked off by a lucky shot from the swaying zeppelins.

By this time, both sides had landed some troops. Some had been killed between the sky and the ground; several more were wounded, and lay on the cliff or among the trees. But neither force had yet reached the cave, and still the power inside it lay with Mrs Coulter.

Will said above the noise:

"What are you going to do?"

"Hold you captive."

"What, as hostages? Why should they take any notice of that? They want to kill us all anyway."

"One force does, certainly," she said, "but I'm not sure about the other. We must hope the Africans win."

She sounded happy, and in the glare from outside, Will saw her face full of joy and life and energy.

"You broke the knife," he said.

"No, I didn't. I wanted it whole, so we could get away. You were the one who broke it."

Lyra's voice came urgently: "Will?" she muttered. "Is that Will?"

"Lyra!" he said, and knelt quickly beside her. Ama was helping her sit up.

"What's happening?" Lyra said. "Where are we? Oh, Will, I had this dream…"

"We're in a cave. Don't move too fast, you'll get dizzy. Just take it carefully. Find your strength. You've been asleep for days and days."

Her eyes were still heavy, and she was racked by deep

yawns, but she was desperate to be awake, and he helped her up, putting her arm over his shoulder and taking much of her weight. Ama watched timidly, for now the strange girl was awake, she was nervous of her. Will breathed in the scent of Lyra's sleepy body with a happy satisfaction: she was here, she was real.

They sat on a rock. Lyra held his hand and rubbed her eyes. "What's happening, Will?" she whispered.

"Ama here got some powder to wake you up," he said speaking very quietly, and Lyra turned to the girl, seeing her for the first time, and put her hand on Ama's shoulder in thanks. "I got here as soon as I could," Will went on, "but some soldiers did too. I don't know who they are. We'll get out as soon as we can."

Outside, the noise and confusion was reaching a height; one of the gyropters had taken a fusillade from a zeppelin's machine gun while the riflemen were jumping out on the clifftop, and it burst into flames, not only killing the crew but also preventing the remaining gyropters from landing.

Another zeppelin, meanwhile, had found a clear space further down the valley, and the crossbow-men who disembarked from it were now running up the path to reinforce those already in action. Mrs Coulter was following as much as she could see from the cave-mouth, and now she raised her pistol, supporting it with both hands, and took careful aim before firing. Will saw the flash from the muzzle, but heard nothing over the explosions and gunfire from outside.

If she does that again, he thought, I'll rush and knock her over, and he turned to whisper that to Balthamos; but the angel was nowhere near. Instead, Will saw with dismay, he was cowering against the wall of the cave, back in his angel form, trembling and whimpering.

"Balthamos!" Will said urgently. "Come on, they can't hurt you! And you have to help us! You can fight – you know that – you're not a coward – and we need you –"

But before the angel could reply, something else happened.

Mrs Coulter cried out and reached down to her ankle, and simultaneously the golden monkey snatched at something in mid-air, with a snarl of glee.

A voice – a woman's voice – but somehow *minute* – came from the thing in the monkey's paw:

"Tialys! Tialys!"

It was a tiny woman, no bigger than Lyra's hand, and the monkey was already pulling and pulling at one of her arms so that she cried out in pain. Ama knew he wouldn't stop till he'd torn it off, but Will leapt forward as he saw the pistol fall from Mrs Coulter's hand.

And he caught the gun – but then Mrs Coulter fell still, and Will became aware of a strange stalemate.

The golden monkey and Mrs Coulter were both utterly motionless. Her face was distorted with pain and fury, but she dared not move, because standing on her shoulder was a tiny man with his heel pressed against her neck, his hands entwined in her hair; and Will, through his astonishment, saw on that heel a glistening horny spur, and knew what had caused her to cry out a moment before. He must have stung her ankle.

But the little man couldn't hurt Mrs Coulter any more, because of the danger his partner was in at the hands of the monkey; and the monkey couldn't harm *her*, in case the little man dug his poison spur into Mrs Coulter's jugular vein. None of them could move.

Breathing deeply and swallowing hard to govern the pain, Mrs Coulter turned her tear-dashed eyes to Will and said calmly, "So, Master Will, what do you think we should do now?"

13

Tialys and Salmakia

*H*olding the heavy gun, Will swept his hand sideways and knocked the golden monkey off his perch, stunning him so that Mrs Coulter groaned aloud, and the monkey's paw relaxed enough to let the tiny woman struggle free.

In a moment she leapt up to the rocks, and the man sprang away from Mrs Coulter, both of them moving as quickly as grasshoppers. The three children had no time to be astonished. The man was concerned: he felt his companion's shoulder and arm tenderly, and embraced her swiftly before calling to Will.

"You! Boy!" he said, and although his voice was small in volume, it was as deep as a grown man's. "Have you got the knife?"

"Of course I have," said Will. If they didn't know it was broken, he wasn't going to tell them.

"You and the girl will have to follow us. Who is the other child?"

"Ama, from the village," said Will.

"Tell her to return there. Move now, before the Swiss come."

Will didn't hesitate. Whatever these two intended, he and

Lyra could still get away through the window he'd opened behind the bush on the path below.

So he helped her up, and watched curiously as the two small figures leapt on – what? Birds? No, dragonflies, almost as long as his forearm, which had been waiting in the darkness. They darted forward to the cave-mouth, where Mrs Coulter lay. She was half-stunned with pain and drowsy from the chevalier's sting, but she reached up as they went past her, and cried:

"Lyra! Lyra, my daughter, my dear one! Lyra, don't go! Don't go!"

Lyra looked down at her, anguished; but then she stepped over her mother's body and loosened Mrs Coulter's feeble clutch from her ankle. The woman was sobbing now; Will saw the tears glistening on her cheeks.

Crouching just beside the cave-mouth, the three children waited until there was a brief pause in the shooting, and then followed the dragonflies as they darted down the path. The light had changed: as well as the cold anbaric gleam from the zeppelins' flood-lights, there was the leaping orange of flames.

Will looked back once. In the glare Mrs Coulter's face was a mask of tragic passion, and her dæmon clung piteously to her as she knelt and held out her arms, crying:

"Lyra! Lyra my love! My heart's treasure, my little child, my only one! Oh Lyra, Lyra, don't go, don't leave me! My darling daughter – you're tearing my heart –"

And a great and furious sob shook Lyra herself, for after all Mrs Coulter was the only mother she would ever have, and Will saw a cascade of tears run down the girl's cheeks.

But he had to be ruthless. He pulled at Lyra's hand, and as the dragonfly-rider darted close to his head, urging them to hurry, he led her at a crouching run down the path and away from the cave. In Will's left hand, bleeding again from the blow he'd landed on the monkey, was Mrs Coulter's pistol.

"Make for the top of the cliff," said the dragonfly-rider, "and give yourself up to the Africans. They're your best hope."

Mindful of those sharp spurs, Will said nothing, though he hadn't the least intention of obeying. There was only one place he was making for, and that was the window behind the bush; so he kept his head low and ran fast, and Lyra and Ama ran behind him.

"Halt!"

There was a man, three men, blocking the path ahead – uniformed – white men with cross-bows and snarling wolf-dog dæmons – the Swiss Guard.

"Iorek!" cried Will at once. "Iorek Byrnison!" He could hear the bear crashing and snarling not far away, and hear the screams and cries of the soldiers unlucky enough to meet him.

But someone else came from nowhere to help them: Balthamos, in a blur of desperation, hurled himself between the children and the soldiers. The men fell back, amazed, as this apparition shimmered into being in front of them.

But they were trained warriors, and a moment later their dæmons leapt at the angel, savage teeth flashing white in the gloom – and Balthamos flinched: he cried out in fear and shame, and shrank back. Then he sprang upwards, beating his wings hard. Will watched in dismay as the figure of his guide and friend soared up to vanish out of sight among the tree-tops.

Lyra was following it all with still-dazed eyes. It had taken no more than two or three seconds, but it was enough for the Swiss to re-group, and now their leader was raising his cross-bow, and Will had no choice: he swung up the pistol and clamped his right hand to the butt and pulled the trigger, and the blast shook his bones, but the bullet found the man's heart.

The soldier fell back as if he'd been kicked by a horse. Simultaneously the two little spies launched themselves at the other two, leaping from the dragonflies at their victims before Will could blink. The woman found a neck, the man a wrist, and each made a quick backward stab with a heel. A choking anguished gasp, and the two Swiss died, their dæmons vanishing in mid-howl.

Will leapt over the bodies, and Lyra went with him, running hard and fast with Pantalaimon racing wildcat-formed at their heels. *Where's Ama?* Will thought, and he saw her in the same moment dodging down a different path. Now she'll be safe, he thought, and a second later he saw the pale gleam of the window deep behind the bushes. He seized Lyra's arm and pulled her towards it. Their faces were scratched, their clothes were snagged, their ankles twisted on roots and rocks, but they found the window and tumbled through, into the other world, on to the bone-white rocks under the glaring moon, where only the scraping of the insects broke the immense silence.

And the first thing Will did was to hold his stomach and retch, heaving and heaving with a mortal horror. That was two men now that he'd killed, not to mention the youth in the Tower of the Angels... Will *did not want* this. His body revolted at what his instinct had made him do, and the result was a dry, sour, agonizing spell of kneeling and vomiting until his stomach and his heart were empty.

Lyra watched helpless nearby, nursing Pan, rocking him against her breast.

Finally Will recovered a little and looked around. And at

once he saw that they weren't alone in this world, because the little spies were there too, with their packs laid on the ground nearby. Their dragonflies were skimming over the rocks, snapping up moths. The man was massaging the shoulder of the woman, and both of them looked at the children sternly. Their eyes were so bright and their features so distinct that there was no doubt about their feelings, and Will knew they were a formidable pair, whoever they were.

He said to Lyra, "The alethiometer's in my rucksack, there."

"Oh, Will – I did so hope you'd find it – whatever *happened*? Did you find your father? And my *dream*, Will – it's too much to believe, what we got to do, oh, I daren't even think of it... And it's *safe*! You brung it all this way safe for me..."

The words tumbled out of her so urgently that even she didn't expect answers. She turned the alethiometer over and over, her fingers stroking the heavy gold and the smooth crystal and the knurled wheels they knew so well.

Will thought: *It'll tell us how to mend the knife!*

But he said first, "Are you all right? Are you hungry or thirsty?"

"I dunno ... yeah. But not too much. Anyway –"

"We should move away from this window," Will said, "just in case they find it and come through."

"Yes, that's true," she said, and they moved up the slope, Will carrying his rucksack and Lyra happily carrying the little bag she kept the alethiometer in. Out of the corner of his eye Will saw the two small spies following, but they kept their distance and made no threat.

Over the brow of the rise there was a ledge of rock that offered a narrow shelter, and they sat beneath it, having carefully checked it for snakes, and shared some dried fruit and some water from Will's canteen.

Will said quietly, "The knife's broken. I don't know how it happened. Mrs Coulter did something, or said something, and I thought of my mother and that made the knife twist, or catch, or – I don't know what happened. But we're stuck till we can get it mended. I didn't want those two little people to know, because while they think I can still use it, I've got the upper hand. I thought you could ask the alethiometer, maybe, and –"

"Yeah!" she said at once. "Yeah, I will."

She had the golden instrument out in a moment, and moved into the moonlight so she could see the dial clearly. Looping back the hair behind her ears, just as Will had seen her mother do, she began to turn the wheels in the old familiar way, and Pantalaimon, mouse-formed now, sat on her knee. But it wasn't as easy to see as she'd thought; perhaps the moonlight was deceptive. She had to turn it around once or twice, and blink to clear her eyes, before the symbols became clear, and then she had it again.

She had hardly started before she gave a little gasp of excitement, and she looked up at Will with shining eyes as the needle swung. But it hadn't finished yet, and she looked back, frowning, until the instrument fell still.

She put it away, saying, "Iorek? Is he nearby, Will? I thought I heard you call him, but then I thought I was just wishing. Is he *really*?"

"Yes. Could he mend the knife? Is that what the alethiometer said?"

"Oh, he can do anything with metal, Will! Not only armour – he can make little delicate things as well…" She told him about the small tin box Iorek had made for her to shut the spy-fly in. "But where is he?"

"Close by. He would have come when I called, but obviously

he was fighting... And Balthamos! Oh, he must have been so frightened..."

"Who?"

He explained briefly, feeling his cheeks warm with the shame that the angel must be feeling.

"But I'll tell you more about him later," he said. "It's so strange... He told me so many things, and I think I understand them, too..." He ran his hands through his hair and rubbed his eyes.

"You got to tell me *everything*," she said firmly. "Everything you did since she caught me. Oh, Will, you en't still bleeding? Your poor hand..."

"No. My father cured it. I just opened it up when I hit the golden monkey, but it's better now. He gave me some ointment that he'd made –"

"You *found* your father?"

"That's right, on the mountain, that night..."

He let her clean his wound and put on some fresh ointment from the little horn box while he told her some of what had happened: the fight with the stranger, the revelation that came to them both a second before the witch's arrow struck home, his meeting with the angels, his journey to the cave and his meeting with Iorek.

"All that happening, and I was asleep," she marvelled. "D'you know, I think she was kind to me, Will – I *think* she was – I don't think she ever wanted to hurt me... She did such bad things, but..."

She rubbed her eyes.

"Oh, but my *dream*, Will – I can't tell you how strange it was! It was like when I read the alethiometer, all that clearness and understanding going so deep you can't see the bottom, but clear all the way down.

"It was... Remember I told you about my friend Roger, and how the Gobblers caught him and I tried to rescue him, and it went wrong and Lord Asriel killed him?

"Well, I saw him. In my dream I saw him again, only he was dead, he was a ghost, and he was like beckoning to me, calling to me, only I couldn't hear. He didn't want me to be *dead*, it wasn't that. He wanted to speak to me.

"And... It was me that took him there, to Svalbard, where he got killed, it was my fault he was dead. And I thought back to when we used to play in Jordan College, Roger and me, on the roof, all through the town, in the markets and by the river and down the Claybeds... Me and Roger and all the others... And I went to Bolvangar to fetch him safe home, only I made it worse, and if I don't say sorry it'll all be no good, just a huge waste of time. I got to do that, you see, Will. I got to go down into the land of the dead and find him, and ... and say sorry. I don't care what happens after that. Then we can... I can... It doesn't matter after that."

Will said, "This place where the dead are. Is it a world like this one, like mine or yours or any of the others? Is it a world I could get to with the knife?"

She looked at him, struck by the idea.

"You could ask," he went on. "Do it now. Ask where it is, and how we get there."

She bent over the alethiometer, having to rub her eyes and peer closely again, and her fingers moved swiftly. A minute later she had the answer.

"Yes," she said, "but it's a strange place, Will... *So* strange... Could we really do that? Could we really go to the land of the dead? But – what part of us does that? Because dæmons fade away when we die – I've seen them – and our bodies, well, they just stay in the grave and decay, don't they?"

"Then there must be a third part. A different part."

"You know," she said, full of excitement, "I think that must be true! Because I can think about my body and I can think about my dæmon – so there *must* be another part, to do the thinking!"

"Yes. And that's the ghost."

Lyra's eyes blazed. She said, "Maybe we could get Roger's ghost out. Maybe we could rescue him."

"Maybe. We could try."

"Yeah, we'll do it!" she said at once. "We'll go together! That's *exactly* what we'll do!"

But if they didn't get the knife mended, Will thought, they'd be able to do nothing at all.

As soon as his head cleared and his stomach felt calmer, he sat up and called to the little spies. They were busy with some minute apparatus nearby.

"Who are you?" he said. "And whose side are you on?"

The man finished what he was doing and shut a wooden box, like a violin-case no longer than a walnut. The woman spoke first.

"We are Gallivespian," she said. "I am the Lady Salmakia, and my companion is the Chevalier Tialys. We are spies for Lord Asriel."

She was standing on a rock three or four paces away from Will and Lyra, distinct and brilliant in the moonlight. Her little voice was perfectly clear and low, her expression confident. She wore a loose skirt of some silver material and a sleeveless top of green, and her spurred feet were bare, like the man's. His costume was similarly coloured, but his sleeves were long and his wide trousers reached to mid-calf. Both of them looked strong, capable, ruthless and proud.

"What world do you come from?" said Lyra. "I never seen people like you before."

"Our world has the same problems as yours," said Tialys. "We are outlaws. Our leader Lord Roke heard of Lord Asriel's revolt, and pledged our support."

"And what did you want to do with me?"

"To take you to your father," said the Lady Salmakia. "Lord Asriel sent a force under King Ogunwe to rescue you and the boy and bring you both to his fortress. We are here to help."

"Ah, but suppose I don't want to go to my father? Suppose I don't trust him?"

"I'm sorry to hear that," she said, "but those are our orders: to take you to him."

Lyra couldn't help it: she laughed out loud at the notion of these tiny people making her do anything. But it was a mistake. Moving suddenly, the woman seized Pantalaimon, and holding his mouse-body in a fierce grip, she touched the tip of a spur to his leg. Lyra gasped: it was like the shock when the men at Bolvangar had seized him. No one should touch someone else's dæmon – it was a violation.

But then she saw that Will had swept up the man in his right hand, holding him tightly around the legs so he couldn't use his spurs, and was holding him high.

"Stalemate again," said the lady calmly. "Put the chevalier down, boy."

"Let go of Lyra's dæmon first," said Will. "I'm not in the mood to argue."

Lyra saw with a cold thrill that Will was perfectly ready to dash the Gallivespian's head against the rock. And both little people knew it.

Salmakia lifted her foot away from Pantalaimon's leg, and at once he fought free of her grasp and changed into a wildcat, hissing ferociously, fur on end, tail lashing. His bared teeth were a hand's breadth from the lady's face, and she gazed at him with perfect composure. After a moment he turned and fled to Lyra's breast, ermine-shaped, and Will carefully placed Tialys back on the rock beside his partner.

"You should show some respect," the chevalier said to Lyra. "You are a thoughtless insolent child, and several brave men have died this evening in order to make you safe. You'd do better to act politely."

"Yes," she said humbly, "I'm sorry, I will. Honest."

"As for you —" he went on, turning to Will.

But Will interrupted: "As for me, I'm not going to be spoken to like that, so don't try. Respect goes two ways. Now listen carefully. You are not in charge here; we are. If you want to stay and help, then you do as we say. Otherwise, go back to Lord Asriel now. There's no arguing about it."

Lyra could see the pair of them bristling, but Tialys was looking at Will's hand, which was on the sheath at his belt, and she knew he was thinking that while Will had the knife, he was stronger than they were. At all costs they mustn't know it was broken, then.

"Very well," said the chevalier. "We shall help you, because that's the task we've been given. But you must let us know what you intend to do."

"That's fair," said Will. "I'll tell you. We're going back into Lyra's world as soon as we've rested, and we're going to find a friend of ours, a bear. He's not far away."

"The bear with the armour? Very well," said Salmakia. "We saw him fight. We'll help you do that. But then you must come with us to Lord Asriel."

"Yes," said Lyra, lying earnestly, "oh yes, we'll do that then all right."

Pantalaimon was calmer now, and curious, so she let him climb to her shoulder and change. He became a dragonfly, as big as the two that were skimming through the air as they spoke, and darted up to join them.

"That poison," Lyra said, turning back to the Gallivespians, "in your spurs I mean, is it deadly? Because you stung my mother, Mrs Coulter, didn't you? Will she die?"

"It was only a light sting," said Tialys. "A full dose would have killed her, yes, but a small scratch will make her weak and drowsy for half a day or so."

And full of maddening pain, he knew, but he didn't tell her that.

"I need to talk to Lyra in private," said Will. "We're just going to move away for a minute."

"With that knife," said the chevalier, "you can cut through from one world to another, isn't that so?"

"Don't you trust me?"

"No."

"All right, I'll leave it here then. If I haven't got it, I can't use it."

He unbuckled the sheath and laid it on the rock, and then he and Lyra walked away and sat where they could see the Gallivespians. Tialys was looking closely at the knife handle, but he wasn't touching it.

"We'll just have to put up with them," Will said. "As soon as the knife's mended, we'll escape."

"They're so *quick*, Will," she said. "And they wouldn't care, they'd kill you."

"I just hope Iorek can mend it. I hadn't realized how much we need it."

"He will," she said confidently.

She was watching Pantalaimon as he skimmed and darted

through the air, snapping up tiny moths like the other dragonflies. He couldn't go as far as they could, but he was just as fast, and even more brightly patterned. She raised her hand, and he settled on it, his long transparent wings vibrating.

"Do you think we can trust them while we sleep?" Will said.

"Yes. They're fierce, but I think they're honest."

They went back to the rock, and Will said to the Gallivespians, "I'm going to sleep now. We'll move on in the morning."

The chevalier nodded, and Will curled up at once and fell asleep.

Lyra sat down beside him, with Pantalaimon cat-formed and warm in her lap. How lucky Will was that she was awake now to look after him! He was truly fearless, and she admired that beyond measure; but he wasn't good at lying and betraying and cheating, which all came to her as naturally as breathing. When she thought of that she felt warm and virtuous, because she did it for Will, never for herself.

She had intended to look at the alethiometer again, but to her deep surprise she found herself as weary as if she'd been awake all that time instead of unconscious, and she lay down close by and closed her eyes, just for a brief nap, as she assured herself before she fell asleep.

14
Know What It Is

*W*ill and Lyra slept through the night, and woke up when the sun struck their eyelids. They actually awoke within seconds of each other, with the same thought: but when they looked around, the Chevalier Tialys was calmly on guard close by.

"The force of the Consistorial Court has retreated," he told them. "Mrs Coulter is in the hands of King Ogunwe, and on her way to Lord Asriel."

"How do you know?" said Will, sitting up stiffly. "Have you been back through the window?"

"No. We talk through the lodestone resonator. I reported our conversation," Tialys said to Lyra, "to my commander Lord Roke, and he has agreed that we should go with you to the bear, and that once you have seen him, you will come with us. So we are allies, and we shall help you as much as we can."

"Good," said Will. "Then let's eat together. Do you eat our food?"

"Thank you, yes," said the lady.

Will took out his last few dried peaches and the stale flat loaf of rye bread which was all he had left, and shared it all out among them, though of course the spies did not take much.

"As for water, there doesn't seem to be any round here on this world," Will said. "We'll have to wait till we go back through before we can have a drink."

"Then we better do that soon," said Lyra.

First, though, she took out the alethiometer. She could see it clearly, unlike the night before, but her fingers were slow and stiff after her long sleep. She asked if there was still any danger in the valley. No, came the answer, all the soldiers have gone, and the villagers are in their homes; so they prepared to leave.

The window looked strange in the dazzling air of the desert, giving on to the deep-shaded bush, a square of thick green vegetation hanging in the air like a painting. The Gallivespians wanted to look at it, and were astounded to see how it was just not there from the back, and how it only sprang into being when you came round from the side.

"I'll have to close it once we're through," Will said.

Lyra tried to pinch the edges together, but her fingers couldn't find it at all; nor could the spies, despite the fineness of their hands. Only Will could feel exactly where the edges were, and he did it cleanly and quickly.

"How many worlds can you enter with the knife?" said Tialys.

"As many as there are," said Will. "No one would ever have time to find out."

He swung his rucksack up and led the way along the forest path. The dragonflies relished the fresh moist air, and darted like needles through the shafts of sunlight. The movement of the trees above was less violent, and the air was cool and tranquil; so it was all the more shocking to see the twisted wreckage of a gyropter suspended among the branches, with the body of its African pilot tangled in his seat-belt half out

of the door, and to find the charred remains of the zeppelin
a little further up – soot-black strips of cloth, blackened
struts and pipework, broken glass, and then the bodies: three
men burnt to cinders, their limbs contorted and drawn up as
if they were still threatening to fight.

And they were only the ones who had fallen near the path.
There were other bodies and more wreckage on the cliff above
and among the trees further down. Shocked and silenced, the
two children moved through the carnage, while the spies on
their dragonflies looked around more coolly, accustomed to
battle, noting how it had gone and who had lost most.

When they reached the top of the valley, where the trees
thinned out and the rainbow-waterfalls began, they stopped
to drink deeply of the ice-cold water.

"I hope that little girl's all right," said Will. "We'd never
have got you away if she hadn't woken you up. She went to a
holy man to get that powder specially."

"She is all right," said Lyra, "cause I asked the
alethiometer, last night. She thinks we're devils though. She's
afraid of us. She probably wishes she'd never got mixed up in
it, but she's safe all right."

They climbed up beside the waterfalls, and refilled Will's
canteen before striking off across the plateau towards the
ridge where the alethiometer told Lyra that Iorek had gone.

And then there came a day of long, hard walking: no
trouble for Will, but a torment to Lyra, whose limbs were
weakened and softened after her long sleep. But she would
sooner have her tongue torn out than confess how bad she
felt: limping, tight-lipped, trembling, she kept pace with Will
and said nothing. Only when they sat down at noon did she
allow herself so much as a whimper, and then only when Will
had gone apart to relieve himself.

The Lady Salmakia said, "Rest. There is no disgrace in being weary."

"But I don't want to let Will down! I don't want him to think I'm weak and holding him back."

"That's the last thing he thinks."

"You don't know," said Lyra rudely. "You don't know him any more than you know me."

"I know impertinence when I hear it," said the lady calmly. "Do as I tell you now and rest. Save your energy for the walking."

Lyra felt mutinous, but the lady's glittering spurs were very clear in the sunlight, so she said nothing.

Her companion the chevalier was opening the case of the lodestone resonator, and, curiosity overcoming resentment, Lyra watched to see what he did. The instrument looked like a short length of pencil made of dull grey-black stone, resting on a stand of wood, and the chevalier swept a tiny bow like a violinist's across the end while he pressed his fingers at various points along the surface. The places weren't marked, so he seemed to be touching it at random, but from the intensity of his expression and the certain fluency of his movements, Lyra knew it was as skilful and demanding a process as her own reading of the alethiometer.

After several minutes the spy put the bow away and took up a pair of headphones, the earpieces no larger than Lyra's little fingernail, and wrapped one end of the wire tightly around a peg in the end of the stone, leading the rest along to another peg at the other end and wrapping it around that. By manipulating the two pegs and the tension on the wire between them, he could obviously hear a response to his own message.

"How does that work?" she said when he'd finished.

Tialys looked at her as if to judge whether she was genuinely interested, and then said, "Your scientists, what do you call them, experimental theologians, would know of something called quantum entanglement. It means that two particles can exist that only have properties in common, so that whatever happens to one happens to the other at the same moment, no matter how far apart they are. Well, in our world there is a way of taking a common lodestone and entangling all its particles, and then splitting it in two so that both parts resonate together. The counterpart to this is with Lord Roke, our commander. When I play on this one with my bow, the other one reproduces the sounds exactly, and so we communicate."

He put everything away and said something to the lady. She joined him and they went a little apart, talking too quietly for Lyra to hear, though Pantalaimon became an owl and turned his great ears in their direction.

Presently Will came back and then they moved on, more slowly as the day went by, and the track got steeper and the snow line nearer. They rested once more at the head of a rocky valley, because even Will could tell that Lyra was nearly finished: she was limping badly and her face was grey.

"Let me see your feet," he said to her, "because if they're blistered, I'll put some ointment on."

They were, badly, and she let him rub in the bloodmoss salve, closing her eyes and gritting her teeth.

Meanwhile, the chevalier was busy, and after a few minutes he put his lodestone away and said, "I have told Lord Roke of our position, and they are sending a gyropter to bring us away as soon as you have spoken to your friend."

Will nodded. Lyra took no notice. Presently she sat up wearily and pulled on her socks and shoes, and they set off once more.

Another hour, and most of the valley was in shadow, and

Will was wondering whether they would find any shelter before night fell; but then Lyra gave a cry of relief and joy.

"Iorek! Iorek!"

She had seen him before Will had. The bear-king was some way off still, his white coat indistinct against a patch of snow, but when Lyra's voice echoed out he turned his head, raised it to sniff, and bounded down the mountainside towards them.

Ignoring Will, he let Lyra clasp his neck and bury her face in his fur, growling so deep that Will felt it through his feet; but Lyra felt it as pleasure, and forgot her blisters and her weariness in a moment.

"Oh, Iorek, my dear, I'm so glad to see you! I never thought I'd ever see you again – after that time on Svalbard – and all the things that've happened – is Mr Scoresby safe? How's your kingdom? Are you all alone here?"

The little spies had vanished; at all events, there seemed to be only the three of them now on the darkening mountainside, the boy and the girl and the great white bear. As if she had never wanted to be anywhere else, Lyra climbed up as Iorek offered his back and rode proud and happy as her dear friend carried her up the last stretch of the way to his cave.

Will, preoccupied, didn't listen as Lyra talked to Iorek, though he did hear a cry of dismay at one point, and heard her say:

"Mr Scoresby – oh no! Oh, it's too cruel! *Really* dead? You're sure, Iorek?"

"The witch told me he set out to find the man called Grumman," said the bear.

Will listened more closely now, for Baruch and Balthamos had told him some of this.

"What happened? Who killed him?" said Lyra, her voice shaky.

"He died fighting. He kept a whole company of Muscovites at bay while the man escaped. I found his body. He died bravely. I shall avenge him."

Lyra was weeping freely, and Will didn't know what to say, for it was his father whom this unknown man had died to save; and Lyra and the bear had both known and loved Lee Scoresby, and he had not.

Soon Iorek turned aside, and made for the entrance to a cave, very dark against the snow. Will didn't know where the spies were, but he was perfectly sure they were nearby. He wanted to speak quietly to Lyra, but not till he could see the Gallivespians and know he wasn't being overheard.

He laid his rucksack in the cave-mouth and sat down wearily. Behind him the bear was kindling a fire, and Lyra watched, curious despite her sorrow. Iorek held a small rock of some sort of ironstone in his left forepaw and struck it no more than three or four times on a similar one on the floor. Each time a scatter of sparks burst out, and went exactly where Iorek directed them: into a heap of shredded twigs and dried grass. Very soon that was ablaze, and Iorek calmly placed one log and then another and another until the fire was burning strongly.

The children welcomed it, because the air was very cold now, and then came something even better: a haunch of something that might have been goat. Iorek ate his meat raw, of course, but he spitted this joint on a sharp stick and laid it to roast across the fire for the two of them.

"Is it easy, hunting up in these mountains, Iorek?" she said.

"No. My people can't live here. I was wrong, but luckily so, since I found you. What are your plans now?"

Will looked around the cave. They were sitting close to the

fire, and the fire-light threw warm yellows and oranges on the bear-king's fur. Will could see no sign of the spies, but there was nothing for it: he had to ask.

"King Iorek," he began, "my knife is broken –" and then he looked past the bear and said, "No, wait." He was pointing at the wall. "If you're listening," he went on more loudly, "come out and do it honestly. Don't spy on us."

Lyra and Iorek Byrnison turned to see who he was talking to. The little man came out of the shadow and stood calmly in the light, on a ledge higher than the children's heads. Iorek growled.

"You haven't asked Iorek Byrnison for permission to enter his cave," Will said. "And he is a king, and you're just a spy. You should show more respect."

Lyra loved hearing that. She looked at Will with pleasure, and saw him fierce and contemptuous.

But the chevalier's expression, as he looked at Will, was displeased.

"We have been truthful with you," he said. "It was dishonourable to deceive us."

Will stood up. His dæmon, Lyra thought, would have the form of a tigress, and she shrank back from the anger she imagined the great animal to show.

"If we deceived you, it was necessary," he said. "Would you have agreed to come here if you knew the knife was broken? Of course you wouldn't. You'd have used your venom to make us unconscious, and then you'd call for help and have us kidnapped and taken to Lord Asriel. So we had to trick you, Tialys, and you'll just have to put up with it."

Iorek Byrnison said, "Who is this?"

"Spies," said Will. "Sent by Lord Asriel. They helped us escape yesterday, but if they're on our side they shouldn't hide and eavesdrop on us. And if they do, they're the last people who should talk about dishonour."

The spy's glare was so ferocious that he looked ready to take on Iorek himself, never mind the unarmed Will; but Tialys was in the wrong, and he knew it. All he could do was bow and apologize.

"Your Majesty," he said to Iorek, who growled at once.

The chevalier's eyes flashed hatred at Will, and defiance and warning at Lyra, and a cold and wary respect at Iorek. The clarity of his features made all these expressions vivid and bright, as if a light shone on him. Beside him the Lady Salmakia was emerging from the shadow, and, ignoring the children completely, she made a curtsey to the bear.

"Forgive us," she said to Iorek. "The habit of concealment is hard to break, and my companion the Chevalier Tialys and I, the Lady Salmakia, have been among our enemies for so long that out of pure habit we neglected to pay you the proper courtesy. We're accompanying this boy and girl to make sure they arrive safely in the care of Lord Asriel. We have no other aim, and certainly no harmful intentions towards you, King Iorek Byrnison."

If Iorek wondered how any such tiny beings could cause him harm, he didn't show it; not only was his expression naturally hard to read, but he had his courtesy too, and the lady had spoken graciously enough.

"Come down by the fire," he said. "There is food enough and plenty if you are hungry. Will, you began to speak about the knife."

"Yes," said Will, "and I thought it could never happen, but it's broken. And the alethiometer told Lyra that you'd be able to mend it. I was going to ask more politely, but there it is: can you mend it, Iorek?"

"Show me."

Will shook all the pieces out of the sheath and laid them on the rocky floor, pushing them about carefully until they were in their right places and he could see that they were all there. Lyra held a burning branch up, and in its light Iorek bent low to look closely at each piece, touching it delicately with his massive claws and lifting it up to turn it this way and that and examine the break. Will marvelled at the deftness in those huge black hooks.

Then Iorek sat up again, his head rearing high into the shadow.

"Yes," he said, answering exactly the question and no more.

Lyra said, knowing what he meant, "Ah, but *will* you, Iorek? You couldn't believe how important this is – if we can't get it mended then we're in desperate trouble, and not only us –"

"I don't like that knife," Iorek said. "I fear what it can do. I have never known anything so dangerous. The most deadly fighting machines are little toys compared to that knife; the harm it can do is unlimited. It would have been infinitely better if it had never been made."

"But with it –" began Will.

Iorek didn't let him finish, but went on, "With it you can do strange things. What you don't know is what the knife does on its own. Your intentions may be good. The knife has intentions too."

"How can that be?" said Will.

"The intentions of a tool are what it does. A hammer intends to strike, a vice intends to hold fast, a lever intends to lift. They are what it is made for. But sometimes a tool may have other uses that you don't know. Sometimes in doing what *you* intend, you also do what the knife intends, without knowing. Can you see the sharpest edge of that knife?"

"No," said Will, for it was true: the edge diminished to a thinness so fine that the eye could not reach it.

"Then how can you know everything it does?"

"I can't. But I must still use it, and do what I can to help good things come about. If I did nothing I'd be worse than useless. I'd be guilty."

Lyra was following this closely, and seeing Iorek still unwilling, she said:

"Iorek, you *know* how wicked those Bolvangar people were. If we can't win, then they're going to be able to carry on doing those kind of things for ever. And besides, if we don't have the knife, then they might get hold of it theirselves. We never knew about it when I first met you, Iorek, and nor did anyone, but now that we do, we *got* to use it ourselves – we can't just *not*. That'd be feeble, and it'd be wrong too, it'd be just like handing it over to 'em and saying go on, use it, we won't stop you. All right, we don't know what it does, but I can ask the alethiometer, can't I? Then we'd know. And we could think about it properly instead of just guessing and being afraid."

Will didn't want to mention his own most pressing reason: if the knife were not repaired, he'd never get home, never see his mother again; she would never know what had happened; she'd think he'd abandoned her as his father had done. The knife had been directly responsible for both their desertions. He *must* use it to return to her, or never forgive himself.

Iorek Byrnison said nothing for a long time, but turned his head to look out at the darkness. Then he slowly got to his feet and stalked to the cave-mouth, and looked up at the stars: some the same as those he knew, from the north, and some that were strange to him.

Behind him, Lyra turned the meat over on the fire, and Will looked at his wounds, to see how they were healing. Tialys and Salmakia sat silent on their ledge.

Then Iorek turned around.

"Very well, I shall do it on one condition," he said. "Though I feel it is a mistake. My people have no gods, no ghosts or dæmons. We live and die and that is that. Human affairs bring us nothing but sorrow and trouble, but we have language and we make war and we use tools; maybe we should take sides. But full knowledge is better than half-knowledge. Lyra, read your instrument. Know what it is that you're asking. If you still want it then, I shall mend the knife."

At once Lyra took out the alethiometer and edged nearer to the fire so that she could see the face. The inconstant flicker made it hard to see, or perhaps the smoke was getting in her eyes, and the reading took her longer than usual. When she blinked and sighed and came out of the trance her face was troubled.

"I never known it so confused," she said. "There was lots of things it said. I think I got it clear. I *think* so. It said about balance first. It said the knife could be harmful or it could do good, but it was so slight, such a delicate kind of a balance, that the faintest thought or wish could tip it one way or the other... And it meant *you*, Will, it meant what you wished or thought, only it didn't say what would be a good thought or a bad one.

"Then ... it said yes," she said, her eyes flashing at the spies. "It said yes, do it, repair the knife."

Iorek looked at her steadily, and then nodded once.

Tialys and Salmakia climbed down to watch more closely, and Lyra said, "D'you need more fuel, Iorek? Me and Will could go and fetch some, I'm sure."

Will understood what she meant: away from the spies they could talk.

Iorek said, "Below the first spur on the track there is a bush with resinous wood. Bring as much of that as you can."

She jumped up at once, and Will went with her.

The moon was brilliant, the path a track of scumbled footprints in the snow, the air cutting and cold. Both of them felt brisk and hopeful and alive. They didn't talk till they were well away from the cave.

"What else did it say?" Will said.

"It said some things I didn't understand then and I still don't understand now. It said the knife would be the death of Dust, but then it said it was the only way to keep Dust alive. I didn't understand it, Will. But it said again it was dangerous, it kept saying that. It said if we – you know – what I thought –"

"If we go to the world of the dead –"

"Yeah – if we do that – it said that we might never come back, Will. We might not survive."

He said nothing, and they walked along more soberly now, watching out for the bush that Iorek had mentioned, and silenced by the thought of what they might be taking on.

"We've got to, though," he said, "haven't we?"

"I don't know."

"Now we *know*, I mean. You have to speak to Roger, and I have to speak to my father. We have to, now."

"I'm frightened," she said.

And he knew she'd never admit that to anyone else.

"Did it say what would happen if we *didn't*?" he asked.

"Just emptiness. Just blankness. I really didn't understand it, Will. But I *think* it meant that even if it *is* that dangerous, we should still try and rescue Roger. But it won't be like when

I rescued him from Bolvangar; I didn't know what I was doing then, really, I just set off, and I was lucky. I mean there was all kinds of other people to help, like the gyptians and the witches. There won't be any help where we'd have to go. And I can see... In my dream I saw... The place was... It was worse than Bolvangar. That's why I'm afraid."

"What *I'm* afraid of," said Will after a minute, not looking at her at all, "is getting stuck somewhere and never seeing my mother again."

From nowhere, a memory came to him: he was very young, and it was before her troubles began, and he was ill. All night long, it seemed, his mother had sat on his bed in the dark, singing nursery rhymes, telling him stories, and as long as her dear voice was there, he knew he was safe. He *couldn't* abandon her now. He couldn't! He'd look after her all his life long if she needed it.

And as if Lyra had known what he was thinking, she said warmly:

"Yeah, that's true, that would be awful... You know, with my mother, I never realized... I just grew up on my own, really; I don't remember anyone ever holding me or cuddling me, it was just me and Pan as far back as I can go... I can't remember Mrs Lonsdale being like that to me; she was the housekeeper at Jordan College, all she did was make sure I was clean, that's all she thought about, oh and manners... But in the cave, Will, I really felt – oh it's *strange*, I know she's done terrible things, but I really felt she was loving me and looking after me... She must have thought I was going to die, being asleep all that time – I suppose I must've caught some disease – but she never stopped looking after me. And I remember waking up once or twice and she was holding me in her arms... I *do* remember that, I'm sure... That's what I'd do in her place, if I had a child."

So she didn't know why she'd been asleep all that time. Should he tell her, and betray that memory, even if it was false? No, of course he shouldn't.

"Is that the bush?" Lyra said.

The moonlight was brilliant enough to show every leaf. Will snapped off a twig, and the piny resinous smell stayed strongly on his fingers.

"And we en't going to say anything to those little spies," she added.

They gathered armfuls of the bush, and carried them back up towards the cave.

15

The Forge

*A*t that moment, the Gallivespians were talking about the knife. Having made a suspicious peace with Iorek Byrnison, they climbed back to their ledge to be out of the way, and as the crackle of flames rose and the snapping and roaring of the fire filled the air, Tialys said, "We must never leave his side. As soon as the knife is mended, we must keep closer than a shadow."

"He is too alert. He watches everywhere for us," said Salmakia. "The girl is more trusting. I think we could win her round. She's innocent, and she loves easily. We could work on her. I think we should do that, Tialys."

"But he has the knife. He is the one who can use it."

"He won't go anywhere without her."

"But she has to follow him, if he has the knife. And I think that as soon as the knife's intact again, they'll use it to slip into another world so as to get away from us. Did you see how he stopped her from speaking when she was going to say something more? They have some secret purpose, and it's very different from what we want them to do."

"We'll see. But you're right, Tialys, I think. We must stay close to the boy at all costs."

They both watched with some scepticism as Iorek Byrnison laid out the tools in his improvised workshop. The mighty workers in the ordnance factories under Lord Asriel's fortress, with their blast furnaces and rolling mills, their anbaric forges and hydraulic presses, would have laughed at the open fire, the stone hammer, the anvil consisting of a piece of Iorek's armour. Nevertheless, the bear had taken the measure of the task, and in the certainty of his movements the little spies began to see some quality that muffled their scorn.

When Lyra and Will came in with the bushes, Iorek directed them in placing branches carefully on the fire. He looked at each branch, turning it from side to side, and then told Will or Lyra to place it at such-and-such an angle, or to break off part and place it separately at the edge. The result was a fire of extraordinary ferocity, with all its energy concentrated at one side.

By this time the heat in the cave was intense. Iorek continued to build the fire, and made the children take two more trips down the path to ensure that there was enough fuel for the whole operation.

Then the bear turned over a small stone on the floor, and told Lyra to find some more stones of the same kind. He said that those stones, when heated, gave off a gas which would surround the blade and keep the air from it, for if the hot metal came in contact with the air it would absorb some and be weakened by it.

Lyra set about searching, and with owl-eyed Pantalaimon's help soon had a dozen or more stones to hand. Iorek told her how to place them, and where, and showed her exactly the kind of draught she should get moving, with a leafy branch, to make sure the gas flowed evenly over the work piece.

Will was placed in charge of the fire, and Iorek spent several minutes directing him and making sure he understood the principles he was to use. So much depended on exact placement, and Iorek could not stop and correct each one: Will had to understand, and then he'd do it properly.

Furthermore, he mustn't expect the knife to look exactly the same when it was mended. It would be shorter, because each section of the blade would have to overlap the next by a little way, so they could be forged together; and the surface would have oxidized a little, despite the stone-gas, so some of the play of colour would be lost; and no doubt the handle would be charred. But the blade would be just as sharp, and it would work.

So Will watched as the flames roared along the resinous twigs, and with streaming eyes and scorched hands he adjusted each fresh branch till the heat was focused as Iorek wanted it.

Meanwhile Iorek himself was grinding and hammering a fist-sized stone, having rejected several until he found one of the right weight. With massive blows he shaped it and smoothed it, the cordite-smell of smashed rocks joining the smoke in the nostrils of the two spies, watching from high up. Even Pantalaimon was active, changing to a crow so he could flap his wings and make the fire burn faster.

Eventually the hammer was formed to Iorek's satisfaction, and he set the first two pieces of the blade of the subtle knife among the fierce-burning wood at the heart of the fire, and told Lyra to begin wafting the stone-gas over them. The bear watched, his long white face lurid in the glare, and Will saw the surface of the metal begin to glow red and then yellow and then white.

Iorek was watching closely, his paw held ready to snatch

the pieces out. After a few moments the metal changed again, and the surface became shiny and glistening, and sparks just like those from a firework sprayed up from it.

Then Iorek moved. His right paw darted in and seized first one piece and then the other, holding them between the tips of his massive claws and placing them on the slab of iron that was the backplate of his armour. Will could smell the claws burning, but Iorek took no notice of that, and moving with extraordinary speed he adjusted the angle at which the pieces overlapped and then raised his left paw high and struck a blow with the rock hammer.

The knife-tip leaped on the rock under the massive blow. Will was thinking that the whole of the rest of his life depended on what happened in that tiny triangle of metal, that point that searched out the gaps inside the atoms, and all his nerves trembled, sensing every flicker of every flame and the loosening of every atom in the lattice of the metal. Before this began, he had supposed that only a full-scale furnace, with the finest tools and equipment, could work on that blade; but now he saw that these were the finest tools, and that Iorek's artistry had constructed the best furnace there could be.

Iorek roared above the clangour: "Hold it still in your mind! You have to forge it too! This is your task as much as mine!"

Will felt his whole being quiver under the blows of the stone hammer in the bear's fist. The second piece of the blade was heating too, and Lyra's leafy branch sent the hot gas along to bathe both pieces in its flow and keep out the iron-eating air. Will sensed it all, and felt the atoms of the metal linking each to each across the fracture, forming new crystals again, strengthening and straightening themselves in the invisible lattice as the join came good.

"The edge!" roared Iorek. "Hold the edge in line!"

He meant *with your mind*, and Will did it instantly, sensing the minute snags and then the minute easement as the edges lined up perfectly. Then that join was made, and Iorek turned to the next piece.

"A new stone," he called to Lyra, who knocked the first one aside and placed a second on the spot to heat.

Will checked the fuel and snapped a branch in two to direct the flames better, and Iorek began to work with the hammer once more. Will felt a new layer of complexity added to his task, because he had to hold the new piece in a precise relation with both the previous two, and he understood that only by doing that accurately could he help Iorek mend it.

So the work continued. He had no idea how long it took; Lyra, for her part, found her arms aching, her eyes streaming, her skin scorched and red, and every bone in her body aching with fatigue; but still she placed each stone as Iorek had told her, and still the weary Pantalaimon raised his wings readily and beat them over the flames.

When it came to the final joint, Will's head was ringing, and he was so exhausted by the intellectual effort he could barely lift the next branch on to the fire. He had to understand every connection, or the knife would not hold together; and when it came to the most complex one, the last, which would fix the nearly-finished blade on to the small part remaining at the handle – if he couldn't hold it in his full consciousness together with all the others, then the knife would simply fall apart as if Iorek had never begun.

The bear sensed this, too, and paused before he began heating the last piece. He looked at Will, and in his eyes Will could see nothing, no expression, just a bottomless black brilliance. Nevertheless, he understood: this was work, and it was hard, but they were equal to it, all of them.

That was enough for Will, so he turned back to the fire and sent his imagination out to the broken end of the haft, and braced himself for the last and fiercest part of the task.

So he and Iorek and Lyra between them forged the knife, and how long the final joint took he had no idea; but when Iorek had struck the final blow, and Will had felt the final tiny settling as the atoms connected across the break, he sank down on to the floor of the cave and let exhaustion possess him. Lyra nearby was in the same state, her eyes glassy and red-rimmed, her hair full of soot and smoke; and Iorek himself stood heavy-headed, his fur singed in several places, dark streaks of ash marking its rich cream-white.

Tialys and Salmakia had slept in turns, one of them always alert. Now she was awake and he was sleeping, but as the blade cooled from red to grey and finally to silver, and as Will reached out for the handle, she woke her partner with a hand on his shoulder. He was alert at once.

But Will didn't touch the knife: he held his palm close by, and the heat was still too great for his hand. The spies relaxed on the rocky shelf as Iorek said to Will:

"Come outside."

Then he said to Lyra: "Stay here, and don't touch the knife."

Lyra sat close to the anvil, where the knife lay cooling, and Iorek told her to bank the fire up and not let it burn down: there was a final operation yet.

Will followed the great bear out on to the dark mountain-side. The cold was bitter and instantaneous, after the inferno in the cave.

"They should not have made that knife," said Iorek, after they had walked a little way. "Maybe I should not have mended it. I'm troubled, and I have never been troubled before, never in doubt. Now I am full of doubt. Doubt is a human thing, not a bear thing. If I am becoming human, something's wrong, something's bad. And I've made it worse."

"But when the first bear made the first piece of armour, wasn't that bad too, in the same way?"

Iorek was silent. They walked on till they came to a big drift of snow, and Iorek lay in it and rolled this way and that, sending flurries of snow up into the dark air so that it looked as if he himself were made of snow, he was the personification of all the snow in the world.

When had finished he rolled over and stood up and shook himself vigorously, and then, seeing Will still waiting for an answer to his question, said:

"Yes, I think it might have been, too. But before that first armoured bear, there were no others. We know of nothing before that. That was when custom began. We know our customs, and they are firm and solid and we follow them without change. Bear-nature is weak without custom, as bear-flesh is unprotected without armour.

"But I think I have stepped outside bear-nature in mending this knife. I think I've been as foolish as Iofur Raknison. Time will tell. But I am uncertain and doubtful. Now you must tell me: why did the knife break?"

Will rubbed his aching head with both hands.

"The woman looked at me and I thought she had the face of my mother," he said, trying to recollect the experience with all the honesty he had. "And the knife came up against something it couldn't cut, and because my mind was pushing it through and forcing it back both at the same time, it snapped. That's what I think. The woman knew what she was doing, I'm sure. She's very clever."

"When you talk of the knife, you talk of your mother and father."

"Do I? Yes... I suppose I do."

"What are you going to do with it?"

"I don't know."

Suddenly Iorek lunged at Will and cuffed him hard with his left paw: so hard that Will fell half-stunned into the snow and tumbled over and over until he ended some way down the slope with his head ringing.

Iorek came down slowly to where Will was struggling up, and said, "Answer me truthfully."

Will was tempted to say, "You wouldn't have done that if I'd had the knife in my hand." But he knew that Iorek knew that, and knew that he knew it, and that it would be discourteous and stupid to say it; but he was tempted, all the same.

He held his tongue until he was standing upright, facing Iorek directly.

"I said I don't know," he said, trying hard to keep his voice calm, "because I haven't looked clearly at what it is that I'm going to do. At what it means. It frightens me. And it frightens Lyra too. Anyway, I agreed as soon as I heard what she said."

"And what was that?"

"We want to go down to the land of the dead and talk to the ghost of Lyra's friend Roger, the one who got killed on Svalbard. And if there really is a world of the dead, then my father will be there too, and if we can talk to ghosts, I want to talk to him.

"But I'm divided, I'm pulled apart, because also I want to go back and look after my mother, because I *could*, and also because my father and the angel Balthamos told me I should go to Lord Asriel and offer it to him, and I think maybe they were right as well..."

"The angel fled," said the bear.

"He wasn't a warrior. He did as much as he could, and then he couldn't do any more. He wasn't the only one to be afraid; I'm afraid, too. So I have to think it through. Maybe sometimes we don't do the right thing because the wrong thing looks more dangerous, and we don't want to look scared, so we go and do the wrong thing just *because* it's dangerous. We're more concerned with not looking scared than with judging right. It's very hard. That's why I didn't answer you."

"I see," said the bear.

They stood in silence for what felt like a long time, especially to Will, who had little protection from the bitter cold. But Iorek hadn't finished yet, and Will was still weak and dizzy from the blow, and didn't quite trust his feet, so they stayed where they were.

"Well, I have compromised myself in many ways," said the bear-king. "It may be that in helping you I have brought final destruction on my kingdom. And it may be that I have not, and that destruction was coming anyway; maybe I have held it off. So I am troubled, having to do un-bearlike deeds and speculate and doubt like a human.

"And I shall tell you one thing. You know it already, but you don't want to, which is why I tell you openly, so that you don't mistake it. If you want to succeed in this task, you must no longer think about your mother. You must put her aside. If your mind is divided, the knife will break.

"Now I'm going to say farewell to Lyra. You must wait in the cave; those two spies will not let you out of their sight, and I do not want them listening when I speak to her."

Will had no words, though his breast and his throat were full. He managed to say, "Thank you, Iorek Byrnison," but that was all he could say.

He walked with Iorek up the slope towards the cave, where the fire-glow shone warmly still in the vast surrounding dark.

There Iorek carried out the last process in the mending of the subtle knife. He laid it among the brighter cinders until the blade was glowing, and Will and Lyra saw a hundred colours swirling in the smoky depths of the metal, and when he judged the moment was right, Iorek told Will to take it and plunge it directly into the snow that had drifted outside.

The rosewood handle was charred and scorched, but Will wrapped his hand in several folds of a shirt and did as Iorek told him. In the hiss and flare of steam he felt the atoms finally settle together, and he knew that the knife was as keen as before, the point as infinitely rare.

But it did look different. It was shorter, and much less elegant, and there was a dull silver surface over each of the joins. It looked ugly now; it looked like what it was, wounded.

When it was cool enough, he packed it away in the rucksack, and sat, ignoring the spies, to wait for Lyra to come back.

Iorek had taken her a little further up the slope, to a point out of sight of the cave, and there he had let her sit cradled in the shelter of his great arms, with Pantalaimon nestling mouse-formed at her breast. Iorek bent his head over her, and nuzzled at her scorched and smoky hands. Without a word he began to lick them clean; his tongue was soothing on the burns, and she felt as safe as she had ever felt in her life.

But when her hands were free of soot and dirt, Iorek spoke. She felt his voice vibrate against her back.

"Lyra Silvertongue, what is this plan to visit the dead?"

"It came to me in a dream, Iorek. I saw Roger's ghost, and I knew he was calling to me... You remember Roger; well, after we left you he was killed, and it was my fault, at least I felt it was. And I think I should just finish what I began, that's all: I should go and say sorry, and if I can, I should rescue him from there. If Will can open a way to the world of the dead, then we must do it."

"Can is not the same as must."

"But if you must and you can, then there's no excuse."

"While you are alive, your business is with life."

"No, Iorek," she said gently, "our business is to keep promises, no matter how difficult they are. You know, secretly, I'm deadly scared. And I wish I'd never had that dream, and I wish Will hadn't thought of using the knife to go there. But we did, so we can't get out of it."

Lyra felt Pantalaimon trembling, and stroked him with her sore hands.

"We don't know how to get there, though," she went on. "We won't know anything till we try. What are *you* going to do, Iorek?"

"I'm going back north, with my people. We can't live in the mountains. Even the snow is different. I thought we could live here, but we can live more easily in the sea, even if it is warm. That was worth learning. And besides, I think we will be needed. I can feel war, Lyra Silvertongue; I can smell it; I can hear it. I spoke to Serafina Pekkala before I came this way, and she told me she was going to Lord Faa and the gyptians. If there is war, we shall be needed."

Lyra sat up, excited at hearing the names of her old friends. But Iorek hadn't finished. He went on:

"If you do not find a way out of the world of the dead, we shall not meet again, because I have no ghost. My body will remain on the earth, and then become part of it. But if it turns out that you and I both survive, then you will always be a welcome and honoured visitor to Svalbard; and the same is true of Will. Has he told you what happened when we met?"

"No," said Lyra, "except that it was by a river."

"He outfaced me. I thought no one could ever do that, but this half-grown boy was too daring for me, and too clever. I am not happy that you should do what you plan, but there is no one I would trust to go with you, except that boy. You are worthy of each other. Go well, Lyra Silvertongue, my dear friend."

She reached up and put her arms around his neck, and pressed her face into his fur, unable to speak.

After a minute he stood up gently and disengaged her arms, and then he turned and walked silently away into the dark. Lyra thought his outline was lost almost at once against the pallor of the snow-covered ground, but it might have been that her eyes were full of tears.

When Will heard her footsteps on the path, he looked at the spies and said, "Don't you move. Look – here's the knife – I'm not going to use it. Stay here."

He went outside and found Lyra standing still, weeping, with Pantalaimon as a wolf raising his face to the black sky. She was quite silent. The only light came from the pale reflection in the snow-bank of the remains of the fire, and that in turn was reflected from her wet cheeks, and her tears found their own reflection in Will's eyes, and so those photons wove the two together in a silent web.

"I love him so much, Will!" she managed to whisper shakily. "And he looked *old*! He looked hungry and old and sad... Is it all coming on to us now, Will? We can't rely on anyone else now, can we... It's just us. But we en't old enough yet. We're only young... We're *too* young... If poor Mr Scoresby's dead and Iorek's old... It's all coming on to us, what's got to be done."

"We can do it," he said. "I'm not going to look back any

more. We can do it. But we've got to sleep now, and if we stay in this world those gyropter things might come, that the spies sent for... I'm going to cut through now and we'll find another world to sleep in, and if the spies come with us, that's too bad; we'll have to get rid of them another time."

"Yes," she said, and sniffed and wiped the back of her hand across her nose and rubbed her eyes with both palms. "Let's do that. You sure the knife will work? You tested it?"

"I know it'll work."

With Pantalaimon tiger-formed to deter the spies, they hoped, Will and Lyra went back and picked up their rucksacks.

"What are you doing?" said Salmakia.

"Going into another world," said Will, taking out the knife. It felt like being whole again; he hadn't realized how much he loved it.

"But you must wait for Lord Asriel's gyropters," said Tialys, his voice hard.

"We're not going to," said Will. "If you come near the knife I'll kill you. Come through with us if you must, but you can't make us stay here. We're leaving."

"You lied!"

"No," said Lyra, "I lied. Will doesn't lie. You didn't think of that."

"But where are you going?"

Will didn't answer. He felt forward in the dim air and cut an opening.

Salmakia said, "This is a mistake. You should realize that, and listen to us. You haven't thought –"

"Yes we have," said Will, "we've thought hard, and we'll tell you what we've thought tomorrow. You can come where we're going, or you can go back to Lord Asriel."

The window opened on to the world into which he had

escaped with Baruch and Balthamos, and where he'd slept safely: the warm endless beach with the fern-like trees behind the dunes. He said:

"Here – we'll sleep here – this'll do."

He let them through, and closed it behind them at once. While he and Lyra lay down where they were, exhausted, the Lady Salmakia kept watch, and the chevalier opened his lodestone resonator and began to play a message into the dark.

16

The Intention Craft

" *My child!* My *daughter!* Where is she? What have you done? My Lyra – you'd do better to tear the fibres from my heart – she was safe with me, *safe*, and now where is she?"

Mrs Coulter's cry resounded through the little chamber at the top of the adamant tower. She was bound to a chair, her hair dishevelled, her clothing torn, her eyes wild; and her monkey-dæmon thrashed and struggled on the floor in the coils of a silver chain.

Lord Asriel sat nearby, scribbling on a piece of paper, taking no notice. An orderly stood beside him, glancing nervously at the woman. When Lord Asriel handed him the paper he saluted and hurried out, his terrier-dæmon close at his heels with her tail tucked low.

Lord Asriel turned to Mrs Coulter.

"Lyra? Frankly, I don't care," he said, his voice quiet and hoarse. "The wretched child should have stayed where she was put, and done what she was told. I can't waste any more time or resources on her; if she refuses to be helped, let her deal with the consequences."

"You don't mean that, Asriel, or you wouldn't have –"

"I mean every word of it. The fuss she's caused is out of all proportion to her merits. An ordinary English girl, not very clever –"

"She is!" said Mrs Coulter.

"All right; bright but not intellectual; impulsive, dishonest, greedy –"

"Brave, generous, loving."

"A perfectly ordinary child, distinguished by nothing –"

"Perfectly ordinary? Lyra? She's unique. Think of what she's done already. Dislike her if you will, Asriel, but don't you dare patronize your daughter. And she was safe with me, until –"

"You're right," he said, getting up. "She *is* unique. To have tamed and softened you – that's no everyday feat. She's drawn your poison, Marisa. She's taken your teeth out. Your fire's been quenched in a drizzle of sentimental piety. Who would have thought it? The pitiless agent of the church, the fanatical persecutor of children, the inventor of hideous machines to slice them apart and look in their terrified little beings for any evidence of *sin* – and along comes a foulmouthed ignorant little brat with dirty fingernails, and you cluck and settle your feathers over her like a hen. Well, I admit: the child must have some gift I've never seen myself. But if all it does is turn you into a doting mother, it's a pretty thin, drab, puny little gift. And now you might as well be quiet. I've asked my chief commanders to come in for an urgent conference, and if you can't control your noise I'll have you gagged."

Mrs Coulter was more like her daughter than she knew. Her answer to this was to spit in Lord Asriel's face. He wiped it calmly away and said, "A gag would put an end to that kind of behaviour, too."

"Oh, do correct me, Asriel," she said; "someone who displays a captive to his under-officers tied to a chair is clearly a prince of politeness. Untie me, or I'll *force* you to gag me."

"As you wish," he said, and took a silk scarf from the drawer; but before he could tie it around her mouth, she shook her head.

"No, no," she said, "Asriel, don't, I beg you, please don't humiliate me."

Angry tears dashed from her eyes.

"Very well, I'll untie you, but he can stay in his chains," he said, and dropped the scarf back in the drawer before cutting her bonds with a clasp knife.

She rubbed her wrists, stood up, stretched, and only then noticed the condition of her clothes and her hair. She looked haggard and pale; the last of the Gallivespian venom still remained in her body, causing agonizing pains in her joints, but she was not going to show him that.

Lord Asriel said, "You can wash in there," indicating a small room hardly bigger than a closet.

She picked up her chained dæmon, whose baleful eyes glared at Lord Asriel over her shoulder, and went through to make herself tidier.

The orderly came in to announce:

"His Majesty King Ogunwe and the Lord Roke."

The African general and the Gallivespian came in: King Ogunwe in a clean uniform, with a wound on his temple freshly dressed, and Lord Roke gliding swiftly to the table astride his blue hawk.

Lord Asriel greeted them warmly and offered wine. The bird let his rider step off, and then flew to the bracket by the door as the orderly announced the third of Lord Asriel's high commanders, an angel by the name of Xaphania. She was of a much higher rank than Baruch or Balthamos, and visible by a shimmering, disconcerting light that seemed to come from somewhere else.

By this time Mrs Coulter had emerged, much tidied, and all three commanders bowed to her; and if she was surprised at their appearance, she gave no sign, but inclined her head and sat down peaceably, holding the pinioned monkey in her arms.

Without wasting time, Lord Asriel said, "Tell me what happened, King Ogunwe."

The African, powerful and deep-voiced, said, "We killed seventeen Swiss Guards and destroyed two zeppelins. We lost five men and one gyropter. The girl and the boy escaped. We captured the Lady Coulter, despite her courageous defence, and brought her here. I hope she feels we treated her courteously."

"I am quite content with the way you treated me, sir," she said, with the faintest possible stress on the *you*.

"Any damage to the other gyropters? Any wounded?" said Lord Asriel.

"Some damage and some wounds, but all minor."

"Good. Thank you, King; your force did well. My Lord Roke, what have you heard?"

The Gallivespian said, "My spies are with the boy and girl in another world. Both children are safe and well, though the girl has been kept in a drugged sleep for many days. The boy lost the use of his knife during the events in the cave: by some accident, it broke in pieces. But it is now whole again, thanks to a creature from the north of *your* world, Lord Asriel, a giant bear, very skilled at smith-work. As soon as the knife was mended, the boy cut through into another world, where they are now. My spies are with them, of course, but there is a difficulty: while the boy has the knife, he cannot be compelled to do anything; and yet if they were to kill him in his sleep, the knife would be useless to us. For the time being, the Chevalier Tialys and the Lady Salmakia will go with them wherever they go, so at least we can keep track of them. They seem to have a plan in mind; they are refusing to come here, at any rate. My two will not lose them."

"Are they safe in this other world they're in now?" said Lord Asriel.

"They're on a beach near a forest of tree-ferns. There is no sign of animal life nearby. As we speak, both boy and girl are asleep; I spoke to the Chevalier Tialys not five minutes ago."

"Thank you," said Lord Asriel. "Now that your two agents are following the children, of course, we have no eyes in the Magisterium any more. We shall have to rely on the alethiometer. At least –"

Then Mrs Coulter spoke, to their surprise.

"I don't know about the other branches," she said, "but as far as the Consistorial Court is concerned, the reader they rely on is Fra Pavel Rašek. And he's thorough, but slow. They won't know where Lyra is for another few hours."

Lord Asriel said, "Thank you, Marisa. Do *you* have any idea what Lyra and this boy intend to do next?"

"No," she said, "none. I've spoken to the boy, and he seemed to be a stubborn child, and one well used to keeping secrets. I can't guess what he would do. As for Lyra, she is quite impossible to read."

"My Lord," said King Ogunwe, "may we know whether the lady is now part of this commanding council? If so, what is her function? If not, should she not be taken elsewhere?"

"She is our captive and my guest, and as a distinguished

former agent of the Church, she may have information that would be useful."

"Will she reveal anything willingly? Or will she need to be tortured?" said Lord Roke, watching her directly as he spoke.

Mrs Coulter laughed.

"I would have thought Lord Asriel's commanders would know better than to expect truth to come out of torture," she said.

Lord Asriel couldn't help enjoying her barefaced insincerity.

"I will guarantee Mrs Coulter's behaviour," he said. "She knows what will happen if she betrays us; though she will not have the chance. However, if any of you has a doubt, express it now, fearlessly."

"I do," said King Ogunwe, "but I doubt you, not her."

"Why?" said Lord Asriel.

"If she tempted you, you would not resist. It was right to capture her, but wrong to invite her to this council. Treat her with every courtesy, give her the greatest comfort, but place her somewhere else, and stay away from her."

"Well, I invited you to speak," said Lord Asriel, "and I must accept your rebuke. I value your presence more than hers, King. I'll have her taken away."

He reached for the bell, but before he could ring, Mrs Coulter spoke.

"Please," she said urgently, "listen to me first. I can help. I've been closer to the heart of the Magisterium than anyone you're likely to find again. I know how they think, I can guess what they'll do. You wonder why you should trust me, what's made me leave them? It's simple: they're going to kill my daughter. They daren't let her live. The moment I found out who she is – what she is – what the witches prophesy about her – I knew I had to leave the church; I knew I was their enemy, and they were mine; I didn't know what *you* were, or what I was to you – that was a mystery; but I knew that I had to set myself against the church, against everything they believed in, and if need be, against the Authority himself. I..."

She stopped. All the commanders were listening intently. Now she looked Lord Asriel full in the face and seemed to speak to him alone, her voice low and passionate, her brilliant eyes glittering.

"I have been the worst mother in the world. I let my only child be taken away from me when she was a tiny infant, because I didn't care about her; I was concerned only with my own advancement. I didn't think of her for years, and if I did, it was only to regret the embarrassment of her birth.

"But then the church began to take an interest in Dust and in children, and something stirred in my heart, and I remembered that I was a mother and Lyra was ... *my* child.

"And because there was a threat, I saved her from it. Three times now I've stepped in to pluck her out of danger. First when the Oblation Board began its work: I went to Jordan College and I took her to live with me, in London, where I could keep her safe from the Board ... or so I hoped. But she ran away.

"The second time was at Bolvangar, when I found her just in time, under the – under the blade of the... My heart nearly stopped... It was what they – we – what I had done to other children, but when it was *mine*... Oh, you can't conceive the horror of that moment, I hope you never suffer as I did then... But I got her free; I took her out; I saved her a second time.

"But even as I did that, I still felt myself part of the church, a servant, a loyal and faithful and devoted servant, because I was doing the Authority's work.

"And then I learned the witches' prophecy. Lyra will somehow, sometime soon, be tempted, as Eve was – that's what they say. What form this temptation will take, I don't know, but she's growing up, after all. It's not hard to imagine. And now that the church knows that, too, they'll kill her. If it all depends on her, could they risk letting her live? Would they dare take the chance that she'd refuse this temptation, whatever it will be?

"No, they're bound to kill her. If they could, they'd go back to the garden of Eden and kill Eve before *she* was tempted. Killing is not difficult for them; Calvin himself ordered the deaths of children; they'd kill her with pomp and ceremonial and prayers and lamentations and psalms and hymns, but they would kill her. If she falls into their hands, she's dead already.

"So when I heard what the witch said, I saved my daughter for the third time. I took her to a place where I kept her safe, and there I was going to stay."

"You drugged her," said King Ogunwe. "You kept her unconscious."

"I had to," said Mrs Coulter, "because she hated me," and here her voice, which had been full of emotion but under control, spilled over into a sob, and it trembled as she went on: "She feared me and hated me, and she would have fled from my presence like a bird from a cat if I hadn't drugged her into oblivion. Do you know what that means to a mother? But it was the only way to keep her safe! All that time in the cave ... asleep, her eyes closed, her body helpless, her dæmon curled up at her throat... Oh, I felt such a love, such a tenderness, such a deep, deep... My own child, the first time I had ever been able to do these things for her, my little... I washed her and fed her and kept her safe and warm, I made sure her body was nourished as she slept... I lay beside her at night, I cradled her in my arms, I wept into her hair, I kissed her sleeping eyes, my little one..."

She was shameless. She spoke quietly; she didn't declaim or raise her voice; and when a sob shook her, it was muffled almost into a hiccup, as if she were stifling her emotions for the sake of courtesy. Which made her barefaced lies all the more effective, Lord Asriel thought with disgust; she lied in the very marrow of her bones.

She directed her words mainly at King Ogunwe, without seeming to, and Lord Asriel saw that too. Not only was the king her chief accuser, he was also human, unlike the angel, or Lord Roke, and she knew how to play on him.

In fact, though, it was on the Gallivespian that she made the greatest impression. Lord Roke sensed in her a nature as close to that of a scorpion as he had ever encountered, and he was well aware of the power in the sting he could detect under her gentle tone. Better to keep scorpions where you could see them, he thought.

So he supported King Ogunwe when the latter changed his mind and argued that she should stay, and Lord Asriel found himself outflanked: for he now wanted her elsewhere, but he had already agreed to abide by his commanders' wishes.

Mrs Coulter looked at him with an expression of mild and virtuous concern. He was certain that no one else could see the glitter of sly triumph in the depths of her beautiful eyes.

"Stay then," he said. "But you've spoken enough. Stay quiet now. I want to consider this proposal for a garrison on the southern border. You've seen the report: is it workable? Is it desirable? Next I want to look at the armoury. And then I want to hear from Xaphania about the dispositions of the angelic forces. First, the garrison. King Ogunwe?"

The African leader began. They spoke for some time, and Mrs Coulter was impressed by their accurate knowledge of the church's defences, and their clear assessment of its leaders' strengths.

But now that Tialys and Salmakia were with the children, and Lord Asriel no longer had a spy in the Magisterium, their knowledge would soon be dangerously out of date. An idea came to Mrs Coulter's mind, and she and the monkey-dæmon exchanged a glance that felt like a powerful anbaric spark; but she said nothing, and stroked his golden fur as she listened to the commanders.

Then Lord Asriel said, "Enough. That is a problem we'll deal with later. Now for the armoury. I understand they're ready to test the intention craft. We'll go and look at it."

He took a silver key from his pocket and unlocked the chain around the golden monkey's feet and hands, and carefully avoided touching even the tip of one golden hair.

Lord Roke mounted his hawk, and followed with the others as Lord Asriel set off down the stairs of the tower and out on to the battlements.

A cold wind was blowing, snapping at their eye-lids, and the dark-blue hawk soared up in a mighty draught, wheeling and screaming in the wild air. King Ogunwe drew his coat around him and rested his hand on his cheetah-dæmon's head.

Mrs Coulter said humbly to the angel:

"Excuse me, my lady: your name is Xaphania?"

"Yes," said the angel.

Her appearance impressed Mrs Coulter just as her fellows had impressed the witch Ruta Skadi when she found them in the sky: she was not shining, but shone on, though there was no source of light. She was tall, naked, winged, and her lined face was older than any living creature Mrs Coulter had ever seen.

"Are you one of the angels who rebelled so long ago?"

"Yes. And since then I have been wandering between many worlds. Now I have pledged my allegiance to Lord Asriel, because I see in his great enterprise the best hope of destroying the tyranny at last."

"But if you fail?"

"Then we shall all be destroyed, and cruelty will reign for ever."

As they spoke, they followed Lord Asriel's rapid strides along the wind-beaten battlements towards a mighty staircase going down so deep that even the flaring lights on sconces down the walls could not disclose the bottom. Past them swooped the blue hawk, gliding down and down into the gloom, with each flaring light making his feathers flicker as he passed it until he was merely a tiny spark, and then nothing.

The angel had moved on to Lord Asriel's side, and Mrs Coulter found herself descending next to the African king.

"Excuse my ignorance, sir," she said, "but I had never seen or heard of a being like the man on the blue hawk until the fight in the cave yesterday... Where does he come from? Can you tell me about his people? I wouldn't offend him for the world, but if I speak without knowing something about him, I might be unintentionally rude."

"You do well to ask," said King Ogunwe. "His people are proud. Their world developed unlike ours; there are two kinds of conscious being there, humans and Gallivespians. The humans are mostly servants of the Authority, and they have been trying to exterminate the small people since the earliest time anyone can remember. They regard them as diabolic. So the Gallivespians still cannot quite trust those who are our size. But they are fierce and proud warriors, and deadly enemies, and valuable spies."

"Are all his people with you, or are they divided as humans are?"

"There are some who are with the enemy, but most are with us."

"And the angels? You know, I thought until recently that angels were an invention of the Middle Age; they were just imaginary... To find yourself speaking to one is disconcerting, isn't it... How many are with Lord Asriel?"

"Mrs Coulter," said the king, "these questions are just the sort of things a spy would want to find out."

"A fine sort of spy I'd be, to ask you so transparently," she replied. "I'm a captive, sir. I couldn't get away, even if I had a safe place to flee to. From now on, I'm harmless, you can take my word for that."

"If you say so, I am happy to believe you," said the king. "Angels are more difficult to understand than any human being. They're not all of one kind, to begin with; some have greater powers than others; and there are complicated alliances among them, and ancient enmities, that we know little about. The Authority has been suppressing them since he came into being."

She stopped. She was genuinely shocked. The African king halted beside her, thinking she was unwell, and indeed the light of the flaring sconce above her did throw ghastly shadows over her face.

"You say that so casually," she said, "as if it were something I should know too, but... How can it be? The Authority created the worlds, didn't he? He existed before everything. How can he have *come into being?*"

"This is angelic knowledge," said Ogunwe. "It shocked some of us too to learn that the Authority is not the creator. There may have been a creator, or there may not: we don't know. All we know is that at some point the Authority took charge, and since then, angels have rebelled, and human beings have struggled against him too. This is the last rebellion. Never before have humans and angels, and beings from all the worlds, made a common cause. This is the greatest force ever assembled. But it may still not be enough. We shall see."

"But what does Lord Asriel intend? What is this world, and why has he come here?"

"He led us here because this world is empty. Empty of conscious life, that is. We are not colonialists, Mrs Coulter. We haven't come to conquer, but to build."

"And is he going to attack the kingdom of heaven?"

Ogunwe looked at her levelly.

"We're not going to invade the kingdom," he said, "but if the kingdom invades us, they had better be ready for war, because we are prepared. Mrs Coulter, I am a king, but it's my proudest task to join Lord Asriel in setting up a world where there are no kingdoms at all. No kings, no bishops, no priests. The kingdom of heaven has been known by that name since the Authority first set himself above the rest of the angels. And we want no part of it. This world is different. We intend to be free citizens of the republic of heaven."

Mrs Coulter wanted to say more, to ask the dozen questions that rose to her lips, but the king had moved on, unwilling to keep his commander waiting, and she had to follow.

The staircase led so far down that by the time it reached a level floor the sky behind them at the head of the flight was quite invisible. Well before half-way she had little breath left, but she made no complaint, and moved on down till it opened out into a massive hall lit by glowing crystals in the pillars that supported the roof. Ladders, gantries, beams and walkways crossed the gloom above, with small figures moving about them purposefully.

Lord Asriel was speaking to his commanders when Mrs Coulter arrived, and without waiting to let her rest he moved on across the great hall, where occasionally a bright figure would sweep through the air or alight on the floor for a brief snatched word with him. The air was dense and warm. Mrs Coulter noticed that, presumably as a courtesy to Lord Roke, every pillar had an empty bracket at human head-height so that his hawk could perch there and allow the Gallivespian to be included in the discussion.

But they did not stay in the great hall for long. At the far side, an attendant hauled open a heavy double door to let them through, on to the platform of a railway. There waiting was a small closed carriage, drawn by an anbaric locomotive.

The engineer bowed, and his brown monkey-dæmon retreated behind his legs at the sight of the golden monkey. Lord Asriel spoke to the man briefly and showed the others into the carriage, which like the hall was lit by those glowing crystals, held on silver brackets against mirrored mahogany panels.

As soon as Lord Asriel had joined them the train began to move, gliding smoothly away from the platform and into a tunnel, accelerating briskly. Only the sound of the wheels on the smooth track gave any idea of their speed.

"Where are we going?" Mrs Coulter asked.

"To the armoury," Lord Asriel said shortly, and turned away to talk quietly with the angel.

Mrs Coulter said to Lord Roke, "My lord, are your spies always sent out in pairs?"

"Why do you ask?"

"Simple curiosity. My dæmon and I found ourselves at a stalemate when we met them recently in that cave, and I was intrigued to see how well they fought."

"Why *intrigued*? Did you not expect people of our size to be good fighters?"

She looked at him coolly, aware of the ferocity of his pride.

"No," she said. "I thought we would beat you easily, and you very nearly beat us. I'm happy to admit my mistake. But do you always fight in pairs?"

"*You* are a pair, are you not, you and your dæmon? Did you expect us to concede the advantage?" he said, and his haughty stare, brilliantly clear even in the soft light of the crystals, dared her to ask more.

She looked down modestly and said nothing.

Several minutes went past, and Mrs Coulter felt the train taking them downwards, even deeper into the mountain's heart. She couldn't guess how far they went, but when at least fifteen minutes had gone by, the train begin to slow; and presently they drew up to a platform where the anbaric lights seemed brilliant after the darkness of the tunnel.

Lord Asriel opened the doors, and they got out into an atmosphere so hot and sulphur-laden that Mrs Coulter had to gasp. The air rang with the pounding of mighty hammers and the clangorous screech of iron on stone.

An attendant hauled open the doors leading off the platform, and instantly the noise redoubled and the heat swept over them like a breaking wave. A blaze of scorching light made them shade their eyes; only Xaphania seemed unaffected by the onslaught of sound and light and heat. When her senses had adjusted, Mrs Coulter looked around, alive with curiosity.

She had seen forges, iron-works, manufactories in her own world: the biggest seemed like a village smithy beside this.

Hammers the size of houses were lifted in a moment to the distant ceiling and then hurled downwards to flatten baulks of iron the size of tree-trunks, pounding them flat in a fraction of a second with a blow that made the very mountain tremble; from a vent in the rocky wall, a river of sulphurous molten metal flowed until it was cut off by an adamant gate, and the brilliant seething flood rushed through channels and sluices and over weirs into row upon row of moulds, to settle and cool in a cloud of evil smoke; gigantic slicing machines and rollers cut and folded and pressed sheets of inch-thick iron as if it were tissue-paper, and then those monstrous hammers pounded it flat again, layering metal upon metal with such force that the different layers became one tougher one, over and over again.

If Iorek Byrnison could have seen this armoury, he might have admitted that these people knew something about working with metal. Mrs Coulter could only look and wonder. It was impossible to speak and be understood, and no one tried. And now Lord Asriel was gesturing to the small group to follow him along a grated walkway suspended over an even larger vault below, where miners toiled with picks and spades to hack the bright metals from the mother-rock.

They passed over the walkway and down a long rocky corridor, where stalactites hung gleaming with strange colours and where the pounding and grinding and hammering gradually faded. Mrs Coulter could feel a cool breeze on her heated face. The crystals that gave them light were neither mounted on sconces nor enclosed in glowing pillars, but scattered loosely on the floor, and there were no flaring torches to add to the heat, so little by little the party began to feel cold again; and presently they came out, quite suddenly, into the night air.

They were at a place where part of the mountain had been hacked away, making a space as wide and open as a parade-ground. Further along they could see, dimly lit, great iron doors in the mountainside, some open and some shut; and from out of one of the mighty doorways, men were hauling something draped in a tarpaulin.

"What is that?" Mrs Coulter said to the African king, and he replied:

"The intention craft."

Mrs Coulter had no idea what that could mean, and watched with intense curiosity as they prepared to take off the tarpaulin.

She stood close to King Ogunwe as if for shelter and said, "How does it work? What does it do?"

"We're about to see," said the king.

It looked like some kind of complex drilling apparatus, or the cockpit of a gyropter, or the cabin of a massive crane. It had a glass canopy over a seat with at least a dozen levers and handles banked in front of it. It stood on six legs, each jointed and sprung at a different angle to the body, so that it seemed both energetic and ungainly; and the body itself was a mass of pipework, cylinders, pistons, coiled cables, switchgear and valves and gauges. It was hard to tell what was structure and what was not, because it was only lit from behind, and most of it was hidden in gloom.

Lord Roke on his hawk had glided up to it directly, circling above, examining it from all sides. Lord Asriel and the angel were close in discussion with the engineers, and men were clambering down from the craft itself, one carrying a clipboard, another a length of cable.

Mrs Coulter's eyes gazed at the craft hungrily, memorizing every part of it, making sense of its complexity. And as she watched, Lord Asriel swung himself up into the seat, fastening a leather harness around his waist and shoulders and setting a helmet securely on his head. His dæmon, the snow leopard, sprang up to follow him, and he turned to adjust something beside her. The engineer called up, Lord Asriel replied, and the men withdrew to the doorway.

The intention craft moved, though Mrs Coulter was not sure how. It was almost as if it had quivered, though there it was, quite still, poised with a strange energy on those six insect-legs. As she looked it moved again, and then she saw what was happening: various parts of it were revolving, turning this way and that, scanning the dark sky overhead. Lord Asriel sat busily moving this lever, checking that dial, adjusting that control; and then suddenly the intention craft vanished.

Somehow, it had sprung into the air. It was hovering above them now, as high as a tree-top, turning slowly to the left. There was no sound of an engine, no hint of how it was held against gravity. It simply hung in the air.

"Listen," said King Ogunwe. "To the south."

She turned her head and strained to hear. There was a wind that moaned around the edge of the mountain, and there were the deep hammer-blows from the presses which she felt through the soles of her feet, and there was the sound of voices from the lighted doorway, but at some signal the voices stopped and the lights were extinguished. And in the quiet Mrs Coulter could hear, very faintly, the chop-chop-chop of gyropter engines on the gusts of wind.

"Who are they?" she said quietly.

"Decoys," said the king. "My pilots, flying a mission to tempt the enemy to follow. Watch."

She widened her eyes, trying to see anything against the

heavy dark with its few stars. Above them, the intention craft hung as firmly as if it were anchored and bolted there; no gust of wind had the slightest effect on it. No light came from the cockpit, so it was very difficult to see, and the figure of Lord Asriel was out of sight completely.

Then she caught the first sight of a group of lights low in the sky, at the same moment as the engine-sound became loud enough to hear steadily. Six gyropters, flying fast, one of them seemingly in trouble, for smoke trailed from it, and it flew lower than the others. They were making for the mountain, but on a course to take them past it and beyond.

And behind them, in close pursuit, came a motley collection of flyers. It was not easy to make out what they were, but Mrs Coulter saw a heavy gyropter of a strange kind, two straight-winged aircraft, one great bird that glided with effortless speed carrying two armed riders, and three or four angels.

"A raiding party," said King Ogunwe.

They were closing on the gyropters. Then a line of light blazed from one of the straight-winged aircraft, followed a second or two later by the sound, a deep crack. But the shell never reached its target, the crippled gyropter, because in the same instant as they saw the light, and before they heard the crack, the watchers on the mountain saw a flash from the intention craft, and a shell exploded in mid-air.

Mrs Coulter had hardly time to understand that almost instantaneous sequence of light and sound before the battle was under way. Nor was it at all easy to follow, because the sky was so dark and the movement of every flier so quick; but a series of nearly silent flashes lit the mountainside, accompanied by short hisses like the escape of steam. Each flash struck somehow at a different raider: the aircraft caught fire or exploded, the giant bird uttered a scream like the tearing of a mountain-high curtain and plummeted on to the rocks far below; and as for the angels, each of them simply vanished in a drift of glowing air, a myriad particles twinkling and glowing dimmer until they flickered out like a dying firework.

Then there was silence. The wind carried away the sound of the decoy gyropters, which had now disappeared around the flank of the mountain, and no one watching spoke. Flames far below glared on the underside of the intention craft, still somehow hovering in the air and now turning slowly as if to look around. The destruction of the raiding party was so complete that Mrs Coulter, who had seen many things to be shocked by, was nevertheless shocked by this. As she looked up at the intention craft, it seemed to shimmer or dislodge itself and then there it was, solidly on the ground again.

King Ogunwe hurried forward, as did the other commanders and the engineers, who had thrown open the doors and let the light flood out over the proving-ground. Mrs Coulter stayed where she was, puzzling over the workings of the intention craft.

"Why is he showing it to us?" her dæmon said quietly.

"Surely he can't have read our mind," she replied in the same tone.

They were thinking of the moment in the adamant tower when that spark-like idea had flashed between them. They had thought of making Lord Asriel a proposition: of offering to go to the Consistorial Court of Discipline and spy for him. She knew every lever of power; she could manipulate them all. It would be hard at first to convince them of her good faith, but she could do it. And now that the Gallivespian spies had left to go with Will and Lyra, surely Asriel couldn't resist an offer like that.

But now, as they looked at that strange flying machine, another idea struck even more forcibly, and she hugged the golden monkey with glee.

"Asriel," she called innocently, "may I see how the machine works?"

He looked down, his expression distracted and impatient, but full of excited satisfaction too. He was delighted with the intention craft: she knew he wouldn't be able to resist showing it off.

King Ogunwe stood aside, and Lord Asriel reached down and pulled her up into the cockpit. He helped her into the seat, and watched as she looked around the controls.

"How does it work? What powers it?" she said.

"Your intentions," he said. "Hence the name. If you intend to go forward, it will go forward."

"That's no answer. Come on, tell me. What sort of engine is it? How does it fly? I couldn't see anything aerodynamic at all. But these controls ... from inside, it's almost like a gyropter."

He was finding it hard not to tell her; and since she was in his power, he did. He held out a cable at the end of which was a leather grip, deeply marked by his dæmon's teeth.

"Your dæmon," he explained, "has to hold this handle – whether in teeth, or hands, it doesn't matter. And you have to wear that helmet. There's a current flowing between them, and a capacitor amplifies it – oh, it's more complicated than that, but the thing's simple to fly. We put in controls like a gyropter for the sake of familiarity, but eventually we won't need controls at all. Of course, only a human with a dæmon can fly it."

"I see," she said.

And she pushed him hard, so that he fell out of the machine.

In the same moment she slipped the helmet on her head, and the golden monkey snatched up the leather handle. She reached for the control which in a gyropter would tilt the aerofoil, and pushed the throttle forward, and at once the intention craft leapt into the air.

But she didn't quite have the measure of it yet. The craft hung still for some moments, slightly tilted, before she found the controls to move it forward, and in those few seconds, Lord Asriel did three things. He leapt to his feet; he put up his hand to stop King Ogunwe from ordering the soldiers to fire on the intention craft; and he said, "Lord Roke, go with her, if you would be so kind."

The Gallivespian urged his blue hawk upwards at once, and the bird flew straight to the still-open cabin door. The watchers below could see the woman's head looking this way and that, and the golden monkey likewise, and they could see that neither of them noticed the little figure of Lord Roke leaping from his hawk into the cabin behind them.

A moment later, the intention craft began to move, and the hawk wheeled away to skim down to Lord Asriel's wrist. No more than two seconds later, the aircraft was already vanishing from sight in the damp and starry air.

Lord Asriel watched with rueful admiration.

"Well, King, you were quite right," he said, "and I should have listened to you in the first place. She is Lyra's mother; I might have expected something like that."

"Aren't you going to pursue her?" said King Ogunwe.

"What, and destroy a perfectly good aircraft? Certainly not."

"Where d'you think she'll go? In search of the child?"

"Not at first. She doesn't know where to find her. I know exactly what she'll do: she'll go to the Consistorial Court, and give them the intention craft as an earnest of good faith, and then she'll spy. She'll spy on them for us. She's tried every other kind of duplicity: that one'll be a novel experience. And as soon as she finds out where the girl is, she'll go there, and we shall follow."

"And when will Lord Roke let her know he's come with her?"

"Oh, I think he'll keep that as a surprise, don't you?"

They laughed, and moved back into the workshops, where a later, more advanced model of the intention craft was awaiting their inspection.

17
Oil and Lacquer

NOW THE SERPENT WAS MORE SUBTIL THAN ANY BEAST OF THE FIELD WHICH THE LORD GOD HAD MADE · GENESIS

Mary Malone was constructing a mirror. Not out of vanity, for she had little of that, but because she wanted to test an idea she had. She wanted to try and catch Shadows, and without the instruments in her laboratory she had to improvise with the materials to hand.

Mulefa technology had little use for metal. They did extraordinary things with stone and wood and cord and shell and horn, but what metals they had were hammered from native nuggets of copper and other metals which they found in the sand of the river, and they were never used for tool-making. They were ornamental. Mulefa couples, for example, on entering marriage, would exchange strips of bright copper, which were bent around the base of one of their horns with much the meaning of a wedding ring.

So they were fascinated by the Swiss Army knife which was Mary's most valuable possession.

The zalif who was her particular friend, Atal by name, exclaimed with astonishment one day when Mary unfolded the knife, and showed her all the parts and explained as well as she could, with her limited language, what they were for. One attachment was a miniature magnifying glass with which she began to burn a design on to a dry branch, and it was that which set her thinking about Shadows.

They were fishing at the time, but the river was low and the fish must have been elsewhere, so they let the net lie across the water and sat on the grassy bank and talked, until Mary saw the dry branch, which had a smooth white surface. She burned the design – a simple daisy – into the wood, and delighted Atal; but as the thin line of smoke wafted up from the spot where the focused sunlight touched the wood, Mary thought: If this became fossilized, and a scientist in ten million years found it, they could still find Shadows around it, because I've worked on it.

She drifted into a sun-doped reverie until Atal asked:

What are you dreaming?

Mary tried to explain about her work, her research, the laboratory, the discovery of Shadow-particles, the fantastical revelation that they were conscious, and found the whole tale gripping her again, so that she longed to be back among her equipment.

She didn't expect Atal to follow her explanation, partly because of her own imperfect command of their language, but partly because the *mulefa* seemed so practical, so strongly rooted in the physical everyday world, and much of what she was saying was mathematical; but Atal surprised her by saying, *Yes – we know what you mean – we call it...* and then she used a word that sounded like their word for *light*.

Mary said, *Light?* and Atal said, *Not light, but...* and said the word more slowly for Mary to catch, explaining: *like the light on water when it makes small ripples, at sunset, and the light comes off in bright flakes, we call it that, but it is a make-like.*

Make-like was their term for metaphor, Mary had discovered.

So she said, *It is not really light, but you see it and it looks like that light on water at sunset?*

Atal said, *Yes. All the mulefa have this. You have too. That is how we knew you were like us and not like the grazers, who don't have it. Even though you look so bizarre and horrible, you are like us, because you have –* and again came that word that Mary couldn't hear quite clearly enough to say: something like *sraf*, or *sarf*, accompanied by a leftward flick of the trunk.

Mary was excited. She had to keep herself calm enough to find the right words.

What do you know about it? Where does it come from?

From us, and from the oil, was Atal's reply, and Mary knew she meant the oil in the great seed-pod wheels.

From you?

When we are grown-up. But without the trees it would just vanish again. With the wheels and the oil, it stays among us.

When we are grown-up... Again Mary had to keep herself from becoming incoherent. One of the things she'd begun to suspect about Shadows was that children and adults reacted to them differently, or attracted different kinds of Shadow-activity. Hadn't Lyra said that the scientists in her world had discovered something like that about Dust, which was their name for Shadows? Here it was again.

And it was connected to what the Shadows had said to her on the computer screen just before she'd left her own world: whatever it was, this question, it had to do with the great change in human history symbolized in the story of Adam and Eve; with the Temptation, the Fall, Original Sin. In his investigations among fossil skulls, her colleague Oliver Payne had discovered that around thirty thousand years ago, a great increase had taken place in the number of Shadow-particles associated with human remains. Something had happened then, some development in evolution, to make the human brain an ideal channel for amplifying their effects.

She said to Atal:

How long have there been mulefa?

And Atal said:

Thirty-three thousand years.

She was able to read Mary's expressions by this time, or the most obvious of them at least, and she laughed at the way Mary's jaw dropped. Their laughter was free and joyful and so infectious that Mary usually had to join in, but now she remained serious and astounded and said:

How can you know so exactly? Do you have a history of all those years?

Oh, yes, said Atal. *Ever since we have had the sraf, we have had memory and wakefulness. Before that, we knew nothing.*

What happened to give you the sraf?

We discovered how to use the wheels. One day a creature with no name discovered a seed-pod and began to play, and as she played she –

She?

She, yes. She had no name before then. She saw a snake coiling itself through the hole in a seed-pod, and the snake said –

The snake spoke to her?

No! no! It is a make-like. The story tells that the snake said What do you know? What do you remember? What do you see ahead? And she said Nothing, nothing, nothing. So the snake said Put your foot through the hole in the seed-pod where I was playing, and you will become wise. So she put a foot in where the snake had been. And the oil entered her foot and made her see more clearly than before, and the first thing she saw was the sraf. It was so strange and pleasant that she wanted to share it at once with all her kindred. So she and her mate took the first ones, and they discovered that they knew who they were, they knew they were mulefa and not grazers. They gave each other names. They named themselves mulefa. They named the seed-tree, and all the creatures and plants.

Because they were different, said Mary.

Yes, they were. And so were their children, because as more seed-pods fell, they showed their children how to use them. And when the children were old enough, they began to generate the sraf as well, and as they were big enough to ride on the wheels, the sraf came back with the oil and stayed with them. So they saw that they had to plant more seed-pod trees, for the sake of the oil, but the pods were so hard that they very seldom germinated. And the first mulefa saw what they must do to help the trees, which was to ride on the wheels and break them, so mulefa and seed-pod trees have always lived together.

Mary directly understood about a quarter of what Atal was saying, but by questioning and guessing she found out the rest quite accurately; and her own command of the language was increasing all the time. The more she learned, though, the more difficult it became, as each new thing she found out suggested half a dozen questions, each leading in a different direction.

But she pulled her mind after the subject of *sraf*, because that was the biggest; and that was why she thought about the mirror.

It was the comparison of sraf to the sparkles on water that suggested it. Reflected light like the glare off the sea was polarized: it might be that the Shadow-particles, when they behaved like waves as light did, were capable of being polarized too.

I can't see sraf as you can, she said, *but I would like to make a mirror out of the sap-lacquer, because I think that might help me see it.*

Atal was excited by this idea, and they hauled in their net at once and began to gather what Mary needed. As a token of good luck there were three fine fish in the net.

The sap-lacquer was a product of another and much smaller tree, which the mulefa cultivated for that purpose. By boiling the sap and dissolving it in the alcohol they made from distilled fruit juice, the mulefa made a substance like milk in consistency, and delicate amber in colour, which they used as a varnish. They would put up to twenty coats on a base of wood or shell, letting each one cure under wet cloth before applying the next, and gradually build up a surface of great hardness and brilliance. They would usually make it opaque with various oxides, but sometimes they left it transparent, and that was what had interested Mary: because the clear amber-coloured lacquer had the same curious property as the mineral known as Iceland Spar. It split light rays in two, so that when you looked through it you saw double.

She wasn't sure what she wanted to do, except that she knew that if she fooled around for long enough, without fretting, or nagging herself, she'd find out. She remembered quoting the words of the poet Keats to Lyra, and Lyra's understanding at once that that was her own state of mind when she read the alethiometer – that was what Mary had to find now.

So she began by finding herself a more or less flat piece of a wood like pine, and grinding at the surface with a piece of sandstone (no metal: no planes) until it was as flat as she could make it. That was the method the mulefa used, and it worked well enough, with time and effort.

Then she visited the lacquer-grove with Atal, having carefully explained what she was intending, and asked permission to take some sap. The mulefa were happy to let her, but too busy to be concerned. With Atal's help she drew off some of the sticky resinous sap, and then came the long process of boiling, dissolving, boiling again, until the varnish was ready to use.

The mulefa used pads of a cottony fibre from another plant to apply it, and following the instructions of a craftsman, she laboriously painted her mirror over and over again, seeing hardly any difference each time as the layer of lacquer was so thin, but letting them cure unhurriedly and finding gradually that the thickness was building up. She painted on over forty coats – she lost count – but by the time her lacquer had run out, the surface was at least five millimetres thick.

After the final layer came the polishing: a whole day of rubbing the surface gently, in smooth circular movements, until her arms ached and her head was throbbing and she could bear the labour no more.

Then she slept.

Next morning the group went to work in a coppice of what they called knot-wood, making sure the shoots were growing as they had been set, tightening the inter-weaving so that the grown sticks would be properly shaped. They valued Mary's help for this task, as she on her own could squeeze into narrower gaps than the mulefa, and, with her double hands, work in tighter spaces.

It was only when that work was done, and they had returned to the settlement, that Mary could begin to experiment – or rather to play, since she still didn't have a clear idea of what she was doing.

First she tried using the lacquer sheet simply as a mirror, but for lack of a silvered back, all she could see was a doubled reflection faintly in the wood.

Then she thought that what she really needed was the lacquer without the wood, but she quailed at the idea of making another sheet; how could she make it flat without a backing anyway?

The idea came of simply cutting the wood away to leave the lacquer. That would take time too, but at least she had the Swiss Army knife. And she began, splitting it very delicately from the edge, taking the greatest of care not to scratch the lacquer from behind, but eventually removing most of the pine and leaving a mess of torn and splintered wood stuck immovably to the pane of clear hard varnish.

She wondered what would happen if she soaked it in water. Did the lacquer soften if it got wet? *No*, said her master in the craft, *it will remain hard for ever; but why not do it like this?* – and he showed her a liquid kept in a stone bowl, which would eat through any wood in only a few hours. It looked and smelt to Mary like an acid.

That would hurt the lacquer hardly at all, he said, and she could repair any damage easily enough. He was intrigued by her project, and helped her to swab the acid delicately on to the wood, telling her how they made it by grinding and dissolving and distilling a mineral they found at the edge of some shallow lakes she had not yet visited. Gradually the wood softened and came free, and Mary was left with the single sheet of clear brown-yellow lacquer, about the size of a page from a paperback book.

She polished the reverse as highly as the top, until both were as flat and smooth as the finest mirror.

And when she looked through it...

Nothing in particular. It was perfectly clear, but it showed her a double image, the right one quite close to the left and about fifteen degrees upwards.

She wondered what would happen if she looked through two pieces, one on top of the other.

So she took the Swiss Army knife again and tried to score a line across the sheet so she could cut it in two. By working and re-working and by keeping the knife sharp on a smooth stone she managed to score a line deep enough for her to risk snapping the sheet. She laid a thin stick under the score line and pushed sharply down on the lacquer, as she'd seen a glazier cutting glass, and it worked: now she had two sheets.

She put them together and looked through. The amber colour was denser, and like a photographic filter it emphasized some colours and held back others, giving a slightly different cast to the landscape. The curious thing was that the double-ness had disappeared, and everything was single again; but there was no sign of Shadows.

She moved the two pieces apart, watching how the appearance of things changed as she did so. When they were about a hand-span apart, a curious thing happened: the amber colouring disappeared, and everything seemed its normal colour, but brighter and more vivid.

At that point Atal came along to see what she was doing.

Can you see sraf now? she said.

No, but I can see other things, Mary said, and tried to show her.

Atal was interested, but politely, not with the sense of discovery that was animating Mary, and presently the zalif tired of looking through the small pieces of lacquer and settled down on the grass to maintain her wheels. Sometimes the mulefa would groom each other's claws, out of pure sociability, and once or twice Atal had invited Mary to attend to hers. Mary in turn let Atal tidy her hair, enjoying how the soft trunk lifted it and let it fall, stroking and massaging her scalp.

She sensed that Atal wanted this now, so she put down the two pieces of lacquer and ran her hands over the astonishing smoothness of Atal's claws, that surface smoother and slicker than Teflon that rested on the lower rim of the central hole and served as a bearing when the wheel turned. The contours matched exactly, of course, and as Mary ran her hands around the inside of the wheel she could feel no difference in texture: it was as if the mulefa and the seed-pod really were one creature which by a miracle could disassemble itself and put itself together again.

Atal was soothed, and so was Mary, by this contact. Her friend was young and unmarried, and there were no young males in this group, so she would have to marry a zalif from outside; but contact wasn't easy, and sometimes Mary thought that Atal was anxious about her future. So she didn't grudge the time she spent with her, and now she was happy to clean the wheel-holes of all the dust and grime that accumulated there, and smooth the fragrant oil gently over her friend's claws while Atal's trunk lifted and straightened her hair.

When Atal had had enough, she set herself on the wheels again and moved away to help with the evening meal. Mary turned back to her lacquer, and almost at once she made her discovery.

She held the two plates a hand-span apart so that they showed that clear bright image she'd seen before, but something had happened.

As she looked through, she saw a swarm of golden sparkles surrounding the form of Atal. They were only visible through one small part of the lacquer, and then Mary realized why: at that point she had touched the surface of it with her oily fingers.

"Atal!" she called. "Quick! Come back!"

Atal turned and wheeled back.

"Let me take a little oil," Mary said, "just enough to put on the lacquer."

Atal willingly let her run her fingers around the wheel-holes again, and watched curiously as Mary coated one of the pieces with a film of the clear sweet substance.

Then she pressed the plates together and moved them around to spread the oil evenly, and held them a hand-span apart once more.

And when she looked through, everything was changed. She could see Shadows. If she'd been in the Jordan College Retiring Room when Lord Asriel had projected the photo-grams he'd made with the special emulsion, she would have recognized the effect. Everywhere she looked she could see gold, just as Atal had described it: sparkles of light, floating and drifting and sometimes moving in a current of purpose. Among it all was the world she could see with the naked eye, the grass, the river, the trees; but wherever she saw a conscious being, one of the mulefa, the light was thicker and more full of movement. It didn't obscure their shapes in any way; if anything it made them clearer.

I didn't know it was beautiful, Mary said to Atal.

Why, of course it is, her friend replied. *It is strange to think that you couldn't see it. Look at the little one...*

She indicated one of the small children playing in the long grass, leaping clumsily after grasshoppers, suddenly stopping to examine a leaf, falling over, scrambling up again to rush and tell his mother something, being distracted again by a piece of stick, trying to pick it up, finding ants on his trunk and hooting with agitation... There was a golden haze around him as there was around the shelters, the fishing-nets, the evening fire: stronger than theirs, though not by much. But unlike theirs it was full of little swirling currents of intention, that eddied and broke off and drifted about, to disappear as new ones were born.

Around his mother, on the other hand, the golden sparkles were much stronger, and the currents they moved in more settled and powerful. She was preparing food, spreading flour on a flat stone, making the thin bread like chapattis or tortillas, watching her child at the same time, and the Shadows or the sraf or the Dust that bathed her looked like the very image of responsibility and wise care.

So at last you can see, said Atal. *Well, now you must come with me.*

Mary looked at her friend in puzzlement. Atal's tone was strange: it was as if she were saying *Finally you're ready; we've been waiting; now things must change.*

And others were appearing, from over the brow of the hill, from out of their shelters, from along the river: members of the group, but strangers too, mulefa who were new to her, and who looked curiously towards where she was standing. The sound of their wheels on the hard-packed earth was low and steady.

Where must I go? Mary said. *Why are they all coming here?*

Don't worry, said Atal, *come with me, we shall not hurt you.*

It seemed to have been long planned, this meeting, for they all knew where to go and what to expect. There was a low mound at the edge of the village that was regular in shape and packed with hard earth, with ramps at each end, and the crowd – fifty or so at least, Mary estimated – was moving towards it. The smoke of the cooking fires hung in the evening air, and the setting sun spread its own kind of hazy gold over everything; and Mary was aware of the smell of roasting corn, and the warm smell of the mulefa themselves – part oil, part warm flesh, a sweet horse-like smell.

Atal urged her towards the mound.

Mary said, *What is happening? Tell me!*

No, no... Not me. Sattamax will speak...

Mary didn't know the name Sattamax, and the zalif whom Atal indicated was a stranger to her. He was older than anyone she'd seen so far: at the base of his trunk was a scatter of white hairs, and he moved stiffly, as if he had arthritis. The others all moved with care around him, and when Mary stole a glance through the lacquer glass she saw why: the old zalif's Shadow-cloud was so rich and complex that Mary herself felt respect, even though she knew so little of what it meant.

When Sattamax was ready to speak, the rest of the crowd fell silent. Mary stood close to the mound, with Atal nearby for reassurance; but she sensed all their eyes on her, and felt as if she were a new girl at school.

Sattamax began to speak. His voice was deep, the tones rich and varied, the gestures of his trunk low and graceful.

We have all come together to greet the stranger Mary. Those of us who know her have reason to be grateful for her activities since she arrived among us. We have waited until she had some command of our language. With the help of many of us, but especially the zalif Atal, the stranger Mary can now understand us.

But there was another thing she had to understand, and that was sraf. She knew about it, but she could not see it as we can, until she made an instrument to look through.

And now she has succeeded, she is ready to learn more about what she must do to help us.

Mary, come here and join me.

She felt dizzy, self-conscious, bemused, but she did as she

had to and stepped up beside the old zalif. She thought she had better speak, so she began:

You have all made me feel I am a friend. You are kind and hospitable. I came from a world where life is very different, but some of us are aware of sraf, as you are, and I'm grateful for your help in making this glass, through which I can see it. If there is any way in which I can help you, I will be glad to do it.

She spoke more awkwardly than she did with Atal, and she was afraid she hadn't made her meaning clear. It was hard to know where to face when you had to gesture as well as speak, but they seemed to understand.

Sattamax said: *It is good to hear you speak. We hope you will be able to help us. If not, I cannot see how we will survive. The tualapi will kill us all. There are more of them than there ever were, and their numbers are increasing every year. Something has gone wrong with the world. For most of the thirty-three thousand years that there have been mulefa, we have taken care of the earth. Everything balanced. The trees prospered, the grazers were healthy, and even if once in a while the tualapi came, our numbers and theirs remained constant.*

But three hundred years ago the trees began to sicken. We watched them anxiously and tended them with care and still we found them producing fewer seed-pods, and dropping their leaves out of season, and some of them died outright, which had never been known. All our memory could not find a cause for this.

To be sure, it was slow, but so is the rhythm of our lives. We did not know that until you came. We have seen butterflies and birds, but they have no sraf. You do, strange as you seem; but you are swift and immediate, like birds, like butterflies. You realize there is a need for something to help you see sraf and instantly, out of the materials we have known for thousands of years, you put together an instrument to do so. Beside us, you think and act with the speed of a bird. That is how it seems, which is how we know that our rhythm seems slow to you.

But that fact is our hope. You can see things that we cannot, you can see connections and possibilities and alternatives that are invisible to us, just as sraf was invisible to you. And while we cannot see a way to survive, we hope that you may. We hope that you will go swiftly to the cause of the trees' sickness and find a cure; we hope you will invent a means of dealing with the tualapi, who are so numerous and so powerful.

And we hope you can do so soon, or we shall all die.

There was a murmur of agreement and approval from the crowd. They were all looking at Mary, and she felt more than ever like the new pupil at a school where they had high expectations of her. She also felt a strange flattery: the idea of herself as swift and darting and bird-like was new and pleasant, because she had always thought of herself as dogged and plodding. But along with that came the feeling that they'd got it terribly wrong, if they saw her like that; they didn't understand at all; she couldn't possibly fulfil this desperate hope of theirs.

But equally, she must. They were waiting.

Sattamax, she said, *mulefa, you put your trust in me and I shall do my best. You have been kind and your life is good and beautiful and I will try very hard to help you, and now I have seen sraf, I know what it is that I am doing. Thank you for trusting me.*

They nodded and murmured and stroked her with their trunks as she stepped down. She was daunted by what she had agreed to do.

At that very moment in the world of Cittàgazze, the assassin-priest Father Gomez was making his way up a rough track in the mountains between the twisted trunks of olive trees. The evening light slanted through the silvery leaves and the air was full of the noise of crickets and cicadas.

Ahead of him he could see a little farmhouse sheltered among vines, where a goat bleated and a spring trickled down through the grey rocks. There was an old man attending to some task beside the house, and an old woman leading the goat towards a stool and a bucket.

In the village some way behind, they had told him that the woman he was following had passed this way, and that she'd talked of going up into the mountains; perhaps this old couple had seen her. At least there might be cheese and olives to buy, and spring water to drink. Father Gomez was quite used to living frugally, and there was plenty of time.

18

The Suburbs of the Dead

*L*yra was awake before dawn, with Pantalaimon shivering at her breast, and she got up to walk about and warm herself up as the grey light seeped into the sky. She had never known such silence, not even in the snow-blanketed Arctic; there was not a stir of wind, and the sea was so still that not the tiniest ripple broke on the sand; the world seemed suspended between breathing in and breathing out.

Will lay curled up fast asleep, with his head on the rucksack to protect the knife. The cloak had fallen off his shoulder, and she tucked it around him, pretending that she was taking care to avoid his dæmon, and that she had the form of a cat, curled up just as he was. *She must be here somewhere*, she thought.

Carrying the still sleepy Pantalaimon, she walked away from Will and sat down on the slope of a sand dune a little way off, so their voices wouldn't wake him.

"Those little people," Pantalaimon said.

"I don't like 'em," said Lyra decisively. "I think we should get away from 'em as soon as we can. I reckon if we trap 'em in a net or something Will can cut through and close up and that's it, we'll be free."

"We haven't got a net," he said, "or something. Anyway, I bet they're cleverer than that. *He's* watching us now."

Pantalaimon was a hawk as he said that, and his eyes were keener than hers. The darkness of the sky was turning minute by minute into the palest ethereal blue, and as she looked across the sand the first edge of the sun just cleared the rim of the sea, dazzling her. Because she was on the slope of the dune, the light reached her a few seconds before it touched the beach, and she watched it flow around her and along towards Will; and then she saw the hand-high figure of the Chevalier Tialys, standing by Will's head, clear and wide awake and watching them.

"The thing is," said Lyra, "they can't make us do what they want. They got to follow us. I bet they're fed up."

"If they got hold of us," said Pan, meaning him and Lyra, "and got their stings ready to stick in us, Will'd *have* to do what they said."

Lyra thought about it. She remembered vividly the horrible scream of pain from Mrs Coulter, the eye-rolling convulsions, the ghastly lolling drool of the golden monkey as the poison entered her bloodstream... And that was only a scratch, as her mother had recently been reminded elsewhere. Will would *have* to give in and do what they wanted.

"Suppose they thought he wouldn't, though," she said, "suppose they thought he was so cold-hearted he'd just watch us die. Maybe he better make 'em think that, if he can."

She had brought the alethiometer with her, and now it was light enough to see, she took the beloved instrument out and laid it on its black velvet cloth in her lap. Little by little she drifted into that trance in which the many layers of meaning were clear to her, and where she could sense intricate webs of connectedness between them all. As her fingers found the symbols, her mind found the words: how can we get rid of the spies?

Then the needle began to dart this way and that, faster than she had ever seen it move before – so fast, in fact, that she was afraid for the first time that she'd miss some of the swings and stops; but some part of her awareness was counting them, and saw at once the meaning of what the movement said.

It told her: *Do not try, because your lives depend on them.*

That was a surprise, and not a happy one. But she went on and asked: *How can we get to the land of the dead?*

The answer came: *Go down. Follow the knife. Go onwards. Follow the knife.*

And finally she asked hesitantly, half-ashamed: *Is this the right thing to do?*

Yes, said the alethiometer instantly. *Yes.*

She sighed, coming out of her trance, and tucked the hair behind her ears, feeling the first warmth of the sun on her face and shoulders. There were sounds in the world now too: insects were stirring, and a very slight breeze was rustling the dry grass-stems growing higher up the dune.

She put the alethiometer away and wandered back to Will, with Pantalaimon as large as he could make himself and lion-shaped, in the hope of daunting the Gallivespians.

The man was using his lodestone apparatus, and when he'd finished Lyra said:

"You been talking to Lord Asriel?"

"To his representative," said Tialys.

"We en't going."

"That's what I told him."

"What did he say?"

"That was for my ears, not yours."

"Suit yourself," she said. "Are you married to that lady?"

"No. We are colleagues."

"Have you got any children?"

"No."

Tialys continued to pack the lodestone resonator away, and as he did so the Lady Salmakia woke up nearby, sitting up graceful and slow from the little hollow she'd made in the soft sand. The dragonflies were still asleep, tethered with cobweb-thin cord, their wings damp with dew.

"Are there big people on your world, or are they all small like you?" Lyra said.

"We know how to deal with big people," Tialys replied, not very helpfully, and went to talk quietly to the lady. They spoke too softly for Lyra to hear, but she enjoyed watching them sip dew-drops from the marram grass to refresh themselves. Water must be different for them, she thought to Pantalaimon: imagine drops the size of your fist! They'd be hard to get into; they'd have a sort of elastic rind, like a balloon.

By this time Will was waking too, wearily. The first thing he did was to look for the Gallivespians, who looked back at once, fully focused on him.

He looked away and found Lyra.

"I want to tell you something," she said. "Come over here, away from…"

"If you go away from us," said Tialys's clear voice, "you must leave the knife. If you won't leave the knife, you must talk to each other here."

"Can't we be private?" Lyra said indignantly. "We don't want you listening to what we say!"

"Then go away, but leave the knife."

There was no one else nearby, after all, and certainly the Gallivespians wouldn't be able to use it. Will rummaged in the rucksack for the water-canteen and a couple of biscuits, and handing one to Lyra, he went with her up the slope of the dune.

"I asked the alethiometer," she told him, "and it said we shouldn't try and escape from the little people, because they were going to save our lives. So maybe we're stuck with 'em."

"Have you told them what we're going to do?"

"No! And I won't, either. Cause they'll only tell Lord Asriel on that speaking-fiddle and he'd go there and stop us – so we got to just go, and not talk about it in front of them."

"They are spies, though," Will pointed out. "They must be good at listening and hiding. So maybe we better not mention it at all. We know where we're going. So we'll just go and not talk about it, and they'll have to put up with it and come along."

"They can't hear us now. They're too far off. Will, I asked how we get there, too. It said to follow the knife, just that."

"Sounds easy," he said. "But I bet it isn't. D'you know what Iorek told me?"

"No. He said – when I went to say goodbye – he said it would be very difficult for you, but he thought you could do it. But he never told me why..."

"The knife broke because I thought of my mother," he explained. "So I've got to put her out of my mind. But... It's like when someone says don't think about a crocodile, you *do*, you can't help it..."

"Well, you cut through last night all right," she said.

"Yeah, because I was tired, I think. Well, we'll see. Just follow the knife?"

"That's all it said."

"Might as well go now, then. Except there's not much food left. We ought to find something to take with us, bread and fruit or something. So first I'll find a world where we can get food, and then we'll start looking properly."

"All right," said Lyra, quite happy to be moving again, with Pan and Will, alive and awake.

They made their way back to the spies, who were sitting alertly by the knife, packs on their backs.

"We should like to know what you intend," said Salmakia.

"Well, we're not coming to Lord Asriel, anyway," said Will. "We've got something else to do first."

"And will you tell us what that is, since it's clear we can't stop you doing it?"

"No," said Lyra, "because you'd just go and tell them. You'll have to come along without knowing where we're going. Course, you could always give up and go back to them."

"Certainly not," said Tialys.

"We want some kind of guarantee," said Will. "You're spies, so you're bound to be dishonest, that's your trade. We need to know we can trust you. Last night we were all too tired and we couldn't think about it, but there'd be nothing to stop you waiting till we were asleep and then stinging us to make us helpless and calling up Lord Asriel on that lodestone thing. You could do that easily. So we need to have a proper guarantee that you won't. A promise isn't enough."

The two Gallivespians trembled with anger at this slur on their honour.

Tialys, controlling himself, said, "We don't accept one-sided demands. You must give something in exchange. You must tell us what your intentions are, and then I shall give the lodestone resonator into your care. You must let me have it when I want to send a message, but you will always know when that happens, and we shall not be able to use it without your agreement. That will be our guarantee. And now you tell us where you are going, and why."

Will and Lyra exchanged a glance to confirm it.

"All right," Lyra said, "that's fair. So here's where we're going: we're going to the world of the dead. We don't know where it is, but the knife'll find it. That's what we're going to do."

The two spies were looking at her with open-mouthed incredulity.

Then Salmakia blinked and said, "What you say doesn't make sense. The dead are dead, that's all. There is no world of the dead."

"I thought that was true, as well," said Will. "But now I'm not sure. At least with the knife we can find out."

"But *why?*"

Lyra looked at Will, and saw him nod.

"Well," she said, "before I met Will, long before I was asleep, I led this friend into danger, and he was killed. I thought I was rescuing him, only I was making things worse. And while I was asleep I dreamt of him and I thought maybe I could make amends if I went where he's gone and said I was sorry. And Will wants to find his father, who died just when he found him before. See, Lord Asriel wouldn't think of that. Nor would Mrs Coulter. If we went to him we'd have to do what *he* wants, and he wouldn't think of Roger at all – that's my friend who died – it wouldn't matter to him. But it matters to me. To us. So that's what we want to do."

"Child," said Tialys, "when we die, everything is over. There is no other life. You have seen death. You've seen dead bodies, and you've seen what happens to a dæmon when death comes. It vanishes. What else can there be to live on after that?"

"We're going to go and find out," said Lyra. "And now we've told you, I'll take your lodestone resonator."

She held out her hand, and leopard-Pantalaimon stood, tail swinging slowly, to reinforce her demand. Tialys unslung the pack from his back and laid it in her palm. It was surprisingly heavy; no burden for her, of course, but she marvelled at his strength.

"And how long do you think this expedition will take?" said the chevalier.

"We don't know," Lyra told him. "We don't know anything about it, any more than you do. We'll just go there and see."

"First thing," Will said, "we've got to get some water and some more food, something easy to carry. So I'm going to find a world where we can do that, and then we'll set off."

Tialys and Salmakia mounted their dragonflies, and held them quivering on the ground. The great insects were eager for flight, but the command of their riders was absolute, and Lyra, watching them in daylight for the first time, saw the extraordinary fineness of the grey silk reins, the silvery stirrups, the tiny saddles.

Will took the knife, and a powerful temptation made him feel for the touch of his own world: he had the credit card still; he could buy familiar food; he could even telephone Mrs Cooper and ask for news of his mother –

The knife jarred with a sound like a nail being drawn along rough stone, and his heart nearly stopped. If he broke the blade again, it would be the end.

After a few moments he tried again. Instead of trying not to think of his mother he said to himself: *Yes, I know she's there, but I'm just going to look away while I do this...*

And that time it worked. He found a new world and slid the knife along to make an opening, and a few moments later all of them were standing in what looked like a neat and prosperous farmyard in some northern country like Holland or Denmark, where the stone-flagged yard was swept and clean and a row of stable doors stood open. The sun shone down through a hazy sky, and there was the smell of burning in the air, as well as something less pleasant. There was no sound of human life, though a loud buzzing, so active and vigorous that it sounded like a machine, came from the stables.

Lyra went and looked, and came back at once, looking pale.

"There's four –" she gulped, hand to her throat, and recovered – "four dead horses in there. And millions of flies..."

"Look," said Will, swallowing, "or maybe better not."

He was pointing at the raspberry canes that edged the kitchen garden. He'd just seen a man's legs, one with a shoe on and one without, protruding from the thickest part of the bushes.

Lyra didn't want to look, but Will went to see if the man was still alive and needed help. He came back shaking his head, looking uneasy.

The two spies were already at the farmhouse door, which was ajar.

Tialys darted back and said, "It smells sweeter in there," and then he flew back over the threshold while Salmakia scouted further around the outbuildings.

Will followed the chevalier. He found himself in a big square kitchen, an old-fashioned place with white china on a wooden dresser, and a scrubbed pine table, and a hearth where a black kettle stood cold. Next door there was a pantry, with two shelves full of apples that filled the whole room with fragrance. The silence was oppressive.

Lyra said quietly, "Will, is *this* the world of the dead?"

The same thought had occurred to him. But he said, "No, I don't think so. It's one we haven't been in before. Look, we'll load up with as much as we can carry. There's sort of rye bread, that'll be good – it's light – and here's some cheese..."

When they had taken what they could carry, Will dropped a gold coin into the drawer in the big pine table.

"Well?" said Lyra, seeing Tialys raise his eyebrows. "You should always pay for what you take."

At that moment Salmakia came in through the back door, landing her dragonfly on the table in a shimmer of electric blue.

"There are men coming," she said, "on foot, with weapons. They're only a few minutes' walk away. And there is a village burning beyond the fields."

And as she spoke they could hear the sound of boots on gravel, and a voice issuing orders, and the jingle of metal.

"Then we should go," said Will.

He felt in the air with the knife-point. And at once he was aware of a new kind of sensation. The blade seemed to be sliding along a very smooth surface, like a mirror, and then it sank through slowly until he was able to cut. But it was resistant, like heavy cloth, and when he made a opening he blinked with surprise and alarm: because the world he was opening into was the same in every detail as the one they were already standing in.

"What's happening?" said Lyra.

The spies were looking through, puzzled. But it was more than puzzlement they felt. Just as the air had resisted the knife, so something in this opening resisted their going through. Will had to push against something invisible and then help pull Lyra after him, and the Gallivespians could hardly make any headway at all. They had to perch the dragonflies on the children's hands, and even then it was like pulling them against a pressure in the air; their filmy wings bent and twisted, and the little riders had to stroke their heads and whisper to calm their fears.

But after a few seconds of struggle they were all through, and Will found the edge of the window (though it was impossible to see) and closed it, shutting the sound of the soldiers away in their own world.

"Will," said Lyra, and he turned to see that there was another figure in the kitchen with them.

His heart jolted. It was the man he'd seen not ten minutes before, stark dead in the bushes with his throat cut.

He was middle-aged, lean, with the look of a man who spent most of the time in the open air. But now he was looking almost crazed, or paralysed, with shock. His eyes were so wide that the white showed all around the iris, and he was clutching the edge of the table with a trembling hand. His throat, Will was glad to see, was intact.

He opened his mouth to speak, but no words came out. All he could do was point at Will and Lyra.

Lyra said, "Excuse us for being in your house, but we had to escape from the men who were coming. I'm sorry if we startled you. I'm Lyra, and this is Will, and these are our friends, the Chevalier Tialys and the Lady Salmakia. Could you tell us your name and where we are?"

This normal-sounding request seemed to bring the man to his senses, and a shudder passed over him as if he were waking from a dream.

"I'm dead," he said. "I'm lying out there, dead. I know I am. *You* ain't dead. What's happening? God help me, they cut my throat. What's happening?"

Lyra stepped closer to Will when the man said *I'm dead*, and Pantalaimon fled to her breast as a mouse. As for the Gallivespians, they were trying to control their dragonflies, because the great insects seemed to have an aversion for the man, and darted here and there in the kitchen, looking for a way out.

But the man didn't notice them. He was still trying to understand what had happened.

"Are you a ghost?" Will said cautiously.

The man reached out his hand, and Will tried to take it, but his fingers closed on the air. A tingle of cold was all he felt.

When he saw it happen, the man looked at his own hand, appalled. The numbness was beginning to wear off, and he could feel the pity of his state.

"Truly," he said, "I *am* dead... I'm dead, and I'm going to hell..."

"Hush," said Lyra, "we'll go together. What's your name?"

"Dirk Jansen I was," he said, "but already I ... I don't know what to do... Don't know where to go..."

Will opened the door. The barnyard looked the same, the kitchen garden was unchanged, the same hazy sun shone down. And there was the man's body, untouched.

A little groan broke from Dirk Jansen's throat, as if there was no denying it any more. The dragonflies darted out of the door and skimmed over the ground and then shot up high, faster than birds. The man was looking around helplessly, raising his hands, lowering them again, uttering little cries.

"I can't stay here... Can't stay," he was saying. "But this ain't the farm I knew. This is wrong. I got to go..."

"Where are you going, Mr Jansen?" said Lyra.

"Down the road. Dunno. Got to go. Can't stay here…"

Salmakia flew down to perch on Lyra's hand. The dragonfly's little claws pricked as the lady said, "There are people walking from the village – people like this man – all walking in the same direction."

"Then we'll go with them," said Will, and swung his rucksack over his shoulder.

Dirk Jansen was already passing his own body, averting his eyes. He looked almost as if he were drunk, stopping, moving on, wandering to left and right, stumbling over little ruts and stones on the path his living feet had known so well.

Lyra came after Will, and Pantalaimon became a kestrel and flew up as high as he could, making Lyra gasp.

"They're right," he said when he came down. "There's lines of people all coming from the village. Dead people…"

And soon they saw them too: twenty or so men, women and children, all moving as Dirk Jansen had done, uncertain and shocked. The village was half a mile away, and the people were coming towards them, close together in the middle of the road. When Dirk Jansen saw the other ghosts he broke into a stumbling run, and they held out their hands to greet him.

"Even if they don't know where they're going, they're all going there together," Lyra said. "We better just go with them."

"D'you think they had dæmons in this world?" said Will.

"Can't tell. If you saw one of 'em in your world, would you know he was a ghost?"

"It's hard to say. They don't look normal, exactly… There was a man I used to see in my town, and he used to walk about outside the shops always holding the same old plastic bag, and he never spoke to anyone or went inside. And no one ever looked at him. I used to pretend he was a ghost. They look a bit like him. Maybe my world's full of ghosts and I never knew."

"I don't think mine is," said Lyra doubtfully.

"Anyway, this must be the world of the dead. These people have just been killed – those soldiers must've done it – and here they are, and it's just like the world they were alive in. I thought it'd be a lot different..."

"Well, it's fading," she said. "Look!"

She was clutching his arm. He stopped and looked around, and she was right. Not long before he had found the window in Oxford and stepped through into the other world of Cittàgazze, there had been an eclipse of the sun, and like millions of others Will had stood outside at midday and watched as the bright daylight faded and dimmed until a sort of eerie twilight covered the houses, the trees, the park. Everything was just as clear as in full daylight, but there was less light to see it by, as if all the strength were draining out of a dying sun.

What was happening now was like that, but odder, because the edges of things were losing their definition as well and becoming blurred.

"It's not like going blind, even," said Lyra, frightened, "because it's not that we can't see things, it's like the things themselves are fading..."

The colour was slowly seeping out of the world. A dim green-grey for the bright green of the trees and the grass, a dim sand-grey for the vivid yellow of a field of corn, a dim blood-grey for the red bricks of a neat farmhouse...

The people themselves, closer now, had begun to notice too, and were pointing and holding one another's arms for reassurance.

The only bright things in the whole landscape were the brilliant red-and-yellow and electric blue of the dragonflies, and their little riders, and Will and Lyra, and Pantalaimon, who was hovering kestrel-shaped close above.

They were close to the first of the people now, and it was clear: they were all ghosts. Will and Lyra took a step towards each other, but there was nothing to fear, for the ghosts were far more afraid of them, and were hanging back, unwilling to approach.

Will called out, "Don't be afraid. We're not going to hurt you. Where are you going?"

They looked at the oldest man among them, as if he was their guide.

"We're going where all the others go," he said. "Seems as if I know, but I can't remember learning it. Seems as if it's along the road. We'll know it when we get there."

"Mamma," said a child, "why's it getting dark in the daytime?"

"Hush, dear, don't fret," the mother said. "Can't make anything better by fretting. We're dead, I expect."

"But where are we going?" the child said. "I don't want to be dead, mamma!"

"We're going to see Grandpa," the mother said desperately.

But the child wouldn't be consoled, and wept bitterly. Others in the group looked at the mother with sympathy or annoyance, but there was nothing they could do to help, and they all walked on disconsolately through the fading landscape as the child's thin cries went on, and on, and on.

The Chevalier Tialys had spoken to Salmakia before skimming away ahead, and Will and Lyra watched the dragonfly with eyes greedy for its brightness and vigour as it got smaller and smaller. The lady flew down and perched her insect on Will's hand.

"The chevalier has gone to see what's ahead," she said. "We think the landscape is fading because these people are forgetting it. The further they go away from their homes the darker it will get."

"But why d'you think they're moving?" Lyra said. "If I was a ghost I'd want to stay in the places I knew, not wander along and get lost."

"They feel unhappy there," Will said, guessing. "It's where they've just died. They're afraid of it."

"No, they're pulled onwards by something," said the lady. "Some instinct is drawing them down the road."

And indeed the ghosts were moving more purposefully now that they were out of sight of their own village. The sky was as dark as if a mighty storm were threatening, but there was none of the electric tension that comes ahead of a storm. The ghosts walked on steadily, and the road ran straight ahead across a landscape that was almost featureless.

From time to time one of them would glance at Will or Lyra, or at the brilliant dragonfly and its rider, as if they were curious. Finally the oldest man said:

"You, you boy and girl. You ain't dead. You ain't ghosts. What you coming along here for?"

"We came through by accident," Lyra told him before Will could speak. "I don't know how it happened. We were trying to escape from those men, and we just seemed to find ourselves here."

"How will you know when you've got to the place where you've got to go?" said Will.

"I expect we'll be told," said the ghost confidently. "They'll separate out the sinners and the righteous, I dare say. It's no good praying now. It's too late for that now. You should have done that when you were alive. No use now."

It was quite clear which group he expected to be in, and quite clear too that he thought it wouldn't be a big one. The other ghosts heard him uneasily, but he was all the guidance they had, so they followed without arguing.

And on they walked, trudging in silence under a sky that had finally darkened to a dull iron-grey and remained there without getting any darker. The living ones found themselves looking to left and right, above and below, for anything that was bright or lively or joyful, and they were always disappointed until a little spark appeared ahead and raced towards them through the air. It was the chevalier, and Salmakia urged her dragonfly ahead to meet him, with a cry of pleasure.

They conferred, and sped back to the children.

"There's a town ahead," said Tialys. "It looks like a refugee camp, but it's obviously been there for centuries or more. And I think there's a sea or a lake beyond it, but that's covered in mist. I could hear the cries of birds. And there are hundreds of people arriving every minute, from every direction, people like these – ghosts…"

The ghosts themselves listened as he spoke, though without much curiosity. They seemed to have settled into a dull trance, and Lyra wanted to shake them, to urge them to struggle and wake up and look around for a way out.

"How are we going to help these people, Will?" she said.

He couldn't even guess. As they moved on, they could see a movement on the horizon to left and right, and ahead of them a dirty-coloured smoke was rising slowly to add its darkness to the dismal air. The movement was people, or ghosts: in lines or pairs or groups or alone, but all empty-handed, hundreds and thousands of men and women and children were drifting over the plain towards the source of the smoke.

The ground was sloping downwards now, and becoming more and more like a rubbish dump. The air was heavy and full of smoke, and of other smells besides: acrid chemicals, decaying vegetable matter, sewage. And the further down they went, the worse it got. There was not a patch of clean soil in sight, and the only plants growing anywhere were rank weeds and coarse greyish grass.

Ahead of them, above the water, was the mist. It rose like a cliff to merge with the gloomy sky, and from somewhere inside it came those bird cries that Tialys had referred to.

Between the waste heaps and the mist, there lay the first town of the dead.

19
Lyra and her Death

*H*ere and there, fires had been lit among the ruins. The town was a jumble, with no streets, no squares, and no open spaces except where a building had fallen. A few churches or public buildings still stood above the rest, though their roofs were holed or their walls cracked, and in one case a whole portico had crumpled on to its columns. Between the shells of the stone buildings, a mazy clutter of shacks and shanties had been put together out of lengths of roofing timber, beaten-out petrol cans or biscuit tins, torn sheets of polythene, scraps of plywood or hardboard.

The ghosts who had come with them were hurrying towards the town, and from every direction came more of them, so many that they looked like the grains of sand that trickle towards the hole of an hourglass. The ghosts walked straight into the squalid confusion of the town as if they knew exactly where they were going, and Lyra and Will were about to follow them; but then they were stopped.

A figure stepped out of a patched-up doorway and said, "Wait, wait."

A dim light was glowing behind him, and it wasn't easy to

make out his features; but they knew he wasn't a ghost. He was like them, alive. He was a thin man who could have been any age, dressed in a drab and tattered business suit, and he was holding a pencil and a sheaf of papers held together with a bulldog clip. The building he'd stepped out of had the look of a customs post on a rarely-visited frontier.

"What is this place?" said Will. "And why can't we go in?"

"You're not dead," said the man wearily. "You have to wait in the holding area. Go further along the road to the left and give these papers to the official at the gate."

"But excuse me, sir," said Lyra, "I hope you don't mind me asking, but how can we have come this far if we en't dead? Because this *is* the world of the dead, isn't it?"

"It's a suburb of the world of the dead. Sometimes the living come here by mistake, but they have to wait in the holding area before they can go on."

"Wait for how long?"

"Until they die."

Will felt his head swim. He could see Lyra was about to argue, and before she could speak he said, "Can you just explain what happens then? I mean, these ghosts who come here, do they stay in this town for ever?"

"No, no," said the official. "This is just a port of transit. They go on beyond here by boat."

"Where to?" said Will.

"That's not something I can tell you," said the man, and a bitter smile pulled his mouth down at the corners. "You must move along, please. You must go to the holding area."

Will took the papers the man was holding out, and then held Lyra's arm and urged her away.

The dragonflies were flying sluggishly now, and Tialys explained that they needed to rest; so they perched on Will's rucksack, and Lyra let the spies sit on her shoulders. Pantalaimon, leopard-shaped, looked up at them jealously, but he said nothing. They moved along the track, skirting the wretched shanties and the pools of sewage, and watching the never-ending stream of ghosts arriving and passing without hindrance into the town itself.

"We've got to get over the water, like the rest of them," said Will. "And maybe the people in this holding place will tell us how. They don't seem to be angry, anyway, or dangerous. It's strange. And these papers…"

They were simply scraps of paper torn from a notebook, with random words scribbled in pencil and crossed out. It was as if these people were playing a game, and waiting to see when the travellers would challenge them or give in and laugh. And yet it all looked so real.

It was getting darker and colder, and time was hard to keep track of. Lyra thought they walked for half an hour, or maybe it was twice as long; the look of the place didn't change. Finally, they reached a little wooden shack like the one they'd stopped at earlier, where a dim bulb glowed on a bare wire over the door.

As they approached, a man dressed much like the other one came out holding a piece of bread and butter in one hand, and without a word looked at their papers and nodded.

He handed them back and was about to go inside when Will said, "Excuse me, where do we go now?"

"Go and find somewhere to stay," said the man, not unkindly. "Just ask. Everybody's waiting, same as you."

He turned away and shut his door against the cold, and the travellers turned down into the heart of the shanty town where the living people had to stay.

It was very much like the main town: shabby little huts,

repaired a dozen times, patched with scraps of plastic or corrugated iron, leaning crazily against each other over muddy alleyways. At some places, an electric cable looped down from a bracket and provided enough feeble current to power a naked light bulb or two, strung out over the nearby huts. Most of what light there was, however, came from the fires. Their smoky glow flickered redly over the scraps and tatters of building material, as if they were the last remaining flames of a great conflagration, staying alive out of pure malice.

But as Will and Lyra and the Gallivespians came closer and saw more detail, they picked out several – more – many figures, sitting in the darkness by themselves or leaning against the walls or gathered in small groups, talking quietly.

"Why aren't those people inside?" said Lyra. "It's cold."

"They're not people," said the Lady Salmakia. "They're not even ghosts. They're something else, but I don't know what."

The travellers came to the first group of shacks, which were lit by one of those big weak electric bulbs on a cable swinging slightly in the cold wind, and Will put his hand on the knife at his belt. There was a group of those people-shaped things outside, crouching on their heels and rolling dice, and when the children came near they stood up: five of them, all men, their faces in shadow and their clothes shabby, all silent.

"What is the name of this town?" said Will.

There was no reply. Some of them took a step backwards, and all five moved a little closer together, as if *they* were afraid. Lyra felt her skin crawling, and all the tiny hairs on her arms standing on end, though she couldn't have said why. Inside her shirt, Pantalaimon was shivering and whispering, "No, no, Lyra, no, go away, let's go back, please..."

The "people" made no move, and finally Will shrugged and said, "Well, good evening to you anyway," and moved on. They met a similar response from all the other figures they spoke to, and all the time their apprehension grew.

"Will, are they Spectres?" Lyra said quietly. "Are we grown up enough to see Spectres now?"

"I don't think so. If we were, they'd attack us, but they seem to be afraid themselves. I don't know what they are."

A door opened, and light spilled out on the muddy ground. A man – a real man, a human being – stood in the doorway, watching them approach. The little cluster of figures around the door moved back a step or two, as if out of respect, and they saw the man's face: stolid, harmless, and mild.

"Who are you?" he said.

"Travellers," said Will. "We don't know where we are. What is this town?"

"This is the holding area," said the man. "Have you travelled far?"

"A long way, yes, and we're tired," said Will. "Could we buy some food and pay for shelter?"

The man was looking past them, into the dark, and then he came out and looked around further, as if there was someone missing. Then he turned to the strange figures standing by and said:

"Did *you* see any death?"

They shook their heads, and the children heard a murmur of, "No, no, none."

The man turned back. Behind him, in the doorway, there were faces looking out: a woman, two young children, another man. They were all nervous and apprehensive.

"Death?" said Will. "We're not bringing any death."

But that seemed to be the very thing they were worried about, because when Will spoke, there was a soft gasp from the living people, and even the figures outside shrank away a little.

"Excuse me," said Lyra, stepping forward in her best polite way, as if the housekeeper of Jordan College were glaring at her. "I couldn't help noticing, but these gentlemen here, are they dead? I'm sorry for asking, if it's rude, but where we come from it's very unusual, and we never saw anyone like them before. If I'm being impolite I do beg your pardon. But you see, in my world, we have dæmons, everyone has a dæmon, and we'd be shocked if we saw someone without one, just like you're shocked to see us. And now we've been travelling, Will and me – this is Will, and I'm Lyra – I've learned there are some people who don't seem to have dæmons, like Will doesn't, and I was scared till I found out they were just ordinary like me really. So maybe that's why someone from your world might be just a bit sort of nervous when they see us, if you think we're different."

The man said, "Lyra? And Will?"

"Yes, sir," she said humbly.

"Are *those* your dæmons?" he said, pointing to the spies on her shoulder.

"No," said Lyra, and she was tempted to say, "They're our servants," but she felt Will would have thought that a bad idea; so she said, "They're our friends, the Chevalier Tialys and the Lady Salmakia, very distinguished and wise people who are travelling with us. Oh, and this is my dæmon," she said, taking mouse-Pantalaimon out of her pocket. "You see, we're harmless, we promise we won't hurt you. And we do need food and shelter. We'll move on tomorrow. Honest."

Everyone waited. The man's nervousness was soothed a

little by her humble tone, and the spies had the good sense to look modest and harmless. After a pause the man said:

"Well, though it's strange, I suppose these are strange times... Come in then, be welcome..."

The figures outside nodded, one or two of them gave little bows, and they stood aside respectfully as Will and Lyra walked into the warmth and light. The man closed the door behind them and hooked a wire over a nail to keep it shut.

It was a single room, lit by a naphtha lamp on the table, and clean but shabby. The plywood walls were decorated with pictures cut from film-star magazines, and with a pattern made with fingerprints of soot. There was an iron stove against one wall, with a clothes-horse in front of it where some dingy shirts were steaming, and on a dressing-table, there was a shrine of plastic flowers, sea-shells, coloured scent bottles, and other gaudy bits and pieces, all surrounding the picture of a jaunty skeleton with a top hat and dark glasses.

The shanty was crowded: as well as the man and a woman and the two young children, there was a baby in a crib, an older man, and in one corner, in a heap of blankets, a very old woman was lying and watching everything with glittering eyes in a face as wrinkled as the blankets. As Lyra looked at her, she had a shock: the blankets stirred, and a very thin arm emerged, in a black sleeve, and then another face, a man's, so ancient it was almost a skeleton. In fact he looked more like the skeleton in the picture than like a living human being; and then Will too noticed, and all the travellers together realized that he was one of those shadowy polite figures like the ones outside. And all of them felt as nonplussed as the man had been when he'd first seen them.

In fact, all the people in the crowded little shack – all

except the baby, who was asleep – were at a loss for words. It was Lyra who found her voice first.

"That's very kind of you," she said, "thank you, good evening, we're very pleased to be here. And like I said, we're sorry to have arrived without any death, if that's the normal way of things. But we won't disturb you any more than we have to. You see, we're looking for the land of the dead, and that's how we happened to come here. But we don't know where it is, or whether this is part of it, or how to get there, or what. So if you can tell us anything about it, we'll be very grateful."

The people in the shack were still staring, but Lyra's words eased the atmosphere a little, and the woman invited them to sit at the table, drawing out a bench. Will and Lyra lifted the sleeping dragonflies up to a shelf in a dark corner, where Tialys said they would rest till daylight, and then the Gallivespians joined them on the table.

The woman had been preparing a dish of stew, and she peeled a couple of potatoes and cut them into it to make it go further, urging her husband to offer the travellers some other refreshment while it cooked. He brought out a bottle of clear and pungent spirit that smelt to Lyra like the gyptians' jenniver, and the two spies accepted a glass into which they dipped little vessels of their own.

Lyra would have expected the family to stare most at the Gallivespians, but their curiosity was directed just as much, she thought, at her and Will. She didn't wait long to ask why.

"You're the first people we ever saw without a death," said the man, whose name, they'd learned, was Peter. "Since we come here, that is. We're like you, we come here before we was dead, by some chance or accident. We got to wait till our death tells us it's time."

"Your *death* tells you?" said Lyra.

"Yes. What we found out when we come here, oh, long ago for most of us, we found we all brought our deaths with us. This is where we found out. We had 'em all the time, and we never knew. See, everyone has a death. It goes everywhere with 'em, all their life long, right close by. Our deaths, they're outside, taking the air; they'll come in by and by. Granny's death, he's there with her, he's close to her, very close."

"Doesn't it scare you, having your death close by all the time?" said Lyra.

"Why ever would it? If he's there, you can keep an eye on him. I'd be a lot more nervous not knowing where he was."

"And everyone has their own death?" said Will, marvelling.

"Why yes, the moment you're born, your death comes into the world with you, and it's your death that takes you out."

"Ah," said Lyra, "that's what we need to know, because we're trying to find the land of the dead, and we don't know how to get there. Where do we go then, when we die?"

"Your death taps you on the shoulder, or takes your hand, and says, come along o' me, it's time. It might happen when you're sick with a fever, or when you choke on a piece of dry bread, or when you fall off a high building; in the middle of your pain and travail, your death comes to you kindly and says easy now, easy, child, you come along o' me, and you go with them in a boat out across the lake into the mist. What happens there, no one knows. No one's ever come back."

The woman told a child to call the deaths in, and he scampered to the door and spoke to them. Will and Lyra watched in wonder, and the Gallivespians drew closer together, as the deaths – one for each of the family – came in through the door: pale, unremarkable figures in shabby clothes, just drab and quiet and dull.

"These are your deaths?" said Tialys.

"Indeed, sir," said Peter.

"Do you know when they'll tell you it's time to go?"

"No. But you know they're close by, and that's a comfort."

Tialys said nothing, but it was clear that he felt it would be anything but a comfort. The deaths stood politely along the wall, and it was strange to see how little space they took up, and to find how little notice they attracted. Lyra and Will soon found themselves ignoring them altogether, though Will thought: those men I killed – their deaths were close beside them all the time – they didn't know, and I didn't know...

The woman, Martha, dished up the stew on to chipped enamel plates, and put some in a bowl for the deaths to pass about among themselves. They didn't eat, but the good smell kept them content. Presently all the family and their guests were eating hungrily, and Peter asked the children where they'd come from, and what their world was like.

"I'll tell you all about it," said Lyra.

As she said that, as she took charge, part of her felt a little stream of pleasure rising upwards in her breast like the bubbles in champagne. And she knew Will was watching, and she was happy that he could see her doing what she was best at, doing it for him and for all of them.

She started by telling about her parents. They were a duke and duchess, very important and wealthy, who had been cheated out of their estate by a political enemy and thrown into prison. But they managed to escape by climbing down a rope with the baby Lyra in her father's arms, and they regained the family fortune only to be attacked and murdered by outlaws. Lyra would have been killed as well, and roasted and eaten, had not Will rescued her just in time and taken her back to the wolves, in the forest where he was being brought up as one of them. He had fallen overboard as a baby from the side of his father's ship and been washed up on a desolate shore, where a female wolf had suckled him and kept him alive.

The people ate up this nonsense with placid credulity, and even the deaths crowded close to listen, perching on the bench or lying on the floor close by, gazing at her with their mild and courteous faces as she spun out the tale of her life with Will in the forest.

He and Lyra stayed with the wolves for a while, and then moved to Oxford to work in the kitchens of Jordan College. There they met Roger, and when Jordan was attacked by the brick-burners who lived in the Claybeds, they had to escape in a hurry; so she and Will and Roger captured a gyptian narrow boat and sailed it all the way down the Thames, nearly getting caught at Abingdon Lock, and then they'd been sunk by the Wapping pirates and had to swim for safety to a three-masted clipper just setting off for Hang Chow in Cathay to trade for tea.

And on the clipper they'd met the Gallivespians, who were strangers from the Moon, blown down to the earth by a fierce gale out of the Milky Way. They'd taken refuge in the crow's nest, and she and Will and Roger used to take it in turns going up there to see them, only one day Roger lost his footing and plunged down into Davy Jones's Locker.

They tried to persuade the captain to turn the ship round and look for him, but he was a hard fierce man only interested in the profit he'd make by getting to Cathay quickly, and he clapped them in irons. But the Gallivespians brought them a file, and...

And so on. From time to time she'd turn to Will or the spies for confirmation, and Salmakia would add a detail or two, or Will would nod, and the story wound itself up to the point where the children and their friends from the Moon had to find their way to the land of the dead in order to learn, from her parents, the secret of where the family fortune had been buried.

"And if we knew our deaths, in our land," she said, "like you do here, it would be easier, probably; but I think we're really lucky to find our way here, so's we could get your advice. And thank you very much for being so kind and listening, and for giving us this meal, it was really nice.

"But what we need now, you see, or in the morning maybe, is we need to find a way out across the water where the dead people go, and see if we can get there too. Is there any boats we could sort of hire?"

They looked doubtful. The children, flushed with tiredness, looked with sleepy eyes from one grown-up to the other, but no one could suggest where they could find a boat.

Then came a voice that hadn't spoken before. From the depths of the bedclothes in the corner came a dry-cracked-nasal tone – not a woman's voice – not a living voice: it was the voice of the grandmother's death.

"The only way you'll cross the lake and go to the land of the dead," he said, and he was leaning up on his elbow, pointing with a skinny finger at Lyra, "is with your own deaths. You must call up your own deaths. I have heard of people like you, who keep their deaths at bay. You don't like them, and out of courtesy they stay out of sight. But they're not far off. Whenever you turn your head, your deaths dodge behind you. Wherever you look, they hide. They can hide in a teacup. Or in a dewdrop. Or in a breath of wind. Not like me and old Magda here," he said, and he pinched her withered cheek, and she pushed his hand away. "We live together in kindness and friendship. That's the answer, that's it, that's what you've got to do, say welcome, make friends, be kind, invite your deaths to come close to you, and see what you can get them to agree to."

His words fell into Lyra's mind like heavy stones, and Will, too, felt the deadly weight of them.

"How should we do that?" he said.

"You've only got to wish for it, and the thing is done."

"Wait," said Tialys.

Every eye turned to him, and those deaths lying on the floor sat up to turn their blank mild faces to his tiny passionate one. He was standing close by Salmakia, his hand on her shoulder. Lyra could see what he was thinking: he was going to say that this had gone too far, they must turn back, they were taking this foolishness to irresponsible lengths.

So she stepped in. "Excuse me," she said to the man Peter, "but me and our friend the chevalier, we've got to go outside for a minute, because he needs to talk to his friends in the Moon through my special instrument. We won't be long."

And she picked him up carefully, avoiding his spurs, and took him outside into the dark, where a loose piece of corrugated iron roofing was banging in the cold wind with a melancholy sound.

"You must stop," he said, as she set him on an upturned oil drum, in the feeble light of one of those electric bulbs that swung on its cable overhead. "This is far enough. No more."

"But we made an agreement," Lyra said.

"No, no. Not to these lengths."

"All right. Leave us. You fly on back. Will can cut a window into your world, or any world you like, and you can fly through and be safe, that's all right, we don't mind."

"Do you realize what you're doing?"

"Yes."

"You don't. You're a thoughtless irresponsible lying child. Fantasy comes so easily to you that your whole nature is riddled with dishonesty, and you don't even admit the truth when it stares you in the face. Well, if you can't see it, I'll tell you plainly: you cannot, you must not risk your death. You must come back with us now. I'll call Lord Asriel and we can be safe in the fortress in hours."

Lyra felt a great sob of rage building up in her chest, and stamped her foot, unable to keep still.

"You *don't know*," she cried, "you just don't know what I got in my head or my heart, do you? I don't know if you people ever have children, maybe you lay *eggs* or something, I wouldn't be surprised, because you're not kind, you're not generous, you're not considerate – you're not *cruel*, even – that would be *better*, if you were cruel, because it'd mean you took us serious, you didn't just go along with us when it suited you... Oh, I can't trust you at all now! You said you'd help and we'd do it together, and now you want to stop us – *you're* the dishonest one, Tialys!"

"I wouldn't let a child of my own speak to me in the insolent high-handed way you're speaking, Lyra – why I haven't punished you before –"

"Then go ahead! Punish me, since you *can*! Take your bloody spurs and dig 'em in hard, go on! Here's my hand – do it! You got no idea what's in my heart, you proud selfish creature – you got no notion how I feel sad and wicked and sorry about my friend Roger – you kill people just like *that*," snapping her finger, "they don't matter to you – but it's a torment and a sorrow to me that I never said goodbye to my friend Roger, and I want to say sorry and make it as good as I can – you'd never understand that, for all your pride, for all your grown-up cleverness – and if I have to *die* to do what's proper, then I *will*, and be happy while I do. I seen worse than that. So you want to kill me, you hard man, you strong man, you poison-bearer, you chevalier, you do it, go on, kill me. Then me and Roger can play in the land of the dead for ever, and laugh at you, you pitiful thing."

What Tialys might have done then wasn't hard to see, for he was ablaze from head to foot with a passionate anger, shaking with it; but he didn't have time to move before a voice spoke behind Lyra, and they both felt a chill fall over them. Lyra turned around, knowing what she'd see and dreading it despite her bravado.

The death stood very close, smiling kindly, his face exactly like those of all the others she'd seen; but this was hers, her very own death, and Pantalaimon at her breast howled and shivered, and his ermine-shape flowed up around her neck and tried to push her away from the death. But by doing that, he only pushed himself closer, and realizing it he shrank back towards her again, to her warm throat and the strong pulse of her heart.

Lyra clutched him to her and faced the death directly. She couldn't remember what he'd said, and out of the corner of her eye she could see Tialys quickly preparing the lodestone resonator, busy.

"You're my death, en't you?" she said.

"Yes, my dear," he said.

"You en't going to take me yet, are you?"

"You wanted me. I am always here."

"Yes, but … I *did*, yes, but … I want to go to the land of the dead, that's true. But not to die. I don't want to die. I love being alive, and I love my dæmon, and… Dæmons don't go down there, do they? I seen 'em vanish and just go out like candles when people die. Do they have dæmons in the land of the dead?"

"No," he said. "Your dæmon vanishes into the air, and you vanish under the ground."

"Then I want to take my dæmon with me when I go to the land of the dead," she said firmly. "And I want to come back again. Has it ever been known, for people to do that?"

"Not for many, many ages. Eventually, child, you will come to the land of the dead with no effort, no risk, a safe calm journey, in the company of your own death, your special devoted friend, who's been beside you every moment of your life, who knows you better than yourself –"

"But *Pantalaimon* is my special and devoted friend! I don't know you, Death, I know Pan and I love Pan and if he ever – if we ever –"

The death was nodding. He seemed interested and kindly, but she couldn't for a moment forget what he was: her very own death, and so close.

"I *know* it'll be an effort to go on now," she said more steadily, "and dangerous, but I want to, Death, I do truly. And so does Will. We both had people taken away too soon, and we need to make amends, at least I do."

"Everyone wishes they could speak again to those who've gone to the land of the dead. Why should there be an exception for you?"

"Because," she began, lying, "because there's something I've got to do there, not just seeing my friend Roger, something else. It was a task put on me by an angel, and no one else can do it, only me. It's too important to wait till I die in the natural way, it's got to be done now. See, the angel *commanded* me. That's why we came here, me and Will. We *got* to."

Behind her, Tialys put away his instrument, and sat

watching the child plead with her own death to be taken where no one should go.

The death scratched his head and held up his hands, but nothing could stop Lyra's words, nothing could deflect her desire, not even fear: she'd seen worse than death, she claimed, and she had, too.

So eventually her death said:

"If nothing can put you off, then all I can say is, come with me, and I will take you there, into the land of the dead. I'll be your guide. I can show you the way in, but as for getting out again, you'll have to manage by yourself."

"And my friends," said Lyra. "My friend Will and the others."

"Lyra," said Tialys, "against every instinct, we'll go with you. I was angry with you a minute ago. But you make it hard…"

Lyra knew that this was a time to conciliate, and she was happy to do that, having got her way.

"Yes," she said, "I *am* sorry, Tialys, but if you hadn't got angry we'd never have found this gentleman to guide us. So I'm glad you were here, you and the lady, I'm really grateful to you for being with us."

So Lyra persuaded her own death to guide her and the others into the land where Roger had gone, and Will's father, and Tony Makarios, and so many others; and her death told her to go down to the jetty when the first light came to the sky, and prepare to leave.

But Pantalaimon was trembling and shivering, and nothing Lyra could do could soothe him into stillness, or quieten the soft little moan he couldn't help uttering. So her sleep was broken and shallow, on the floor of the shack with all the other sleepers, and her death sat watchfully beside her.

20
Climbing

-I GAINED IT
SO-BY CLIMB-
ING SLOW-BY
CATCHING AT
THE TWIGS
THAT GROW
BETWEEN THE
BLISS-AND ME-
EMILY DICKINSON

The mulefa made many kinds of rope and cord, and Mary Malone spent a morning inspecting and testing the ones Atal's family had in their stores before choosing what she wanted. The principle of twisting and winding hadn't caught on in their world, so all the cords and ropes were braided; but they were strong and flexible, and Mary soon found exactly the sort she wanted.

What are you doing? said Atal.

The mulefa had no term for *climb*, so Mary had to do a lot of gesturing and roundabout explaining. Atal was horrified.

To go into the high part of the trees?

I must see what is happening, Mary explained. *Now you can help me prepare the rope.*

Once in California Mary had met a mathematician who spent every weekend climbing among the trees. Mary had done a little rock-climbing, and she'd listened avidly as he had talked about the techniques and equipment, and had decided to try it herself as soon as she had the chance. Of course, she'd never expected to be climbing trees in another universe, and climbing solo didn't greatly appeal either, but there was no choice about that. What she could do was make it as safe as possible beforehand.

She took a coil long enough to reach over one of the branches of a high tree and back down to the ground, and strong enough to bear several times her weight. Then she cut a large number of short pieces of a smaller but very tough cord and made slings with them: short loops tied with a fisherman's knot, which could make hand and footholds when she tied them to the main line.

Then there was the problem of getting the rope over the branch in the first place. An hour or two's experimenting with some fine tough cord and a length of springy branch produced a bow; the Swiss Army knife cut some arrows, with stiff leaves in place of feathers to stabilize them in flight; and finally, after a day's work, Mary was ready to begin. But the sun was setting, and her hands were tired, and she ate and slept, preoccupied, while the mulefa discussed her endlessly in their quiet musical whispers.

First thing in the morning, she set off to shoot the arrow over a branch. Some of the mulefa gathered to watch, anxious for her safety. Climbing was so alien to creatures with wheels that the very thought of it horrified them.

Privately, Mary knew how they felt. She swallowed her nervousness, and tied an end of the thinnest, lightest line to one of her arrows, and sent it flying upwards from the bow.

She lost the first arrow: it stuck in the bark part way up, and wouldn't come out. She lost the second because, although it did clear the branch, it didn't fall far enough to reach the ground on the other side, and pulling it back, she caught it and snapped it. The long line fell back attached to the broken shaft, and she tried again with the third and last, and this time it worked.

Pulling carefully and steadily so as not to snag the line and break it, she hauled the prepared rope up and over until both ends were on the ground. Then she tied them both securely to a massive buttress of one of the roots, as thick around as her own hips, so it should be fairly solid, she thought. It had better be. What she couldn't tell from the ground, of course, was what kind of branch the whole thing, including her, would be depending on. Unlike climbing on rock, where you could fasten the rope to pitons on the cliff-face every few metres so you never had far to fall, this business involved one very long free length of rope, and one very long fall if anything went wrong. To make herself a little more secure, she braided together three small ropes into a harness, and passed it around both hanging ends of the main rope with a loose knot that she could tighten the moment she began to slip.

Mary put her foot in the first sling, and began to climb.

She reached the canopy in less time than she'd anticipated. The climbing was straightforward, the rope was kindly on her hands, and although she hadn't wanted to think about the problem of getting on top of the first branch, she found that the deep fissures in the bark helped her to get a solid purchase and feel secure. In fact, only fifteen minutes after she'd left the ground, she was standing on the first branch and planning her route to the next.

She had brought two more coils of rope with her, intending to make a web of fixed lines to serve in place of the pitons and anchors and "friends" and other hardware she relied on when climbing a rock face. Tying them in place took her some minutes more, and once she'd secured herself, she chose what looked like the most promising branch, coiled her spare rope again, and set off.

After ten minutes' careful climbing she found herself right in the thickest part of the canopy. She could reach the long leaves and run them through her hands; she found flower after flower, off-white and absurdly small, each growing the little coin-sized thing that would later become one of those great iron-hard seed-pods.

She reached a comfortable spot where three branches forked, tied the rope securely, fastened her harness, and rested.

Through the gaps in the leaves she could see the blue sea, clear and sparkling as far as the horizon; and in the other direction over her right shoulder she could see the succession of low rises in the gold-brown prairie, laced across by the black highways.

There was a light breeze, which lifted a faint scent out of the flowers and rustled the stiff leaves, and Mary imagined a huge dim benevolence holding her up, like a pair of giant hands. As she lay in the fork of the great branches, she felt a kind of bliss she had only felt once before; and that was not when she made her vows as a nun.

Eventually she was brought back to her normal state of mind by cramp in her right ankle, which was resting awkwardly in the crook of the fork. She eased it away and turned her attention to the task, still dizzy from the sense of oceanic gladness that surrounded her.

She'd explained to the mulefa how she had to hold the sap-lacquer plates a hand-span apart in order to see the sraf; and at once they'd seen the problem and made a short tube of bamboo, fixing the amber-coloured plates at each end like a telescope. This spyglass was tucked in her breast pocket, and she took it out now. When she looked through it, she saw those drifting golden sparkles, the sraf, the Shadows, Lyra's Dust, like a vast cloud of tiny beings floating through the wind. For the most part they drifted randomly like dust motes in a shaft of sunlight, or molecules in a glass of water. For the most part.

But the longer she looked, the more she began to see another kind of motion. Underlying the random drifting was a deeper, slower, universal movement, out from the land towards the sea.

Well, that was curious. Securing herself to one of her fixed ropes, she crawled out along a horizontal branch, looking closely at all the flower-heads she could find. And presently she began to see what was happening. She watched and waited till she was perfectly sure, and then began the careful, lengthy, strenuous process of climbing down.

Mary found the mulefa in a fearful state, having suffered a thousand anxieties for their friend so far off the ground.

Atal was especially relieved, and touched her nervously all over with her trunk, uttering gentle whinnies of pleasure to find her safe, and carrying her swiftly down to the settlement along with a dozen or so others.

As soon as they came over the brow of the hill, the call went out among those in the village, and by the time they reached the speaking ground, the throng was so thick that Mary guessed there were many visitors from elsewhere, come to hear what she said. She wished she had better news for them.

The old zalif, Sattamax, mounted the platform and welcomed her warmly, and she responded with all the mulefa-courtesy she could remember. As soon as the greetings were over, she began to speak.

Haltingly and with many roundabout phrasings, she said:
My good friends, I have been into the high canopy of your

trees and looked closely at the growing leaves and the young flowers and the seed-pods.

I could see that there is a current of sraf high in the tree-tops, she went on, *and it moves against the wind. The air is moving inland off the sea, but the sraf is moving slowly against it. Can you see that from the ground? Because I could not.*

No, said Sattamax. *That is the first we ever heard about that.*

Well, she continued, *the trees are filtering the sraf as it moves through them, and some of it is attracted to the flowers. I could see it happening: the flowers are turned upwards, and if the sraf were falling straight down it would enter their petals and fertilize them like pollen from the stars.*

But the sraf isn't falling down, it's moving out towards the sea. When a flower happens to be facing the land, the sraf can enter it. That's why there are still some seed-pods growing. But most of them face upwards, and the sraf just drifts past without entering. The flowers must have evolved like that because in the past all the sraf fell straight down. Something has happened to the sraf, not to the trees. And you can only see that current from high up, which is why you never knew about it.

So if you want to save the trees, and mulefa life, we must find out why the sraf is doing that. I can't think of a way yet, but I will try.

She saw many of them craning to look upwards at this drift of Dust. But from the ground you couldn't see it: she looked herself through the spyglass, but the dense blue of the sky was all she could see.

They spoke for a long time, trying to recall any mention of the sraf-wind among their legends and histories, but there was none. All they had ever known was that sraf came from the stars, as it had always done.

Finally they asked if she had any more ideas, and she said:

*I need to make more observations. I need to find out whether
the wind goes always in that direction or whether it alters like the
air-currents during the day and the night. So I need to spend more
time in the tree-tops, and sleep up there and observe at night. I
will need your help to build a platform of some kind so I can sleep
safely. But we do need more observations.*

The mulefa, practical and anxious to find out, offered at
once to build her whatever she needed. They knew the
techniques of using pulleys and tackle, and presently one
suggested a way of lifting Mary easily into the canopy so as to
save her the dangerous labour of climbing.

Glad to have something to do, they set about gathering
materials at once, braiding and tying and lashing spars and
ropes and lines under her guidance, and assembling everything she needed for a tree-top observation platform.

After speaking to the old couple by the olive grove, Father
Gomez lost the track. He spent several days searching and
enquiring in every direction round about, but the woman
seemed to have vanished completely.

He would never have given up, although it was discourag-
ing; the crucifix around his neck and the rifle at his back were
twin tokens of his absolute determination to complete the task.

But it would have taken him much longer, if it hadn't been
for a difference in the weather. In the world he was in, it was
hot and dry, and he was increasingly thirsty; and seeing a wet
patch of rock at the top of a scree, he climbed up to see if
there was a spring there. There wasn't, but in the world of
the wheel-pod trees, there had just been a shower of rain; and
so it was that he discovered the window, and found where
Mary had gone.

21

The Harpies

I HATE THINGS ALL FICTION... THERE SHOULD ALWAYS BE SOME FOUNDATION OF FACT ...BYRON

Lyra and Will each awoke with a heavy dread: it was like being a condemned prisoner on the morning fixed for the execution. Tialys and Salmakia were attending to their dragonflies, bringing them moths lassoed near the anbaric lamp over the oil-drum outside, flies cut from spider-webs, and water in a tin plate. When she saw the expression on Lyra's face and the way that Pantalaimon, mouse-formed, was pressing himself close to her breast, the Lady Salmakia left what she was doing to come and speak with her. Will, meanwhile, left the hut to walk about outside.

"You can still decide differently," said Salmakia.

"No, we can't. We decided already," said Lyra, stubborn and fearful at once.

"And if we don't come back?"

"*You* don't have to come," Lyra pointed out.

"We're not going to abandon you."

"Then what if *you* don't come back?"

"We shall have died doing something important."

Lyra was silent. She hadn't really looked at the lady before; but she could see her very clearly now, in the smoky light of the naphtha lamp, standing on the table just an arm's length away. Her face was calm and kindly, not beautiful, not pretty, but the very sort of face you would be glad to see if you were ill or unhappy or frightened. Her voice was low and expressive, with a current of laughter and happiness under the clear surface. In all the life she could remember Lyra had never been read to in bed; no one had told her stories or sung nursery rhymes with her before kissing her and putting out the light. But she suddenly thought now that if ever there was a voice that would lap you in safety and warm you with love, it would be a voice like the Lady Salmakia's, and she felt a wish in her heart to have a child of her own, to lull and soothe and sing to, one day, in a voice like that.

"Well," Lyra said, and found her throat choked, so she swallowed and shrugged.

"We'll see," said the lady, and turned back.

Once they had eaten the thin dry bread and drunk the bitter tea which was all the people had to offer them, they thanked their hosts, took their rucksacks and set off through the shanty town for the lake shore. Lyra looked around for her death, and sure enough, there he was, walking politely a little way ahead; but he didn't want to come closer, though he kept looking back to see they were following.

The day was overhung with a gloomy mist. It was more like dusk than daylight, and wraiths and streamers of the fog rose dismally from puddles in the road, or clung like forlorn lovers to the anbaric cables overhead. They saw no people, and few deaths, but the dragonflies skimmed through the damp air as if they were sewing it all together with invisible threads, and it was a delight to the eyes to watch their bright colours flashing back and forth.

Before long they had reached the edge of the settlement, and made their way beside a sluggish stream through bare-twigged scrubby bushes. Occasionally they would hear a harsh croak or a splash as some amphibian was disturbed, but the only creature they saw was a toad as big as Will's foot, which could only flop in a pain-filled sideways heave as if it were horribly injured. It lay across the path, trying to move out of the way and looking at them as if it knew they meant to hurt it.

"It would be merciful to kill it," said Tialys.

"How do you know?" said Lyra. "It might still like being alive, in spite of everything."

"If we killed it, we'd be taking it with us," said Will. "It wants to stay here. I've killed enough living things. Even a filthy stagnant pool might be better than being dead."

"But if it's in pain?" said Tialys.

"If it could tell us, we'd know. But since it can't, I'm not going to kill it. That would be considering our feelings rather than the toad's."

They moved on. Before long the changing sound their footsteps made told them that there was an openness nearby, although the mist was even thicker. Pantalaimon was a lemur, with the biggest eyes he could manage, clinging to Lyra's shoulder, pressing himself into her fog-pearled hair, peering all round and seeing no more than she did. And still he was trembling and trembling.

Suddenly they all heard a little wave breaking. It was quiet, but it was very close by. The dragonflies returned with their riders to the children, and Pantalaimon crept into Lyra's breast as she and Will moved closer together, treading carefully along the slimy path.

And then they were at the shore. The oily, scummy water lay still in front of them, an occasional ripple breaking languidly on the pebbles.

The path turned to the left, and a little way along, more like a thickening of the mist than a solid object, a wooden jetty stood crazily out over the water. The piles were decayed and the planks were green with slime, and there was nothing else; nothing beyond it; the path ended where the jetty began, and where the jetty ended, the mist began. Lyra's death, having guided them there, bowed to her and stepped into the fog and vanished before she could ask him what to do next.

"Listen," said Will.

There was a slow sound out on the invisible water: a creak of wood and a quiet regular splash. Will put his hand on the knife at his belt, and moved forward carefully on to the rotting planks. Lyra followed close behind. The dragonflies perched on the two weed-covered mooring posts, looking like heraldic guardians, and the children stood at the end of the jetty, pressing their open eyes against the mist, and having to brush their lashes free of the drops that settled on them. The only sound was that slow creak and splash that was getting closer and closer.

"Don't let's go!" Pantalaimon whispered.

"Got to," Lyra whispered back.

She looked at Will. His face was set hard and grim and eager: he wouldn't turn aside. And the Gallivespians, Tialys on Will's shoulder, Salmakia on Lyra's, were calm and watchful. The dragonflies' wings were pearled with mist, like cobwebs, and from time to time they'd beat them quickly to clear them, because the drops must make them heavy, Lyra thought. She hoped there would be food for them in the land of the dead.

Then suddenly there was the boat.

It was an ancient rowing boat, battered, patched, rotting; and the figure rowing it was aged beyond age, huddled in a robe of sacking bound with string, crippled and bent, his bony hands crooked permanently around the oar-handles, and his moist pale eyes sunk deep among folds and wrinkles of grey skin.

He let go of an oar and reached his crooked hand up to the iron ring set in the post at the corner of the jetty. With the other hand he moved the oar to bring the boat right up against the planks.

There was no need to speak. Will got in first, and then Lyra came forward to step down too.

But the boatman held up his hand.

"Not him," he said, in a harsh whisper.

"Not who?"

"Not him."

He extended a yellow-grey finger, pointing directly at Pantalaimon, whose red-brown stoat-form immediately became ermine-white.

"But he *is* me!" Lyra said.

"If you come, he must stay."

"But we can't! We'd die!"

"Isn't that what you want?"

And then for the first time Lyra truly realized what she was doing. This was the real consequence. She stood aghast, trembling, and clutched her dear dæmon so tightly that he whimpered in pain.

"*They*..." said Lyra helplessly, then stopped: it wasn't fair to point out that the other three didn't have to give anything up.

Will was watching her anxiously. She looked all around, at the lake, at the jetty, at the rough path, the stagnant puddles, the dead and sodden bushes... Her Pan, alone here: how could he live without her? He was shaking inside her shirt, against her bare flesh, his fur needing her warmth. Impossible! Never!

"He must stay here if you are to come," the boatman said again.

The Lady Salmakia flicked the rein, and her dragonfly skimmed away from Lyra's shoulder to land on the gunwale of the boat, where Tialys joined her. They said something to the boatman. Lyra watched as a condemned prisoner watches the stir at the back of the courtroom that might be a messenger with a pardon.

The boatman bent to listen, and then shook his head.

"No," he said. "If she comes, he has to stay."

Will said, "That's not right. We don't have to leave part of ourselves behind. Why should Lyra?"

"Oh, but you do," said the boatman. "It's her misfortune that she can see and talk to the part she must leave. You will not know until you are on the water, and then it will be too late. But you all have to leave that part of yourselves here. There is no passage to the land of the dead for such as him."

No, Lyra thought, and Pantalaimon thought with her: *We didn't go through Bolvangar for this, no; how will we ever find each other again?*

And she looked back again at the foul and dismal shore, so bleak and blasted with disease and poison, and thought of her dear Pan waiting there alone, her heart's companion, watching her disappear into the mist, and she fell into a storm of weeping. Her passionate sobs didn't echo, because the mist muffled them, but all along the shore in innumerable ponds and shallows, in wretched broken tree stumps, the damaged creatures that lurked there heard her full-hearted cry and drew themselves a little closer to the ground, afraid of such passion.

"If he could come —" cried Will, desperate to end her grief, but the boatman shook his head.

"He can come in the boat, but if he does, the boat stays here," he said.

"But how will she find him again?"

"I don't know."

"When we leave, will we come back this way?"

"Leave?"

"We're going to come back. We're going to the land of the dead and we are going to come back."

"Not this way."

"Then some other way, but we will!"

"I have taken millions, and none came back."

"Then we shall be the first. We'll find our way out. And since we're going to do that, be kind, boatman, be compassionate, let her take her dæmon!"

"No," he said and shook his ancient head. "It's not a rule you can break. It's a law like this one..." He leant over the side and cupped a handful of water, and then tilted his hand so it ran out again. "The law that makes the water fall back into the lake, it's a law like that. I can't tilt my hand and make the water fly upwards. No more can I take her dæmon to the land of the dead. Whether or not *she* comes, he must stay."

Lyra could see nothing: her face was buried in Pantalaimon's cat-fur. But Will saw Tialys dismount from his dragonfly and prepare to spring at the boatman, and he half-agreed with the spy's intention: but the old man had seen him, and turned his ancient head to say:

"How many ages do you think I've been ferrying people to the land of the dead? D'you think if anything could hurt me, it wouldn't have happened already? D'you think the people I take come with me gladly? They struggle and cry, they try to bribe me, they threaten and fight; nothing works. You can't hurt me, sting as you will. Better comfort the child; she's coming; take no notice of me."

Will could hardly watch. Lyra was doing the cruellest thing she had ever done, hating herself, hating the deed, suffering for Pan and with Pan and because of Pan; trying to put him down on the cold path, disengaging his cat-claws from her clothes, weeping, weeping. Will closed his ears: the sound was too unhappy to bear. Time after time she pushed her dæmon away, and still he cried and tried to cling.

She *could* turn back.

She could say no, this is a bad idea, we mustn't do it.

She could be true to the heart-deep, life-deep bond linking her to Pantalaimon, she could put that first, she could push the rest out of her mind –

But she couldn't.

"Pan, no one's done this before," she whispered shiveringly, "but Will says we're coming back and I *swear*, Pan, I love you, I *swear* we're coming back – I will – take care, my dear – you'll be safe – we will come back, and if I have to spend every minute of my life finding you again I will, I won't stop, I won't rest, I won't – oh Pan – dear Pan – I've got to, I've got to..."

And she pushed him away, so that he crouched bitter and cold and frightened on the muddy ground.

What animal he was now, Will could hardly tell. He seemed to be so young, a cub, a puppy, something helpless and beaten, a creature so sunk in misery that it was more misery than creature. His eyes never left Lyra's face, and Will could see her making herself not look away, not avoid the guilt, and he admired her honesty and her courage at the same time as he was wrenched with the shock of their parting. There were so many vivid currents of feeling between them that the very air felt electric to him.

And Pantalaimon didn't say, "Why?", because he knew; and he didn't ask whether Lyra loved Roger more than him, because he knew the true answer to that, too. And he knew that if he spoke, she wouldn't be able to resist; so the dæmon held himself quiet so as not to distress the human who was abandoning him, and now they were both pretending that it wouldn't hurt, it wouldn't be long before they were together again, it was all for the best. But Will knew that the little girl was tearing her heart out of her breast.

Then she stepped down into the boat. She was so light that it barely rocked at all. She sat beside Will, and her eyes never left Pantalaimon, who stood trembling at the shore end of the jetty; but as the boatman let go of the iron ring and swung his oars out to pull the boat away, the little dog-dæmon trotted helplessly out to the very end, his claws clicking softly on the soft planks, and stood watching, just watching, as the boat drew away and the jetty faded and vanished in the mist.

Then Lyra gave a cry so passionate that even in that muffled mist-hung world it raised an echo, but of course it wasn't an echo, it was the other part of her crying in turn from the land of the living as Lyra moved away into the land of the dead.

"My *heart*, Will..." she groaned, and clung to him, her wet face contorted with pain.

And thus the prophecy that the Master of Jordan College had made to the Librarian, that Lyra would make a great betrayal and it would hurt her terribly, was fulfilled.

But Will too found an agony building inside him, and through the pain he saw that the two Gallivespians, clinging together just as he and Lyra were doing, were moved by the same anguish.

Part of it was physical. It felt as if an iron hand had gripped his heart and was pulling it out between his ribs, so that he pressed his hands to the place and vainly tried to hold it in. It was far deeper and far worse than the pain of losing his fingers. But it was mental, too: something secret and private was being dragged into the open where it had no wish to be, and Will was nearly overcome by a mixture of pain and shame and fear and self-reproach, because he himself had caused it.

And it was worse than that. It was as if he'd said, "No, don't kill me, I'm frightened; kill my mother instead; she doesn't matter, I don't love her," and as if she'd heard him say it, and pretended she hadn't so as to spare his feelings, and offered herself in his place anyway because of her love for him. He felt as bad as that. There was nothing worse to feel.

So Will knew that all those things were part of having a dæmon, and that whatever his dæmon was, she too was left behind, with Pantalaimon, on that poisoned and desolate shore. The thought came to Will and Lyra at the same moment, and they exchanged a tear-filled glance. And for the second time in their lives, but not the last, each of them saw their own expression on the other's face.

Only the boatman and the dragonflies seemed indifferent to the journey they were making. The great insects were fully alive and bright with beauty even in the clinging mist, shaking their filmy wings to dislodge the moisture; and the old man in his sacking robe leaned forward and back, forward and back, bracing his bare feet against the slime-puddled floor.

The journey lasted longer than Lyra wanted to measure. Though part of her was raw with anguish, imagining Pantalaimon abandoned on the shore, another part was adjusting to the pain, measuring her own strength, curious to see what would happen and where they would land.

Will's arm was strong around her, but he too was looking ahead, trying to peer through the wet grey gloom and to hear anything other than the dank splash of the oars. And presently something did change: a cliff or an island lay ahead of them. They heard the enclosing of the sound before they saw the mist darken.

The boatman pulled on one oar to turn the boat a little to the left.

"Where are we?" said the voice of the Chevalier Tialys, small but strong as ever, though there was a harsh edge to it as if he too had been suffering pain.

"Near the island," said the boatman. "Another five minutes, we'll be at the landing stage."

"What island?" said Will. He found his own voice strained too, so tight it hardly seemed his.

"The gate to the land of the dead is on this island," said the boatman. "Everyone comes here, kings, queens, murderers, poets, children; everyone comes this way, and none come back."

"*We* shall come back," whispered Lyra fiercely.

He said nothing, but his ancient eyes were full of pity.

As they moved closer, they could see branches of cypress and yew hanging down low over the water, dark green, dense and gloomy. The land rose steeply, and the trees grew so thickly that hardly a ferret could slip between them, and at that thought, Lyra gave a little half-hiccup-half-sob, for Pan would have shown her how well he could do it; but not now, maybe not ever again.

"Are we dead now?" Will said to the boatman.

"Makes no difference," he said. "There's some that came here never believing they were dead. They insisted all the way that they were alive, it was a mistake, someone would have to pay; made no difference. There's others who longed to be dead when they were alive, poor souls; lives full of pain or misery; killed themselves for a chance of a blessed rest, and found that nothing had changed except for the worse, and this time there was no escape; you can't make yourself alive again. And there's been others so frail and sickly, little infants, sometimes, that they're scarcely born into the living before they come down to the dead. I've rowed this boat with a little crying baby on my lap many, many times, that never knew the difference between up there and down here. And old folk too, the rich ones are the worst, snarling and savage and cursing me, railing and screaming: what did I think I was? Hadn't they gathered and saved all the gold they could garner? Wouldn't I take some now, to put them back ashore? They'd have the law on me, they had powerful friends, they knew the Pope and the King of this and the Duke of that, they were in a position to see I was punished and chastised... But they knew what the truth was in the end: the only position they were in was in my boat going to the land of the dead, and as for those kings and popes, they'd be in here too, in their turn, sooner than they wanted. I let 'em cry and rave; they can't hurt me; they fall silent in the end.

"So if you don't know whether you're dead or not, and the little girl swears blind she'll come out again to the living, I say nothing to contradict you. What you are, you'll know soon enough."

All the time he had been steadily rowing along the shore, and now he shipped the oars, slipping the handles down inside the boat and reaching out to his right for the first wooden post that rose out of the lake.

He pulled the boat alongside the narrow wharf and held it still for them. Lyra didn't want to get out: as long as she was near the boat, then Pantalaimon would be able to think of her properly, because that was how he last saw her, but when she moved away from it, he wouldn't know how to picture her any more. So she hesitated, but the dragonflies flew up, and Will got out, pale and clutching his chest; so she had to as well.

"Thank you," she said to the boatman. "When you go back, if you see my dæmon, tell him I love him the best of everything in the land of the living or the dead, and I swear I'll come back to him, even if no one's ever done it before, I swear I will."

"Yes, I'll tell him that," said the old boatman.

He pushed off, and the sound of his slow oar strokes faded away in the mist.

The Gallivespians flew back, having gone a little way, and perched on the children's shoulders as before, she on Lyra, he on Will. So they stood, the travellers, at the edge of the land of the dead. Ahead of them there was nothing but mist, though they could see from the darkening of it that a great wall rose in front of them.

Lyra shivered. She felt as if her skin had turned into lace and the damp and bitter air could flow in and out of her ribs, scaldingly cold on the raw wound where Pantalaimon had been. Still, she thought, Roger must have felt like that as he plunged down the mountainside, trying to cling to her desperate fingers.

They stood still and listened. The only sound was an endless drip-drip-drip of water from the leaves, and as they looked up they felt one or two drops splash coldly on their cheeks.

"Can't stay here," said Lyra.

They moved off the wharf, keeping close together, and made their way to the wall. Gigantic stone blocks, green with ancient slime, rose higher into the mist than they could see. And now they were closer, they could hear the sound of cries behind it, though whether they were human voices crying was impossible to tell: high mournful shrieks and wails that hung in the air like the drifting filaments of a jellyfish, causing pain wherever they touched.

"There's a door," said Will, in a hoarse strained voice.

It was a battered wooden postern under a slab of stone. Before Will could lift his hand and open it, one of those high harsh cries sounded very close by, jarring their ears and frightening them horribly.

Immediately the Gallivespians darted into the air, the dragonflies like little war-horses eager for battle. But the thing that flew down swept them aside with a brutal blow from her wing, and then settled heavily on a ledge just above the children's heads. Tialys and Salmakia gathered themselves and soothed their shaken mounts.

The thing was a great bird the size of a vulture, with the face and breasts of a woman. Will had seen pictures of creatures like her, and the word *harpy* came to mind as soon as he saw her clearly. Her face was smooth and unwrinkled, but aged beyond even the age of the witches: she had seen thousands of years pass, and the cruelty and misery of all of them had formed the hateful expression on her features. But as the travellers saw her more clearly, she became even more repulsive. Her eye-sockets were clotted with filthy slime, and the redness of her lips was caked and crusted as if she had vomited ancient blood again and again. Her matted, filthy black hair hung down to her shoulders; her jagged claws gripped the stone fiercely; her powerful dark wings were folded along her back, and a drift of putrescent stink wafted from her every time she moved.

Will and Lyra, both of them sick and full of pain, tried to stand upright and face her.

"But you are alive!" the harpy said, her harsh voice mocking them.

Will found himself hating and fearing her more than any human being he had ever known.

"Who are you?" said Lyra, who was just as repelled as Will.

For answer the harpy screamed. She opened her mouth and directed a jet of noise right in their faces, so that their heads rang and they nearly fell backwards. Will clutched at Lyra and they both clung together as the scream turned into wild mocking peals of laughter, which were answered by other harpy-voices in the fog along the shore. The jeering hate-filled sound reminded Will of the merciless cruelty of children in a playground, but there were no teachers here to regulate things, no one to appeal to, nowhere to hide.

He set his hand on the knife at his belt and looked her in the eyes, though his head was ringing and the sheer power of her scream had made him dizzy.

"If you're trying to stop us," he said, "then you'd better be ready to fight as well as scream. Because we're going through that door."

The harpy's sickening red mouth moved again, but this time it was to purse her lips into a mock-kiss.

Then she said, "Your mother is alone. We shall send her nightmares. We shall scream at her in her sleep!"

Will didn't move, because out of the corner of his eye he could see the Lady Salmakia moving delicately along the branch where the harpy was perching. Her dragonfly, wings quivering, was being held by Tialys on the ground, and then two things happened: the lady leapt at the harpy and spun around to dig her spur deep into the creature's scaly leg, and Tialys launched the dragonfly upwards. In less than a second Salmakia had spun away and leapt off the branch, directly on to the back of her electric-blue steed and up into the air.

The effect on the harpy was immediate. Another scream shattered the silence, much louder than before, and she beat her dark wings so hard that Will and Lyra both felt the wind, and staggered. But she clung to the stone with her claws, and her face was suffused with dark-red anger, and her hair stood out from her head like a crest of serpents.

Will tugged at Lyra's hand, and they both tried to run towards the door, but the harpy launched herself at them in a fury and only pulled up from the dive when Will turned, thrusting Lyra behind him and holding up the knife.

The Gallivespians flew at the harpy at once, darting close at her face and then darting away again, unable to get in a blow but distracting her so that she beat her wings clumsily and half-fell on to the ground.

Lyra called out, "Tialys! Salmakia! Stop, stop!"

The spies reined back their dragonflies and skimmed high over the children's heads. Other dark forms were clustering in the fog, and the jeering screams of a hundred more harpies sounded from further along the shore. The first one was shaking her wings, shaking her hair, stretching each leg in turn and flexing her claws. She was unhurt, and that was what Lyra had noticed.

The Gallivespians hovered, and then dived back towards Lyra, who was holding out both hands for them to land on. Salmakia realized what Lyra had meant, and said to Tialys: "She's right. We can't hurt her, for some reason."

Lyra said, "Lady, what's your name?"

The harpy shook her wings wide, and the travellers nearly

fainted in the hideous smells of corruption and decay that wafted from her.

"No-Name!" she cried.

"What do you want with us?" said Lyra.

"What can you give me?"

"We could tell you where we've been, and maybe you'd be interested, I don't know. We saw all kinds of strange things on the way here."

"Oh, and you're offering to tell me a story?"

"If you'd like."

"Maybe I would. And what then?"

"You might let us go in through that door and find the ghost we've come here to look for, I hope you would, anyway. If you'd be so kind."

"Try, then," said No-Name.

And even in her sickness and pain, Lyra felt that she'd just been dealt the ace of trumps.

"Oh, be careful," whispered Salmakia, but Lyra's mind was already racing ahead through the story she'd told the night before, shaping and cutting and improving and adding: *parents dead; family treasure; shipwreck; escape...*

"Well," she said, settling in to her story-telling frame of mind, "it began when I was a baby, really. My father and mother were the Duke and Duchess of Abingdon, you see, and they were as rich as anything. My father was one of the king's advisers, and the king himself used to come and stay, oh, all the time. They'd go hunting in our forest. The house there, where I was born, it was the biggest house in the whole south of England. It was called —"

Without even a cry of warning the harpy launched herself at Lyra, claws outstretched. Lyra just had time to duck, but still one of the claws caught her scalp and tore out a clump of hair.

"Liar! Liar!" the harpy was screaming. "Liar!"

She flew around again, aiming directly for Lyra's face; but Will took out the knife, and threw himself in the way. No-Name swerved out of reach just in time, and Will hustled Lyra over towards the door, because she was numb with shock and half-blinded by the blood running down her face. Where the Gallivespians were, Will had no idea, but the harpy was flying at them again and screaming and screaming in rage and hatred:

"*Liar! Liar! Liar!*"

And it sounded as if her voice was coming from everywhere, and the word echoed back from the great wall in the fog, muffled and changed, so that she seemed to be screaming Lyra's name, so that *Lyra* and *liar* were one and the same thing.

Will had the girl pressed against his chest, with his shoulder curved over to protect her, and he felt her shaking and sobbing against him; but then he thrust the knife into the rotten wood of the door, and cut out the lock with a quick slash of the blade.

Then he and Lyra, with the spies beside them on their darting dragonflies, tumbled through into the realm of the ghosts as the harpy's cry was doubled and redoubled by others on the foggy shore behind them.

22
The Whisperers

THICK AS AUTUM-
NAL LEAVES THAT
STROW THE BROOKS
IN VALLOMBROSA,
WHERE TH'ETRURIAN
SHADES HIGH OVER-
ARCH'T IMBOWR···
JOHN MILTON

The first thing Will did was to make Lyra sit down, and then he took out the little pot of bloodmoss ointment and looked at the wound on her head. It was bleeding freely, as scalp wounds do, but it wasn't deep. He tore a strip off the edge of his shirt and mopped it clean, and spread some of the ointment over the gash, trying not to think of the filthy state of the claw that made it.

Lyra's eyes were glazed, and she was ash-pale.

"Lyra! Lyra!" he said, and shook her gently. "Come on now, we've got to move."

She gave a shudder and took a long shaky breath, and her eyes focused on him, full of a wild despair.

"Will – I can't do it any more – I can't do it! I can't tell lies! I thought it was so easy – but it didn't work – it's all I can do, and it doesn't work!"

"It's *not* all you can do. You can read the alethiometer, can't you? Come on, let's see where we are. Let's look for Roger."

He helped her up, and for the first time they looked around at the land where the ghosts were.

They found themselves on a great plain that extended far ahead into the mist. The light by which they saw was a dull self-luminescence that seemed to exist everywhere equally, so that there were no true shadows and no true light, and everything was the same dingy colour.

Standing on the floor of this huge space were adults and children – ghost-people – so many that Lyra couldn't guess their number. At least, most of them were standing, though some were sitting and some lying down listless or asleep. No one was moving about, or running or playing, though many of them turned to look at these new arrivals, with a fearful curiosity in their wide eyes.

"Ghosts," she whispered. "This is where they all are, everyone that's ever died..."

No doubt it was because she didn't have Pantalaimon any more, but she clung close to Will's arm, and he was glad she did. The Gallivespians had flown ahead, and he could see their bright little forms darting and skimming over the heads of the ghosts, who looked up and followed them with wonder; but the silence was immense and oppressive, and the grey light filled him with fear, and Lyra's warm presence beside him was the only thing that felt like life.

Behind them, outside the wall, the screams of the harpies were still echoing up and down the shore. Some of the ghost-people were looking up apprehensively, but more of them were staring at Will and Lyra, and then they began to crowd forward. Lyra shrank back; she didn't have the strength just yet to face them as she would have liked to do, and it was Will who had to speak first.

"Do you speak our language?" he said. "Can you speak at all?"

Shivering and frightened and full of pain as they were, he and Lyra had more authority than the whole mass of the dead put together. These poor ghosts had little power of their own, and hearing Will's voice, the first clear voice that had sounded there in all the memory of the dead, many of them came forward, eager to respond.

But they could only whisper. A faint pale sound, no more than a soft breath, was all they could utter. And as they thrust forward, jostling and desperate, the Gallivespians flew down and darted to and fro in front of them, to prevent them from crowding too close. The ghost-children looked up with a passionate longing, and Lyra knew at once why: they thought the dragonflies were dæmons; they were wishing with all their hearts that they could hold their own dæmons again.

"Oh, they *en't* dæmons," Lyra burst out, compassionately; "and if my own dæmon was here, you could all stroke him and touch him, I promise –"

And she held out her hands to the children. The adult ghosts hung back, listless or fearful, but the children all came thronging forward. They had as much substance as fog, poor things, and Lyra's hands passed through and through them, as did Will's. They crammed forward, light and lifeless, to warm themselves at the flowing blood and the strong-beating hearts of the two travellers, and both Will and Lyra felt a succession of cold delicate brushing sensations as the ghosts passed through their bodies, warming themselves on the way. The two living children felt that little by little they were becoming dead too; they hadn't got an infinite amount of life and warmth to give, and they were so cold already, and the endless crowds pressing forward looked as if they were never going to stop.

Finally Lyra had to plead with them to hold back.

She held up her hands and said, "Please – we wish we could touch you all, but we came down here to look for someone, and I need you to tell me where he is and how to find him. Oh, Will," she said, leaning her head to his, "I wish I knew what to do!"

The ghosts were fascinated by the blood on Lyra's forehead. It glowed as brightly as a holly berry in the dimness, and several of them had brushed through it, longing for the contact with something so vibrantly alive. One ghost-girl, who when she was alive must have been about nine or ten, reached up shyly to try and touch it, and then shrank back in fear; but Lyra said, "Don't be afraid – we en't come here to hurt you – speak to us, if you can!"

The ghost-girl spoke, but in her thin pale voice it was only a whisper.

"Did the harpies do that? Did they try and hurt you?"

"Yeah," said Lyra, "but if that's all they can do, I en't worried about them."

"Oh, it isn't – oh, they do worse –"

"What? What do they do?"

But they were reluctant to tell her. They shook their heads and kept silent, until one boy said, "It en't so bad for them that's been here hundreds of years, because you get tired after all that time, they can't 'fraid you up so much –"

"It's the new ones that they like talking to most," said the first girl. "It's just... Oh, it's just hateful. They... I can't tell you."

Their voices were no louder than dry leaves falling. And it was only the children who spoke; the adults all seemed sunk in a lethargy so ancient that they might never move or speak again.

"Listen," said Lyra, "please listen. We came here, me and my friends, because we got to find a boy called Roger. He en't been here long, just a few weeks, so he won't know very many people, but if you know where he is..."

But even as she spoke she knew that they could stay here till they grew old, searching everywhere and looking at every face, and still they might never see more than a tiny fraction of the dead. She felt despair sit on her shoulders, as heavy as if the harpy herself were perching there.

However, she clenched her teeth and tried to hold her chin high. We got here, she thought; that's part of it, anyway.

The first ghost-girl was saying something in that lost little whisper.

"Why do we want to find him?" said Will. "Well, Lyra wants to speak to him. But there's someone I want to find as well. I want to find my father, John Parry. He's here too, somewhere, and I want to speak to him before I go back to the world. So please ask, if you can, ask for Roger and for John Parry to come and speak to Lyra and to Will. Ask them —"

But suddenly the ghosts all turned and fled, even the grown-ups, like dry leaves scattered by a sudden gust of wind. In a moment the space around the children was empty, and then they heard why: screams, cries, shrieks came from the air above, and then the harpies were on them, with gusts of rotten stink, battering wings, and those raucous screams, jeering, mocking, cackling, deriding.

Lyra shrank to the ground at once, covering her ears, and Will, knife in hand, crouched over her. He could see Tialys and Salmakia skimming towards them, but they were some way off yet, and he had a moment or two to watch the harpies as they wheeled and dived. He saw their human faces snap at the air as if they were eating insects, and he heard the words they were shouting — scoffing words, filthy words, all about his mother, words that shook his heart; but part of his mind was quite cold and separate, thinking, calculating, observing. None of them wanted to come anywhere near the knife.

To see what would happen, he stood up. One of them – it might have been No-Name herself – had to swerve heavily out of the way, because she'd been diving low, intending to skim just over his head. Her heavy wings beat clumsily, and she only just made the turn. He could have reached out and slashed off her head with the knife.

By this time, the Gallivespians had arrived, and the two of them were about to attack, but Will called: "Tialys! Come here! Salmakia, come to my hand!"

They landed on his shoulders, and he said, "Watch. See what they do. They only come and scream. I think it was a mistake, when she hit Lyra. I don't think they want to touch us at all. We can ignore them."

Lyra looked up, wide-eyed. The creatures flew around Will's head, sometimes only a foot or so away, but they always swerved aside or upwards at the last moment. He could sense the two spies eager for battle, and the dragonflies' wings were quivering with desire to dart through the air with their deadly riders, but they held themselves back: they could see he was right.

And it had an effect on the ghosts, too: seeing Will standing unafraid and unharmed, they began to drift back towards the travellers. They watched the harpies cautiously, but for all that, the lure of the warm flesh and blood, those strong heartbeats, was too much to resist.

Lyra stood up to join Will. Her wound had opened again, and fresh blood was trickling down her cheek, but she wiped it aside.

"Will," she said, "I'm so glad we came down here together..."

He heard a tone in her voice, and he saw an expression on her face, which he knew and liked more than anything he'd ever known: it showed she was thinking of something daring, but she wasn't ready to speak of it yet.

He nodded, to show he'd understood.

The ghost-girl said, "This way – come with us – we'll find them!"

And both of them felt the strangest sensation, as if little ghost-hands were reaching inside and tugging at their ribs to make them follow.

So they set off across the floor of that great desolate plain, and the harpies wheeled higher and higher overhead, screaming and screaming. But they kept their distance, and the Gallivespians flew above, keeping watch.

As they walked along, the ghosts talked to them.

"Excuse me," said one ghost-girl, "but where's your dæmons? Excuse me for asking. But..."

Lyra was conscious every single second of her dear abandoned Pantalaimon. She couldn't speak easily, so Will answered instead.

"We left our dæmons outside," he said, "where it's safe for them. We'll collect them later. Did you have a dæmon?"

"Yes," said the ghost; "his name was Sandling ... oh, I loved him..."

"And had he settled?" said Lyra.

"No, not yet. He used to think he'd be a bird, and I hoped he wouldn't, because I liked him all furry in bed at night. But he was a bird more and more. What's your dæmon called?"

Lyra told her, and the ghosts pressed forward eagerly again. They all wanted to talk about their dæmons, every one.

"Mine was called Matapan –"

"We used to play hide-and-seek, she'd change like a chameleon and I couldn't see her at all, she was ever so good –"

"Once I hurt my eye and I couldn't see and he guided me all the way home –"

"He never wanted to settle, but I wanted to grow up, and we used to argue –"

"She used to curl up in my hand and go to sleep –"

"Are they still there, somewhere else? Will we see them again?"

"No. When you die your dæmon just goes out like a candle flame. I seen it happen. I never saw my Castor, though – I never said goodbye –"

"They en't *nowhere*! They must be *somewhere*! My dæmon's still there somewhere, I know he is!"

The jostling ghosts were animated and eager, their eyes shining and their cheeks warm as if they were borrowing life from the travellers.

Will said, "Is there anyone here from my world, where we don't have dæmons?"

A thin ghost-boy of his own age nodded, and Will turned to him.

"Oh yes," came the answer. "We didn't understand what dæmons were, but we knew what it felt like to be without them. There's people here from all kinds of worlds."

"I knew my death," said one girl, "I knew him all the while I was growing up. When I heard them talk about dæmons, I thought they meant something like our deaths. I miss him now. I won't never see him again. *I'm over and done with*, that's the last thing he said to me, and then he went for ever. When he was with me I always knew there was someone I could trust, someone who knew where we was going and what to do. But I ain't got him no more. I don't know what's going to happen ever again."

"There ain't *nothing* going to happen!" someone else said.

"Nothing, for ever!"

"*You* don't know," said another. "*They* came, didn't they? No one ever knew *that* was going to happen."

She meant Will and Lyra.

"This is the first thing that ever happened here," said a ghost-boy. "Maybe it's all going to change now."

"What would you do, if you could?" said Lyra.

"Go up to the world again!"

"Even if it meant you could only see it once, would you still want to do that?"

"Yes! Yes! Yes!"

"Well, anyway, I've got to find Roger," said Lyra, burning with her new idea; but it was for Will to know first.

On the floor of the endless plain, there was a vast slow movement among the uncountable ghosts. The children couldn't see it, but Tialys and Salmakia, flying above, watched the little pale figures all moving with an effect that looked like the migration of immense flocks of birds or herds of reindeer. At the centre of the movement were the two children who were not ghosts, moving steadily on; not leading, and not following, but somehow focusing the movement into an intention of all the dead.

The spies, their thoughts moving even more quickly than their darting steeds, exchanged a glance and brought the dragonflies to rest side by side on a dry withered branch.

"Do *we* have dæmons, Tialys?" said the lady.

"Since we got into that boat I have felt as if my heart had been torn out and thrown still beating on the shore," he said. "But it wasn't; it's still working in my breast. So something of mine is out there with the little girl's dæmon, and something of yours too, Salmakia, because your face is drawn and your hands are pale and tight. Yes, we have dæmons, whatever they are. Maybe the people in Lyra's world are the only living beings to know they have. Maybe that's why it was one of them who started the revolt."

He slipped off the dragonfly's back and tethered it safely, and then took out the lodestone resonator. But he had hardly begun to touch it when he stopped.

"No response," he said sombrely.

"So we're beyond everything?"

"Beyond help, certainly. Well, we knew we were coming to the land of the dead."

"The boy would go with her to the end of the world."

"Will his knife open the way back, do you think?"

"I'm sure he thinks so. But oh, Tialys, I don't know."

"He's very young. Well, they are both young. You know, if she doesn't survive this, the question of whether she'll choose the right thing when she's tempted won't arise. It won't matter any more."

"Do you think she's chosen already? When she chose to leave her dæmon on the shore? Was that the choice she had to make?"

The chevalier looked down on the slow-moving millions on the floor of the land of the dead, all drifting after that bright and living spark Lyra Silvertongue. He could just make out her hair, the lightest thing in the gloom, and beside it the boy's head, black-haired and solid and strong.

"No," he said, "not yet. That's still to come, whatever it may be."

"Then we must bring her to it safely."

"Bring them both. They're bound together now."

The Lady Salmakia flicked the cobweb-light rein, and her dragonfly darted off the branch at once, and sped down towards the living children, with the chevalier close behind.

But they didn't stop with them; having skimmed low to make sure they were all right, they flew on ahead, partly because the dragonflies were restless, and partly because they wanted to find out how far this dismal place extended.

Lyra saw them flashing overhead and felt a pang of relief that there was still something that darted and glowed with beauty. Then, unable to keep her idea to herself any more, she turned to Will; but she had to whisper. She put her lips to his ear, and in a noisy rush of warmth he heard her say:

"Will, I want us to take *all* these poor dead ghost-kids outside – the grown-ups as well – we could set 'em free! We'll find Roger and your father, and then let's open the way to the world outside, and set 'em all free!"

He turned and gave her a true smile, so warm and happy she felt something stumble and falter inside her; at least, it felt like that, but without Pantalaimon she couldn't ask herself what it meant. It might have been a new way for her heart to beat. Deeply surprised, she told herself to walk straight and stop feeling giddy.

So they moved on. The whisper *Roger* was spreading out faster than they could move; the words "Roger – Lyra's come – Roger – Lyra's here –" passed from one ghost to another like the electric message that one cell in the body passes on to the next.

And Tialys and Salmakia, cruising above on their tireless dragonflies, and looking all around as they flew, eventually noticed a new kind of movement. Some way off there was a little gyration of activity. Skimming down closer they found themselves ignored, for the first time, because something more interesting was gripping the minds of all the ghosts. They were talking excitedly in their near-silent whispers, they were pointing, they were urging someone forward.

Salmakia flew down low, but couldn't land: the press was too great, and none of their hands or shoulders would support her, even if they dared to try. She saw a young ghost-boy with an honest unhappy face, dazed and puzzled by what he was being told, and she called out:

"Roger? Is that Roger?"

He looked up, bemused, nervous, and nodded.

Salmakia flew back up to her companion, and together they sped back to Lyra. It was a long way, and hard to navigate, but by watching the patterns of movement, they finally found her.

"There she is," said Tialys, and called: "Lyra! Lyra! Your friend is there!"

Lyra looked up and held out her hand for the dragonfly. The great insect landed at once, its red and yellow gleaming like enamel, and its filmy wings stiff and still on either side. Tialys kept his balance as she held him at eye-level.

"Where?" she said, breathless with excitement. "Is he far off?"

"An hour's walk," said the chevalier. "But he knows you're coming. The others have told him, and we made sure it was him. Just keep going, and soon you'll find him."

Tialys saw Will make the effort to stand up straight and force himself to find some more energy. Lyra was charged with it already, and plied the Gallivespians with questions: how did Roger seem? Had he spoken to them? Did he seem glad? Were the other children aware of what was happening, and were they helping, or were they just in the way?

And so on. Tialys tried to answer everything truthfully and patiently, and step by step the living girl drew closer to the boy she had brought to his death.

23
No Way Out

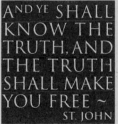

AND YE SHALL KNOW THE TRUTH, AND THE TRUTH SHALL MAKE YOU FREE ~ ST. JOHN

"Will," said Lyra, "what d'you think the harpies will do when we let the ghosts out?"

Because the creatures were getting louder and flying closer, and there were more and more of them all the time, as if the gloom were gathering itself into little clots of malice and giving them wings. The ghosts kept looking up fearfully.

"Are we getting close?" Lyra called to the Lady Salmakia.

"Not far now," she called down, hovering above them. "You could see him, if you climbed that rock."

But Lyra didn't want to waste time. She was trying with all her heart to put on a cheerful face for Roger, but in front of her mind's eye every moment was that terrible image of the little dog-Pan abandoned on the jetty as the mist closed around him, and she could barely keep from howling. She must, though; she must be hopeful for Roger; she always had been.

When they did come face to face, it happened quite suddenly. In among the press of all the ghosts, there he was, his familiar features wan but his expression as full of delight as a ghost could be. He rushed to embrace her.

But he passed like cold smoke through her arms, and though she felt his little hand clutch at her heart, it had no strength to hold on. They could never truly touch again.

But he could whisper, and his voice said, "Lyra, I never thought I'd ever see you again – I thought even if you did come down here when you was dead, you'd be much older, you'd be grown up, and you wouldn't want to speak to me –"

"Why ever not?"

"Because I done the wrong thing when Pan got my dæmon away from Lord Asriel's! We should've run, we shouldn't have tried to fight her! We should've run to you! Then she wouldn't have been able to get my dæmon again and when the cliff fell away she'd've still been with me!"

"But that weren't *your* fault, stupid!" Lyra said. "It was me that brung you there in the first place, and I should've let you go back with the other kids and the gyptians. It was my fault. I'm so sorry, Roger, honest, it was *my* fault, you wouldn't've been here otherwise…"

"Well," he said, "I dunno. Maybe I would've got dead some other way. But it weren't your *fault*, Lyra, see."

She felt herself beginning to believe it; but all the same, it was heart-rending to see the poor little cold thing, so close and yet so out of reach. She tried to grasp his wrist, though her fingers closed in the empty air; but he understood, and sat down beside her.

The other ghosts withdrew a little, leaving them alone, and Will moved apart too, to sit down and nurse his hand. It was bleeding again, and while Tialys flew fiercely at the ghosts to force them away, Salmakia helped Will tend to the wound.

But Lyra and Roger were oblivious to that.

"And you en't dead," he said. "How'd you come here if you're still alive? And where's Pan?"

"Oh, Roger — I had to leave him on the shore — it was the worst thing I ever had to do, it hurt so much — you know how it hurts — and he just stood there, just looking, oh, I felt like a murderer, Roger — but I *had* to, or else I couldn't have come!"

"I been pretending to talk to you all the time since I died," he said. "I been wishing I could, and wishing so hard... Just wishing I could get out, me and all the other dead 'uns, cause this is a terrible place, Lyra, it's hopeless, there's no change when you're dead, and them bird-things... You know what they do? They wait till you're resting — you can't never sleep properly, you just sort of doze — and they come up quiet beside you and they whisper all the bad things you ever did when you was alive, so you can't forget 'em. They know all the worst things about you. They know how to make you feel horrible, just thinking of all the stupid things and bad things you ever did. And all the greedy and unkind thoughts you ever had, they know 'em all, and they shame you up and they make you feel sick with yourself... But you can't get away from 'em."

"Well," she said, "listen."

Dropping her voice and leaning closer to the little ghost, just as she used to do when they were planning mischief at Jordan, she went on:

"You probably don't know, but the witches — you remember Serafina Pekkala — the witches've got a prophecy about me. They don't know I know — no one does. I never spoke to anyone about it before. But when I was in Trollesund, and Farder Coram the gyptian took me to see the witches' consul, Dr Lanselius, he gave me like a kind of a test. He said I had to go outside and pick out the right piece of cloud-pine out of all the others to show I could really read the alethiometer.

"Well, I done that, and then I came in quickly, because it was cold and it only took a second, it was easy. The consul was talking to Farder Coram, and they didn't know I could hear 'em. He said the witches had this prophecy about me, I was going to do something great and important, and it was going to be in another world...

"Only I never spoke of it, and I reckon I must have even forgot it, there was so much else going on. So it sort of sunk out of my mind. I never even talked about it with Pan, 'cause he would have laughed, I reckon.

"But then later on Mrs Coulter caught me and she kept me in a trance, and I was dreaming and I dreamed of that, and I dreamed of you. And I remembered the gyptian boat-mother, Ma Costa – you remember – it was their boat we got on board of, in Jericho, with Simon and Hugh and them –"

"Yes! And we nearly sailed it to Abingdon! That was the best thing we ever done, Lyra! I won't never forget that, even if I'm down here dead for a thousand years –"

"Yes, but *listen* – when I ran away from Mrs Coulter the first time, right, I found the gyptians again and they looked after me and... Oh, Roger, there's so *much* I found out, you'd be amazed – but this is the important thing: Ma Costa said to me, she said I'd got witch-oil in my soul, she said the gyptians were water people but I was a fire person.

"And what I think that means is she was sort of preparing me for the witch-prophecy. I *know* I got something important to do, and Dr Lanselius the consul said it was vital I never found out what my destiny was till it happened, see – I must never *ask* about it... So I never did. I never even thought what it might be. I never asked the alethiometer, even.

"But *now* I think I know. And finding you again is just a sort of proof. What I got to do, Roger, what my destiny is, is

I got to help all the ghosts out of the land of the dead for ever. Me and Will – we got to rescue you all. I'm sure it's that. It must be. And because Lord Asriel, because of something my father said... *Death is going to die*, he said. I dunno what'll happen, though. You mustn't tell 'em yet, promise. I mean you might not *last* up there. But –"

He was desperate to speak, so she stopped.

"That's *just* what I wanted to tell you!" he said. "I told 'em, all the other dead 'uns, I *told* them you'd come! Just like you came and rescued the kids from Bolvangar! I says, Lyra'll do it, if anyone can. They wished it'd be true, they wanted to believe me, but they never really did, I could tell.

"For one thing," he went on, "every kid that's ever come here, every single one, starts by saying I bet my dad'll come and get me, or I bet my mum, as soon as she knows where I am, she'll fetch me home again. If it en't their dad or mum it's their friends, or their grandpa, but *someone*'s going to come and rescue 'em. Only they never do. So no one believed me when I told 'em you'd come. Only I was right!"

"Yeah," she said, "well, I couldn't have done it without Will. That's Will over there, and that's the Chevalier Tialys and the Lady Salmakia. There's so *much* to tell you, Roger..."

"Who's Will? Where's he come from?"

Lyra began to explain, quite unaware of how her voice changed, how she sat up straighter, and how even her eyes looked different when she told the story of her meeting with Will and the fight for the subtle knife. How could she have known? But Roger noticed, with the sad voiceless envy of the unchanging dead.

Meanwhile, Will and the Gallivespians were a little way off, talking quietly.

"What are you going to do, you and the girl?" said Tialys.

"Open this world and let the ghosts out. That's what I've got the knife for."

He had never seen such astonishment on any faces, let alone those of people whose good opinion he valued. He'd acquired a great respect for these two. They sat silent for a few moments, and then Tialys said:

"This will undo everything. It's the greatest blow you could strike. The Authority will be powerless after this."

"How would they ever suspect it?" said the lady. "It'll come at them out of nowhere!"

"And what then?" Tialys asked Will.

"What then? Well, then we'll have to get out ourselves, and find our dæmons, I suppose. Don't think of *then*. It's enough to think of now. I haven't said anything to the ghosts, in case ... in case it doesn't work. So don't you say anything either. Now I'm going to find a world I can open, and those harpies are watching. So if you want to help, you can go and distract them while I do that."

Instantly the Gallivespians urged their dragonflies up into the murk overhead, where the harpies were as thick as blowflies. Will watched the great insects charging fearlessly up at them, for all the world as if the harpies were flies and they could snap them up in their jaws, big as they were. He thought how much the brilliant creatures would love it when the sky was open and they could skim about over bright water again.

Then he took up the knife. And instantly there came back the words the harpies had thrown at him – taunts about his mother – and he stopped. He put the knife down, trying to clear his mind.

He tried again, with the same result. He could hear them clamouring above, despite the ferocity of the Gallivespians;

there were so many of them that two flyers alone could do little to stop them.

Well, this was what it was going to be like. It wasn't going to get any easier. So Will let his mind relax and become disengaged, and just sat there with the knife held loosely until he was ready again.

This time the knife cut straight into the air – and met rock. He had opened a window in this world into the underground of another. He closed it up, and tried again.

And the same thing happened, though he knew it was a different world. He'd opened windows before to find himself above the ground of another world, so he shouldn't have been surprised to find he was underground for a change, but it was disconcerting.

Next time he felt carefully in the way he'd learned, letting the tip search for the resonance that revealed a world where the ground was in the same place. But the touch was wrong wherever he felt. There was no world anywhere he could open into; everywhere he touched, it was solid rock.

Lyra had sensed that something was wrong, and she jumped up from her close conversation with Roger's ghost to hurry to Will's side.

"What is it?" she said quietly.

He told her, and added, "We're going to have to move somewhere else before I can find a world we can open into. And those harpies aren't going to let us. Have you told the ghosts what we were planning?"

"No. Only Roger, and I told him to keep it quiet. He'll do whatever I tell him. Oh, Will, I'm scared, I'm so scared. We might not ever get out. Suppose we get stuck here for ever?"

"The knife can cut through rock. If we need to, we'll just

cut a tunnel. It'll take a long time and I hope we won't have to, but we could. Don't worry."

"Yeah. You're right. Course we could."

But she thought he looked so ill, with his face drawn in pain and with dark rings around his eyes, and his hand was shaking, and his fingers were bleeding again; he looked as sick as she felt. They couldn't go on much longer without their dæmons. She felt her own ghost quail in her body, and hugged her arms tightly, aching for Pan.

But meanwhile the ghosts were pressing close, poor things, and the children especially couldn't leave Lyra alone.

"Please," said one girl, "you won't forget us when you go back, will you?"

"No," said Lyra, "never."

"You'll tell them about us?"

"I promise. What's your name?"

But the poor girl was embarrassed and ashamed: she'd forgotten. She turned away, hiding her face, and a boy said:

"It's better to forget, I reckon. I've forgotten mine. Some en't been here long, and they still know who they are. There's some kids been here thousands of years. They're no older than us, and they've forgotten a whole lot. Except the sunshine. No one forgets that. And the wind."

"Yeah," said another, "tell us about that!"

And more and more of them clamoured for Lyra to tell them about the things they remembered, the sun and the wind and the sky, and the things they'd forgotten, such as how to play; and she turned to Will and whispered, "What should I do, Will?"

"Tell them."

"I'm scared. After what happened back there – the harpies –"

"Tell them the truth. We'll keep the harpies off."

She looked at him doubtfully. In fact, she felt sick with apprehension. She turned back to the ghosts, who were thronging closer and closer.

"Please!" they were whispering. "You've just come from the world! Tell us, tell us! Tell us about the world!"

There was a tree not far away – just a dead trunk with its bone-white branches thrusting into the chilly grey air – and because Lyra was feeling weak, and because she didn't think she could walk and talk at the same time, she made for that so as to have somewhere to sit. The crowd of ghosts jostled and shuffled aside to make room.

When they were nearly at the tree, Tialys landed on Will's hand and indicated that Will should bend his head to listen.

"They're coming back," he said quietly, "those harpies. More and more of them. Have your knife ready. The lady and I will hold them off as long as we can, but you might need to fight."

Without worrying Lyra, Will loosened the knife in its sheath and kept his hand close to it. Tialys took off again, and then Lyra reached the tree and sat down on one of the thick roots.

So many dead figures clustered around, pressing hopefully, wide-eyed, that Will had to make them keep back and leave room; but he let Roger stay close, because he was gazing at Lyra, listening with a passion.

And Lyra began to talk about the world she knew.

She told them the story of how she and Roger had climbed over Jordan College roof and found the rook with the broken leg, and how they had looked after it until it was ready to fly again; and how they had explored the wine cellars, all thick with dust and cobwebs, and drunk some canary, or it might have been Tokay, she couldn't tell, and how drunk they had been. And Roger's ghost listened, proud and desperate, nodding and whispering, "Yes, yes! That's just what happened, that's true, all right!"

Then she told them all about the great battle between the Oxford townies and the clay-burners.

First she described the Claybeds, making sure she got in everything she could remember, the wide ochre-coloured washing pits, the dragline, the kilns like great brick beehives. She told them about the willow trees along the river's edge, with their leaves all silvery underneath; and she told how when the sun shone for more than a couple of days, the clay began to split up into great handsome plates, with deep cracks between, and how it felt to squish your fingers into the cracks and slowly lever up a dried plate of mud, trying to keep it as big as you could without breaking it. Underneath it was still wet, ideal for throwing at people.

And she described the smells around the place: the smoke from the kilns, the rotten-leaf-mould smell of the river when the wind was in the south-west, the warm smell of the baking potatoes the clay-burners used to eat; and the sound of the water slipping slickly over the sluices and into the washing-pits; and the slow thick suck as you tried to pull your foot out of the ground; and the heavy wet slap of the gate-paddles in the clay-thick water.

As she spoke, playing on all their senses, the ghosts crowded closer, feeding on her words, remembering the time when they had flesh and skin and nerves and senses, and willing her never to stop.

Then she told how the clay-burners' children always made war on the townies, but how they were slow and dull, with clay in their brains, and how the townies were as sharp and quick as sparrows by contrast; and how one day all the townies had swallowed their differences and plotted and planned and attacked the Claybeds from three sides, pinning the clay-burners' children back against the river, hurling handfuls and handfuls of heavy claggy clay at one another, rushing their muddy castle and tearing it down, turning the fortifications into missiles until the air and the ground and the water were all mixed inextricably together, and every child looked exactly the same, mud from scalp to sole, and none of them had had a better day in all their lives.

When she'd finished, she looked at Will, exhausted. Then she had a shock.

As well as the ghosts, silent all around, and her companions, close and living, there was another audience too; because the branches of the tree were clustered with those dark bird-forms, their women's faces gazing down at her, solemn and spellbound.

She stood up in sudden fear, but they didn't move.

"You," she said, desperate, "you flew at me before, when I tried to tell you something. What's stopping you now? Go on, tear at me with your claws and make a ghost out of me!"

"That is the least we shall do," said the harpy in the centre, who was No-Name herself. "Listen to me. Thousands of years ago, when the first ghosts came down here, the Authority gave us the power to see the worst in every one, and we have fed on the worst ever since, till our blood is rank with it and our very hearts are sickened.

"But still, it was all we had to feed on. It was all we had. And now we learn that you are planning to open a way to the upper world and lead all the ghosts out into the air –"

And her harsh voice was drowned by a million whispers, as every ghost who could hear cried out in joy and hope; but all the harpies screamed and beat their wings until the ghosts fell silent again.

"Yes," cried No-Name, "to lead them out! What will we do now? I shall tell you what we will do: from now on, we shall hold nothing back. We shall hurt and defile and tear and rend every ghost that comes through, and we shall send them mad with fear and remorse and self-hatred. This is a wasteland now; we shall make it a hell!"

Every single harpy shrieked and jeered, and many of them flew up off the tree and straight at the ghosts, making them scatter in terror. Lyra clung to Will's arm and said, "They've given it away now, and we can't do it – they'll hate us – they'll think we betrayed them! We've made it worse, not better!"

"Quiet," said Tialys. "Don't despair. Call them back and make them listen to us."

So Will cried out, "Come back! Come back, every one of you! Come back and listen!"

One by one the harpies, their faces eager and hungry and suffused with the lust for misery, turned and flew back to the tree, and the ghosts drifted back as well. The chevalier left his dragonfly in the care of Salmakia, and his little tense figure, green-clad and dark-haired, leapt to a rock where they could all see him.

"Harpies," he said, "we can offer you something better than that. Answer my questions truly, and hear what I say, and then judge. When Lyra spoke to you outside the wall, you flew at her. Why did you do that?"

"Lies!" the harpies all cried. "Lies and fantasies!"

"Yet when she spoke just now, you all listened, every one of you, and you kept silent and still. Again, why was that?"

"Because it was true," said No-Name. "Because she spoke the truth. Because it was nourishing. Because it was feeding us. Because we couldn't help it. Because it was true. Because we had no idea that there was anything but wickedness.

Because it brought us news of the world and the sun and the wind and the rain. Because it was true."

"Then," said Tialys, "let's make a bargain with you. Instead of seeing only the wickedness and cruelty and greed of the ghosts that come down here, from now on you will have the right to ask every ghost to tell you the story of their lives, and they will have to tell the truth about what they've seen and touched and heard and loved and known in the world. Every one of these ghosts has a story; every single one that comes down in the future will have true things to tell you about the world. And you'll have the right to hear them, and they will have to tell you."

Lyra marvelled at the nerve of the little spy. How did he dare speak to these creatures as if he had the power to give them rights? Any one of them could have snapped him up in a moment, wrenched him apart in her claws, or carried him high and then hurled him down to the ground to smash in pieces. And yet there he stood, proud and fearless, making a bargain with them! And they listened, and conferred, their faces turning to one another, their voices low.

All the ghosts watched, fearful and silent.

Then No-Name turned back.

"That's not enough," she said. "We want more than that. We had a *task* under the old dispensation. We had a place and a duty. We fulfilled the Authority's commands diligently, and for that we were honoured. Hated and feared, but honoured too. What will happen to our honour now? Why should the ghosts take any notice of us, if they can simply walk out into the world again? We have our pride, and you should not let that be dispensed with. We need an honourable place! We need a duty and a task to do, that will bring us the respect we deserve!"

They shifted on the branches, muttering and raising their wings. But a moment later Salmakia leapt up to join the chevalier, and called out:

"You are quite right. Everyone should have a task to do that's important, one that brings them honour, one they can perform with pride. So here is your task, and it's one that only you can do, because you are the guardians and the keepers of this place. Your task will be to guide the ghosts from the landing-place by the lake all the way through the land of the dead to the new opening out into the world. In exchange, they will tell you their stories as a fair and just payment for this guidance. Does that seem right to you?"

No-Name looked at her sisters, and they nodded. She said:

"And we have the right to refuse to guide them if they lie, or if they hold anything back, or if they have nothing to tell us. If they live in the world, they *should* see and touch and hear and love and learn things. We shall make an exception for infants who have not had time to learn anything, but otherwise, if they come down here bringing nothing, we shall not guide them out."

"That is fair," said Salmakia, and the other travellers agreed.

So they made a treaty. And in exchange for the story of Lyra's that they'd already heard, the harpies offered to take the travellers and their knife to a part of the land of the dead where the upper world was close. It was a long way off, through tunnels and caves, but they would guide them faithfully, and all the ghosts could follow.

But before they could begin, a voice cried out, as loudly as a whisper could cry. It was the ghost of a thin man with an angry, passionate face, and he cried:

"What will happen? When we leave the world of the dead,

will we live again? Or will we vanish as our dæmons did? Brothers, sisters, we shouldn't follow this child anywhere till we know what's going to happen to us!"

Others took up the question: "Yes, tell us where we're going! Tell us what to expect! We won't go unless we know what'll happen to us!"

Lyra turned to Will in despair, but he said, "Tell them the truth. Ask the alethiometer, and tell them what it says."

"All right," she said.

She took out the golden instrument. The answer came at once. She put it away and stood up.

"This is what'll happen," she said, "and it's true, perfectly true. When you go out of here, all the particles that make you up will loosen and float apart, just like your dæmons did. If you've seen people dying, you know what that looks like. But your dæmons en't just *nothing* now; they're part of every-thing. All the atoms that were them, they've gone into the air and the wind and the trees and the earth and all the living things. They'll never vanish. They're just part of everything. And that's exactly what'll happen to you, I swear to you, I promise on my honour. You'll drift apart, it's true, but you'll be out in the open, part of everything alive again."

No one spoke. Those who had seen how dæmons dissolved were remembering it, and those who hadn't were imagining it, and no one spoke until a young woman came forward. She had died as a martyr centuries before. She looked around and said:

"When we were alive, they told us that when we died we'd go to heaven. And they said that heaven was a place of joy and glory and we would spend eternity in the company of saints and angels praising the Almighty, in a state of bliss. That's what they said. And that's what led some of us to give our lives, and others to spend years in solitary prayer, while all the joy of life was going to waste around us, and we never knew.

"Because the land of the dead isn't a place of reward or a place of punishment. It's a place of nothing. The good come here as well as the wicked, and all of us languish in this gloom for ever, with no hope of freedom, or joy, or sleep or rest or peace.

"But now this child has come offering us a way out and I'm going to follow her. Even if it means oblivion, friends, I'll welcome it, because it won't be nothing, we'll be alive again in a thousand blades of grass, and a million leaves, we'll be falling in the raindrops and blowing in the fresh breeze, we'll be glittering in the dew under the stars and the moon out there in the physical world which is our true home and always was.

"So I urge you: come with the child out to the sky!"

But her ghost was thrust aside by the ghost of a man who looked like a monk: thin, and pale even in his death, with dark zealous eyes. He crossed himself and murmured a prayer, and then he said:

"This is a bitter message, a sad and cruel joke. Can't you see the truth? This is not a child. This is an agent of the Evil One himself! The world we lived in was a vale of corruption and tears. Nothing there could satisfy us. But the Almighty has granted us this blessed place for all eternity, this paradise, which to the fallen soul seems bleak and barren, but which the eyes of faith see as it is, overflowing with milk and honey and resounding with the sweet hymns of the angels. *This* is heaven, truly! What this evil girl promises is nothing but lies. She wants to lead you to hell! Go with her at your peril. My companions and I of the true faith will remain here in our blessed paradise, and spend eternity singing the praises of the

Almighty, who has given us the judgement to tell the false from the true."

Once again he crossed himself, and then he and his companions turned away in horror and loathing.

Lyra felt bewildered. Was she wrong? Was she making some great mistake? She looked around: gloom and desolation on every side. But she'd been wrong before about the appearance of things, trusting Mrs Coulter because of her beautiful smile and her sweet scented glamour. It was so easy to get things wrong; and without her dæmon to guide her, maybe she was wrong about this too.

But Will was shaking her arm. Then he put his hands to her face and held it roughly.

"You *know* that's not true," he said, "just as well as you can feel this. Take no notice! *They* can all see he's lying, too. And they're depending on us. Come on, let's make a start."

She nodded. She had to trust her body and the truth of what her senses told her; she knew Pan would have done.

So they set off, and the numberless millions of ghosts began to follow them. Behind them, too far back for the children to see, other inhabitants of the world of the dead had heard what was happening, and were coming to join the great march. Tialys and Salmakia flew back to look, and were overjoyed to see their own people there, and every other kind of conscious being who had ever been punished by the Authority with exile and death. Among them were beings who didn't look human at all, beings like the mulefa, whom Mary Malone would have recognized, and stranger ghosts as well.

But Will and Lyra had no strength to look back; all they could do was move on after the harpies, and hope.

"Have we almost done it, Will?" Lyra whispered. "Is it nearly over?"

He couldn't tell. But they were so weak and sick that he said, "Yes, it's nearly over, we've nearly done it. We'll be out soon."

24
Mrs Coulter in Geneva

AS IS THE
MOTHER,
SO IS HER
DAUGHTER·
EZEKIEL

Mrs Coulter waited till nightfall before she approached the College of St Jerome. After darkness had fallen, she brought the intention craft down through the cloud and moved slowly along the lakeshore at tree-top height. The College was a distinctive shape among the other ancient buildings of Geneva, and she soon found the spire, the dark hollow of the cloisters, the square tower where the President of the Consistorial Court of Discipline had his lodging. She had visited the College three times before; she knew that the ridges and gables and chimneys of the roof concealed plenty of hiding-places, even for something as large as the intention craft.

Flying slowly above the tiles, which glistened with the recent rain, she edged the machine into a little gully between a steep tiled roof and the sheer wall of the tower. The place was only visible from the belfry of the Chapel of the Holy Penitence nearby; it would do very well.

She lowered the aircraft delicately, letting its six feet find their own purchase and adjust themselves to keep the cabin level. She was beginning to love this machine: it sprang to her bidding as fast as she could think, and it was so silent; it could hover above someone's head closely enough for them to touch, and they'd never know it was there. In the day or so since she'd stolen it, Mrs Coulter had mastered the controls, but she still had no idea how it was powered, and that was the only thing she worried about: she had no way of telling when the fuel or the batteries would run out.

Once she was sure it had settled, and that the roof was solid enough to support it, she took off the helmet and climbed down.

Her dæmon was already prising up one of the heavy old tiles. She joined him, and soon they had lifted half a dozen out of the way, and then she snapped off the battens on which they'd been hung, making a gap big enough to get through.

"Go in and look around," she whispered, and the dæmon dropped through into the dark.

She could hear his claws as he moved carefully over the floor of the attic, and then his gold-fringed black face appeared in the opening. She understood at once, and followed him through, waiting to let her eyes adjust. In the dim light she gradually saw a long attic where the dark shapes of cupboards, tables, bookcases, furniture of all kinds had been put to store.

The first thing she did was to push a tall cupboard in front of the gap where the tiles had been. Then she tiptoed to the door in the wall at the far end, and tried the handle. It was locked, of course, but she had a hairpin, and the lock was simple. Three minutes later she and her dæmon were standing at one end of a long corridor, where a dusty skylight let them see a narrow staircase descending at the other.

And five minutes after that, they had opened a window in the pantry next to the kitchen two floors below, and climbed out into the alley. The gatehouse of the College was just around the corner, and as she said to the golden monkey, it was important to arrive in the orthodox way, no matter how they intended to leave.

"Take your hands off me," she said calmly to the guard, "and show me some courtesy, or I shall have you flayed. Tell the President that Mrs Coulter has arrived, and that she wishes to see him at once."

The man fell back, and his pinscher-dæmon, who had been baring her teeth at the mild-mannered golden monkey, instantly cowered and tucked her tail-stump as low as it would go.

The guard cranked the handle of a telephone, and under a minute later a fresh-faced young priest came hastening into the gatehouse, wiping his palms on his robe in case she wanted to shake hands. She didn't.

"Who are you?" she said.

"Brother Louis," said the man, soothing his rabbit-dæmon, "Convenor of the Secretariat of the Consistorial Court. If you would be so kind –"

"I haven't come here to parley with a scrivener," she told him. "Take me to Father MacPhail. And do it now."

The man bowed helplessly, and led her away. The guard behind her blew out his cheeks with relief.

Brother Louis, after trying two or three times to make conversation, gave up and led her in silence to the President's rooms in the tower. Father MacPhail was at his devotions, and poor Brother Louis's hand shook violently as he knocked. They heard a sigh and a groan, and then heavy footsteps crossed the floor.

The President's eyes widened as he saw who it was, and he smiled wolfishly.

"Mrs Coulter," he said, offering his hand. "I am very glad

to see you. My study is cold, and our hospitality is plain, but come in, come in."

"Good evening," she said, following him inside the bleak stone-walled room, allowing him to make a little fuss and show her to a chair. "Thank you," she said to Brother Louis, who was still hovering, "I'll take a glass of chocolatl."

Nothing had been offered, and she knew how insulting it was to treat him like a servant, but his manner was so abject that he deserved it. The President nodded, and Brother Louis had to leave and deal with it, to his great annoyance.

"Of course, you are under arrest," said the President, taking the other chair and turning up the lamp.

"Oh, why spoil our talk before we've even begun?" said Mrs Coulter. "I came here voluntarily, as soon as I could escape from Asriel's fortress. The fact is, Father President, I have a great deal of information about his forces, and about the child, and I came here to give it to you."

"The child, then. Begin with the child."

"My daughter is now twelve years old. Very soon she will approach the cusp of adolescence, and then it will be too late for any of us to prevent the catastrophe; nature and opportunity will come together like spark and tinder. Thanks to your intervention, that is now far more likely. I hope you're satisfied."

"It was your duty to bring her here into our care. Instead you chose to skulk in a mountain cave – though how a woman of your intelligence hoped to remain hidden is a mystery to me."

"There's probably a great deal that's mysterious to you, my Lord President, starting with the relations between a mother and her child. If you thought for one moment that I would release my daughter into the care – the *care!* – of a body of men with a feverish obsession with sexuality, men with dirty fingernails, reeking of ancient sweat, men whose furtive imaginations would crawl over her body like cockroaches – if you thought I would expose my child to *that*, my Lord President, you are more stupid than you take *me* for."

There was a knock on the door before he could reply, and Brother Louis came in with two glasses of chocolatl on a wooden tray. He laid the tray on the table with a nervous bow, smiling at the President in hopes of being asked to stay; but Father MacPhail nodded towards the door, and the young man left reluctantly.

"So what *were* you going to do?" said the President.

"I was going to keep her safe until the danger had passed."

"What danger would that be?" he said, handing her a glass.

"Oh, I think you know what I mean. Somewhere there is a tempter, a serpent, so to speak, and I had to keep them from meeting."

"There is a boy with her."

"Yes. And if you hadn't interfered, they would both be under my control. As it is, they could be anywhere. At least they're not with Lord Asriel."

"I have no doubt he will be looking for them. The boy has a knife of extraordinary power. They would be worth pursuing for that alone."

"I'm aware of that," said Mrs Coulter. "I managed to break it, and he managed to get it mended again."

She was smiling. Surely she didn't approve of this wretched boy?

"We know," he said shortly.

"Well, well," she said. "Fra Pavel must be getting quicker. When I knew him it would have taken him a month at least to read all that."

She sipped her chocolatl, which was thin and weak; how like these tedious priests, she thought, to take their self-righteous abstinence out on their visitors too.

"Tell me about Lord Asriel," said the President. "Tell me everything."

Mrs Coulter settled back comfortably and began to tell him – not everything, but he never thought for a moment that she would. She told him about the fortress, about the allies, about the angels, about the mines and the foundries.

Father MacPhail sat without moving a muscle, his lizard-dæmon absorbing and remembering every word.

"And how did you get here?" he asked.

"I stole a gyropter. It ran out of fuel and I had to abandon it in the countryside not far from here. The rest of the way I walked."

"Is Lord Asriel actively searching for the girl and the boy?"

"Of course."

"I assume he's after that knife. You know it has a name? The cliff-ghasts of the north call it the god-destroyer," he went on, crossing to the window and looking down over the cloisters. "That's what Asriel is aiming to do, isn't it? Destroy the Authority? There are some people who claim that God is dead already. Presumably Asriel is not one of those, if he retains the ambition to kill him."

"Well, where is God," said Mrs Coulter, "if he's alive? And why doesn't he speak any more? At the beginning of the world, God walked in the garden and spoke with Adam and Eve. Then he began to withdraw, and Moses only heard his voice. Later, in the time of Daniel, he was aged – he was the Ancient of Days. Where is he now? Is he still alive, at some inconceivable age, decrepit and demented, unable to think or act or speak and unable to die, a rotten hulk? And if that *is* his condition, wouldn't it be the most merciful thing, the truest proof of our love for God, to seek him out and give him the gift of death?"

Mrs Coulter felt a calm exhilaration as she spoke. She wondered if she'd ever get out alive; but it was intoxicating, to speak like that to this man.

"And Dust?" he said. "From the depths of heresy, what is your view of Dust?"

"I have no view of Dust," she said. "I don't know what it is. No one does."

"I see. Well, I began by reminding you that you are under arrest. I think it's time we found you somewhere to sleep. You'll be quite comfortable; no one will hurt you; but you're not going to get away. And we shall talk more tomorrow."

He rang a bell, and Brother Louis came in almost at once.

"Show Mrs Coulter to the best guest room," said the President. "And lock her in."

The best guest room was shabby and the furniture was cheap, but at least it was clean. After the lock had turned behind her, Mrs Coulter looked around at once for the microphone, and found one in the elaborate light-fitting and another under the frame of the bed. She disconnected them both, and then had a horrible surprise.

Watching her from the top of the chest of drawers behind the door was Lord Roke.

She cried out and put a hand on the wall to steady herself. The Gallivespian was sitting cross-legged, entirely at his ease, and neither she nor the golden monkey had seen him. Once the pounding of her heart had subsided, and her breathing had slowed, she said, "And when would you have done me the courtesy of letting me know you were here, my lord? Before I undressed, or afterwards?"

"Before," he said. "Tell your dæmon to calm down, or I'll disable him."

The golden monkey's teeth were bared, and all his fur was standing on end. The scorching malice of his expression was enough to make any normal person quail, but Lord Roke merely smiled. His spurs glittered in the dim light.

The little spy stood up and stretched.

"I've just spoken to my agent in Lord Asriel's fortress," he went on. "Lord Asriel presents his compliments, and asks you to let him know as soon as you find out what these people's intentions are."

She felt winded, as if Lord Asriel had thrown her hard in wrestling. Her eyes widened, and she sat down slowly on the bed.

"Did you come here to spy on me, or to help?" she said.

"Both, and it's lucky for you I'm here. As soon as you arrived, they set some anbaric work in motion down in the cellars. I don't know what it is, but there's a team of scientists working on it right now. You seem to have galvanized them."

"I don't know whether to be flattered or alarmed. As a matter of fact, I'm exhausted, and I'm going to sleep. If you're here to help me, you can keep watch. You can begin by looking the other way."

He bowed, and faced the wall until she had washed in the chipped basin, dried herself on the thin towel, and undressed and got into bed. Her dæmon patrolled the room, checking the wardrobe, the picture rail, the curtains, the view of the dark cloisters out of the window. Lord Roke watched him every inch of the way. Finally the golden monkey joined Mrs Coulter, and they fell asleep at once.

* * *

Lord Roke hadn't told her everything that he'd learned from Lord Asriel. The allies had been tracking the flight of all kinds of beings in the air above the frontiers of the republic, and had noticed a concentration of what might have been angels, and might have been something else entirely, in the west. They had sent patrols out to investigate, but so far they had learned nothing: whatever it was that hung there had wrapped itself in impenetrable fog.

The spy thought it best not to trouble Mrs Coulter with that, though; she was exhausted. Let her sleep, he decided, and he moved silently about the room, listening at the door, watching out of the window, awake and alert.

An hour after she had first come into the room, he heard a quiet noise outside the door: a faint scratch and a whisper. At the same moment, a dim light outlined the door. Lord Roke moved to the furthest corner, and stood behind one of the legs of the chair on which Mrs Coulter had thrown her clothes.

A minute went by, and then the key turned very quietly in the lock. The door opened an inch, no more, and then the light went out.

Lord Roke could see well enough in the dim glow through the thin curtains, but the intruder was having to wait for his eyes to adjust. Finally the door opened further, very slowly, and the young priest, Brother Louis, stepped in.

He crossed himself, and tiptoed to the bed. Lord Roke prepared to spring, but the priest merely listened to Mrs Coulter's steady breathing, looked closely to see whether she was asleep, and then turned to the bedside table.

He covered the bulb of the battery-light with his hand and switched it on, letting a thin gleam escape through his fingers. He peered at the table so closely that his nose nearly touched the surface, but whatever he was looking for, he didn't find it. Mrs Coulter had put a few things there before she got into bed: a couple of coins, a ring, her watch; but Brother Louis wasn't interested in those.

He turned to her again, and then he saw what he was looking for, uttering a soft hiss between his teeth. Lord Roke could see his dismay: the object of his search was the locket on the gold chain around Mrs Coulter's neck.

Lord Roke moved silently along the skirting board towards the door.

The priest crossed himself again, for he was going to have to touch her. Holding his breath, he bent over the bed – and the golden monkey stirred.

The young man froze, hands outstretched. His rabbit-dæmon trembled at his feet, no use at all: she could at least have kept watch for the poor man, Lord Roke thought. The monkey turned over in his sleep, and fell still again.

After a minute poised like a waxwork, Brother Louis lowered his shaking hands to Mrs Coulter's neck. He fumbled for so long that Lord Roke thought the dawn would break before he got the catch undone, but finally he lifted the locket gently away and stood up.

Lord Roke, as quick and as quiet as a mouse, was out of the door before the priest had turned around. He waited in the dark corridor, and when the young man tiptoed out and turned the key, the Gallivespian began to follow him.

Brother Louis made for the tower, and when the President opened his door, Lord Roke darted through and made for the prie-dieu in the corner of the room. There he found a shadowy ledge where he crouched and listened.

Father MacPhail wasn't alone: the alethiometrist, Fra Pavel, was busy with his books, and another figure stood nervously by the window. This was Dr Cooper, the experimental theologian from Bolvangar. They both looked up.

"Well done, Brother Louis," said the President. "Bring it here, sit down, show me, show me. Well done!"

Fra Pavel moved some of his books, and the young priest laid the gold chain on the table. The others bent over to look as Father MacPhail fiddled with the catch. Dr Cooper offered him a pocket knife, and then there was a soft click.

"Ah!" sighed the President.

Lord Roke climbed to the top of the desk so that he could see. In the naphtha lamplight there was a gleam of dark gold: it was a lock of hair, and the President was twisting it between his fingers, turning it this way and that.

"Are we certain this is the child's?" he said.

"I am certain," came the weary voice of Fra Pavel.

"And is there enough of it, Dr Cooper?"

The pale-faced man bent low and took the lock from Father MacPhail's fingers. He held it up to the light.

"Oh, yes," he said. "One single hair would be enough. This is ample."

"I'm very pleased to hear it," said the President. "Now, Brother Louis, you must return the locket to the good lady's neck."

The priest sagged faintly: he had hoped his task was over. The President placed the curl of Lyra's hair in an envelope and shut the locket, looking up and around as he did so, and Lord Roke had to drop out of sight.

"Father President," said Brother Louis, "I shall of course do as you command, but may I know why you need the child's hair?"

"No, Brother Louis, because it would disturb you. Leave these matters to us. Off you go."

The young man took the locket and left, smothering his resentment. Lord Roke thought of going back with him, and waking Mrs Coulter just as he was trying to replace the chain, in order to see what she'd do; but it was more important to find out what these people were up to.

As the door closed, the Gallivespian went back into the shadows and listened.

"How did you know where she had it?" said the scientist.

"Every time she mentioned the child," the President said, "her hand went to the locket. Now then, how soon can it be ready?"

"A matter of hours," said Dr Cooper.

"And the hair? What do you do with that?"

"We place the hair in the resonating chamber. You understand, each individual is unique, and the arrangement of genetic particles quite distinct... Well, as soon as it's analysed, the information is coded in a series of anbaric pulses and transferred to the aiming device. That locates the, the origin of the material, the hair, wherever she may be. It's a process that actually makes use of the Barnard-Stokes heresy, the many-worlds idea..."

"Don't alarm yourself, Doctor. Fra Pavel has told me that the child is in another world. Please go on. The force of the bomb is directed by means of the hair?"

"Yes. To each of the hairs from which these ones were cut. That's right."

"So when it's detonated, the child will be destroyed, wherever she is?"

There was a heavy indrawn breath from the scientist, and then a reluctant "Yes". He swallowed, and went on, "The power needed is enormous. The anbaric power. Just as an atomic bomb needs a high-explosive to force the uranium together and set off the chain reaction, this device needs a colossal current to release the much greater power of the severance process. I was wondering –"

"It doesn't matter where it's detonated, does it?"

"No. That is the point. Anywhere will do."

"And it's completely ready?"

"Now we have the hair, yes. But the power, you see –"

"I have seen to that. The hydro-anbaric generating station at Saint-Jean-Les-Eaux has been requisitioned for our use. They produce enough power there, wouldn't you say?"

"Yes," said the scientist.

"Then we shall set out at once. Please go and see to the apparatus, Dr Cooper. Have it ready for transportation as soon as you can. The weather changes quickly in the mountains, and there is a storm on the way."

The scientist took the little envelope containing Lyra's hair, and bowed nervously as he left. Lord Roke left with him, making no more noise than a shadow.

As soon as they were out of earshot of the President's room, the Gallivespian sprang. Dr Cooper, below him on the stairs, felt an agonizing stab in his shoulder, and grabbed for the banister: but his arm was strangely weak, and he slipped and tumbled down the whole flight, to land semi-conscious at the bottom.

Lord Roke hauled the envelope out of the man's twitching hand with some difficulty, for it was half as big as he was, and set off in the shadows towards the room where Mrs Coulter was asleep.

The gap at the foot of the door was wide enough for him

to slip through. Brother Louis had come and gone, but he hadn't dared to try and fasten the chain around Mrs Coulter's neck: it lay beside her on the pillow.

Lord Roke pressed her hand to wake her up. She was profoundly exhausted, but she focused on him at once, and sat up, rubbing her eyes.

He explained what had happened, and gave her the envelope.

"You should destroy it at once," he told her; "one single hair would be enough, the man said."

She looked at the little curl of dark blonde hair, and shook her head.

"Too late for that," she said. "This is only half the lock I cut from Lyra. He must have kept back some of it."

Lord Roke hissed with anger.

"When he looked around!" he said. "Ach – I moved to be out of his sight – he must have set it aside then…"

"And there's no way of knowing where he'll have put it," said Mrs Coulter. "Still, if we can find the bomb –"

"Sssh!"

That was the golden monkey. He was crouching by the door, listening, and then they heard it too: heavy footsteps, hurrying towards the room.

Mrs Coulter thrust the envelope and the lock of hair at Lord Roke, who took it and leapt for the top of the wardrobe. Then she lay down next to her dæmon as the key turned noisily in the door.

"Where is it? What have you done with it? How did you attack Dr Cooper?" said the President's harsh voice, as the light fell across the bed.

Mrs Coulter threw up an arm to shade her eyes, and struggled to sit up.

"You do like to keep your guests entertained," she said drowsily. "Is this a new game? What do I have to do? And who is Dr Cooper?"

The guard from the gatehouse came in with Father MacPhail, and shone a torch into the corners of the room and under the bed. The President was slightly disconcerted: Mrs Coulter's eyes were heavy with sleep, and she could hardly see in the glare from the corridor light. It was obvious that she hadn't left her bed.

"You have an accomplice," he said. "Someone has attacked a guest of the college. Who is it? Who came here with you? Where is he?"

"I haven't the faintest idea what you're talking about. And what's this...?"

Her hand, which she'd put down to help herself sit up, had found the locket on the pillow. She stopped, picked it up, looked at the President with wide-open sleepy eyes, and Lord Roke saw a superb piece of acting as she said, puzzled, "But this is my ... what's it doing here? Father MacPhail, who's been in here? Someone has taken this from around my neck. And – *where is Lyra's hair?* There was a lock of my child's hair in here. Who's taken it? Why? What's going on?"

And now she was standing, her hair disordered, passion in her voice – plainly just as bewildered as the President himself.

Father MacPhail took a step backwards, and put his hand to his head.

"Someone else must have come with you. There must be an accomplice," he said, his voice rasping at the air. "Where is he hiding?"

"I have no accomplice," she said angrily. "If there's an invisible assassin in this place, I can only imagine it's the Devil himself. I dare say he feels quite at home."

Father MacPhail said to the guard, "Take her to the cellars. Put her in chains. I know just what we can do with this woman; I should have thought of it as soon as she appeared."

She looked wildly around, and met Lord Roke's eyes for a fraction of a second, glittering in the darkness near the ceiling. He caught her expression at once, and understood exactly what she meant him to do.

25

Saint-Jean-les-Eaux

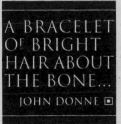

A BRACELET OF BRIGHT HAIR ABOUT THE BONE...
JOHN DONNE

*T*he cataract of Saint-Jean-les-Eaux plunged between pinnacles of rock at the eastern end of a spur of the Alps, and the generating station clung to the side of the mountain above it. It was a wild region, a bleak and battered wilderness, and no one would have built anything there at all had it not been for the promise of driving great anbaric generators with the power of the thousands of tons of water that roared through the gorge.

It was the night following Mrs Coulter's arrest, and the weather was stormy. Near the sheer stone front of the generating station, a zeppelin slowed to a hover in the buffeting wind. The search-lights below the craft made it look as if it was standing on several legs of light and gradually lowering itself to lie down.

But the pilot wasn't satisfied; the wind was swept into eddies and cross-gusts by the edges of the mountain. Besides, the cables, the pylons, the transformers were too close: to be swept in among them, with a zeppelin full of inflammable gas, would be instantly fatal. Sleet drummed slantwise at the great rigid envelope of the craft, making a noise that almost drowned the clatter and howl of the straining engines, and obscuring the view of the ground.

"Not here," the pilot shouted over the noise. "We'll go around the spur."

Father MacPhail watched fiercely as the pilot moved the throttle forward and adjusted the trim of the engines. The zeppelin rose with a lurch and moved over the rim of the mountain. Those legs of light suddenly lengthened, and seemed to feel their way down the ridge, their lower ends lost in the whirl of sleet and rain.

"You can't get closer to the station than this?" said the President, leaning forward to let his voice carry to the pilot.

"Not if you want to land," the pilot said.

"Yes, we want to land. Very well, put us down below the ridge."

The pilot gave orders for the crew to prepare to moor. As the equipment they were going to unload was heavy as well as delicate, it was important to make the craft secure. The President settled back, tapping his fingers on the arm of his seat, gnawing his lip, but saying nothing and letting the pilot work unflustered.

From his hiding-place in the transverse bulkheads at the rear of the cabin, Lord Roke watched. Several times during the flight, his little shadowy form had passed along behind the metal mesh, clearly visible to anyone who might have looked, if only they had turned their heads; but in order to hear what was happening, he had to come to a place where they could see him. The risk was unavoidable.

He edged forward, listening hard through the roar of the engines, the thunder of the hail and sleet, the high-pitched singing of the wind in the wires, and the clatter of booted feet on metal walkways. The flight engineer called some figures to the pilot, who confirmed them, and Lord Roke sank back into the shadows, holding tight to the struts and beams as the airship plunged and tilted.

Finally, sensing from the movement that the craft was nearly anchored, he made his way back through the skin of the cabin to the seats on the starboard side.

There were men passing through in both directions: crew members, technicians, priests. Many of their dæmons were dogs, too, brimming with curiosity. On the other side of the aisle, Mrs Coulter sat awake and silent, her golden dæmon watching everything from her lap and exuding malice.

Lord Roke waited for the chance and then darted across to Mrs Coulter's seat, and was up in the shadow of her shoulder in a moment.

"What are they doing?" she murmured.

"Landing. We're near the generating station."

"Are you going to stay with me, or work on your own?" she whispered.

"I'll stay with you. I'll have to hide under your coat."

She was wearing a heavy sheepskin coat, uncomfortably hot in the heated cabin, but with her hands manacled she couldn't take it off.

"Go on, now," she said, looking around, and he darted inside the breast, finding a fur-lined pocket where he could sit securely. The golden monkey tucked Mrs Coulter's silk collar inside solicitously, for all the world like a fastidious couturier attending to his favourite model, while all the time making sure that Lord Roke was completely hidden in the folds of the coat.

He was just in time. Not a minute later, a soldier armed with a rifle came to order Mrs Coulter out of the airship.

"Must I have these handcuffs on?" she said.

"I haven't been told to remove them," he replied. "On your feet, please."

"But it's hard to move if I can't hold on to things. I'm stiff – I've been sitting here for the best part of a day without moving – and you know I haven't got any weapons, because you searched me. Go and ask the President if it's really necessary to manacle me. Am I going to try and run away in this wilderness?"

Lord Roke was impervious to her charm, but interested in its effect on others. The guard was a young man: they should have sent a grizzled old warrior.

"Well," said the guard, "I'm sure you won't, ma'am, but I can't do what I en't been ordered to do. You see that, I'm sure. Please to stand up, ma'am, and if you stumble I'll catch hold of your arm."

She stood up, and Lord Roke felt her move clumsily forwards. She was the most graceful human the Gallivespian had ever seen: this clumsiness was feigned. As they reached the head of the gangway Lord Roke felt her stumble, and cry out in alarm, and felt the jar as the guard's arm caught her. He heard the change in the sounds around them, too; the howl of the wind, the engines turning over steadily to generate power for the lights, voices from somewhere nearby giving orders.

They moved down the gangway, Mrs Coulter leaning heavily on the guard. She was speaking softly, and Lord Roke could just make out his reply.

"The sergeant, ma'am – over there by the large crate – he's got the keys. But I daren't ask him, ma'am, I'm sorry."

"Oh well," she said with a pretty sigh of regret. "Thank you anyway."

Lord Roke heard booted feet moving away over rock, and then she whispered: "You heard about the keys?"

"Tell me where the sergeant is. I need to know where and how far."

"About ten of my paces away. To the right. A big man. I can see the keys in a bunch at his waist."

"No good unless I know which one. Did you see them lock the manacles?"

"Yes. A short stubby key with black tape wound around it."

Lord Roke climbed down hand over hand in the thick fleece of her coat, until he reached the hem at the level of her knees. There he clung and looked around.

They had rigged a flood-light, which cast a glare over the wet rocks. But as he looked down, casting around for shadows, he saw the glare begin to swing sideways in a gust of wind. He heard a shout, and the light went out abruptly.

He dropped to the ground at once, and sprang through the dashing sleet towards the sergeant, who had lurched forward to try and catch the falling flood-light.

In the confusion, Lord Roke leapt at the big man's leg as it swung past him, seized the camouflage cotton of the trousers – heavy and sodden with rain already – and kicked a spur into the flesh just above the boot.

The sergeant gave a grunting cry and fell clumsily, grasping his leg, trying to breathe, trying to call out. Lord Roke let go and sprang away from the falling body.

No one had noticed: the noise of the wind and the engines and the pounding hail covered the man's cry, and in the darkness his body couldn't be seen. But there were others close by, and Lord Roke had to work quickly. He leapt to the fallen man's side, where the bunch of keys lay in a pool of icy water, and hauled aside the great shafts of steel, as big around as his arm and half as long as he was, till he found the one with the black tape. And then there was the clasp of the key-ring to wrestle with, and the perpetual risk of the hail, which for a Gallivespian was deadly: blocks of ice as big as his two fists.

And then a voice above him said, "You all right, Sergeant?"

The soldier's dæmon was growling and nuzzling at the sergeant's, who had fallen into a semi-stupor. Lord Roke couldn't wait: a spring and a kick, and the other man fell beside the sergeant.

Hauling, wrestling, heaving, Lord Roke finally snapped open the key-ring, and then he had to lift six other keys out of the way before the black-taped one was free. Any second now they'd get the light back on, but even in the half-dark they could hardly miss two men lying unconscious –

And as he hoisted the key out, a shout went up. He hauled up the massive shaft with all the strength he had, tugging, heaving, lifting, crawling, dragging, and hid beside a small boulder just as pounding feet arrived and voices called for light.

"Shot?"

"Didn't hear a thing –"

"Are they breathing?"

Then the flood-light, secure again, snapped on once more. Lord Roke was caught in the open, as clear as a fox in the headlights of a car. He stood stock still, his eyes moving to left and right, and once he was sure that everyone's attention was on the two men who had fallen so mysteriously, he hauled the key to his shoulder and ran around the puddles and the boulders until he reached Mrs Coulter.

A second later she had unlocked the handcuffs and lowered them silently to the ground. Lord Roke leapt for the hem of her coat and ran up to her shoulder.

"Where's the bomb?" he said, close to her ear.

"They've just begun to unload it. It's the big crate on the ground over there. I can't do anything till they take it out, and even then –"

"All right," he said, "run. Hide yourself. I'll stay here and watch. Run!"

He leapt down to her sleeve, and sprang away. Without a sound she moved away from the light, slowly at first so as not to catch the eye of the guard, and then she crouched and ran into the rain-lashed darkness further up the slope, the golden monkey darting ahead to see the way.

Behind her she heard the continuing roar of the engines, the confused shouts, the powerful voice of the President trying to impose some order on the scene. She remembered the long horrible pain and hallucination that she'd suffered at the spur of the Chevalier Tialys, and didn't envy the two men their waking up.

But soon she was higher up, clambering over the wet rocks, and all she could see behind her was the wavering glow of the flood-light reflected back from the great curved belly of the zeppelin; and presently that went out again, and all she could hear was the engine-roar, straining vainly against the wind and the thunder of the cataract below.

The engineers from the hydro-anbaric station were struggling over the edge of the gorge to bring a power cable to the bomb.

The problem for Mrs Coulter was not how to get out of this situation alive: that was a secondary matter. The problem was how to get Lyra's hair out of the bomb before they set it off. Lord Roke had burned the hair from the envelope after her arrest, letting the wind take the ashes away into the night sky; and then he'd found his way to the laboratory, and watched as they placed the rest of the little dark-golden curl in the resonating chamber in preparation. He knew exactly where it was, and how to open the chamber, but the brilliant light and the glittering surfaces in the laboratory, not to mention the constant coming and going of technicians, made it impossible for him to do anything about it there.

So they'd have to remove the lock of hair after the bomb was set up.

And that was going to be even harder, because of what the President intended to do with Mrs Coulter. The energy of the bomb came from cutting the link between human and dæmon, and that meant the hideous process of intercision: the cages of mesh, the silver guillotine. He was going to sever the lifelong connection between her and the golden monkey, and use the power released by that to destroy her daughter. She and Lyra would perish by the means she herself had invented. It was neat, at least, she thought.

Her only hope was Lord Roke. But in their whispered exchanges in the zeppelin, he'd explained about the power of his poison spurs: he couldn't go on using them continually, because with each sting, the venom weakened. It took a day for the full potency to build up again. Before long his main weapon would lose its force, and then they'd only have their wits.

She found an overhanging rock next to the roots of a spruce tree which clung to the side of the gorge, and settled herself beneath it to look around.

Behind her and above, over the lip of the ravine and in the full force of the wind, stood the generating station. The engineers were rigging a series of lights to help them bring the cable to the bomb: she could hear their voices not far away, shouting commands, and see the lights wavering through the trees. The cable itself, as thick as a man's arm, was being hauled from a gigantic reel on a truck at the top of the slope, and at the rate they were edging their way down over the rocks, they'd reach the bomb in five minutes or less.

At the zeppelin, Father MacPhail had rallied the soldiers. Several men stood guard, looking out into the sleet-filled dark with rifles at the ready, while others opened the wooden crate containing the bomb and made it ready for the cable. Mrs Coulter could see it clearly in the wash of the flood-lights, streaming with rain, an ungainly mass of machinery and wiring slightly tilted on the rocky ground. She heard a high-tension crackle and hum from the lights, whose cables swung in the wind, scattering the rain and throwing shadows up over the rocks and down again, like a grotesque skipping-rope.

Mrs Coulter was horribly familiar with one part of the structure: the mesh cages, the silver blade above. They stood at one end of the apparatus. The rest of it was strange to her; she could see no principle behind the coils, the jars, the banks of insulators, the lattice of tubing. Nevertheless, somewhere in all that complexity was the little lock of hair on which everything depended.

To her left, the slope fell away into the dark, and far below was a glimmer of white and a thunder of water from the cataract of Saint-Jean-Les-Eaux.

There came a cry. A soldier dropped his rifle and stumbled forwards, to fall to the ground kicking and thrashing and groaning with pain. In response the President looked up to the sky, put his hands to his mouth, and uttered a piercing yell.

What was he doing?

A moment later Mrs Coulter found out. Of all unlikely

things, a witch flew down and landed beside the President as
he shouted above the wind:

"Search nearby! There is a creature of some kind helping
the woman. It's attacked several of my men already. You can
see through the dark. Find it and kill it!"

"There is something coming," said the witch, in a tone
that carried clearly to Mrs Coulter's shelter. "I can see it in
the north."

"Never mind that. Find the creature and destroy it," said
the President. "It can't be far away. And look for the woman
too. Go!"

The witch sprang into the air again.

Suddenly the monkey seized Mrs Coulter's hand, and
pointed.

There was Lord Roke, lying in the open on a patch of
moss. How could they not have seen him? But something had
happened, for he wasn't moving.

"Go and bring him back," she said, and the monkey,
crouching low, darted from one rock to another, making for
the little patch of green among the rocks. His golden fur was
soon darkened by the rain and plastered close to his body,
making him smaller and less easy to see, but all the same he
was horribly conspicuous.

Father MacPhail, meanwhile, had turned to the bomb
again. The engineers from the generating station had brought
their cable right down to it, and the technicians were busy
securing the clamps and making ready the terminals.

Mrs Coulter wondered what he intended to do, now that
his victim had escaped. Then the President turned to look
over his shoulder, and she saw his expression. It was so fixed
and intense that he looked more like a mask than a man. His
lips were moving in prayer, his eyes were turned up wide

open as the rain beat into them, and altogether he looked like some gloomy Spanish painting of a saint in the ecstasy of martyrdom. Mrs Coulter felt a sudden bolt of fear, because she knew exactly what he intended: he was going to sacrifice himself. The bomb would work whether or not she was part of it.

Darting from rock to rock, the golden monkey reached Lord Roke.

"My left leg is broken," said the Gallivespian calmly. "The last man stepped on me. Listen carefully –"

As the monkey lifted him away from the lights, Lord Roke explained exactly where the resonating chamber was, and how to open it. They were practically under the eyes of the soldiers, but step by step, from shadow to shadow, the dæmon crept with his little burden.

Mrs Coulter, watching and biting her lip, heard a rush of air and felt a heavy knock – not to her body, but to the tree. An arrow stuck there quivering less than a hand's breadth from her left arm. At once she rolled away, before the witch could shoot another, and tumbled down the slope towards the monkey.

And then everything was happening at once, too quickly: there was a burst of gunfire, and a cloud of acrid smoke billowed across the slope, though she saw no flames. The golden monkey, seeing Mrs Coulter attacked, set Lord Roke down and sprang to her defence, just as the witch flew down, knife at the ready. Lord Roke pushed himself back against the nearest rock, and Mrs Coulter grappled directly with the witch. They wrestled furiously among the rocks, while the golden monkey set about tearing all the needles from the witch's cloud-pine branch.

Meanwhile, the President was thrusting his lizard-dæmon

into the smaller of the silver mesh cages. She writhed and screamed and kicked and bit, but he struck her off his hand and slammed the door shut quickly. The technicians were making the final adjustments, checking their meters and gauges.

Out of nowhere a seagull flew down with a wild cry, and seized the Gallivespian in his claw. It was the witch's dæmon. Lord Roke fought hard, but the bird had him too tightly, and then the witch tore herself from Mrs Coulter's grasp, snatched the tattered pine branch, and leapt into the air to join her dæmon.

Mrs Coulter hurled herself towards the bomb, feeling the smoke attack her nose and throat like claws: tear-gas. The soldiers, most of them, had fallen or stumbled away choking (and where had the gas come from, she wondered?), but now, as the wind dispersed it, they were beginning to gather themselves again. The great ribbed belly of the zeppelin bulked over the bomb, straining at its cables in the wind, its silver sides running with moisture.

But then a sound from high above made Mrs Coulter's ears ring: a scream so high and horrified that even the golden monkey clutched her in fear. And a second later, pitching down in a swirl of white limbs, black silk, and green twigs, the witch fell right at the feet of Father MacPhail, her bones crunching audibly on the rock.

Mrs Coulter darted forward to see if Lord Roke had survived the fall. But the Gallivespian was dead. His right spur was deep in the witch's neck.

The witch herself was still just alive, and her mouth moved shudderingly, saying, "Something coming – something else – coming –"

It made no sense. The President was already stepping over

her body to reach the larger cage. His dæmon was running up and down the sides of the other, her little claws making the silver mesh ring, her voice crying for pity.

The golden monkey leapt for Father MacPhail, but not to attack: he scrambled up and over the man's shoulders to reach the complex heart of the wires and the pipework, the resonating chamber. The President tried to grab him, but Mrs Coulter seized the man's arm and tried to pull him back. She couldn't see: the rain was driving into her eyes, and there was still gas in the air.

And all around there was gunfire: what was happening?

The flood-lights swung in the wind so that nothing seemed steady, not even the black rocks of the mountainside. The President and Mrs Coulter fought hand-to-hand, scratching, punching, tearing, pulling, biting, and she was tired and he was strong; but she was desperate too, and she might have pulled him away, but part of her was watching her dæmon as he manipulated the handles, his fierce black paws snapping the mechanism this way, that way, pulling, twisting, reaching in –

Then came a blow to her temple. She fell stunned, and the President broke free and hauled himself bleeding into the cage, dragging the door shut after him.

And the monkey had the chamber open – a glass door on heavy hinges, and he was reaching inside – there was the lock of hair: held between rubber pads in a metal clasp! Still more to undo; and Mrs Coulter was hauling herself up with shaking hands. She shook the silvery mesh with all her might, looking up at the blade, the sparking terminals, the man inside. The monkey was unscrewing the clasp, and the President, his face a mask of grim exultation, was twisting wires together.

There was a flash of intense white, a lashing *crack*, and the monkey's form was flung high in the air. With him came a little cloud of gold: was it Lyra's hair? Was it his own fur? Whatever it was, it blew away at once in the dark. Mrs Coulter's right hand had convulsed so tightly that it clung to the mesh, leaving her half-lying, half-hanging, while her head rang and her heart pounded.

But something had happened to her sight. A terrible clarity had come over her eyes, the power to see the most tiny details, and they were focused on the one detail in the universe that mattered: stuck to one of the pads of the clasp in the resonating chamber, there was a single dark-gold hair.

She cried a great wail of anguish, and shook and shook the cage, trying to loosen the hair with the little strength she had left. The President passed his hands over his face, wiping it clear of the rain. His mouth moved as though he were speaking, but she couldn't hear a word. She tore at the mesh, helpless, and then hurled her whole weight against the machine as he brought two wires together with a spark. In utter silence the brilliant silver blade shot down.

Something exploded, somewhere, but Mrs Coulter was beyond feeling it.

There were hands lifting her up: Lord Asriel's hands. There was nothing to be surprised at any more; the intention craft stood behind him, poised on the slope and perfectly level. He lifted her in his arms and carried her to the craft, ignoring the gunfire, the billowing smoke, the cries of alarm and confusion.

"Is he dead? Did it go off?" she managed to say.

Lord Asriel climbed in beside her, and the snow leopard leapt in too, the half-stunned monkey in her mouth. Lord Asriel took the controls and the craft sprang at once into the air. Through pain-dazed eyes Mrs Coulter looked down at the mountain slope. Men were running here and there like ants; some lay dead, while others crawled brokenly over the rocks; the great cable from the generating station snaked down through the chaos, the only purposeful thing in sight, making its way to the glittering bomb where the President's body lay crumpled inside the cage.

"Lord Roke?" said Lord Asriel.

"Dead," she whispered.

He pressed a button, and a lance of flame jetted towards the tossing, swaying zeppelin. An instant later the whole airship bloomed into a rose of white fire, engulfing the intention craft, which hung motionless and unharmed in the middle of it. Lord Asriel moved the craft unhurriedly away, and they watched as the blazing zeppelin fell slowly, slowly down on top of the whole scene, bomb, cable, soldiers and all, and everything began to tumble in a welter of smoke and flames down the mountainside, gathering speed and incinerating the resinous trees as it went, until it plunged into the white waters of the cataract, which whirled it all away into the dark.

Lord Asriel touched the controls again, and the intention craft began to speed away northwards. But Mrs Coulter couldn't take her eyes off the scene; she watched behind them for a long time, gazing with tear-filled eyes at the fire, until it was no more than a vertical line of orange scratched on the dark and wreathed in smoke and steam, and then it was nothing.

26
The Abyss

THE SUN HAS
LEFT HIS BLACKNESS
& HAS FOUND A FRESHER
MORNING,
& THE FAIR MOON
REJOICES IN THE
CLEAR & CLOUDLESS
NIGHT...
WILLIAM BLAKE

*I*t was dark, with an enfolding black-ness that pressed on Lyra's eyes so heavily that she almost felt the weight of the thousands of tons of rock above them. The only light they had came from the luminous tail of the Lady Salmakia's dragonfly, and even that was fading; for the poor insects had found no food in the world of the dead, and the chevalier's had died not long before.

So while Tialys sat on Will's shoulder, Lyra held the lady's dragonfly in her hands as the lady soothed it and whispered to the trembling creature, feeding it first on crumbs of biscuit and then on her own blood. If Lyra had seen her do that, she would have offered hers, since there was more of it; but it was all she could do to concentrate on placing her feet safely and avoiding the lowest parts of the rock above.

No-Name the harpy had led them into a system of caves which would bring them, she said, to the nearest point in the world of the dead from which they could open a window to another world. Behind them came the endless column of ghosts. The tunnel was full of whispers, as the foremost encouraged those behind, as the brave urged on the faint-hearted, as the old gave hope to the young.

"Is it much further, No-Name?" said Lyra quietly. "Because this poor dragonfly's dying, and then his light'll go out."

The harpy stopped and turned to say:

"Just follow. If you can't see, listen. If you can't hear, feel."

Her eyes shone fierce in the gloom. Lyra nodded and said, "Yes, I will, but I'm not as strong as I used to be, and I'm not brave, not very anyway. Please don't stop. I'll follow you – we all will. Please keep going, No-Name."

The harpy turned back and moved on. The dragonfly-shine was getting dimmer by the minute, and Lyra knew it would soon be completely gone.

But as she stumbled forward, a voice spoke just beside her – a familiar voice.

"Lyra – Lyra, child..."

And she turned in delight.

"Mr Scoresby! Oh, I'm so glad to hear you! And it *is* you – I can see, just – oh, I wish I could touch you!"

In the faint, faint light she made out the lean form and the sardonic smile of the Texan aëronaut, and her hand reached forward of its own accord, in vain.

"Me too, honey. But listen to me – they're working some trouble out there, and it's aimed at you – don't ask me how. Is this the boy with the knife?"

Will had been looking at him, eager to see this old companion of Lyra's; but now his eyes went right past Lee to look at the ghost beside him. Lyra saw at once who it was, and marvelled at this grown-up vision of Will – the same jutting jaw, the same way of holding his head.

Will was speechless, but his father said:

"Listen – there's no time to talk about this – just do exactly as I say. Take the knife now and find a place where a lock has been cut from Lyra's hair."

His tone was urgent, and Will didn't waste time asking why. Lyra, her eyes wide with alarm, held up the dragonfly with one hand and felt her hair with the other.

"No," said Will, "take your hand away – I can't see."

And in the faint gleam, he could see it: just above her left temple, there was a little patch of hair that was shorter than the rest.

"Who did that?" said Lyra. "And –"

"Hush," said Will, and asked his father's ghost, "What must I do?"

"Cut the short hair off right down to her scalp. Collect it carefully, every single hair. Don't miss even one. Then open another world – any will do – and put the hair through into it, and then close it again. Do it now, at once."

The harpy was watching; the ghosts behind were crowding close. Lyra could see their faint faces in the dimness. Frightened and bewildered, she stood biting her lip while Will did as his father told him, his face close up to the knife-point in the pale dragonfly-light. He cut a little hollow space in the rock of another world, put all the tiny golden hairs into it, and replaced the rock before closing the window.

And then the ground began to shake. From somewhere very deep there came a growling, grinding noise, as if the whole centre of the earth were turning on itself like a vast millwheel, and little fragments of stone began to fall from the roof of the tunnel. The ground lurched suddenly to one side. Will seized Lyra's arm, and they clung together as the rock under their feet began to shift and slide, and loose pieces of stone came tumbling past and bruising their legs and feet –

The two children, sheltering the Gallivespians, crouched down with their arms over their heads; and then in a horrible sliding movement they found themselves being borne away down to the left, and they held each other fiercely, too breath-less and shaken even to cry out. Their ears were filled with the roar of thousands of tons of rock tumbling and rolling down with them.

Finally their movement stopped, though all around them smaller rocks were still tumbling and bounding down a slope that hadn't been there a minute before. Lyra was lying on Will's left arm. With his right hand he felt for the knife: it was still there at his belt.

"Tialys? Salmakia?" said Will, shakily.

"Both here, both alive," said the chevalier's voice near his ear.

The air was full of dust, and of the cordite-smell of smashed rock. It was hard to breathe, and impossible to see: the dragonfly was dead.

"Mr Scoresby?" said Lyra. "We can't see anything... What happened?"

"I'm here," said Lee, close by. "I guess the bomb went off, and I guess it missed."

"Bomb?" said Lyra, frightened; but then she said, "Roger – are you there?"

"Yeah," came the little whisper. "Mr Parry, he saved me. I was going to fall, and he caught hold."

"Look," said the ghost of John Parry. "But hold still to the rock, and don't move."

The dust was clearing, and from somewhere there was light: a strange faint golden glimmer, like a luminous misty rain falling all around them. It was enough to strike their hearts ablaze with fear, for it lit up what lay to their left, the place into which it was all falling – or flowing, like a river over the edge of a waterfall.

It was a vast black emptiness, like a shaft into the deepest darkness. The golden light flowed into it and died. They could see the other side, but it was much further away than Will could have thrown a stone. To their right, a slope of rough stones, loose and precariously balanced, rose high into the dusty gloom.

The children and their companions were clinging to what was not even a ledge – just some lucky hand and footholds – on the edge of that abyss, and there was no way out except forwards, along the slope, among the shattered rocks and the teetering boulders which, it seemed, the slightest touch would send hurtling down below.

And behind them, as the dust cleared, more and more of the ghosts were gazing in horror at the abyss. They were crouching on the slope, too frightened to move. Only the harpies were unafraid; they took to their wings and soared above, scanning backwards and forwards, flying back to reassure those still in the tunnel, flying ahead to search for the way out.

Lyra checked: at least the alethiometer was safe. Suppressing her fear, she looked around, found Roger's little face, and said:

"Come on then, we're all still here, we en't been hurt. And we can see now, at least. So just keep going, just keep on moving. We can't go any other way than round the edge of this..." She gestured at the abyss. "So we just got to keep going ahead. I swear Will and me'll just keep on till we do. So don't be scared, don't give up, don't lag behind. Tell the others. I can't look back all the time because I got to watch where I'm going, so I got to trust you to come on steady after us, all right?"

The little ghost nodded. And so, in a shocked silence, the column of the dead began their journey along the edge of the abyss. How long it took, neither Lyra nor Will could guess; how fearful and dangerous it was, they were never able to forget. The darkness below was so profound that it seemed to pull the eyesight down into it, and a ghastly dizziness swam over their minds when they looked. Whenever they could, they looked ahead of them fixedly, on this rock, that foothold, this projection, that loose slope of gravel, and kept their eyes from the gulf; but it pulled, it tempted, and they couldn't help glancing into it, only to feel their balance tilting and their eyesight swimming and a dreadful nausea gripping their throats.

From time to time the living ones looked back, and saw the infinite line of the dead winding out of the crack they'd come through: mothers pressing their infants' faces to their breasts, aged fathers clambering slowly, little children clutching the skirts of the person in front, young boys and girls of Roger's age keeping staunch and careful, so many of them... And all following Will and Lyra, so they still hoped, towards the open air.

But some didn't trust them. They crowded close behind, and both children felt cold hands on their hearts and their entrails, and they heard vicious whispers:

"Where is the upper world? How much further?"

"We're frightened here!"

"We should never have come – at least back in the world of the dead we had a little light and a little company – this is far worse!"

"You did a wrong thing when you came to our land! You should have stayed in your own world and waited to die before you came down to disturb us!"

"By what right are you leading us? You are only children! Who gave you the authority?"

Will wanted to turn and denounce them, but Lyra held his arm; they were unhappy and frightened, she said.

Then the Lady Salmakia spoke, and her clear calm voice carried a long way in the great emptiness.

"Friends, be brave! Stay together and keep going! The way is hard, but Lyra can find it. Be patient and cheerful and we'll lead you out, don't fear!"

Lyra felt herself strengthened by hearing this, and that was really the lady's intention. And so they toiled on, with painful effort.

"Will," said Lyra after some minutes, "can you hear that wind?"

"Yes, I can," said Will. "But I can't *feel* it at all. And I tell you something about that hole down there. It's the same kind of thing as when I cut a window. The same kind of edge. There's something special about that kind of edge; once you've felt it you never forget it. And I can see it there, just where the rock falls away into the dark. But that big space down there, that's not another world like all the others. It's different. I don't like it. I wish I could close it up."

"You haven't closed every window you've made."

"No, because I couldn't, some of them. But I know I *should*. Things go wrong if they're left open. And one that big..." He gestured downwards, not wanting to look. "It's wrong. Something bad will happen."

While they were talking together, another conversation had been taking place a little way off: the Chevalier Tialys was talking quietly with the ghosts of Lee Scoresby and John Parry.

"So what are you saying, John?" said Lee. "You're saying we ought *not* to go out into the open air? Man, every single part of me is aching to join the rest of the living universe again!"

"Yes, and so am I," said Will's father. "But I believe that if those of us who are used to fighting could manage to hold ourselves back, we might be able to throw ourselves into the battle on Asriel's side. And if it came at the right moment, it might make all the difference."

"Ghosts?" said Tialys, trying to hold the scepticism from his voice, and failing. "How could you fight?"

"We couldn't hurt living creatures, that's quite true. But Asriel's army is going to contend with other kinds of being as well."

"Those Spectres," said Lee.

"Just what I was thinking. They make for the dæmon, don't they? And our dæmons are long gone. It's worth a try, Lee."

"Well, I'm with you, my friend."

"And you, sir," said John Parry's ghost to the chevalier: "I have spoken to the ghosts of your people. Will you live long enough to see the world again, before you die and come back as a ghost?"

"It's true, our lives are short compared to yours. I have a few days more to live," said Tialys, "and the Lady Salmakia a little longer, perhaps. But thanks to what those children are doing, our exile as ghosts will not be permanent. I have been proud to help them."

They moved on. And that abominable fall yawned all the time, and one little slip, one footstep on a loose rock, one careless handhold, would send you down for ever and ever, thought Lyra, so far down you'd die of starvation before you ever hit the bottom, and then your poor ghost would go on falling and falling into an infinite gulf, with no one to help, no hands to reach down and lift you out, for ever conscious and for ever falling...

Oh, that would be far worse than the grey silent world they were leaving, wouldn't it?

A strange thing happened to her mind then. The thought of falling induced a kind of vertigo in Lyra, and she swayed. Will was ahead of her, just too far to reach, or she might have taken his hand; but at that moment she was more conscious of Roger, and a little flicker of vanity blazed up for a moment in her heart. There'd been an occasion once on Jordan College roof, when just to frighten him she'd defied her vertigo and walked along the edge of the stone gutter.

She looked back to remind him of it now. She was Roger's Lyra, full of grace and daring; she didn't need to creep along like an insect.

But the little boy's whispering voice said, "Lyra, be *careful* –,remember, you en't dead like us –"

And it seemed to happen so slowly, but there was nothing she could do: her weight shifted, the stones moved under her feet, and helplessly she began to slide. In the first moment it was annoying, and then it was comic: she thought *how silly!* But as she utterly failed to hold on to anything, as the stones rolled and tumbled beneath her, as she slid down towards the edge, gathering speed, the horror of it slammed into her. She was going to fall. There was nothing to stop her. It was already too late.

Her body convulsed with terror. She wasn't aware of the ghosts who flung themselves down to try and catch her, only to find her hurtling through them like a stone through mist; she didn't know that Will was yelling her name so loudly that the abyss resounded with it. Instead her whole being was a vortex of roaring fear. Faster and faster she tumbled, down and down, and some ghosts couldn't bear to watch: they hid their eyes and cried aloud.

Will felt electric with fear. He watched in anguish as Lyra slid further and further, knowing he could do nothing, and knowing he had to watch. He couldn't hear the desperate wail he was uttering any more than she could. Another two seconds – another second – she was at the edge, she couldn't stop, she was there, she was falling –

And out of the dark swooped that creature whose claws had raked her scalp not long before, No-Name the harpy, woman-faced, bird-winged; and those same claws closed tight around the girl's wrist. Together they plunged on down, the extra weight almost too much for the harpy's strong wings, but they beat and beat and beat, and her claws held firm, and slowly, heavily, slowly, heavily, the harpy carried the child up and up out of the gulf and brought her limp and fainting to Will's reaching arms.

He held her tight, pressing her to his chest, feeling the wild beat of her heart against his ribs. She wasn't Lyra just then, and he wasn't Will; she wasn't a girl, and he wasn't a boy. They were the only two human beings in that vast gulf of death. They clung together, and the ghosts clustered around, whispering comfort, blessing the harpy. Closest at hand were Will's father and Lee Scoresby, and how they longed to hold her too; and Tialys and Salmakia spoke to No-Name, praising her, calling her the saviour of them all, generous one, blessing her kindness.

As soon as Lyra could move, she reached out trembling for the harpy and put her arms around her neck, kissing and kissing her ravaged face. She couldn't speak. All the words, all the confidence, all the vanity had been shaken out of her.

They lay still for some minutes. Once the terror had begun to subside, they set off again, Will holding Lyra's hand tightly in his good one, and crept forward testing each spot before they put any weight on it, a process so slow and wearisome that they thought they might die of fatigue; but they couldn't rest, they couldn't stop. How could anyone rest, with that fearful gulf below them?

And after another hour of toil, he said to her:

"Look ahead. I think there's a way out..."

It was true: the slope was getting easier, and it was even possible to climb slightly, up and away from the edge. And ahead: wasn't that a fold in the wall of the cliff? Could that really be a way out?

Lyra looked into Will's brilliant strong eyes, and smiled.

They clambered on, up and further up, with every step moving further from the abyss. And as they climbed, they found the ground firmer, the handholds more secure, the footholds less liable to roll and twist their ankles.

"We must have climbed a fair way now," Will said. "I could try the knife and see what I find."

"Not yet," said the harpy. "Further to go yet. This is a bad place to open. Better place higher up."

They carried on quietly, hand, foot, weight, move, test, hand, foot... Their fingers were raw, their knees and hips were trembling with the effort, their heads ached and rang with exhaustion. They climbed the last few feet up to the foot of the cliff, where a narrow defile led a little way into the shadow.

Lyra watched with aching eyes as Will took the knife and began to search the air, touching, withdrawing, searching, touching again.

"Ah," he said.

"You found an open space?"

"I think so..."

"Will," said his father's ghost, "stop a moment. Listen to me."

Will put down the knife and turned. In all the effort he hadn't been able to think of his father, but it was good to know he was there. Suddenly he realized that they were going to part for the last time.

"What will happen when you go outside?" Will said. "Will you just vanish?"

"Not yet. Mr Scoresby and I have an idea. Some of us will remain here for a little while, and we shall need you to let us into Lord Asriel's world, because he might need our help. What's more," he went on sombrely, looking at Lyra, "you'll need to travel there yourselves, if you want to find your dæmons again. Because that's where they've gone."

"But Mr Parry," said Lyra, "how do you know our dæmons have gone into my father's world?"

"I was a shaman when I was alive. I learned how to see things. Ask your alethiometer – it'll confirm what I say. But remember this about dæmons," he said, and his voice was intense and emphatic. "The man you knew as Sir Charles Latrom had to return to his own world periodically; he could not live permanently in mine. The philosophers of the Guild of the Torre degli Angeli, who travelled between worlds for three hundred years or more, found the same thing to be true, and gradually their world weakened and decayed as a result.

"And then there is what happened to me. I was a soldier; I was an officer in the Marines, and then I earned my living as an explorer; I was as fit and healthy as it's possible for a human to be. Then I walked out of my own world by accident, and couldn't find the way back. I did many things and learned a great deal in the world I found myself in, but ten years after I arrived there, I was mortally sick.

"And this is the reason for all those things: your dæmon can only live its full life in the world it was born in. Elsewhere it will eventually sicken and die. We can travel, if there are openings into other worlds, but we can only live in our own. Lord Asriel's great enterprise will fail in the end for the same reason: we have to build the republic of heaven where we are, because for us there is no elsewhere.

"Will, my boy, you and Lyra can go out now for a brief rest; you need that, and you deserve it; but then you must come back into the dark with me and Mr Scoresby for one last journey."

Will and Lyra exchanged a look. Then he cut a window, and it was the sweetest thing they had ever seen.

The night air filled their lungs, fresh and clean and cool; their eyes took in a canopy of dazzling stars, and the shine of water somewhere below, and here and there groves of great trees, as high as castles, dotting the wide savannah.

Will enlarged the window as wide as he could, moving across the grass to left and right, making it big enough for six, seven, eight to walk through abreast, out of the land of the dead.

The first ghosts trembled with hope, and their excitement passed back like a ripple over the long line behind them, young children and aged parents alike looking up and ahead with delight and wonder as the first stars they had seen for centuries shone through into their poor starved eyes.

The first ghost to leave the world of the dead was Roger. He took a step forward, and turned to look back at Lyra, and laughed in surprise as he found himself turning into the night, the starlight, the air ... and then he was gone, leaving behind such a vivid little burst of happiness that Will was reminded of the bubbles in a glass of champagne.

The other ghosts followed him, and Will and Lyra fell exhausted on the dew-laden grass, every nerve in their bodies blessing the sweetness of the good soil, the night air, the stars.

27

The Platform

*O*nce the mulefa began to build the platform for Mary, they worked quickly and well. She enjoyed watching them, because they could discuss without quarrelling and co-operate without getting in each other's way, and because their techniques of splitting and cutting and joining wood were so elegant and effective.

Within two days, the observation platform was designed and built and lifted into place. It was firm and spacious and comfortable, and when she had climbed up to it she was as happy, in one way, as she had ever been. That one way was physically. In the dense green of the canopy, with the rich blue of the sky between the leaves; with a breeze keeping her skin cool, and the faint scent of the flowers delighting her whenever she sensed it; with the rustle of the leaves, the song of the hundreds of birds, and the distant murmur of the waves on the seashore, all her senses were lulled and nurtured, and if she could have stopped thinking, she would have been entirely lapped in bliss.

But of course thinking was what she was there for.

And when she looked through her spyglass and saw the relentless outward drift of the sraf, the Shadow-particles, it seemed to her as if happiness and life and hope were drifting away with them. She could find no explanation at all.

Three hundred years, the mulefa had said: that was how long the trees had been failing. Given that the Shadow-particles passed through all the worlds alike, presumably the same thing was happening in her universe too, and in every other one. Three hundred years ago, the Royal Society was set up: the first true scientific society in her world. Newton was making his discoveries about optics and gravitation.

Three hundred years ago in Lyra's world, someone invented the alethiometer.

At the same time in that strange world through which she'd come to get here, the subtle knife was invented.

She lay back on the planks, feeling the platform move in a very slight, very slow rhythm as the great tree swayed in the sea-breeze. Holding the spyglass to her eye, she watched the myriad tiny sparkles drift through the leaves, past the open mouths of the blossoms, through the massive boughs, moving against the wind, in a slow deliberate current that looked all but conscious.

What had happened three hundred years ago? Was it the cause of the Dust-current, or was it the other way round? Or were they both the results of a different cause altogether? Or were they simply not connected at all?

The drift was mesmerizing. How easy it would be to fall into a trance, and let her mind drift away with the floating particles...

Before she knew what she was doing, and because her body was lulled, that was exactly what happened. She suddenly snapped awake to find herself outside her body, and she panicked.

She was a little way above the platform, and a few feet off

among the branches. And something had happened to the Dust-wind: instead of that slow drift, it was racing like a river in flood. Had it speeded up, or was time moving differently for her, now she was outside her body? Either way, she was conscious of the most horrible danger, because the flood was threatening to sweep her loose completely, and it was immense. She flung out her arms to seize hold of anything solid – but she had no arms. Nothing connected. Now she was almost over that abominable drop, and her body was further and further from reach, sleeping so hoggishly below her. She tried to shout and wake herself up: not a sound. The body slumbered on, and the self that observed was being borne away out of the canopy of leaves altogether and into the open sky.

And no matter how she struggled she could make no headway. The force that carried her out was as smooth and powerful as water pouring over a weir: the particles of Dust were streaming along as if they too were pouring over some invisible edge.

And carrying her away from her body.

She flung a mental lifeline to that physical self, and tried to recall the feeling of being in it: all the sensations that made up being alive. The exact touch of her friend Atal's soft-tipped trunk caressing her neck. The taste of bacon and eggs. The triumphant strain in her muscles as she pulled herself up a rockface. The delicate dancing of her fingers on a computer keyboard. The smell of roasting coffee. The warmth of her bed on a winter night.

And gradually she stopped moving; the lifeline held fast, and she felt the weight and strength of the current pushing against her as she hung there in the sky.

And then a strange thing happened. Little by little (as she

reinforced those sense-memories, adding others: tasting an iced Margarita in California, sitting under the lemon trees outside a restaurant in Lisbon, scraping the frost off the windscreen of her car) she felt the Dust-wind easing. The pressure was lessening.

But only on *her*: all around, above and below, the great flood was streaming as fast as ever. Somehow there was a little patch of stillness around her, where the particles were resisting the flow.

They *were* conscious! They felt her anxiety, and responded to it. And they began to carry her back to her deserted body, and when she was close enough to see it once more, so heavy, so warm, so safe, a silent sob convulsed her heart.

And then she sank back into her body, and awoke.

She took in a deep shuddering breath. She pressed her hands and her legs against the rough planks of the platform, and having a minute ago nearly gone mad with fear, she was now suffused with a deep slow ecstasy at being one with her body and the earth and everything that was matter.

Finally she sat up and tried to take stock. Her fingers found the spyglass, and she held it to her eye, supporting one trembling hand with the other. There was no doubt about it: that slow sky-wide drift had become a flood. There was nothing to hear and nothing to feel, and without the spyglass, nothing to see, but even when she took the glass from her eye, the sense of that swift silent inundation remained vividly, together with something she hadn't noticed in the terror of being outside her body: the profound, helpless regret that was abroad in the air.

The Shadow-particles knew what was happening, and were sorrowful.

And she herself was partly Shadow-matter. Part of her was

subject to this tide that was moving through the cosmos. And so were the mulefa, and so were human beings in every world, and every kind of conscious creature, wherever they were.

And unless she found out what was happening, they might all find themselves drifting away to oblivion, every one.

Suddenly she longed for the earth again. She put the spyglass in her pocket and began the long climb down to the ground.

Father Gomez stepped through the window as the evening light lengthened and mellowed. He saw the great stands of wheel-trees and the roads lacing through the prairie, just as Mary had done from the same spot some time before. But the air was free of haze, for it had rained a little earlier, and he could see further than she had; in particular, he could see the glimmer of a distant sea, and some flickering white shapes that might be sails.

He lifted the rucksack higher on his shoulders, and turned towards them, to see what he could find. In the calm of the long evening it was pleasant to walk on this smooth road, with the sound of some cicada-like creatures in the long grass and the setting sun warm in his face. The air was fresh, too, clear and sweet and entirely free of the taint of naphtha-fumes, kerosene-fumes, whatever they were, which had lain so heavily on the air in one of the worlds he'd passed through: the world his target, the tempter herself, belonged to.

He came out at sunset on a little headland beside a shallow bay. If they had tides in this sea, the tide was high, because there was only a narrow fringe of soft white sand above the water.

And floating in the calm bay were a dozen or more... Father Gomez had to stop and think carefully. A dozen or more enormous snow-white birds, each the size of a rowing-boat, with long straight wings which trailed on the water behind them: very long wings, six feet or more in length. *Were* they birds? They had feathers, and heads and beaks not unlike swans', but those wings were situated one in front of the other, surely...

Suddenly they saw him. Heads turned with a snap, and at once all those wings were raised high, exactly like the sails of a yacht, and they all leaned in with the breeze, making for the shore.

Father Gomez was impressed by the beauty of those wing-sails, by how they were flexed and trimmed so perfectly, and by the speed of the birds. Then he saw that they were paddling, too: they had legs under the water, placed not fore-and-aft like the wings but side by side, and with the wings and the legs together, they had an extraordinary speed and grace in the water.

As the first one reached the shore it lumbered up through the dry sand, making directly for the priest. It was hissing with malice, stabbing its head forward as it waddled heavily up the shore, and the beak snapped and clacked. There were teeth in the beak, too, like a series of sharp incurved hooks.

Father Gomez was about a hundred yards from the edge of the water, on a low grassy promontory, and he had plenty of time to put down his rucksack, take out the rifle, load and aim and fire.

The bird's head exploded in a mist of red and white, and the dead creature blundered on clumsily for several steps before sinking on to its breast. It didn't die for a minute or more; the legs kicked, the wings rose and fell, and the great bird beat itself round and round in a bloody circle, kicking up the rough grass, until a long bubbling expiration from its lungs ended with a coughing spray of red, and it fell still.

The other birds had stopped as soon as the first one fell, and stood watching it, and watching the man, too. There was a quick, ferocious intelligence in their eyes. They looked from him to the dead bird, from that to the rifle, from the rifle to his face.

He raised the rifle to his shoulder again, and saw them react, shifting backwards clumsily, crowding together. They understood.

They were fine strong creatures, large and broad-backed; like living boats, in fact. If they knew what death was, thought Father Gomez, and if they could see the connection between death and himself, then there was the basis of a fruitful understanding between them. Once they had truly learned to fear him, they would do exactly as he said.

28
Midnight

FOR MANY A
TIME I HAVE
BEEN HALF
IN LOVE
WITH EASEFUL
DEATH...
JOHN KEATS

Lord Asriel said, "Marisa, wake up. We're about to land."

A blustery dawn was breaking over the basalt fortress as the intention craft flew in from the south. Mrs Coulter, sore and heartsick, opened her eyes; she had not been asleep. She could see the angel Xaphania gliding above the landing ground, and then rising and wheeling up to the tower as the craft made for the ramparts.

As soon as the craft had landed, Lord Asriel leapt out and ran to join King Ogunwe on the western watch-tower, ignoring Mrs Coulter entirely. The technicians who came at once to attend to the flying machine took no notice of her, either; no one questioned her about the loss of the aircraft she'd stolen; it was as if she'd become invisible. She made her way sadly up to the room in the adamant tower, where the orderly offered to bring her some food and coffee.

"Whatever you have," she said. "And thank you. Oh, by the way," she went on as the man turned to go: "Lord Asriel's alethiometrist, Mr..."

"Mr Basilides?"

"Yes. Is he free to come here for a moment?"

"He's working with his books at the moment, ma'am. I'll ask him to step up here when he can."

She washed, and changed into the one clean shirt she had left. The cold wind that shook the windows, and the grey morning light made her shiver. She put some more coals on the iron stove, hoping it would stop her trembling, but the cold was in her bones, not just her flesh.

Ten minutes later there was a knock on the door. The pale, dark-eyed alethiometrist, with his nightingale-dæmon on his shoulder, came in and bowed slightly. A moment later the orderly arrived with a tray of bread, cheese and coffee, and Mrs Coulter said:

"Thank you for coming, Mr Basilides. May I offer you some refreshment?"

"I will take some coffee, thank you."

"Please tell me," she said as soon as she'd poured the drink, "because I'm sure you've been following what's happened: is my daughter alive?"

He hesitated. The golden monkey clutched her arm.

"She is alive," said Basilides carefully, "but also..."

"Yes? Oh, please, what do you mean?"

"She is in the world of the dead. For some time I could not interpret what the instrument was telling me: it seemed impossible. But there is no doubt. She and the boy have gone into the world of the dead, and they have opened a way for the ghosts to come out. As soon as the dead reach the open they dissolve as their dæmons did, and it seems that this is the most sweet and desirable end for them. And the alethiometer tells me that the girl did this because she overheard a prophecy that there would come an end to death, and she thought that this was a task for her to accomplish. As a result, there is now a way out of the world of the dead."

Mrs Coulter couldn't speak. She had to turn away and go to the window to conceal the emotion on her face. Finally she said:

"And will she come out alive? But no, I know you can't predict. Is she – how is she – has she…"

"She is suffering, she is in pain, she is afraid. But she has the companionship of the boy, and of the two Gallivespian spies, and they are still all together."

"And the bomb?"

"The bomb did not hurt her."

Mrs Coulter felt suddenly exhausted. She wanted nothing more than to lie down and sleep for months, for years. Outside, the flag-rope snapped and clattered in the wind, and the rooks cawed as they wheeled around the ramparts.

"Thank you, sir," she said, turning back to the reader. "I'm very grateful. Please would you let me know if you discover anything more about her, or where she is, or what she's doing?"

The man bowed and left. Mrs Coulter went to lie down on the camp bed, but try as she would, she couldn't keep her eyes closed.

"What do you make of that, King?" said Lord Asriel.

He was looking through the watch-tower telescope at something in the western sky. It had the appearance of a mountain hanging in the sky a hand's breadth above the horizon, and covered in cloud. It was a very long way off; so far, in fact, that it was no bigger than a thumb-nail held out at arm's length. But it had not been there for long, and it hung there absolutely still.

The telescope brought it closer, but there was no more detail: cloud still looks like cloud, however much it's magnified.

"The Clouded Mountain," said Ogunwe. "Or – what do they call it? The Chariot?"

"With the Regent at the reins. He's concealed himself well, this Metatron. They speak of him in the apocryphal scriptures: he was a man once, a man called Enoch, the son of Jared – six generations away from Adam. And now he rules the kingdom. And he's intending to do more than that, if that angel they found by the sulphur lake was correct – the one who entered the Clouded Mountain to spy. If he wins this battle, he intends to intervene directly in human life. Imagine that, Ogunwe – a permanent Inquisition, worse than anything the Consistorial Court of Discipline could dream up, staffed by spies and traitors in every world and directed personally by the intelligence that's keeping that mountain aloft... The old Authority at least had the grace to withdraw; the dirty work of burning heretics and hanging witches was left to his priests. This new one will be far, far worse."

"Well, he's begun by invading the republic," said Ogunwe. "Look – is that smoke?"

A drift of grey was leaving the Clouded Mountain, a slowly spreading smudge against the blue sky. But it couldn't have been smoke: it was drifting *against* the wind that tore at the clouds.

The king put his field-glasses to his eyes, and saw what it was.

"Angels," he said.

Lord Asriel came away from the telescope and stood up, hand shading his eyes. In hundreds, and then thousands, and tens of thousands, until half that part of the sky was darkened, the minute figures flew and flew and kept on coming. Lord Asriel had seen the billion-strong flocks of blue starlings that wheeled at sunset around the palace of the

Emperor K'ang-Po, but he had never seen so vast a multitude in all his life. The flying beings gathered themselves and then streamed away slowly, slowly, to the north and the south.

"Ah! And what's that?" said Lord Asriel, pointing. "That's not the wind."

The cloud was swirling on the southern flank of the mountain, and long tattered banners of vapour streamed out in the powerful winds. But Lord Asriel was right: the movement was coming from within, not from the air outside. The cloud roiled and tumbled, and then it parted for a second.

There was more than a mountain there, but they only saw it for a moment; and then the cloud swirled back, as if drawn across by an unseen hand, to conceal it again.

King Ogunwe put down his field-glasses.

"That's not a mountain," he said. "I saw gun emplacements..."

"So did I. A whole complexity of things. Can he see out through the cloud, I wonder? In some worlds, they have machines to do that. But as for his army, if those angels are all they've got –"

The king gave a brief exclamation, half of astonishment, half of despair. Lord Asriel turned and gripped his arm with fingers that all but bruised him to the bone.

"They haven't got *this*!" he said, and shook Ogunwe's arm violently. "They haven't got *flesh*!"

He laid his hand against his friend's rough cheek.

"Few as we are," he went on, "and short-lived as we are, and weak-sighted as we are – in comparison with them, we're still *stronger*. They *envy* us, Ogunwe! That's what fuels their hatred, I'm sure of it. They long to have our precious bodies, so solid and powerful, so well adapted to the good earth! And if we *drive* at them with force and determination, we can sweep aside those infinite numbers as you can sweep your hand through mist. They have no more power than that!"

"Asriel, they have allies from a thousand worlds, living beings like us."

"We shall win."

"And suppose he's sent those angels to look for your daughter?"

"My daughter!" cried Lord Asriel, exulting. "Isn't it something to bring a child like that into the world? You'd think it was enough to go alone to the king of the armoured bears and trick his kingdom out of his paws – but to go down into the world of the dead and calmly let them all out –! And that boy; I want to meet that boy; I want to shake his hand. Did we know what we were taking on when we started this rebellion? No. But did *they* know – the Authority and his Regent, this Metatron – did they know what they were taking on when my daughter got involved?"

"Lord Asriel," said the king, "do you understand her importance for the future?"

"Frankly, no. That's why I want to see Basilides. Where did he go?"

"To the lady Coulter. But the man is worn out; he can do no more until he's rested."

"He should have rested before. Send for him, would you? Oh, one more thing: please ask Madame Oxentiel to come to the tower as soon as it's convenient. I must give her my condolences."

Madame Oxentiel had been the Gallivespians' second-in-command. Now she would have to take over Lord Roke's responsibilities. King Ogunwe bowed, and left his commander scanning the grey horizon.

* * *

All through that day the army assembled. Angels of Lord Asriel's force flew high over the Clouded Mountain, looking for an opening, but without success. Nothing changed; no more angels flew out or inwards; the high winds tore at the clouds, and the clouds endlessly renewed themselves, not parting even for a second. The sun crossed the cold blue sky and then moved down to the south-west, gilding the clouds and tinting the vapour around the mountain every shade of cream and scarlet, of apricot and orange. When the sun sank, the clouds glowed faintly from within.

Warriors were now in place from every world where Lord Asriel's rebellion had supporters; mechanics and artificers were fuelling aircraft, loading weapons, and calibrating sights and measures. As the darkness came, some welcome re-inforcements arrived: padding silently over the cold ground from the north, separately, singly, came a number of armoured bears – a large number, and among them was their king. Not long afterwards, there arrived the first of several witch-clans, the sound of the air through their pine-branches whispering in the dark sky for a long time.

Along the plain to the south of the fortress glimmered thousands of lights, marking the camps of those who had arrived from far off. Further away, in all four corners of the compass, flights of spy-angels cruised tirelessly, keeping watch.

At midnight in the adamant tower, Lord Asriel sat in discussion with King Ogunwe, the angel Xaphania, Madame Oxentiel the Gallivespian, and Teukros Basilides. The alethiometrist had just finished speaking, and Lord Asriel stood up, crossed to the window, and looked out at the distant glow of the Clouded Mountain hanging in the western sky.

The others were silent; they had just heard something that had made Lord Asriel turn pale and tremble, and none of them quite knew how to respond.

Finally Lord Asriel spoke.

"Mr Basilides," he said, "you must be very fatigued. I am grateful for all your efforts. Please take some wine with us."

"Thank you, my lord," said the reader.

His hands were trembling. King Ogunwe poured the golden Tokay and handed him the glass.

"What will this mean, Lord Asriel?" said the clear voice of Madame Oxentiel.

Lord Asriel came back to the table.

"Well," he said, "it will mean that when we join battle, we shall have a new objective. My daughter and this boy have become separated from their dæmons, somehow, and managed to survive; and their dæmons are somewhere in this world – correct me if I'm summarizing wrongly, Mr Basilides – their dæmons are in this world, and Metatron is intent on capturing them. If he captures their dæmons, the children will have to follow; and if he can control those two children, the future is his, for ever. Our task is clear: we have to find the dæmons before he does, and keep them safe till the girl and the boy rejoin them."

The Gallivespian leader said, "What form do they have, these two lost dæmons?"

"They are not yet fixed, madame," said Teukros Basilides. "They might be any shape."

"So," said Lord Asriel, "to sum it up: all of us, our republic, the future of every conscious being – we all depend on my daughter's remaining alive, and on keeping her dæmon and the boy's out of the hands of Metatron?"

"That is so."

Lord Asriel sighed, almost with satisfaction; it was as if he'd come to the end of a long and complex calculation, and reached an answer that made quite unexpected sense.

"Very well," he said, spreading his hands wide on the table. "Then this is what we shall do when the battle begins. King Ogunwe, you will assume command of all the armies defending the fortress. Madame Oxentiel, you are to send your people out at once to search in every direction for the girl and the boy, and the two dæmons. When you find them, guard them with your lives until they come together again. At that point, I understand, the boy will be able to escape to another world, and safety."

The lady nodded. Her stiff grey hair caught the lamplight, glinting like stainless steel, and the blue hawk she had inherited from Lord Roke spread his wings briefly on the bracket by the door.

"Now, Xaphania," said Lord Asriel. "What do you know of this Metatron? He was once a man: does he still have the physical strength of a human being?"

"He came to prominence long after I was exiled," the angel said. "I have never seen him close to. But he would not have been able to dominate the kingdom unless he was very strong indeed, strong in every way. Most angels would avoid fighting hand-to-hand. Metatron would relish the combat, and win."

Ogunwe could tell that Lord Asriel had been struck by an idea. His attention suddenly withdrew, his eyes lost focus for an instant, and then snapped back to the moment with an extra charge of intensity.

"I see," he said. "Finally, Xaphania, Mr Basilides tells us that their bomb not only opened an abyss below the worlds, but also fractured the structure of things so profoundly that there are fissures and cracks everywhere. Somewhere nearby there must be a way down to the edge of that abyss. I want you to look for it."

"What are you going to do?" said King Ogunwe harshly.

"I'm going to destroy Metatron. But my part is nearly over. It's my daughter who has to live, and it's our task to keep all the forces of the kingdom away from her so that she has a chance to find her way to a safer world – she and that boy, and their dæmons."

"And what about Mrs Coulter?" said the king.

Lord Asriel passed a hand over his forehead.

"I would not have her troubled," he said. "Leave her alone, and protect her if you can. Although... Maybe I'm doing her an injustice. Whatever else she's done, she's never failed to surprise me. But we all know what *we* must do, and why we must do it: we have to protect Lyra until she has found her dæmon and escaped. Our republic might have come into being for the sole purpose of helping her do that. Well, let us do it as well as we can."

Mrs Coulter lay in Lord Asriel's bed next door. Hearing voices in the other room, she stirred, for she wasn't deeply asleep. She came out of her troubled slumber uneasy and heavy with longing.

Her dæmon sat up beside her, but she didn't want to move closer to the door; it was simply the sound of Lord Asriel's voice she wanted to hear rather than any particular words. She thought they were both doomed. She thought they were all doomed.

Finally she heard the door closing in the other room, and roused herself to stand up.

"Asriel," she said, going through into the warm naphtha light.

His dæmon growled softly: the golden monkey dropped his head low to propitiate her. Lord Asriel was rolling up a large map, and did not turn.

"Asriel, what will happen to us all?" she said, taking a chair.

He pressed the heels of his hands into his eyes. His face was ravaged with fatigue. He sat down and rested an elbow on the table. Their dæmons were very still: the monkey crouching on the chair-back, the snow leopard sitting upright and alert at Lord Asriel's side, watching Mrs Coulter unblinkingly.

"You didn't hear?" he said.

"I heard a little. I couldn't sleep, but I wasn't listening. Where is Lyra, does anyone know?"

"No."

He still hadn't answered her first question, and he wasn't going to, and she knew it.

"We should have married," she said, "and brought her up ourselves."

It was such an unexpected remark that he blinked. His dæmon uttered the softest possible growl at the back of her throat, and settled down with her paws outstretched in the manner of the Sphinx. He said nothing.

"I can't bear the thought of oblivion, Asriel," she continued. "Sooner anything than that. I used to think pain would be worse – to be tortured for ever – I thought that must be worse... But as long as you were conscious, it would be better, wouldn't it? Better than feeling nothing, just going into the dark, everything going out for ever and ever?"

His part was simply to listen. His eyes were locked on hers, and he was paying profound attention; there was no need to respond. She said:

"The other day, when you spoke about her so bitterly, and

about me… I thought you hated her. I could understand your hating me. I've never hated you, but I could understand … I could see why you might hate me. But I couldn't see why you hated Lyra."

He turned his head away slowly, and then looked back.

"I remember you said something strange, on Svalbard, on the mountaintop, just before you left our world," she went on. "You said: come with me, and we'll destroy Dust for ever. You remember saying that? But you didn't mean it. You meant the very opposite, didn't you? I see now. Why didn't you tell me what you were really doing? Why didn't you tell me you were really trying to preserve Dust? You could have told me the truth."

"I wanted you to come and join me," he said, his voice hoarse and quiet, "and I thought you would prefer a lie."

"Yes," she whispered, "that's what I thought."

She couldn't sit still, but she didn't really have the strength to stand up. For a moment she felt faint, her head swam, sounds receded, the room darkened, but almost at once her senses came back even more pitilessly than before, and nothing in the situation had changed.

"Asriel…" she murmured.

The golden monkey put a tentative hand out to touch the paw of the snow leopard. The man watched without a word, and Stelmaria didn't move; her eyes were fixed on Mrs Coulter.

"Oh, Asriel, what will happen to us?" Mrs Coulter said again. "Is this the end of everything?"

He said nothing.

Moving like someone in a dream, she got to her feet, picked up the rucksack which lay in the corner of the room, and reached inside it for her pistol; and what she would have done next, no one knew, because at that moment there came the sound of footsteps running up the stairs.

Both man and woman, and both dæmons, turned to look at the orderly who came in and said breathlessly:

"Excuse me, my lord – the two dæmons – they've been seen, not far from the eastern gate – in the form of cats – the sentry tried to talk to them, bring them inside, but they wouldn't come near. It was only a minute or so ago..."

Lord Asriel sat up, transfigured. All the fatigue had been wiped off his face in a moment. He sprang to his feet and seized his greatcoat.

Ignoring Mrs Coulter, he flung the coat around his shoulders and said to the orderly:

"Tell Madame Oxentiel at once. Put this order out: the dæmons are not to be threatened, or frightened, or coerced in any way. Anyone seeing them should first..."

Mrs Coulter heard no more of what he was saying, because he was already half-way down the stairs. When his running footsteps had faded too, the only sounds were the gentle hiss of the naphtha lamp, and the moan of the wild wind outside.

Her eyes found the eyes of her dæmon. The golden monkey's expression was as subtle and complex as it had ever been, in all their thirty-five years of life.

"Very well," she said. "I can't see any other way. I think ... I think we'll..."

He knew at once what she meant. He leapt to her breast, and they embraced. Then she found her fur-lined coat, and they very quietly left the chamber and made their way down the dark stairs.

29

The Battle on the Plain

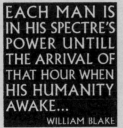

EACH MAN IS IN HIS SPECTRE'S POWER UNTILL THE ARRIVAL OF THAT HOUR WHEN HIS HUMANITY AWAKE...

WILLIAM BLAKE

*I*t was desperately hard for Lyra and Will to leave that sweet world where they had slept the night before, but if they were ever going to find their dæmons, they knew they had to go into the dark once more. And now, after hours of weary crawling through the dim tunnel, Lyra bent over the alethiometer for the twentieth time, making little unconscious sounds of distress – whimpers and catches of breath that would have been sobs if they were any stronger. Will, too, felt the pain where his dæmon had been, a scalded place of acute tenderness which every breath tore at with cold hooks.

How wearily she turned the wheels; on what leaden feet her thoughts moved. The ladders of meaning that led from every one of the alethiometer's thirty-six symbols, down which she used to move so lightly and confidently, felt loose and shaky. And holding the connections between them in her mind... It had once been like running, or singing, or telling a story: something natural. Now she had to do it laboriously, and her grip was failing, and she mustn't fail because otherwise everything would fail...

"It's not far," she said at last. "And there's all kinds of

danger – there's a battle, there's... But we're nearly in the right place now. Just at the end of this tunnel there's a big smooth rock running with water. You cut through there."

The ghosts who were going to fight pressed forward eagerly, and she felt Lee Scoresby close at her side.

He said, "Lyra, gal, it won't be long now. When you see that old bear, you tell him Lee went out fighting. And when the battle's over, there'll be all the time in the world to drift along the wind and find the atoms that used to be Hester, and my mother in the sagelands, and my sweethearts – all my sweethearts... Lyra, child, you rest when this is done, you hear? Life is good, and death is over..."

His voice faded. She wanted to put her arms around him, but of course that was impossible. So she just looked at his pale form instead, and the ghost saw the passion and brilliance in her eyes, and took strength from it.

And on Lyra's shoulder, and on Will's, rode the two Gallivespians. Their short lives were nearly over; each of them felt a stiffness in their limbs, a coldness around the heart. They would both return soon to the world of the dead, this time as ghosts, but they caught each other's eye, and vowed that they would stay with Will and Lyra for as long as they could, and not say a word about their dying.

Up and up the children clambered. They didn't speak. They heard each other's harsh breathing, they heard their footfalls, they heard the little stones their steps dislodged. Ahead of them all the way, the harpy scrambled heavily, her wings dragging, her claws scratching, silent and grim.

Then came a new sound: a regular drip-drip, echoing in the tunnel. And then a faster dripping, a trickle, a running of water.

"Here!" said Lyra, reaching forward to touch a sheet of

rock that blocked the way, smooth and wet and cold. "Here it is."

She turned to the harpy.

"I been thinking," she said, "how you saved me, and how you promised to guide all the other ghosts that'll come through the world of the dead to that land we slept in last night. And I thought, if you en't got a name, that can't be right, not for the future. So I thought I'd give you a name, like King Iorek Byrnison gave me my name Silvertongue. I'm going to call you Gracious Wings. So that's your name now, and that's what you'll be for evermore: Gracious Wings."

"One day," said the harpy, "I will see you again, Lyra Silvertongue."

"And if I know you're here, I shan't be afraid," Lyra said. "Goodbye, Gracious Wings, till I die."

She embraced the harpy, hugging her tightly and kissing her on both cheeks.

Then the Chevalier Tialys said: "This is the world of Lord Asriel's republic?"

"Yes," she said, "that's what the alethiometer says. It's close to his fortress."

"Then let me speak to the ghosts."

She held him high, and he called, "Listen, because the Lady Salmakia and I are the only ones among us who have seen this world before. There is a fortress on a mountaintop: that is what Lord Asriel is defending. Who the enemy is I do not know. Lyra and Will have only one task now, which is to search for their dæmons. Our task is to help them. Let's be of good courage and fight well."

Lyra turned to Will.

"All right," he said, "I'm ready."

He took out the knife, and looked into the eyes of his

father's ghost, who stood close by. They wouldn't know each other for much longer, and Will thought how glad he would have been to see his mother beside them as well, all three together –

"Will," said Lyra, alarmed.

He stopped. The knife was stuck in the air. He took his hand away, and there it hung, fastened in the substance of an invisible world. He let out a deep breath.

"I nearly..."

"I could see," she said. "Look at *me*, Will."

In the ghost-light he saw her bright hair, her firm-set mouth, her candid eyes: he felt the warmth of her breath; he caught the friendly scent of her flesh.

The knife came loose.

"I'll try again," he said.

He turned away. Focusing hard, he let his mind flow down to the knife-tip, touching, withdrawing, searching, and then he found it. In, along, down, and back: the ghosts crowded so close that Will's body and Lyra's felt little jolts of cold along every nerve.

And he made the final cut.

The first thing they sensed was *noise*. The light that struck in was dazzling, and they had to cover their eyes, ghosts and living alike, so they could see nothing for several seconds; but the pounding, the explosions, the rattle of gunfire, the shouts and screams were all instantly clear, and horribly frightening.

John Parry's ghost, and the ghost of Lee Scoresby, recovered their senses first. Because both had been soldiers, experienced in battle, they weren't so disoriented by the noise. Will and Lyra simply watched in fear and amazement.

Explosive rockets were bursting in the air above, showering fragments of rock and metal over the slopes of the mountain, which they saw a little way off; and in the skies, angels were fighting angels, and witches, too, swooped and soared screaming their clan-cries as they shot arrows at their enemies. They saw a Gallivespian, mounted on a dragonfly, diving to attack a flying machine whose human pilot tried to fight him off hand-to-hand. While the dragonfly darted and skimmed above, its rider leapt off to clamp his spurs deep in the pilot's neck; and then the insect returned, swooping low to let its rider leap on the brilliant green back as the flying machine droned straight into the rocks at the foot of the fortress.

"Open it wider," said Lee Scoresby. "Let us out!"

"Wait, Lee," said John Parry. "Something's happening – look over there."

Will cut another small window in the direction he indicated, and as they looked out, they could all see a change in the pattern of the fighting. The attacking force began to withdraw: a group of armed vehicles stopped moving forward, and under covering fire, turned laboriously and moved back. A squadron of flying machines, which had been getting the better of a ragged battle with Lord Asriel's gyropters, wheeled in the sky and made off to the west. The kingdom's forces on the ground – columns of riflemen, troops equipped with flame-throwers, with poison-spraying cannons, with weapons such as none of the watchers had ever seen – began to disengage and pull back.

"What's going on?" said Lee. "They're leaving the field – but why?"

There seemed to be no reason for it: Lord Asriel's allies were outnumbered, their weapons were less potent, and many more of them were lying wounded.

Then Will felt a sudden movement among the ghosts. They were pointing out at something drifting in the air.

"Spectres!" said John Parry. "That's the reason."

And for the first time, Will and Lyra thought they could see those things, like veils of shimmering gauze, falling from the sky like thistledown. But they were very faint, and when they reached the ground they were much harder to see.

"What are they doing?" said Lyra.

"They're making for that platoon of riflemen –"

And Will and Lyra knew what would happen, and they both called out in fear: "Run! Get away!"

Some of the soldiers, hearing children's voices crying out from close by, looked around startled. Others, seeing a Spectre making for them, so strange and blank and greedy, raised their guns and fired, but of course with no effect. And then it struck the first man it came to.

He was a soldier from Lyra's own world, an African. His dæmon was a long-legged tawny cat spotted with black, and she drew back her teeth and prepared to spring.

They all saw the man aiming his rifle, fearless, not giving an inch – and then they saw the dæmon in the toils of an invisible net, snarling, howling, helpless, and the man trying to reach to her, dropping his rifle, crying her name, and sinking and fainting himself with pain and brutal nausea.

"Right, Will," said John Parry. "Let us out now; we can fight those things."

So Will opened the window wide, and ran out at the head of the army of ghosts; and then began the strangest battle he could imagine.

The ghosts clambered out of the earth, pale forms paler still in the midday light. They had nothing to fear any more, and they threw themselves against the invisible Spectres, grappling and wrestling and tearing at things Will and Lyra couldn't see at all.

The riflemen and the other living allies were bemused: they could make nothing of this ghostly, spectral combat. Will made his way through the middle of it, brandishing the knife, remembering how the Spectres had fled from it before.

Wherever he went Lyra went too, wishing she had something to fight with as Will was doing, but looking around, watching more widely. She thought she could see the Spectres from time to time, in an oily glistening of the air; and it was Lyra who felt the first shiver of danger.

With Salmakia on her shoulder, she found herself on a slight rise, just a bank of earth surmounted by hawthorn bushes, from which she could see the great sweep of country the invaders were laying waste.

The sun was above her. Ahead, on the western horizon, clouds lay heaped and brilliant, riven with chasms of darkness, their tops drawn out in the high-altitude winds. That way too, on the plain, the enemy's ground forces waited: machines glinting brightly, flags astir with colour, regiments drawn up, waiting.

Behind, and to her left, was the ridge of jagged hills leading up to the fortress. They shone bright grey in the lurid pre-storm light, and on the distant ramparts of black basalt, she could even see little figures moving about, repairing the damaged battlements, bringing more weapons to bear, or simply watching.

And it was about then that Lyra felt the first distant lurch of nausea, pain, and fear that was the unmistakable touch of the Spectres.

She knew what it was at once, though she'd never felt it before. And it told her two things: first, that she must have grown up enough now to become vulnerable to the Spectres; and secondly, that Pan must be somewhere close by.

"Will – Will –" she cried.

He heard her and turned, knife in hand and eyes ablaze.

But before he could speak, he gave a gasp, a choking lurch, and clutched his breast, and she knew the same thing was happening to him.

"Pan! Pan!" she cried, standing on tiptoe to look all around.

Will was bending over trying not to be sick. After a few moments the feeling passed away, as if their dæmons had escaped; but they were no nearer to finding them, and all around the air was full of gunshots, cries, voices crying in pain or terror, the distant *yowk-yowk-yowk* of cliff-ghasts circling overhead, the occasional *whiz* and *thock* of arrows, and then a new sound: the rising of the wind.

Lyra felt it first on her cheeks, and then she saw the grass bending under it, and then she heard it in the hawthorns. The sky ahead was huge with storm: all the whiteness had gone from the thunderheads, and they rolled and swirled with sulphur-yellow, sea-green, smoke-grey, oil-black, a queasy churning miles high and as wide as the horizon.

Behind her the sun was still shining, so that every grove and every single tree between her and the storm blazed ardent and vivid, little frail things defying the dark with leaf and twig and fruit and flower.

And through it all went the two no-longer-quite-children, seeing the Spectres almost clearly now. The wind was snapping at Will's eyes and lashing Lyra's hair across her face, and it should have been able to blow the Spectres away; but the things drifted straight down through it towards the ground. Boy and girl, hand in hand, picked their way over the dead and the wounded, Lyra calling for her dæmon, Will alert in every sense for his.

And now the sky was laced with lightning, and then the first almighty crack of thunder hit their eardrums like an axe. Lyra put her hands to her head, and Will nearly stumbled, as if driven downwards by the sound. They clung to each other and looked up, and saw a sight no one had ever seen before in any of the millions of worlds.

Witches, Ruta Skadi's clan, and Reina Miti's, and half-a-dozen others, every single witch carrying a torch of flaring pitch-pine dipped in bitumen, were streaming over the fortress from the east, from the last of the clear sky, and flying straight towards the storm.

Those on the ground could hear the roar and crackle as the volatile hydrocarbons flamed high above. A few Spectres still remained in the upper airs, and some witches flew into them unseeing, to cry out and tumble blazing to the ground; but most of the pallid things had reached the earth by this time, and the great flight of witches streamed like a river of fire into the heart of the storm.

A flight of angels, armed with spears and swords, had emerged from the Clouded Mountain to meet the witches head-on. They had the wind behind them, and they sped forward faster than arrows; but the witches were equal to that, and the first ones soared up high and then dived into the ranks of the angels, lashing to left and right with their flaring torches. Angel after angel, outlined in fire, their wings ablaze, tumbled screaming from the air.

And then the first great drops of rain came down. If the commander in the storm-clouds meant to douse the witch-fires, he was disappointed; the pitch-pine and the bitumen blazed defiance at it, spitting and hissing the louder the more rain splashed into them. The raindrops hit the ground as if they'd been hurled in malice, breaking and splashing up into the air. Within a minute Lyra and Will were both soaked to the skin and shaking with cold, and the rain stung their heads and arms like tiny stones.

Through it all they stumbled and struggled, wiping the water from their eyes, calling: "Pan! Pan!" in the tumult.

The thunder overhead was almost constant now, ripping and grinding and crashing as if the very atoms were being torn open. Between thunder-crash and pang of fear ran Will and Lyra, howling, both of them: "Pan! My Pantalaimon! Pan!" and a wordless cry from Will, who knew what he had lost, but not what she was named.

With them everywhere went the two Gallivespians, warning them to look this way, to go that way, watching out for the Spectres the children could still not fully see. But Lyra had to hold Salmakia in her hands, because the lady had little strength left to cling to Lyra's shoulder. Tialys was scanning the skies all around, searching for his kindred and calling out whenever he saw a needle-bright darting movement through the air above. But his voice had lost much of its power, and in any case the other Gallivespians were looking for the clan-colours of their two dragonflies, the electric blue and the red-and-yellow; and those colours had long since faded, and the bodies that had shone with them lay in the world of the dead.

And then came a movement in the sky that was different from the rest. As the children looked up, sheltering their eyes from the lashing raindrops, they saw an aircraft unlike any they'd seen before: ungainly, six-legged, dark, and totally silent. It was flying low, very low, from the fortress. It skimmed overhead, no higher than a rooftop above them, and then moved away into the heart of the storm.

But they had no time to wonder about it, because another

head-wrenching throb of nausea told Lyra that Pan was in danger again, and then Will felt it too, and they stumbled blindly through the puddles and the mud and the chaos of wounded men and fighting ghosts, helpless, terrified, and sick.

30
The Clouded Mountain

*T*he intention craft was being piloted by Mrs Coulter. She and her dæmon were alone in the cockpit.

The barometric altimeter was little use in the storm, but she could judge her altitude roughly by watching the fires on the ground that blazed where angels fell; despite the hurtling rain, they were still flaring high. As for the course, that wasn't difficult either: the lightning that flickered around the mountain served as a brilliant beacon. But she had to avoid the various flying beings who were still fighting in the air, and keep clear of the rising land below.

She didn't use the lights, because she wanted to get close and find somewhere to land before they saw her and shot her down. As she flew closer, the up-draughts became more violent, the gusts more sudden and brutal. A gyropter would have had no chance: the savage air would have slammed it to the ground like a fly. In the intention craft she could move lightly with the wind, adjusting her balance like a wave-rider in the Peaceable Ocean.

Cautiously she began to climb, peering forward, ignoring the instruments and flying by sight and by instinct. Her dæmon leapt from one side of the little glass cabin to the other, looking ahead, above, to left and right, and calling to her constantly. The lightning, great sheets and lances of brilliance, flared and cracked above and around the machine. Through it all she flew in the little aircraft, gaining height little by little, and always moving on towards the cloud-hung palace.

And as Mrs Coulter approached, she found her attention dazzled and bewildered by the nature of the mountain itself.

It reminded her of a certain abominable heresy, whose author was now deservedly languishing in the dungeons of the Consistorial Court. He had suggested that there were more spatial dimensions than the three familiar ones; that on a very small scale, there were up to seven or eight other dimensions, but that they were impossible to examine directly. He had even constructed a model to show how they might work, and Mrs Coulter had seen the object before it was exorcised and burnt. Folds within folds, corners and edges both containing and being contained: its inside was everywhere and its outside was everywhere else. The Clouded Mountain affected her in a similar way: it was less like a rock than like a force-field, manipulating space itself to enfold and stretch and layer it into galleries and terraces, chambers and colonnades and watch-towers of air and light and vapour.

She felt a strange exultation welling slowly in her breast, and she saw at the same time how to bring the aircraft safely up to the clouded terrace on the southern flank. The little craft lurched and strained in the turbid air, but she held the course firm, and her dæmon guided her down to land on the terrace.

The light she'd seen by till now had come from the lightning, the occasional gashes in the cloud where the sun struck through, the fires from the burning angels, the beams of anbaric search-lights; but the light here was different. It came from the substance of the mountain itself, which glowed and faded in a slow breath-like rhythm, with a mother-of-pearl radiance.

Woman and dæmon got down from the craft, and looked around to see which way they should go.

She had the feeling that other beings were moving rapidly above and below, speeding through the substance of the mountain itself with messages, orders, information. She couldn't see them; all she could see was confusing infolded perspectives of colonnade, staircase, terrace and façade.

Before she could make up her mind which way to go, she heard voices, and withdrew behind a column. The voices were singing a psalm, and coming closer, and then she saw a procession of angels carrying a litter.

As they neared the place where she was hiding, they saw the intention craft and stopped. The singing faltered, and some of the bearers looked around in doubt and fear.

Mrs Coulter was close enough to see the being in the litter: an angel, she thought, and indescribably aged. He wasn't easy to see, because the litter was enclosed all round with crystal that glittered and threw back the enveloping light of the mountain, but she had the impression of terrifying decrepitude, of a face sunken in wrinkles, of trembling hands and a mumbling mouth and rheumy eyes.

The aged being gestured shakily at the intention craft, and cackled and muttered to himself, plucking incessantly at his beard, and then threw back his head and uttered a howl of such anguish that Mrs Coulter had to cover her ears.

But evidently the bearers had a task to do, for they gathered themselves and moved further along the terrace, ignoring the cries and mumbles from inside the litter. When they reached an open space they spread their wings wide, and at a word from their leader they began to fly, carrying the litter between them, until they were lost to Mrs Coulter's sight in the swirling vapours.

But there wasn't time to think about that. She and the golden monkey moved on quickly, climbing great staircases, crossing bridges, always moving upwards. The higher they went, the more they felt that sense of invisible activity all around them, until finally they turned a corner into a wide space like a mist-hung piazza, and found themselves confronted by an angel with a spear.

"Who are you? What is your business?" he said.

Mrs Coulter looked at him curiously. These were the beings who had fallen in love with human women, with the daughters of men, so long ago.

"No, no," she said gently, "please don't waste time. Take me to the Regent at once. He's waiting for me."

Disconcert them, she thought, keep them off balance; and this angel did not know what he should do, so he did as she told him. She followed him for some minutes, through those confusing perspectives of light, until they came to an ante-chamber. How they had entered she didn't know, but there they were, and after a brief pause, something in front of her opened like a door.

Her dæmon's sharp nails were pressing into the flesh of her upper arms, and she gripped his fur for reassurance.

Facing them was a being made of light. He was man-shaped, man-sized, she thought, but she was too dazzled to see. The golden monkey hid his face in her shoulder, and she threw up an arm to hide her eyes.

Metatron said, "Where is she? Where is your daughter?"

"I've come to tell you, my Lord Regent," she said.

"If she was in your power, you would have brought her."

"She is not, but her dæmon is."

"How can that be?"

"I swear, Metatron, her dæmon is in my power. Please, great Regent, hide yourself a little – my eyes are dazzled..."

He drew a veil of cloud in front of himself. Now it was like looking at the sun through smoked glass, and her eyes could see him more clearly, though she still pretended to be dazzled by his face. He was exactly like a man in early middle age, tall, powerful, and commanding. Was he clothed? Did he have wings? She couldn't tell, because of the force of his eyes. She could look at nothing else.

"Please, Metatron, hear me. I have just come from Lord Asriel. He has the child's dæmon, and he knows that the child will soon come to search for him."

"What does he want with the child?"

"To keep her from you until she comes of age. He doesn't know where I've gone, and I must go back to him soon. I'm telling you the truth. Look at me, great Regent, as I can't easily look at you. Look at me clearly, and tell me what you see."

The prince of the angels looked at her. It was the most searching examination Marisa Coulter had ever undergone. Every scrap of shelter and deceit was stripped away, and she stood naked, body and ghost and dæmon together, under the ferocity of Metatron's gaze.

And she knew that her nature would have to answer for her, and she was terrified that what he saw in her would be insufficient. Lyra had lied to Iofur Raknison with her words: her mother was lying with her whole life.

"Yes, I see," said Metatron.

"What do you see?"

"Corruption and envy and lust for power. Cruelty and coldness. A vicious probing curiosity. Pure, poisonous, toxic malice. You have never from your earliest years shown a shred of compassion or sympathy or kindness without calculating how it would return to your advantage. You have tortured and killed without regret or hesitation; you have betrayed and intrigued and gloried in your treachery. You are a cess-pit of moral filth."

That voice, delivering that judgement, shook Mrs Coulter profoundly. She knew it was coming, and she dreaded it; and yet she hoped for it too, and now it had been said, she felt a little gush of triumph.

She moved closer to him.

"So you see," she said, "I can betray him easily. I can lead you to where he's taking my daughter's dæmon, and you can destroy Asriel, and the child will walk unsuspecting into your hands."

She felt the movement of vapour about her, and her senses became confused: his next words pierced her flesh like darts of scented ice.

"When I was a man," he said, "I had wives in plenty, but none was as lovely as you."

"When you were a man?"

"When I was a man I was known as Enoch, the son of Jared, the son of Mahalalel, the son of Kenan, the son of Enosh, the son of Seth, the son of Adam. I lived on earth for sixty-five years, and then the Authority took me to his kingdom."

"And you had many wives."

"I loved their flesh. And I understood it when the sons of heaven fell in love with the daughters of earth, and I pleaded their cause with the Authority. But his heart was fixed against them, and he made me prophesy their doom."

"And you have not known a wife for thousands of years..."

"I have been Regent of the kingdom."

"And is it not time you had a consort?"

That was the moment she felt most exposed and in most danger. But she trusted to her flesh, and to the strange truth she'd learned about angels, perhaps especially those angels who had once been human: lacking flesh, they coveted it and longed for contact with it. And Metatron was close now, close enough to smell the perfume of her hair and to gaze at the texture of her skin, close enough to touch her with scalding hands.

There was a strange sound, like the murmur and crackle you hear before you realize that what you're hearing is your house on fire.

"Tell me what Lord Asriel is doing, and where he is," he said.

"I can take you to him now," she said.

The angels carrying the litter left the Clouded Mountain and flew south. Metatron's orders had been to take the Authority to a place of safety away from the battlefield, because he wanted him kept alive for a while yet; but rather than give him a bodyguard of many regiments, which would only attract the enemy's attention, he had trusted to the obscurity of the storm, calculating that in these circumstances, a small party would be safer than a large one.

And so it might have been, if a certain cliff-ghast, busy feasting on a half-dead warrior, had not looked up just as a random search-light caught the side of the crystal litter.

Something stirred in the cliff-ghast's memory. He paused,

one hand on the warm liver, and as his brother knocked him aside, the recollection of a babbling Arctic fox came to his mind.

At once he spread his leathery wings and bounded upwards, and a moment later the rest of the troop followed.

Xaphania and her angels had searched diligently all the night and some of the morning, and finally they had found a minute crack in the mountainside to the south of the fortress, which had not been there the day before. They had explored it and enlarged it, and now Lord Asriel was climbing down into a series of caverns and tunnels extending a long way below the fortress.

It wasn't totally dark, as he'd thought. There was a faint source of illumination, like a stream of billions of tiny particles, faintly glowing. They flowed steadily down the tunnel like a river of light.

"Dust," he said to his dæmon.

He had never seen it with the naked eye, but then he had never seen so much Dust together. He moved on, until quite suddenly the tunnel opened out, and he found himself at the top of a vast cavern: a vault immense enough to contain a dozen cathedrals. There was no floor; the sides sloped vertiginously down towards the edge of a great pit hundreds of feet below, and darker than darkness itself, and into the pit streamed the endless Dust-fall, pouring ceaselessly down. Its billions of particles were like the stars of every galaxy in the sky, and every one of them was a little fragment of conscious thought. It was a melancholy light to see by.

He climbed with his dæmon down towards the abyss, and as they went they gradually began to see what was happening along the far side of the gulf, hundreds of yards away in the gloom. He had thought there was a movement there, and the further down he climbed, the more clearly it resolved itself: a procession of dim pale figures picking their way along the perilous slope, men, women, children, beings of every kind he had seen and many he had not. Intent on keeping their balance, they ignored him altogether, and Lord Asriel felt the hair stir at the back of his neck when he realized that they were ghosts.

"Lyra came here," he said quietly to the snow leopard.

"Tread carefully," was all she said in reply.

By this time, Will and Lyra were soaked through, shivering, racked with pain, and stumbling blindly through mud and over rocks and into little gullies where storm-fed streams ran red with blood. Lyra was afraid that the Lady Salmakia was dying: she hadn't uttered a word for several minutes, and she lay faint and limp in Lyra's hand.

As they sheltered in one river-bed where the water was white, at least, and scooped up handfuls to their thirsty mouths, Will felt Tialys rouse himself and say:

"Will – I can hear horses coming – Lord Asriel has no cavalry. It must be the enemy. Get across the stream and hide – I saw some bushes that way..."

"Come on," said Will to Lyra, and they splashed through the icy bone-aching water and scrambled up the far side of the gully just in time. The riders who came over the slope and clattered down to drink didn't look like cavalry: they seemed to be of the same kind of close-haired flesh as their horses, and they had neither clothes nor harness. They carried weapons, though: tridents, nets, and scimitars.

Will and Lyra didn't stop to look: they stumbled over the rough ground at a crouch, intent only on getting away unseen.

But they had to keep their heads low, to see where they were treading and avoid twisting an ankle, or worse; and thunder exploded overhead as they ran, so they couldn't hear the screeching and snarling of the cliff-ghasts until they ran into them.

The creatures were surrounding something that lay glittering in the mud: something slightly taller than they were, which lay on its side, a large cage, perhaps, with walls of crystal. They were hammering at it with fists and rocks, shrieking and yelling.

And before Will and Lyra could stop and run the other way, they had stumbled right into the middle of the troop.

31
Authority's End

FOR EMPIRE
IS NO MORE,
AND NOW THE
LION & WOLF
SHALL CEASE.
WILLIAM BLAKE

Mrs Coulter whispered to the shadow beside her:

"Look how he hides, Metatron! He creeps through the dark like a rat..."

They stood on a ledge high up in the great cavern, watching Lord Asriel and the snow leopard make their careful way down, a long way below.

"I could strike him now," the shadow whispered.

"Yes, of course you could," she whispered back, leaning close; "but I want to see his face, dear Metatron; I want him to *know* I've betrayed him. Come, let's follow and catch him..."

The Dust-fall shone like a great pillar of faint light as it descended smoothly and never-endingly into the gulf. Mrs Coulter had no attention to spare for it, because the shadow beside her was trembling with desire, and she had to keep him by her side, under what control she could manage.

They moved down, silent, following Lord Asriel. The further down they climbed, the more she felt a great weariness fall over her.

"What? What?" whispered the shadow, feeling her emotions, and suspicious at once.

"I was thinking," she said with a sweet malice, "how glad I am that the child will never grow up to love and be loved. I thought I loved her when she was a baby; but now –"

"There was *regret*," the shadow said, "in your heart there was *regret* that you will not see her grow up."

"Oh, Metatron, how long it is since you were a man! Can you really not tell what it is I'm regretting? It's not *her* coming of age, but mine. How bitterly I regret that I didn't know of you in my own girlhood; how passionately I would have devoted myself to you..."

She leaned towards the shadow, as if she couldn't control the impulses of her own body, and the shadow hungrily sniffed and seemed to gulp at the scent of her flesh.

They were moving laboriously over the tumbled and broken rocks towards the foot of the slope. The further down they went, the more the Dust-light gave everything a nimbus of golden mist. Mrs Coulter kept reaching for where his hand might be, if the shadow had been a human companion, and then seemed to recollect herself, and whispered:

"Keep behind me, Metatron – wait here – Asriel is suspicious – let me lull him first. When he's off guard I'll call you. But come as a shadow, in this small form, so he doesn't see you – otherwise he'll just let the child's dæmon fly away."

The Regent was a being whose profound intellect had had thousands of years to deepen and strengthen itself, and whose knowledge extended over a million universes. Nevertheless, at that moment he was blinded by his twin obsessions: to destroy Lyra and to possess her mother. He nodded, and stayed where he was, while the woman and the monkey moved forward as quietly as they could.

Lord Asriel was waiting behind a great block of granite, out of sight of the Regent. The snow leopard heard them coming, and Lord Asriel stood up as Mrs Coulter came around the corner. Everything, every surface, every cubic centimetre of air, was permeated by the falling Dust, which gave a soft clarity to every tiny detail; and in the Dust-light Lord Asriel saw that her face was wet with tears, and that she was gritting her teeth so as not to sob.

He took her in his arms, and the golden monkey embraced the snow leopard's neck and buried his black face in her fur.

"Is Lyra safe? Has she found her dæmon?" she whispered.

"The ghost of the boy's father is protecting both of them."

"Dust is beautiful... I never knew."

"What did you tell him?"

"I lied and lied, Asriel... Let's not wait too long, I can't bear it... We won't live, will we? We won't survive like the ghosts?"

"Not if we fall into the abyss. We came here to give Lyra time to find her dæmon, and then time to live and grow up. If we take Metatron to extinction, Marisa, she'll have that time, and if we go with him, it doesn't matter."

"And Lyra *will* be safe?"

"Yes, yes," he said gently.

He kissed her. She felt as soft and light in his arms as she'd done when Lyra was conceived thirteen years before.

She was sobbing quietly. When she could speak she whispered:

"I told him I was going to betray you, and betray Lyra, and he believed me because I was corrupt and full of wickedness; he looked so deep I felt sure he'd see the truth. But I lied too well. I was lying with every nerve and fibre and everything I'd ever done... I wanted him to find no good in me, and he didn't. There is none. But I love Lyra. Where did this love come from? I don't know; it came to me like a thief in the night, and now I love her so much my heart is bursting with it. All I could hope was that my crimes were so monstrous that the love was no bigger than a mustard-seed in the shadow of them, and I wished I'd committed even greater ones to hide it more deeply still... But the mustard-seed had taken root and was growing, and the little green shoot was splitting my heart wide open, and I was so afraid he'd see..."

She had to stop to gather herself. He stroked her shining hair, all set about with golden Dust, and waited.

"Any moment now he'll lose patience," she whispered. "I told him to make himself small. But he's only an angel after all, even if he was once a man. And we can wrestle with him and bring him to the edge of the gulf, and we'll both go down with him..."

He kissed her, and said, "Yes. Lyra will be safe, and the kingdom will be powerless against her. Call him now, Marisa, my love."

She took a deep breath and let it out in a long shuddering sigh. Then she smoothed her skirt down over her thighs and tucked the hair back behind her ears.

"Metatron," she called softly. "It's time."

Metatron's shadow-cloaked form appeared out of the golden air, and took in at once what was happening: the two dæmons, crouching and watchful, the woman with the nimbus of Dust, and Lord Asriel –

Who leapt at him at once, seizing him around the waist, and tried to hurl him to the ground. The angel's arms were free, though, and with fists, palms, elbows, knuckles, forearms, he battered Lord Asriel's head and body: great pummelling blows that forced the breath from his lungs and rebounded from his ribs, that cracked against his skull and shook his senses.

However, his arms encircled the angel's wings, cramping them to his side. And a moment later, Mrs Coulter had leapt up between those pinioned wings and seized Metatron's hair. His strength was enormous: it was like holding the mane of a bolting horse. As he shook his head furiously, she was flung this way and that, and she felt the power in the great folded wings as they strained and heaved at the man's arms locked so tightly around them.

The dæmons had seized hold of him, too. Stelmaria had her teeth firmly in his leg, and the golden monkey was tearing at one of the edges of the nearest wing, snapping feathers, ripping at the vanes, and this only roused the angel to greater fury. With a sudden massive effort he flung himself sideways, freeing one wing and crushing Mrs Coulter against a rock.

Mrs Coulter was stunned for a second, and her hands came loose. At once the angel reared up again, beating his one free wing to fling off the golden monkey; but Lord Asriel's arms were firm around him still, and in fact the man had a better grip now there wasn't so much to enclose. Lord Asriel set himself to crushing the breath out of Metatron, grinding his ribs together, and trying to ignore the savage blows that were landing on his skull and his neck.

But those blows were beginning to tell. And as Lord Asriel tried to keep his footing on the broken rocks, something shattering happened to the back of his head. When he flung himself sideways, Metatron had seized a fist-sized rock, and now he brought it down with brutal force on the point of Lord Asriel's skull. The man felt the bones of his head move against each other, and he knew that another blow like that would kill him outright. Dizzy with pain – pain that was worse for the pressure of his head against the angel's side – he still clung fast, the fingers of his right hand crushing the bones of his left, and stumbled for a footing among the fractured rocks.

And as Metatron raised the bloody stone high, a golden-furred shape sprang up like a flame leaping to a tree-top, and the monkey sank his teeth into the angel's hand. The rock came loose and clattered down towards the edge, and Metatron swept his arm to left and right, trying to dislodge the dæmon; but the golden monkey clung with teeth, claws, and tail, and then Mrs Coulter gathered the great white beating wing to herself and smothered its movement.

Metatron was hampered, but he still wasn't hurt. Nor was he near the edge of the abyss.

And by now Lord Asriel was weakening. He was holding fast to his blood-soaked consciousness, but with every movement a little more was lost. He could feel the edges of the bones grinding together in his skull; he could hear them. His senses were disordered: all he knew was *hold tight and drag down*.

Then Mrs Coulter found the angel's face under her hand, and she dug her fingers deep into his eyes.

Metatron cried out. From far off across the great cavern, echoes answered, and his voice bounded from cliff to cliff, doubling and diminishing and causing those distant ghosts to pause in their endless procession and look up.

And Stelmaria the snow-leopard dæmon, her own consciousness dimming with Lord Asriel's, made one last effort and leapt for the angel's throat.

Metatron fell to his knees. Mrs Coulter, falling with him, saw the blood-filled eyes of Lord Asriel gaze at her. And she scrambled up, hand over hand, forcing the beating wing aside, and seized the angel's hair to wrench back his head and bare his throat for the snow leopard's teeth.

And now Lord Asriel was dragging him, dragging him backwards, feet stumbling and rocks falling, and the golden monkey was leaping down with them, snapping and scratching and tearing, and they were almost there, almost at the edge; but Metatron forced himself up, and with a last effort spread both wings wide – a great white canopy that beat down and down and down, again and again and again, and then Mrs Coulter had fallen away, and Metatron was upright, and the wings beat harder and harder, and he was aloft – he was leaving the ground, with Lord Asriel still clinging tight, but weakening fast. The golden monkey's fingers were entwined in the angel's hair, and he would never let go –

But they were over the edge of the abyss. They were rising. And if they flew higher, Lord Asriel would fall, and Metatron would escape.

"Marisa! Marisa!"

The cry was torn from Lord Asriel, and with the snow leopard beside her, with a roaring in her ears, Lyra's mother stood and found her footing and leapt with all her heart, to hurl herself against the angel and her dæmon and her dying lover, and seize those beating wings, and bear them all down together into the abyss.

The cliff-ghasts heard Lyra's exclamation of dismay, and their flat heads all snapped round at once.

Will sprang forward and slashed the knife at the nearest of them. He felt a little kick on his shoulder as Tialys leapt off and landed on the cheek of the biggest, seizing her hair and kicking hard below the jaw before she could throw him off. The creature howled and thrashed as she fell into the mud, and the other looked stupidly at the stump of his arm, and then in horror at his own ankle, which his sliced-off hand had seized as it fell. A second later, the knife was in his breast: Will felt the handle jump three or four times with the dying heart-beats, and pulled it out before the cliff-ghast could twist it away in falling.

He heard the others cry and shriek in hatred as they fled, and he knew that Lyra was unhurt beside him; but he threw himself down in the mud with only one thing in his mind.

"Tialys! Tialys!" he cried, and avoiding the snapping teeth, he hauled the biggest cliff-ghast's head aside. Tialys was dead, his spurs deep in her neck. The creature was kicking and biting still, so he cut off her head and rolled it away before lifting the dead Gallivespian clear of the leathery neck.

"Will," said Lyra behind him, "Will, look at this..."

She was gazing into the crystal litter. It was unbroken, although the crystal was stained and smeared with mud and the blood from what the cliff-ghasts had been eating before they found it. It lay tilted crazily among the rocks, and inside it –

"Oh, Will, he's still alive! But – the poor thing..."

Will saw her hands pressing against the crystal, trying to reach to the angel and comfort him; because he was so old, and he was terrified, crying like a baby and cowering away into the lowest corner.

"He must be so old – I've never seen anyone suffering like that – oh, Will, can't we let him out?"

Will cut through the crystal in one movement and reached in to help the angel out. Demented and powerless, the aged being could only weep and mumble in fear and pain and misery, and he shrank away from what seemed like yet another threat.

"It's all right," Will said, "we can help you hide, at least. Come on, we won't hurt you."

The shaking hand seized his and feebly held on. The old one was uttering a wordless groaning whimper that went on and on, and grinding his teeth, and compulsively plucking at himself with his free hand; but as Lyra reached in too to help him out, he tried to smile, and to bow, and his ancient eyes deep in their wrinkles blinked at her with innocent wonder.

Between them they helped the ancient of days out of his crystal cell; it wasn't hard, for he was as light as paper, and he would have followed them anywhere, having no will of his own, and responding to simple kindness like a flower to the sun. But in the open air there was nothing to stop the wind from damaging him, and to their dismay his form began to loosen and dissolve. Only a few moments later he had vanished completely, and their last impression was of those eyes, blinking in wonder, and a sigh of the most profound and exhausted relief.

Then he was gone: a mystery dissolving in mystery. It had all taken less than a minute, and Will turned back at once to the fallen chevalier. He picked up the little body, cradling it in his palms, and found his tears flowing fast.

But Lyra was saying something urgently.

"Will — we've got to move — we've *got* to — the lady can hear those horses coming —"

Out of the indigo sky an indigo hawk swooped low, and Lyra cried out and ducked; but Salmakia cried with all her strength, "No, Lyra! No! Stand high, and hold out your fist!"

So Lyra held still, supporting one arm with the other, and the blue hawk wheeled and turned and swooped again, to seize her knuckles in sharp claws.

On the hawk's back sat a grey-haired lady, whose clear-eyed face looked first at Lyra, then at Salmakia clinging to her collar.

"Madame..." said Salmakia faintly, "we have done..."

"You have done all you need. Now we are here," said Madame Oxentiel, and twitched the reins.

At once the hawk screamed three times, so loud that Lyra's head rang. In response there darted from the sky first one, then two and three and more, then hundreds of brilliant warrior-bearing dragonflies, all skimming so fast it seemed they were bound to crash into one another; but the reflexes of the insects and the skills of their riders were so acute that instead, they seemed to weave a tapestry of swift and silent needle-bright colour over and around the children.

"Lyra," said the lady on the hawk, "and Will: follow us now, and we shall take you to your dæmons."

As the hawk spread its wings and lifted away from one hand, Lyra felt the little weight of Salmakia fall into the other, and knew in a moment that only the lady's strength of mind had kept her alive this long. She cradled her body close, and ran with Will under the cloud of dragonflies, stumbling and falling more than once, but holding the lady gently against her heart all the time.

"Left! Left!" cried the voice from the blue hawk, and in the lightning-riven murk they turned that way; and to their right Will saw a body of men in light grey armour, helmeted, masked, their grey wolf-dæmons padding in step beside them. A stream of dragonflies made for them at once, and the men faltered: their guns were no use, and the Gallivespians were among them in a moment, each warrior springing from his insect's back, finding a hand, an arm, a bare neck, and plunging his spur in before leaping back to the insect as it wheeled and skimmed past again. They were so quick it was almost impossible to follow. The soldiers turned and fled in panic, their discipline shattered.

But then came hoofbeats in a sudden thunder from behind, and the children turned in dismay: those horse-people were bearing down on them at a gallop, and already one or two had nets in their hands, whirling them around over their heads and entrapping the dragonflies, to snap the nets like whips and fling the broken insects aside.

"This way!" came the lady's voice, and then she said, "Duck, now – get down low!"

They did, and felt the earth shake under them. Could that be hoofbeats? Lyra raised her head and wiped the wet hair from her eyes, and saw something quite different from horses.

"Iorek!" she cried, joy leaping in her chest. "Oh, Iorek!"

Will pulled her down again at once, for not only Iorek Byrnison but a regiment of his bears were making directly for them. Just in time Lyra tucked her head down, and then Iorek bounded over them, roaring orders to his bears to go left, go right, and crush the enemy between them.

Lightly, as if his armour weighed no more than his fur, the bear-king spun to face Will and Lyra, who were struggling upright.

"Iorek – behind you – they've got nets!" Will cried, because the riders were almost on them.

Before the bear could move, the rider's net hissed through the air, and instantly Iorek was enveloped in steel-strong cobweb. He roared, rearing high, slashing with huge paws at the rider. But the net was strong, and although the horse whinnied and reared back in fear, Iorek couldn't fight free of the coils.

"Iorek!" Will shouted. "Keep still! Don't move!"

He scrambled forward through the puddles and over the tussocks as the rider tried to control the horse, and reached Iorek just at the moment when a second rider arrived and another net hissed through the air.

But Will kept his head: instead of slashing wildly and getting in more of a tangle, he watched the flow of the net and cut it through in a matter of moments. The second net fell useless to the ground, and then Will leapt at Iorek, feeling with his left hand, cutting with his right. The great bear stood motionless as the boy darted here and there over his vast body, cutting, freeing, clearing the way.

"Now go!" Will yelled, leaping clear, and Iorek seemed to explode upwards full into the chest of the nearest horse.

The rider had raised his scimitar to sweep down at the bear's neck, but Iorek Byrnison in his armour weighed nearly two tons, and nothing at that range could withstand him. Horse and rider, both of them smashed and shattered, fell harmlessly aside. Iorek gathered his balance, looked around to see how the land lay, and roared to the children:

"On my back! Now!"

Lyra leapt up, and Will followed. Pressing the cold iron between their legs, they felt the massive surge of power as Iorek began to move.

Behind them, the rest of the bears were engaging with the strange cavalry, helped by the Gallivespians, whose stings enraged the horses. The lady on the blue hawk skimmed low, and called: "Straight ahead now! Among the trees in the valley!"

Iorek reached the top of a little rise in the ground, and paused. Ahead of them the broken ground sloped down towards a grove about a quarter of a mile away. Somewhere beyond that, a battery of great guns was firing shell after shell howling high overhead, and someone was firing flares, too, that burst just under the clouds and drifted down towards the trees, making them blaze with cold green light as a fine target for the guns.

And fighting for control of the grove itself were a score or more Spectres, being held back by a ragged band of ghosts. As soon as they saw that little group of trees, Lyra and Will both knew that their dæmons were in there, and that if they didn't reach them soon, they would die. More Spectres were arriving there every minute, streaming over the ridge from the right. Will and Lyra could see them very clearly now.

An explosion just over the ridge shook the ground and flung stones and clods of earth high into the air. Lyra cried out, and Will had to clutch his chest.

"Hold on," Iorek growled, and began to charge.

A flare burst high above, and another and another, drifting slowly downwards with a magnesium-bright glare. Another shell burst, closer this time, and they felt the shock of the air and a second or two later the sting of earth and stones on their faces. Iorek didn't falter, but they found it hard to hold on: they couldn't dig their fingers into his fur – they had to grip the armour between their knees, and his back was so broad that both of them kept slipping.

"Look!" cried Lyra, pointing up as another shell burst nearby.

A dozen witches were making for the flares, carrying thick-leafed, bushy branches, and with them they brushed the glaring lights aside, sweeping them away into the sky beyond. Darkness fell over the grove again, hiding it from the guns.

And now the trees were only a few yards away. Will and Lyra both felt their missing selves close by – an excitement, a wild hope chilled with fear: because the Spectres were thick among the trees, and they would have to go in directly among them, and the very sight of them evoked that nauseating weakness at the heart.

"They're afraid of the knife," said a voice beside them, and the bear-king stopped so suddenly that Will and Lyra tumbled off his back.

"Lee!" said Iorek. "Lee, my comrade, I have never seen this before. You are dead – what am I speaking to?"

"Iorek, old feller, you don't know the half of it. We'll take over now – the Spectres aren't afraid of bears. Lyra, Will – come this way, and hold up that knife –"

The blue hawk swooped once more to Lyra's fist, and the grey-haired lady said, "Don't waste a second – go in and find your dæmons and escape! There's more danger coming."

"Thank you, lady! Thank you all!" said Lyra, and the hawk took wing.

Will could see Lee Scoresby's ghost dimly beside them, urging them into the grove, but they had to say farewell to Iorek Byrnison.

"Iorek, my dear, there en't words – bless you, bless you!"

"Thank you, King Iorek," said Will.

"No time. Go. Go!"

He pushed them away with his armoured head.

Will plunged after Lee Scoresby's ghost into the under-growth, slashing to right and left with the knife. The light here was broken and muted, and the shadows were thick, tangled, confusing.

"Keep close," he called to Lyra, and then cried out as a bramble sliced across his cheek.

All around them there was movement, noise, and struggle. The shadows moved to and fro like branches in a high wind.

They might have been ghosts; both children felt the little dashes of cold they knew so well, and then they heard voices all around:

"This way!"

"Over here!"

"Keep going – we're holding them off!"

"Not far now!"

And then came a cry in a voice that Lyra knew and loved better than any other:

"Oh, come quick! Quick, Lyra!"

"Pan, darling – I'm here –"

She hurled herself into the dark, sobbing and shaking, and Will tore down branches and ivy and slashed at brambles and nettles, while all around them the ghost-voices rose in a clamour of encouragement and warning.

But the Spectres had found their target too, and they pressed in through the snagging tangle of bush and briar and root and branch, meeting no more resistance than smoke. A dozen, a score of the pallid malignities seemed to pour in towards the centre of the grove, where John Parry's ghost marshalled his companions to fight them off.

Will and Lyra were both trembling and weak with fear, exhaustion, nausea, and pain, but giving up was inconceivable. Lyra tore at the brambles with her bare hands, Will slashed and hacked to left and right, as around them the combat of the shadowy beings became more and more savage.

"There!" cried Lee. "See 'em? By that big rock –"

A wildcat, two wildcats, spitting and hissing and slashing. Both were dæmons, and Will felt that if there were time he'd easily be able to tell which was Pantalaimon; but there wasn't time, because a Spectre eased horribly out of the nearest patch of shadow and glided towards them.

Will leapt over the last obstacle, a fallen tree trunk, and plunged the knife into the unresisting shimmer in the air. He felt his arm go numb, but he clenched his teeth as he was clenching his fingers around the hilt, and the pale form seemed to boil away and melt back into the darkness again.

Almost there; and the dæmons were mad with fear, because more Spectres and still more came pressing through the trees, and only the valiant ghosts were holding them back.

"Can you cut through?" said John Parry's ghost.

Will held up the knife, and had to stop as a racking bout of nausea shook him from head to toe. There was nothing left in his stomach, and the spasm hurt dreadfully. Lyra beside him was in the same state. Lee's ghost, seeing why, leapt for the dæmons and wrestled with the pale thing that was coming through the rock from behind them.

"Will – please –" said Lyra, gasping.

In went the knife, along, down, back. Lee Scoresby's ghost looked through, and saw a wide quiet prairie under a brilliant moon, so very like his own homeland that he thought he'd been blessed.

Will leapt across the clearing and seized the nearest dæmon while Lyra scooped up the other.

And even in that horrible urgency, even at that moment of utmost peril, each of them felt the same little shock of excitement: for Lyra was holding Will's dæmon, the nameless wildcat, and Will was carrying Pantalaimon.

They tore their glance away from each other's eyes.

"Goodbye, Mr Scoresby!" Lyra cried, looking around for him. "I wish – oh, thank you, thank you – goodbye!"

"Goodbye, my dear child – goodbye, Will – go well!"

Lyra scrambled through, but Will stood still and looked

into the eyes of his father's ghost, brilliant in the shadows. Before he left him, there was something he had to say.

Will said to his father's ghost, "You said I was a warrior. You told me that was my nature, and I shouldn't argue with it. Father, you were wrong. I fought because I had to. I can't choose my nature, but I can choose what I do. And I *will* choose, because now I'm free."

His father's smile was full of pride and tenderness. "Well done, my boy. Well done indeed," he said.

Will couldn't see him any more. He turned and climbed through after Lyra.

And now that their purpose was achieved, now the children had found their dæmons and escaped, the dead warriors allowed their atoms to relax and drift apart, at long long last.

Out of the little grove, away from the baffled Spectres, out of the valley, past the mighty form of his old companion the armour-clad bear, the last little scrap of the consciousness that had been the aëronaut Lee Scoresby floated upwards, just as his great balloon had done so many times. Untroubled by the flares and the bursting shells, deaf to the explosions and the shouts and cries of anger and warning and pain, conscious only of his movement upwards, the last of Lee Scoresby passed through the heavy clouds and came out under the brilliant stars, where the atoms of his beloved dæmon Hester were waiting for him.

32
Morning

THE MORN~
ING COMES, THE
NIGHT DECAYS,
THE WATCHMEN
LEAVE THEIR
STATIONS...
WILLIAM BLAKE

The wide golden prairie that Lee Scoresby's ghost had seen briefly through the window was lying quiet under the first sun of morning.

Golden, but also yellow, brown, green, and every one of the million shades between them; and black, in places, in lines and streaks of bright pitch; and silvery, too, where the sun caught the tops of a particular kind of grass just coming into flower; and blue, where a wide lake some way off and a small pond closer by reflected back the wide blue of the sky.

And quiet, but not silent, for a soft breeze rustled the billions of little stems, and a billion insects and other small creatures scraped and hummed and chirruped in the grass, and a bird too high in the blue to be seen sang little looping falls of bell-notes now close by, now far off, and never twice the same.

In all that wide landscape the only living things that were silent and still were the boy and the girl lying asleep, back to back, under the shade of an outcrop of rock at the top of a little bluff.

They were so still, so pale, that they might have been dead. Hunger had drawn the skin over their faces, pain had left lines around their eyes, and they were covered in dust and mud and not a little blood. And from the absolute passivity of their limbs, they seemed in the last stages of exhaustion.

Lyra was the first to wake. As the sun moved up the sky, it came past the rock above and touched her hair, and she began to stir, and when the sunlight reached her eyelids she found herself pulled up from the depths of sleep like a fish, slow and heavy and resistant.

But there was no arguing with the sun, and presently she moved her head and threw her arm across her eyes and murmured: "Pan – Pan…"

Under the shadow of her arm she opened her eyes and came properly awake. She didn't move for some time, because her arms and legs were so sore, and every part of her body felt limp with weariness; but still she was awake, and she felt the little breeze and the sun's warmth and she heard the little insect-scrapings and the bell-song of that bird high above. It was all good. She had forgotten how good the world was.

Presently she rolled over and saw Will, still fast asleep. His hand had bled a lot; his shirt was ripped and filthy, his hair was stiff with dust and sweat. She looked at him for a long time, at the little pulse in his throat, at his chest rising and falling slowly, at the delicate shadows his eyelashes made when the sun finally reached them.

He murmured something and stirred. Not wanting to be caught looking at him, she looked the other way at the little grave they'd dug the night before, just a couple of hand-breadths wide, where the bodies of the Chevalier Tialys and the Lady Salmakia now lay at rest. There was a flat stone nearby: she got up and prised it loose from the soil, and set it upright at the head of the grave, and then sat up and shaded her eyes to gaze across the plain.

It seemed to stretch for ever and ever. It was nowhere entirely flat; gentle undulations and little ridges and gullies varied the surface wherever she looked, and here and there she saw a stand of trees so tall they seemed to be constructed rather than grown: their straight trunks and dark green canopy seemed to defy distance, being so clearly visible at what must have been many miles away.

Closer, though – in fact at the foot of the bluff, not more than a hundred yards away – there was a little pond fed by a spring coming out of the rock, and Lyra realized how thirsty she was.

She got up on shaky legs and walked slowly down towards it. The spring gurgled and trickled through mossy rocks, and she dipped her hands in it again and again, washing them clear of the mud and grime before lifting the water to her mouth. It was teeth-achingly cold, and she swallowed it with delight.

The pond was fringed with reeds, where a frog was croaking. It was shallow and warmer than the spring, as she discovered when she took off her shoes and waded into it. She stood for a long time with the sun on her head and her body and relishing the cool mud under her feet and the cold flow of spring water around her calves.

She bent down to dip her face under the water, and wet her hair thoroughly, letting it trail out and flicking it back again, stirring it with her fingers to lift all the dust and grime out.

When she felt a little cleaner and her thirst was satisfied, she looked up the slope again, to see that Will was awake. He was sitting with his knees drawn up and his arms across them, looking out across the plain as she'd done, and marvelling at the extent of it. And at the light, and at the warmth, and at the quiet.

She climbed slowly back to join him, and found him cutting the names of the Gallivespians on the little headstone, and setting it more firmly in the soil.

"Are they..." he said, and she knew he meant the dæmons.

"Don't know. I haven't seen Pan. I got the feeling he's not far away, but I don't know. D'you remember what happened?"

He rubbed his eyes and yawned so deeply she heard little cracking noises in his jaw. Then he blinked and shook his head.

"Not much," he said. "I picked up Pantalaimon and you picked up – the other one and we came through, and it was moonlight everywhere, and I put him down to close the window."

"And your – the other dæmon just jumped out of my arms," she said. "And I was trying to see Mr Scoresby through the window, and Iorek, and to see where Pan had gone, and when I looked around they just weren't there."

"It doesn't feel like when we went into the world of the dead, though. Like when we were really separated."

"No," she agreed. "They're somewhere near all right. I remember when we were young we used to try and play hide-and-seek except it never really worked, because I was too big to hide from him and I always used to know exactly where he was, even if he was camouflaged as a moth or something. But this is strange," she said, passing her hands over her head involuntarily as if she were trying to dispel some enchantment; "he en't here, but I don't feel torn apart, I feel safe, and I know he is."

"They're together, I think," Will said.

"Yeah. They must be."

He stood up suddenly.

"Look," he said, "over there…"

He was shading his eyes and pointing. She followed his gaze, and saw a distant tremor of movement, quite different from the shimmer of the heat-haze.

"Animals?" she said doubtfully.

"And listen," he said, putting his hand behind his ear.

Now he'd pointed it out, she could hear a low persistent rumble, almost like thunder, a very long way off.

"They've disappeared," Will said, pointing.

The little patch of moving shadows had vanished, but the rumble went on for a few moments. Then it became suddenly quieter, though it had been very quiet already. The two of them were still gazing in the same direction, and shortly afterwards they saw the movement start up again. And a few moments later came the sound.

"They went behind a ridge or something," said Will. "Are they closer?"

"Can't really see. Yes, they're turning, look, they're coming this way."

"Well, if we have to fight them, I want a drink first," said Will, and he took the rucksack down to the stream, where he drank deep and washed off most of the dirt. His wound had bled a lot. He was a mess; he longed for a hot shower with plenty of soap, and for some clean clothes.

Lyra was watching the … whatever they were; they were very strange.

"Will," she called, "they're riding on wheels…"

But she said it uncertainly. He climbed back a little way up the slope and shaded his eyes to look. It was possible to see individuals now. The group or herd or gang was about a dozen strong, and they were moving, as Lyra said, on wheels. They looked like a cross between antelopes and motorcycles, but they were stranger than that, even: they had trunks like small elephants.

And they were making for Will and Lyra, with an air of intention. Will took out the knife, but Lyra, sitting on the grass beside him, was already turning the hands of the alethiometer.

It responded quickly, while the creatures were still a few hundred yards away. The needle darted swiftly left and right and left and left, and Lyra watched it anxiously, for her last few readings had been so difficult, and her mind felt awkward and tentative as she stepped down through the branches of understanding. Instead of darting like a bird from one foothold to the next, she moved hand over hand for security; but the meaning was there as solid as ever, and soon she understood what it was saying.

"They're friendly," she said, "it's all right, Will, they're looking for us, they knew we were here... And it's odd, I can't quite make it out ... Dr Malone?"

She said the name half to herself, because she couldn't believe Dr Malone would be in this world. Still, the alethiometer indicated her clearly, although of course it couldn't give her name. Lyra put it away and stood up slowly beside Will.

"I think we should go down to them," she said. "They en't going to hurt us."

Some of them had stopped, waiting. The leader moved ahead a little, trunk raised, and they could see how he propelled himself, with powerful backward strokes of his lateral limbs. Some of the creatures had gone to the pond to drink; the others waited, but not with the mild passive curiosity of cows gathering at a gate. These were individuals, lively with intelligence and purpose. They were people.

Will and Lyra moved down the slope until they were close enough to speak to them. In spite of what Lyra had said, Will kept his hand on the knife.

"I don't know if you understand me," Lyra said cautiously, "but I know you're friendly. I think we should —"

The leader moved his trunk and said, "Come see Mary. You ride. We carry. Come see Mary."

"Oh!" she said, and turned to Will, smiling with delight.

Two of the creatures were fitted with bridles and stirrups of braided cord. Not saddles; their diamond-shaped backs turned out to be comfortable enough without them. Lyra had ridden a bear, and Will had ridden a bicycle, but neither had ridden a horse, which was the closest comparison. However, riders of horses are usually in control, and the children soon found that they were not: the reins and the stirrups were there simply to give them something to hold on to and balance with. The creatures themselves made all the decisions.

"Where are —" Will began to say, but had to stop and regain his balance as the creature moved under him.

The group swung around and moved down the slight slope, going slowly through the grass. The movement was bumpy, but not uncomfortable, because the creatures had no spine: Will and Lyra felt that they were sitting on chairs with a well-sprung seat.

Soon they came to what they hadn't seen clearly from the bluff: one of those patches of black or dark-brown ground. And they were as surprised to find roads of smooth rock lacing through the prairie as Mary Malone had been some time before.

The creatures rolled on to the surface and set off, soon picking up speed. The road was more like a watercourse than a highway, because in places it broadened into wide areas like small lakes, and at others it split into narrow channels only to combine again unpredictably. It was quite unlike the brutal rational way roads in Will's world sliced through hillsides and leapt across valleys on bridges of concrete. This was part of the landscape, not an imposition on it.

They were going faster and faster. It took Will and Lyra a while to get used to the living impulse of the muscles and the shuddering thunder of the hard wheels on the hard stone. Lyra found it more difficult than Will at first, because she had never ridden a bicycle, and she didn't know the trick of leaning into the corner; but she saw how he was doing it, and soon she was finding the speed exhilarating.

The wheels made too much noise for them to speak. Instead they had to point: at the trees, in amazement at their size and splendour; at a flock of birds, the strangest they had ever seen, their fore-and-aft wings giving them a twisting, screwing motion through the air; at a fat blue lizard as long as a horse basking in the very middle of the road (the wheeled creatures divided to ride on either side of it, and it took no notice at all).

The sun was high in the sky when they began to slow down. And in the air, unmistakable, was the salt smell of the sea. The road was rising towards a bluff, and presently they were moving no faster than a walk.

Lyra, stiff and sore, said, "Can you stop? I want to get off and walk."

Her creature felt the tug at the bridle, and whether or not he understood her words, he came to a halt. Will's did too, and both children climbed down, finding themselves stiff and shaken after the continued jolting and tensing.

The creatures wheeled around to talk together, their trunks moving elegantly in time with the sounds they made.

After a minute they moved on, and Will and Lyra were happy to walk among the hay-scented, grass-warm creatures who trundled beside them. One or two had gone on ahead to the top of the rise, and the children, now they no longer had to concentrate on hanging on, were able to watch how they moved, and admire the grace and power with which they propelled themselves forward and leaned and turned.

As they came to the top of the rise, they stopped, and Will and Lyra heard the leader say, "Mary close. Mary there."

They looked down. On the horizon there was the blue gleam of the sea. A broad slow-moving river wound through rich grassland in the middle distance, and at the foot of the long slope, among copses of small trees and rows of vegetables, stood a village of thatched houses. More creatures like these moved about among the houses, or tended crops, or worked among the trees.

"Now ride again," said the leader.

There wasn't far to go. Will and Lyra climbed up once more, and the other creatures looked closely at their balance and checked the stirrups with their trunks, as if to make sure they were safe.

Then they set off, beating the road with their lateral limbs, and urging themselves forward down the slope until they were moving at a terrific pace. Will and Lyra clung tight with hands and knees and felt the air whip past their faces and fling their hair back and press on their eyeballs. The thundering of the wheels, the rush of the grassland on either side, the sure and powerful lean into the broad curve ahead, the clear-headed rapture of speed – the creatures loved this, and Will and Lyra felt their joy and laughed in happy response.

They stopped in the centre of the village, and the others,

who had seen them coming, gathered around raising their trunks and speaking words of welcome.

And then Lyra cried, "Dr Malone!"

Mary had come out of one of the huts, her faded blue shirt, her stocky figure, her warm ruddy cheeks both strange and familiar.

Lyra ran and embraced her, and the woman hugged her tight, and Will stood back, careful and doubtful.

Mary kissed Lyra warmly, and then came forward to welcome Will. And then came a curious little mental dance of sympathy and awkwardness, which took place in a second or less.

Moved by compassion for the state they were in, Mary first meant to embrace him as well as Lyra. But Mary was grown up, and Will was nearly grown, and she could see that that kind of response would have made a child of him, because while she might have embraced a child, she would never have done that to a man she didn't know; so she drew back mentally, wanting above all to honour this friend of Lyra's and not cause him to lose face.

So instead she held out her hand and he shook it, and a current of understanding and respect passed between them so powerful that it became liking at once, and each of them felt that they had made a life-long friend; as indeed they had.

"This is Will," said Lyra, "he's from your world – remember, I told you about him –"

"I'm Mary Malone," she said, "and you're hungry, the pair of you, you look half-starved."

She turned to the creature by her side and spoke some of those singing, hooting sounds, moving her arm as she did so.

At once the creatures moved away, and some of them

brought cushions and rugs from the nearest house and laid them on the firm soil under a tree nearby, whose dense leaves and low-hanging branches gave a cool and fragrant shade.

And as soon as they were comfortable, their hosts brought smooth wooden bowls brimming with milk, which had a faint lemony astringency and was wonderfully refreshing; and small nuts like hazels, but with a richer buttery taste; and salad plucked fresh from the soil, sharp peppery leaves mingled with soft thick ones that oozed a creamy sap, and little cherry-sized roots tasting like sweet carrots.

But they couldn't eat much. It was too rich. Will wanted to do justice to their generosity, but the only thing he could easily swallow, apart from the drink, was some flat, slightly scorched floury bread like chapattis or tortillas. It was plain and nourishing, and that was all Will could cope with. Lyra tried some of everything, but like Will she soon found that a little was quite enough.

Mary managed to avoid asking any questions. These two had passed through an experience that had marked them deeply: they didn't want to talk about it yet.

So she answered their questions about the mulefa, and told them briefly how she had arrived in this world; and then she left them under the shade of the tree, because she could see their eyelids drooping and their heads nodding.

"You don't have to do anything now but sleep," she said.

The afternoon air was warm and still, and the shade of the tree was drowsy and murmurous with crickets. Less than five minutes after they'd swallowed the last of the drink, both Will and Lyra were fast asleep.

They are of two sexes? said Atal, surprised. *But how can you tell?*

It's easy, said Mary. *Their bodies are different shapes. They move differently.*

They are not much smaller than you. But they have less sraf. When will that come to them?

I don't know, Mary said. *I suppose some time soon. I don't know when it happens to us.*

No wheels, said Atal sympathetically.

They were weeding the vegetable garden. Mary had made a hoe to save having to bend down; Atal used her trunk, so their conversation was intermittent.

But you knew they were coming, said Atal.

Yes.

Was it the sticks that told you?

No, said Mary, blushing. She was a scientist; it was bad enough to have to admit to consulting the I Ching, but this was even more embarrassing. *It was a night-picture*, she confessed.

The mulefa had no single word for dream. They dreamed vividly, though, and took their dreams very seriously.

You don't like night-pictures, Atal said.

Yes, I do. But I didn't believe them until now. I saw the boy and the girl so clearly, and a voice told me to prepare for them.

What sort of voice? How did it speak if you couldn't see it?

It was hard for Atal to imagine speech without the trunk-movements that clarified and defined it. She'd stopped in the middle of a row of beans and faced Mary with fascinated curiosity.

Well, I did see it, said Mary. *It was a woman, or a female wise one, like us, like my people. But very old and yet not old at all.*

Wise one was what the mulefa called their leaders. She saw that Atal was looking intensely interested.

How could she be old and also not old? said Atal.

It is a make-like, said Mary.

Atal swung her trunk, reassured.

Mary went on as best she could: *She told me that I should expect the children, and when they would appear, and where. But not why. I must just look after them.*

They are hurt and tired, said Atal. *Will they stop the sraf leaving?*

Mary looked up uneasily. She knew without having to check through the spyglass that the Shadow-particles were streaming away faster than ever.

I hope so, she said. *But I don't know how.*

In the early evening, when the cooking-fires were lit and the first stars were coming out, a group of strangers arrived. Mary was washing; she heard the thunder of their wheels, and the agitated murmur of their talk, and hurried out of her house, drying herself.

Will and Lyra had been asleep all afternoon, and they were just stirring now, hearing the noise. Lyra sat up groggily to see Mary talking to five or six of the mulefa, who were surrounding her, clearly excited; but whether they were angry or joyful, she couldn't tell.

Mary saw her and broke away.

"Lyra," she said, "something's happened – they've found something they can't explain and it's... I don't know what it is... I've got to go and look. It's an hour or so away. I'll come back as soon as I can. Help yourself to anything you need from my house – I can't stop, they're too anxious –"

"All right," said Lyra, still dazed from her long sleep.

Mary looked under the tree. Will was rubbing his eyes.

"I really won't be too long," she said. "Atal will stay with you."

The leader was impatient. Mary swiftly threw her bridle and stirrups over his back, excusing herself for being clumsy, and mounted at once. They wheeled and turned and drove away into the dusk.

They set off in a new direction, along the ridge above the coast to the north. Mary had never ridden in the dark before, and she found the speed even more alarming than by day. As they climbed, Mary could see the glitter of the moon on the sea far off to the left, and its silver-sepia light seemed to envelop her in a cool sceptical wonder. The wonder was in her and the scepticism was in the world, and the coolness was in both.

She looked up from time to time and touched the spyglass in her pocket, but she couldn't use it till they'd stopped moving. And these mulefa were moving urgently, with the air of not wanting to stop for anything. After an hour's hard riding they swung inland, leaving the stone road and moving slowly along a trail of beaten earth that ran between knee-high grass past a stand of wheel-trees and up towards a ridge. The landscape glowed under the moon: wide bare hills with occasional little gullies where streams trickled down among the trees that clustered there.

It was towards one of these gullies that they led her. She had dismounted when they left the road, and she walked steadily at their pace over the brow of the hill and down into the gully.

She heard the trickling of the spring, and the night-wind in the grass. She heard the quiet sound of the wheels crunching over the hard-packed earth, and she heard the mulefa ahead of her murmuring to one another, and then they stopped.

In the side of the hill, just a few yards away, was one of

those openings made by the subtle knife. It was like the mouth of a cave, because the moonlight shone into it a little way, just as if inside the opening there was the inside of the hill: but it wasn't. And out of it was coming a procession of ghosts.

Mary felt as if the ground had given way beneath her mind. She caught herself with a start, and seized the nearest branch for reassurance that there still was a physical world, and she was still part of it.

She moved closer. Old men and women, children, babes in arms, humans and other beings too, more and more thickly they came out of the dark into the world of solid moonlight – and vanished.

That was the strangest thing. They took a few steps in the world of grass and air and silver light, and looked around, their faces transformed with joy – Mary had never seen such joy – and held out their arms as if they were embracing the whole universe; and then, as if they were made of mist or smoke, they simply drifted away, becoming part of the earth and the dew and the night breeze.

Some of them came towards Mary as if they wanted to tell her something, and reached out their hands, and she felt their touch like little shocks of cold. One of the ghosts – an old woman – beckoned, urging her to come close.

Then she spoke, and Mary heard her say:

"Tell them stories. That's what we didn't know. All this time, and we never knew! But they need the truth. That's what nourishes them. You must tell them true stories, and everything will be well, everything. Just tell them stories."

That was all, and then she was gone. It was one of those moments when we suddenly recall a dream that we've unaccountably forgotten, and back in a flood comes all the emotion we felt in our sleep. It was the dream she'd tried to describe to Atal, the night-picture; but as Mary tried to find it again, it dissolved and drifted apart, just as these presences did in the open air. The dream was gone.

All that was left was the sweetness of that feeling, and the injunction to *tell them stories*.

She looked into the darkness. As far as she could see into that endless silence, more of these ghosts were coming, thousands upon thousands, like refugees returning to their homeland.

"Tell them stories," she said to herself.

33

Marzipan

Next morning Lyra woke up from a dream in which Pantalaimon had come back to her, and revealed his final shape; and she had loved it, but now she had no idea what it was.

The sun hadn't long risen, and the air had a fresh bloom. She could see the sunlight through the open door of the little thatched hut she slept in, Mary's house. She lay for a while listening. There were birds outside, and some kind of cricket, and Mary was breathing quietly in her sleep nearby.

Lyra sat up, and found herself naked. She was indignant for a moment, and then she saw some clean clothes folded beside her on the floor: a shirt of Mary's, a length of soft light patterned cloth that she could tie into a skirt. She put them on, feeling swamped in the shirt, but at least decent.

She left the hut. Pantalaimon was nearby: she was sure of it. She could almost hear him talking and laughing. It must mean that he was safe, and they were still connected somehow. And when he forgave her and came back – the hours they'd spend just talking, just telling each other everything...

Will was still asleep under the tree, the lazy thing. Lyra thought of waking him up, but if she was on her own, she could swim in the river. She happily used to swim naked in the river Cherwell, with all the other Oxford children, but it would be quite different with Will, and she blushed even to think of it.

So she went down to the water alone in the pearl-coloured morning. Among the reeds at the edge there was a tall slender bird like a heron, standing perfectly still on one leg. She walked quietly and slowly so as not to disturb it, but the bird took no more notice of her than if she'd been a twig on the water.

"Well," she said.

She left the clothes on the bank and slipped into the river. She swam hard to keep warm, and then came out and huddled on the bank, shivering. Pan would help dry her, normally: was he a fish, laughing at her from under the water? Or a beetle, creeping into the clothes to tickle her, or a bird? Or was he somewhere else entirely with the other dæmon, and with Lyra not on his mind at all?

The sun was warm now, and she was soon dry. She dressed in Mary's loose shirt again and, seeing some flat stones by the bank, went to fetch her own clothes to wash them. But she found that someone had already done that: hers, and Will's too, were laid over the springy twigs of a fragrant bush, nearly dry.

Will was stirring. She sat nearby and called him softly.

"Will! Wake up!"

"Where are we?" he said at once, and sat up, reaching for the knife.

"Safe," she said, looking away. "And they washed our clothes too, or Dr Malone did. I'll get yours. They're nearly dry…"

She passed them in and sat with her back to him till he was dressed.

"I swam in the river," she said. "I went to look for Pan, but I think he's hiding."

"That's a good idea. I mean a swim. I feel as if I've got years and years of dirt on me... I'll go down and wash."

While he was gone, Lyra wandered around the village, not looking too closely at anything in case she broke some code of politeness, but curious about everything she saw. Some of the houses were very old and some quite new, but they were all built in much the same way out of wood and clay and thatch. There was nothing crude about them; each door and window-frame and lintel was covered in subtle patterns, but patterns that weren't carved in the wood: it was as if they'd persuaded the wood to grow in that shape naturally.

The more she looked, the more she saw all kinds of order and carefulness in the village, like the layers of meaning in the alethiometer. Part of her mind was eager to puzzle it all out, to step lightly from similarity to similarity, from one meaning to another as she did with the instrument; but another part was wondering how long they'd be able to stay here before they had to move on.

Well, I'm not going anywhere till Pan comes back, she said to herself.

Presently Will came up from the river, and then Mary came out of her house and offered them breakfast; and soon Atal came along too, and the village came to life around them. The two young mulefa children, without wheels, kept peeping around the edge of their houses to stare, and Lyra would suddenly turn and look at them directly to make them jump and laugh with terror.

"Well now," Mary said when they'd eaten some bread and fruit and drunk a scalding infusion of something like mint. "Yesterday you were too tired and all you could do was rest.

But you look a lot more lively today, both of you, and I think we need to tell each other everything we've found out. And it'll take us a good long time, and we might as well keep our hands busy while we're doing it, so we'll make ourselves useful and mend some nets."

They carried the pile of stiff, tarry netting to the river bank and spread it out on the grass, and Mary showed them how to knot a new piece of cord where it was worn. She was wary, because Atal had told her that the families further along the coast had seen large numbers of the tualapi, the white birds, gathering out at sea, and everyone was prepared for a warning to leave at once; but work had to go on in the meantime.

So they sat working in the sun by the placid river, and Lyra told her story, from the moment so long ago when she and Pan decided to look in the Retiring Room at Jordan College.

The tide came in and turned, and still there was no sign of the tualapi. In the late afternoon Mary took Will and Lyra along the river bank, past the fishing-posts where the nets were tied, and through the wide salt-marsh towards the sea. It was safe to go there when the tide was out, because the white birds only came inland when the water was high. Mary led the way along a hard path above the mud; like many things the mulefa had made, it was ancient and perfectly maintained, more like a part of nature than something imposed on it.

"Did they make the stone roads?" Will said.

"No. I think the roads made them, in a way," Mary said. "I mean they'd never have developed the use of the wheels if there hadn't been plenty of hard flat surfaces to use them on. I think they're lava flows from ancient volcanoes.

"So the roads made it possible for them to use the wheels.

And other things came together as well. Like the wheel-trees themselves, and the way their bodies are formed – they're not vertebrates, they don't have a spine. Some lucky chance in our worlds long ago must have meant that creatures with backbones had it a bit easier, so all kinds of other shapes developed, all based on the central spine. In this world, chance went another way, and the diamond-frame was successful. There are vertebrates, to be sure, but not many. There are snakes, for example. Snakes are important here. The people look after them and try not to hurt them.

"Anyway, their shape, and the roads, and the wheel-trees coming together all made it possible. A lot of little chances, all coming together. When did your part of the story begin, Will?"

"Lots of little chances for me, too," he began, thinking of the cat under the hornbeam trees. If he'd arrived there thirty seconds earlier or later, he would never have seen the cat, never have found the window, never have discovered Cittàgazze and Lyra; none of this would have happened.

He started from the very beginning, and they listened as they walked. By the time they reached the mud-flats, he had reached the point where he and his father were fighting on the mountaintop.

"And then the witch killed him…"

He had never really understood that. He explained what she'd told him before she killed herself: she had loved John Parry, and he had scorned her.

"Witches are fierce, though," Lyra said.

"But if she loved him…"

"Well," said Mary, "love is ferocious too."

"But he loved my mother," said Will. "And I can tell her that he was never unfaithful."

Lyra, looking at Will, thought that if he fell in love, he would be like that.

All around them the quiet noises of the afternoon hung in the warm air: the endless trickling sucking of the marsh, the scraping of insects, the calling of gulls. The tide was fully out, so the whole extent of the beach was clear and glistening under the bright sun. A billion tiny mud-creatures lived and ate and died in the top layer of sand, and the little casts and breathing-holes and invisible movements showed that the whole landscape was aquiver with life.

Without telling the others why, Mary looked out to the distant sea, scanning the horizon for white sails. But there was only hazy glitter where the blue of the sky paled at the edge of the sea, and the sea took up the pallor and made it sparkle through the shimmering air.

She showed Will and Lyra how to gather a particular kind of mollusc by finding their breathing-tubes just above the sand. The mulefa loved them, but it was hard for them to move on the sand and gather them. Whenever Mary came to the shore she harvested as many as she could, and now with three pairs of hands and eyes at work there would be a feast.

She gave each of them a cloth bag, and they worked as they listened to the next part of the story. Steadily they filled their bags, and Mary led them unobtrusively back to the edge of the marsh, for the tide was turning.

The story was taking a long time; they wouldn't get to the world of the dead that day. As they neared the village, Will was telling Mary what he and Lyra had come to realize about the three-part nature of human beings.

"You know," Mary said, "the church – the Catholic Church that I used to belong to – wouldn't use the word dæmon, but St Paul talks about spirit *and* soul *and* body. So the idea of three parts in human nature isn't so strange."

"But the best part is the body," Will said. "That's what Baruch and Balthamos told me. Angels wish they had bodies. They told me that angels can't understand why *we* don't enjoy the world more. It would be sort of ecstasy for them to have our flesh and our senses. In the world of the dead –"

"Tell it when we get to it," said Lyra, and she smiled at him, a smile of such sweet knowledge and joy that his senses felt confused. He smiled back, and Mary thought his expression showed more perfect trust than she'd ever seen on a human face.

By this time they had reached the village, and there was the evening meal to prepare. So Mary left the other two by the river-bank where they sat to watch the tide flooding in, and went to join Atal by the cooking fire. Her friend was overjoyed by the shellfish-harvest.

But Mary, she said, *the tualapi destroyed a village further up the coast, and then another and another. They've never done that before. They usually attack one and then go back to sea. And another tree fell today...*

No! Where?

Atal mentioned a grove not far from a hot spring. Mary had been there only three days before, and nothing had seemed wrong. She took the spyglass and looked at the sky; sure enough, the great stream of shadow-particles was flowing more strongly, and at incomparably greater speed and volume, than the tide now rising between the river-banks.

What can you do? said Atal.

Mary felt the weight of responsibility like a heavy hand between her shoulder-blades, but made herself sit up lightly.

Tell them stories, she said.

* * *

When supper was over, the three humans and Atal sat on rugs outside Mary's house, under the warm stars. They lay back, well fed and comfortable in the flower-scented night, and listened to Mary tell her story.

She began just before she first met Lyra, telling them about the work she was doing at the Dark Matter Research group, and the funding crisis. How much time she'd had to spend asking for money, and how little time there'd been left for research!

But Lyra's coming had changed everything, and so quickly: within a matter of days she'd left her world altogether.

"I did as you told me," she said. "I made a program – that's a set of instructions – to let the Shadows talk to me through the computer. They told me what to do. They said they were angels, and – well…"

"If you were a scientist," said Will, "I don't suppose that was a good thing for them to say. You might not have believed in angels."

"Ah, but I knew about them. I used to be a nun, you see. I thought physics could be done to the glory of God, till I saw there wasn't any God at all and that physics was more interesting anyway. The Christian religion is a very powerful and convincing mistake, that's all."

"When did you stop being a nun?" said Lyra.

"I remember it exactly," Mary said, "even to the time of day. Because I was good at physics, they let me keep up my university career, you see, and I finished my doctorate and I was going to teach. It wasn't one of those orders where they shut you away from the world. In fact we didn't even wear the habit; we just had to dress soberly and wear a crucifix. So I was going into university to teach and do research into particle physics.

"And there was a conference on my subject and they asked

me to come and read a paper. The conference was in Lisbon, and I'd never been there before; in fact I'd never been out of England. The whole business – the plane flight, the hotel, the bright sunlight, the foreign languages all around me, the well-known people who were going to speak, and the thought of my own paper and wondering whether anyone would turn up to listen and whether I'd be too nervous to get the words out... Oh, I was keyed up with excitement, I can't tell you.

"And I was so innocent – you have to remember that. I'd been such a good little girl, I'd gone to Mass regularly, I'd thought I had a vocation for the spiritual life. I wanted to serve God with all my heart. I wanted to take my whole life and offer it up like this," she said, holding up her hands together, "and place it in front of Jesus to do as he liked with. And I suppose I was pleased with myself. Too much. I was holy *and* I was clever. Ha! That lasted until, oh, half past nine on the evening of August the tenth, seven years ago."

Lyra sat up and hugged her knees, listening closely.

"It was the evening after I'd given my paper," Mary went on, "and it had gone well, and there'd been some well-known people listening, and I'd dealt with the questions without making a mess of it, and altogether I was full of relief and pleasure... And pride too, no doubt.

"Anyway, some of my colleagues were going to a restaurant a little way down the coast, and they asked if I'd like to go. Normally I'd have made some excuse, but this time I thought well, I'm a grown woman, I've presented a paper on an important subject and it was well received and I'm among good friends... And it was so warm, and the talk was about all the things I was most interested in, and we were all in high spirits, I thought I'd loosen up a bit. I was discovering another side of myself, you know, one that liked the taste of wine and grilled sardines and the feeling of warm air on my skin and the beat of music in the background. I relished it.

"So we sat down to eat in the garden. I was at the end of a long table under a lemon tree, and there was a sort of bower next to me with passion flowers, and my neighbour was talking to the person on the other side, and... Well, sitting opposite was a man I'd seen once or twice around the conference. I didn't know him to speak to; he was Italian, and he'd done some work that people were talking about, and I thought it would be interesting to hear about it.

"Anyway. He was only a little older than me, and he had soft black hair and beautiful olive-coloured skin and dark, dark eyes. His hair kept falling across his forehead and he kept pushing it back like that, slowly..."

She showed them. Will thought she looked as if she remembered it very well.

"He wasn't handsome," she went on. "He wasn't a ladies' man or a charmer. If he had been, I'd have been shy, I wouldn't have known how to talk to him. But he was nice and clever and funny and it was the easiest thing in the world to sit there in the lantern light under the lemon tree with the scent of the flowers and the grilled food and the wine, and talk and laugh and feel myself hoping that he thought I was pretty. Sister Mary Malone, flirting! What about my vows? What about dedicating my life to Jesus and all that?

"Well, I don't know if it was the wine or my own silliness or the warm air or the lemon tree, or whatever... But it gradually seemed to me that I'd made myself believe something that wasn't true. I'd made myself believe that I was fine and happy and fulfilled on my own without the love of anyone else. Being in love was like China: you knew it was there, and no doubt it was very interesting, and some people went there, but I never would. I'd spend all my life without ever going to China, but it wouldn't matter, because there was all the rest of the world to visit.

"And then someone passed me a bit of some sweet stuff and I suddenly realized I *had* been to China. So to speak. And I'd forgotten it. It was the taste of the sweet stuff that brought it back – I think it was marzipan – sweet almond paste," she explained to Lyra, who was looking puzzled.

Lyra said, "Ah! Marchpane!" and settled back comfortably to hear what happened next.

"Anyway –" Mary went on – "I remembered the taste, and all at once I was back tasting it for the first time as a young girl.

"I was twelve years old. I was at a party at the house of one of my friends, a birthday party, and there was a disco – that's where they play music on a kind of recording machine and people dance," she explained, seeing Lyra's puzzlement. "Usually girls dance together because the boys are too shy to ask them. But this boy – I didn't know him – he asked me to dance, and so we had the first dance and then the next and by that time we were talking... And you know what it is when you like someone, you know it at once; well, I liked him such a lot. And we kept on talking and then there was a birthday cake. And he took a bit of marzipan and he just gently put it in my mouth – I remember trying to smile, and blushing, and feeling so foolish – and I fell in love with him just for that, for the gentle way he touched my lips with the marzipan."

As Mary said that, Lyra felt something strange happen to her body. She felt a stirring at the roots of her hair: she found herself breathing faster. She had never been on a roller-coaster, or anything like one, but if she had, she would have recognized the sensations in her breast: they were exciting and frightening at the same time, and she had not the slightest idea why. The sensation continued, and deepened, and changed, as more parts of her body found themselves affected too. She felt as if she had been handed the key to a great house she hadn't known was there, a house that was somehow inside her, and as she turned the key, deep in the darkness of the building she felt other doors opening too, and lights coming on. She sat trembling, hugging her knees, hardly daring to breathe, as Mary went on:

"And I think it was at that party, or it might have been at another one, that we kissed each other for the first time. It was in a garden, and there was the sound of music from inside, and the quiet and the cool among the trees, and I was *aching* – all my body was *aching* for him, and I could tell he felt the same – and we were both almost too shy to move. Almost. But one of us did and then without any interval between – it was like a quantum leap, *suddenly* – we were kissing each other and oh, it was more than China, it was paradise.

"We saw each other about half a dozen times, no more. And then his parents moved away and I never saw him again. It was such a sweet time, so short... But there it was. I'd known it. I *had* been to China."

It was the strangest thing: Lyra knew exactly what she meant, and half an hour earlier she would have had no idea at all. And inside her, that rich house with all its doors open and all its rooms lit stood waiting, quiet, expectant.

"And at half-past nine in the evening at that restaurant table in Portugal," Mary continued, quite unaware of the silent drama going on in Lyra, "someone gave me a piece of marzipan and it all came back. And I thought: am I really going to spend the rest of my life without ever feeling that again? I thought: I *want* to go to China. It's full of treasures and strangeness and mystery and joy. I thought, will anyone be better off if I go straight back to the hotel and say my prayers and confess to the priest and promise never to fall into temptation again? Will anyone be the better for making me miserable?

"And the answer came back – no. No one will. There's no one to fret, no one to condemn, no one to bless me for being a good girl, no one to punish me for being wicked. Heaven was empty. I didn't know whether God had died, or whether there never had been a God at all. Either way, I felt free and lonely and I didn't know whether I was happy or unhappy, but something very strange had happened. And all that huge change came about as I had the marzipan in my mouth, before I'd even swallowed it. A taste – a memory – a landslide…

"When I did swallow it and looked at the man across the table I could tell he knew something had happened. I couldn't tell him there and then; it was still too strange and private almost for me. But later on we went for a walk along the beach in the dark, and the warm night breeze kept stirring my hair about, and the Atlantic was being very well-behaved – little quiet waves around our feet…

"And I took the crucifix from around my neck and I threw it in the sea. That was it. All over. Gone.

"So that was how I stopped being a nun," she said.

"Was that man the same one that found out about the skulls?" Lyra said, intent.

"Oh – no. The skull man was Dr Payne, Oliver Payne. He came along much later. No, the man at the conference was called Alfredo Montale. He was very different."

"Did you kiss him?"

"Well," said Mary, smiling, "yes, but not then."

"Was it hard to leave the church?" said Will.

"In one way it was, because everyone was so disappointed. Everyone, from the Mother Superior to the priests to my parents – they were so upset and reproachful… I felt as if something *they* all passionately believed in depended on *me* carrying on with something I didn't.

"But in another way it was easy, because it made sense. For the first time ever I felt I was doing something with all of my nature and not only a part of it. So it was lonely for a while but then I got used to it."

"Did you marry him?" said Lyra.

"No. I didn't marry anyone. I lived with someone – not Alfredo, someone else. I lived with him for four years, nearly. My family was scandalized. But then we decided we'd be happier not living together. So I'm on my own. The man I lived with used to like mountain climbing, and he taught me to climb, and I walk in the mountains and... And I've got my work. Well, I *had* my work. So I'm solitary but happy, if you see what I mean."

"What was the boy called?" said Lyra. "At the party?"

"Tim."

"What did he look like?"

"Oh... Nice. That's all I remember."

"When I first saw you, in your Oxford," Lyra said, "you said one of the reasons you became a scientist was that you wouldn't have to think about good and evil. Did you think about them when you were a nun?"

"H'mm. No. But I knew what I *should* think: it was whatever the church taught me to think. And when I did science I had to think about other things altogether. So I never had to think about them for myself at all."

"But do you now?" said Will.

"I think I *have* to," Mary said, trying to be accurate.

"When you stopped believing in God," he went on, "did you stop believing in good and evil?"

"No. But I stopped believing there was a power of good and

a power of evil that were outside us. And I came to believe that good and evil are names for what people do, not for what they are. All we can say is that this is a good deed, because it helps someone, or that's an evil one, because it hurts them. People are too complicated to have simple labels."

"Yes," said Lyra firmly.

"Did you miss God?" asked Will.

"Yes," Mary said, "terribly. And I still do. And what I miss most is the sense of being connected to the whole of the universe. I used to feel I was connected to God like that, and because he was there, I was connected to the whole of his creation. But if he's not there, then..."

Far out on the marshes, a bird called with a long melancholy series of falling tones. Embers settled in the fire; the grass was stirring faintly with the night breeze. Atal seemed to be dozing like a cat, her wheels flat on the grass beside her, her legs folded under her body, eyes half closed, attention half-there and half-elsewhere. Will was lying on his back, eyes open to the stars.

As for Lyra, she hadn't moved a muscle since that strange thing had happened, and she held the memory of those sensations inside her like a fragile vessel brim-full of new knowledge, which she hardly dared touch for fear of spilling it. She didn't know what it was, or what it meant, or where it had come from: so she sat still, hugging her knees, and tried to stop herself trembling with excitement. *Soon*, she thought, *soon I'll know. I'll know very soon.*

Mary was tired: she had run out of stories. No doubt she'd think of more tomorrow.

34
There Is Now

SHEW YOU ALL
ALIVE THE WORLD,
WHERE EVERY
PARTICLE OF
DUST BREATHES
FORTH ITS JOY.
WILLIAM BLAKE

*M*ary couldn't sleep. Every time she closed her eyes, something made her sway and lurch as if she were at the brink of a precipice, and she snapped awake, tense with fear.

This happened three, four, five times, until she realized that sleep was not going to come; so she got up and dressed quietly, and stepped out of the house and away from the tree with its tent-like branches under which Will and Lyra were sleeping.

The moon was bright and high in the sky. There was a lively wind, and the great landscape was mottled with cloud-shadows, moving, Mary thought, like the migration of some herd of unimaginable beasts. But animals migrated for a purpose; when you saw herds of reindeer moving across the tundra, or wildebeest crossing the savannah, you knew they were going where the food was, or to places where it was good to mate and bear offspring. Their movement had a meaning. These clouds were moving as the result of pure chance, the effect of utterly random events at the level of atoms and molecules; their shadows speeding over the grassland had no meaning at all.

Nevertheless, they looked as if they did. They looked tense

and driven with purpose. The whole night did. Mary felt it too, except that she didn't know what that purpose was. But unlike her, the clouds seemed to *know* what they were doing and why, and the wind knew, and the grass knew. The entire world was alive and conscious.

Mary climbed the slope and looked back across the marshes, where the incoming tide laced a brilliant silver through the glistening dark of the mud flats and the reed beds. The cloud-shadows were very clear down there: they looked as if they were fleeing something frightful behind them, or hastening to embrace something wonderful ahead. But what that was, Mary would never know.

She turned towards the grove where her climbing tree stood. It was twenty minutes' walk away; she could see it clearly, towering high and tossing its great head in a dialogue with the urgent wind. They had things to say, and she couldn't hear them.

She hurried towards it, moved by the excitement of the night, and desperate to join in. This was the very thing she'd told Will about when he asked if she missed God: it was the sense that the whole universe was alive, and that everything was connected to everything else by threads of meaning. When she'd been a Christian, she had felt connected too; but when she left the Church, she felt loose and free and light, in a universe without purpose.

And then had come the discovery of the Shadows and her journey into another world, and now this vivid night, and it was plain that everything was throbbing with purpose and meaning, but she was cut off from it. And it was impossible to find a connection, because there was no God.

Half in exultation and half in despair, she resolved to climb her tree and try once again to lose herself in the Dust.

But she hadn't got half-way towards the grove before she heard a different sound among the lashing of the leaves and the streaming of the wind through the grass. Something was groaning, a deep, sombre note like an organ. And above that, the sound of cracking – snapping and breaking, and the squeal and scream of wood on wood.

Surely it couldn't be *her* tree?

She stopped where she was, in the open grassland, with the wind lashing her face and the cloud-shadows racing past her and the tall grasses whipping her thighs, and watched the canopy of the grove. Boughs groaned, twigs snapped, great baulks of green wood snapped off like dry sticks and fell all the long way to the ground, and then the crown itself – the crown of the very tree she knew so well – leaned and leaned and slowly began to topple.

Every fibre in the trunk, the bark, the roots, seemed to cry out separately against this murder. But it fell and fell, all the great length of it smashed its way out of the grove and seemed to lean towards Mary before crashing into the ground like a wave against a break-water; and the colossal trunk rebounded up a little way, and settled down finally, with a groaning of torn wood.

She ran up to touch the tossing leaves. There was her rope; there were the splintered ruins of her platform. Her heart thudding painfully, she climbed in among the fallen branches, hauling herself through the familiar boughs at their unfamiliar angles, and balanced herself as high up as she could get.

She braced herself against a branch and took out the spyglass. Through it she saw two quite different movements in the sky.

One was that of the clouds, driven across the moon in one

direction, and the other was that of the stream of Dust, seeming to cross it in quite another.

And of the two, the Dust was flowing more quickly and at much greater volume. In fact the whole sky seemed to be flowing with it, a great inexorable flood pouring out of the world, out of all the worlds, into some ultimate emptiness.

Slowly, as if they were moving themselves in her mind, things joined up.

Will and Lyra had said that the subtle knife was three hundred years old at least. So the old man in the tower had told them.

The mulefa had told her that the sraf, which had nurtured their lives and their world for thirty-three thousand years, had begun to fail just over three hundred years ago.

According to Will the Guild of the Torre degli Angeli, the owners of the subtle knife, had been careless; they hadn't always closed the windows they opened. Well, Mary had found one, after all, and there must be many others.

Suppose that all this time, little by little, Dust had been leaking out of the wounds the subtle knife had made in nature...

She felt dizzy, and it wasn't only the swaying and rising and falling of the branches she was wedged among. She put the spyglass carefully in her pocket and hooked her arms over the branch in front, gazing at the sky, the moon, the scudding clouds.

The subtle knife was responsible for the small-scale, low-level leakage. It was damaging, and the universe was suffering because of it, and she must talk to Will and Lyra and find a way to stop it.

But the vast flood in the sky was another matter entirely. That was new, and it was catastrophic. And if it wasn't stopped, all conscious life would come to an end. As the mulefa had shown her, Dust came into being when living things became conscious of themselves; but it needed some feedback system to reinforce it and make it safe, as the mulefa had their wheels and the oil from the trees. Without something like that, it would all vanish. Thought, imagination, feeling, would all wither and blow away, leaving nothing but a brutish automatism; and that brief period when life was conscious of itself would flicker out like a candle in every one of the billions of worlds where it had burned brightly.

Mary felt the burden of it keenly. It felt like age. She felt eighty years old, worn out and weary and longing to die.

She climbed heavily out of the branches of the great fallen tree, and with the wind still wild in the leaves and the grass and her hair, set off back to the village.

At the summit of the slope she looked for the last time at the Dust-stream, with the clouds and the wind blowing across it and the moon standing firm in the middle.

And then she saw what they were doing, at last: she saw what that great urgent purpose was.

They were trying to hold back the Dust-flood. They were striving to put some barriers up against the terrible stream: wind, moon, clouds, leaves, grass, all those lovely things were crying out and hurling themselves into the struggle to keep the Shadow-particles in this universe, which they so enriched.

Matter *loved* Dust. It didn't want to see it go. That was the meaning of this night, and it was Mary's meaning too.

Had she thought there was no meaning in life, no purpose, when God had gone? Yes, she had thought that.

"Well, there is now," she said aloud, and again, louder: "There is now!"

As she looked again at the clouds and the moon in the Dust-flow, they looked as frail and doomed as a dam of little twigs and tiny pebbles trying to hold back the Mississippi. But they were trying, all the same. They'd go on trying till the end of everything.

How long she stayed out, Mary didn't know. When the intensity of her feeling began to subside, and exhaustion took its place, she made her way slowly down the hill towards the village.

And when she was half-way down, near a little grove of knotwood bushes, she saw something strange out on the mud-flats. There was a glow of white, a steady movement: something coming up with the tide.

She stood still, gazing intently. It couldn't be the tualapi, because they always moved in a flock, and this was on its own; but everything about it was the same – the sail-like wings, the long neck – it was one of the birds, no doubt about it. She had never heard of their moving about alone, and she hesitated before running down to warn the villagers, because the thing had stopped, in any case. It was floating on the water close to the path.

And it was coming apart... No, something was getting off its back.

The something was a man.

She could see him quite clearly, even at that distance; the moonlight was brilliant, and her eyes were adjusted to it. She looked through the spyglass, and put the matter beyond doubt: it was a human figure, radiating Dust.

He was carrying something: a long stick of some kind. He came along the path quickly and easily, not running, but moving like an athlete or a hunter. He was dressed in simple dark clothes that would normally conceal him well; but through the spyglass, he showed up as if he was under a spotlight.

And as he came closer to the village, she realized what that stick was. He was carrying a rifle.

She felt as if someone had poured icy water over her heart. Every separate hair on her flesh stirred.

She was too far away to do anything: even if she'd shouted, he wouldn't have heard. She had to watch as he stepped into the village, looking to left and right, stopping every so often to listen, moving from house to house.

Mary's mind felt like the moon and the clouds trying to hold back the Dust as she cried out silently: *Don't look under the tree – go away from the tree –*

But he moved closer and closer to it, finally stopping outside her own house. She couldn't bear it; she put the spyglass in her pocket and began to run down the slope. She was about to call out, anything, a wild cry, but just in time she realized that it might wake Will or Lyra and make them reveal themselves, and she choked it back.

Then, because she couldn't bear not knowing what the man was doing, she stopped and fumbled for the spyglass again, and had to stand still while she looked through it.

He was opening the door of her house. He was going inside it. He vanished from sight, although there was a stir in the Dust he left behind, like smoke when a hand is passed through it. Mary waited for an endless minute, and then he appeared again.

He stood in her doorway, looking around slowly from left to right, and his gaze swept past the tree.

Then he stepped off the threshold and stood still, almost at a loss. Mary was suddenly conscious of how exposed she was on the bare hillside, an easy rifle-shot away, but he was only interested in the village; and when another minute or so had gone by, he turned and walked quietly away.

She watched every step he took down the river path, and saw quite clearly how he stepped on to the bird's back and sat cross-legged as it turned to glide away. Five minutes later they were lost to sight.

35
Over the Hills and Far Away

THE BIRTH-
DAY OF MY
LIFE IS COME,
MY LOVE IS
COME TO ME
CHRISTINA ROSSETTI

"Dr Malone," said Lyra in the morning, "Will and me have got to look for our dæmons. When we've found them we'll know what to do. But we can't be without them for much longer. So we just want to go and look."

"Where will you go?" said Mary, heavy-eyed and headachy after her disturbed night. She and Lyra were on the river bank, Lyra to wash, and Mary to look, surreptitiously, for the man's footprints. So far she hadn't found any.

"Don't know," said Lyra. "But they're out there somewhere. As soon as we came through from the battle, they ran away as if they didn't trust us any more. Can't say I blame them either. But we know they're in this world, and we thought we saw them a couple of times, so maybe we can find them."

"Listen," Mary said reluctantly, and told Lyra what she'd seen the night before.

As she spoke, Will came to join them, and both he and Lyra listened, wide-eyed and serious.

"He's probably just a traveller and he found a window and wandered through from somewhere else," Lyra said when

Mary had finished. Privately, she had quite different things to think about, and this man wasn't as interesting as they were. "Like Will's father did," she went on. "There's bound to be all kinds of openings now. Anyway, if he just turned around and left he can't have meant to do anything bad, can he?"

"I don't know. I didn't like it. And I'm worried about you going off on your own – or I would be if I didn't know you'd already done far more dangerous things than that. Oh, I don't know. But please be careful. Please look all around. At least out on the prairie you can see someone coming from a long way off…"

"If we do, we can escape straight away into another world, so he won't be able to hurt us," Will said.

They were determined to go, and Mary was reluctant to argue.

"At least," she said, "promise that you won't go in among the trees. If that man is still around, he might be hiding in a wood or a grove and you wouldn't see him in time to escape."

"We promise," said Lyra.

"Well, I'll pack you some food in case you're out all day."

Mary took some flat bread and cheese and some sweet thirst-quenching red fruits, wrapped them in a cloth, and tied a cord around it for one of them to carry over a shoulder.

"Good hunting," she said as they left. "Please take care."

She was still anxious. She stood watching them all the way to the foot of the slope.

"I wonder why she's so sad," Will said, as he and Lyra climbed the road up to the ridge.

"She's probably wondering if she'll ever go home again," said Lyra. "And if her laboratory'll still be hers when she does. And maybe she's sad about the man she was in love with."

"Mmm," said Will. "D'you think *we'll* ever go home?"

"Dunno. I don't suppose I've got a home anyway. They probably couldn't have me back at Jordan College, and I can't live with the bears or the witches. Maybe I could live with the gyptians. I wouldn't mind that, if they'd have me."

"What about Lord Asriel's world? Wouldn't you want to live there?"

"It's going to fail, remember," she said.

"Why?"

"Because of what your father's ghost said, just before we came out. About dæmons, and how they can only live for a long time if they stay in their own world. But probably Lord Asriel, I mean my father, couldn't have thought about that, because no one knew enough about other worlds when he started... All that," she said wonderingly, "all that bravery and skill... All that, all wasted! All for nothing!"

They climbed on, finding the going easy on the rock road, and when they reached the top of the ridge they stopped and looked back.

"Will," she said, "supposing we *don't* find them?"

"I'm sure we will. What I'm wondering is what my dæmon will be like."

"You saw her. And I picked her up," Lyra said, blushing, because of course it was a gross violation of manners to touch something so private as someone else's dæmon. It was forbidden not only by politeness, but by something deeper than that – something like shame. A quick glance at Will's warm cheeks showed that he knew that just as well as she did. She couldn't tell whether he also felt that half-frightened, half-excited feeling, as she did, the one that had come over her the night before: here it was again.

They walked on side by side, suddenly shy with each other.

But Will, not put off by being shy, said, "When does your dæmon stop changing shape?"

"About... I suppose about our age, or a bit older. Maybe more sometimes. We used to talk about Pan settling, him and me. We used to wonder what he'd be –"

"Don't people have any idea?"

"Not when they're young. As you grow up you start thinking, well, they might be this or they might be that... And usually they end up something that fits. I mean something like your real nature. Like if your dæmon's a dog, that means you like doing what you're told, and knowing who's boss, and following orders, and pleasing people who are in charge. A lot of servants are people whose dæmons are dogs. So it helps to know what you're like and to find what you'd be good at. How do people in your world know what they're like?"

"I don't know. I don't know much about my world. All I know is keeping secret and quiet and hidden, so I don't know much about ... grown-ups, and friends. Or lovers. I think it'd be difficult having a dæmon because everybody would know so much about you just by looking. I like to keep secret and stay out of sight."

"Then maybe your dæmon'd be an animal that's good at hiding. Or one of those animals that looks like another – a butterfly that looks like a wasp, for disguise. They must have creatures like that in your world, because we have, and we're so much alike."

They walked on together in a friendly silence. All around them the wide clear morning lay limpid in the hollows and pearly-blue in the warm air above. As far as the eye could see the great savannah rolled, brown, gold, buff-green, shimmering towards the horizon, and empty. They might have been the only people in the world.

"But it's not empty really," Lyra said.

"You mean that man?"

"No. You know what I mean."

"Yes, I do. I can see shadows in the grass … maybe birds," Will said.

He was following the little darting movements here and there. He found it easier to see the shadows if he didn't look at them. They were more willing to show themselves to the corners of his eye, and when he said so to Lyra she said, "It's negative capability."

"What's that?"

"The poet Keats said it first. Dr Malone knows. It's how I read the alethiometer. It's how you use the knife, isn't it?"

"Yes, I suppose it is. But I was just thinking that they might be the dæmons."

"So was I, but…"

She put her finger to her lips. He nodded.

"Look," he said, "there's one of those fallen trees."

It was Mary's climbing tree. They went up to it carefully, keeping an eye on the grove in case another one should fall. In the calm morning, with only a faint breeze stirring the leaves, it seemed impossible that a mighty thing like this should ever topple, but here it was.

The vast trunk, supported in the grove by its torn-up roots and out on the grass by the mass of branches, was high above their heads. Some of those branches, crushed and broken, were themselves as big around as the biggest trees Will had ever seen; the crown of the tree, tight-packed with boughs that still looked sturdy, leaves that were still green, towered like a ruined palace into the mild air.

Suddenly Lyra gripped Will's arm.

"Ssh," she whispered. "Don't look. I'm sure they're up

there. I saw something move and I *swear* it was Pan…"

Her hand was warm. He was more aware of that than of
the great mass of leaves and branches above them.
Pretending to gaze vacantly at the horizon, he let his attention wander upwards into the confused mass of green, brown
and blue, and there – she was right! – there was a something
that was *not* the tree. And beside it, another.

"Walk away," Will said under his breath. "We'll go somewhere else and see if they follow us."

"Suppose they don't… But yes, all right," Lyra whispered
back.

They pretended to look all around; they set their hands on
one of the branches resting on the ground, as if they were
intending to climb; they pretended to change their minds, by
shaking their heads and walking away.

"I wish we could look behind," Lyra said when they were
a few hundred yards away.

"Just go on walking. They can see us, and they won't get
lost. They'll come to us when they want to."

They stepped off the black road and into the knee-high
grass, swishing their legs through the stems, watching the
insects hovering, darting, fluttering, skimming, hearing the
million-voiced chorus chirrup and scrape.

"What are you going to do, Will?" Lyra said quietly after
they'd walked some way in silence.

"Well, I've got to go home," he said.

She thought he sounded unsure, though. She hoped he
sounded unsure.

"But they might still be after you," she said. "Those men."

"We've seen worse than them, after all."

"Yes, I suppose… But I wanted to show you Jordan
College, and the Fens. I wanted us to…"

"Yes," he said, "and I wanted… It would be good to go to Cittàgazze again, even. It was a beautiful place, and if the Spectres are all gone … But there's my mother. I've got to go back and look after her. I just left her with Mrs Cooper, and it's not fair on either of them."

"But it's not fair on *you* to have to do that."

"No," he said, "but that's a different sort of not fair. That's just like an earthquake or a rainstorm. It might not be fair, but no one's to blame. But if I just leave my mother with an old lady who isn't very well herself, then that's a different kind of not fair. That would be wrong. I've just got to go home. But probably it's going to be difficult to go back as we were. Probably the secret's out now. I don't suppose Mrs Cooper will have been able to look after her, not if my mother's in one of those times when she gets frightened of things. So she's probably had to get help, and when I go back I'll be made to go into some kind of institution."

"No! Like an orphanage?"

"I think that's what they do. I just don't know. I'll hate it."

"You could escape with the knife, Will! You could come to my world!"

"I still belong there where I can be with her. When I'm grown up I'll be able to look after her properly, in my own house. No one can interfere then."

"D'you think you'll get married?"

He was quiet for a long time. She knew he was thinking, though.

"I can't see that far ahead," he said. "It would have to be someone who understands about… I don't think there's anyone like that in my world. Would *you* get married?"

"Me too," she said, and her voice wasn't quite steady. "Not to anyone in my world, I shouldn't think."

They walked on slowly, wandering towards the horizon. They had all the time in the world: all the time the world had.

After a while Lyra said, "You *will* keep the knife, won't you? So you could visit my world?"

"Of course. I certainly wouldn't give it to anyone else, ever."

"Don't look –" she said, not altering her pace. "There they are again. On the left."

"They *are* following us," said Will, delighted.

"Ssh!"

"I thought they would. OK, we'll just pretend now, we'll just wander along as if we're looking for them, and we'll look in all sorts of stupid places."

It became a game. They found a pond and searched among the reeds and in the mud, saying loudly that the dæmons were bound to be shaped like frogs or water-beetles or slugs; they peeled off the bark of a long-fallen tree at the edge of a string-wood grove, pretending to have seen the two dæmons creeping underneath it in the form of earwigs; Lyra made a great fuss of an ant she claimed to have trodden on, sympathizing with its bruises, saying its face was just like Pan's, asking in mock-sorrow why it was refusing to speak to her.

But when she thought they were genuinely out of earshot, she said earnestly to Will, leaning close to speak quietly:

"We *had* to leave them, didn't we? We didn't have a choice really?"

"Yes, we had to. It was worse for you than for me, but we didn't have any choice at all. Because you made a promise to Roger, and you had to keep it."

"And you had to speak to your father again..."

"And we had to let them all out."

"Yes, we did. I'm so glad we did. Pan will be glad one day

too, when *I* die. We won't be split up. It was a *good* thing we did."

As the sun rose higher in the sky and the air became warmer, they began to look for shade. Towards noon they found themselves on the slope rising towards the summit of a ridge, and when they'd reached it, Lyra flopped down on the grass and said, "Well! If we don't find somewhere shady soon..."

There was a valley leading down on the other side, and it was thick with bushes, so they guessed there might be a stream as well. They traversed the slope of the ridge till it dipped into the head of the valley, and there sure enough, among ferns and reeds, a spring bubbled out of the rock.

They dipped their hot faces in the water and swallowed gratefully, and then they followed the stream downwards, seeing it gather in miniature whirlpools and pour over tiny ledges of stone, and all the time get fuller and wider.

"How does it do that?" Lyra marvelled. "There's no *more* water coming into it from anywhere else, but there's so much more of it here than up there."

Will, watching the shadows out of the corner of his eye, saw them slip ahead, leaping over the ferns to disappear into the bushes further down. He pointed silently.

"It just goes slower," he said. "It doesn't flow as fast as the spring comes out, so it gathers in these pools... They've gone in there," he whispered, indicating a little group of trees at the foot of the slope.

Lyra's heart was beating so fast she felt the pulse in her throat. She and Will looked at each other, a curiously formal and serious look, before setting off to follow the stream. The undergrowth got thicker as they went down the valley; the stream went into tunnels of green and emerged in dappled clearings, only to tumble over a lip of stone and bury itself in the green again, and they had to follow it as much by hearing as by sight.

At the foot of the hill it ran into a little wood of silver-barked trees.

Father Gomez watched from the top of the ridge. It hadn't been hard to follow them; despite Mary's confidence in the open savannah, there was plenty of concealment in the grass and the occasional thickets of string-wood and sap-lacquer bushes. The two young people had spent a lot of time earlier looking all around as if they thought they were being followed, and he had had to keep some distance away, but as the morning passed they became more and more absorbed in each other, and paid less attention to the landscape.

The one thing he didn't want to do was hurt the boy. He had a horror of harming an innocent person. The only way to make sure of his target was to get close enough to see her clearly, which meant following them into the wood.

Quietly and cautiously he moved down the course of the stream. His dæmon the green-backed beetle flew overhead, tasting the air; her eyesight was less good than his, but her sense of smell was acute, and she caught the scent of the young people's flesh very clearly. She would go a little ahead, perch on a stem of grass and wait for him, then move on again; and as she caught the trail in the air that their bodies left behind, Father Gomez found himself praising God for his mission, because it was clearer than ever that the boy and the girl were walking into mortal sin.

And there it was: the dark-blonde movement that was the girl's hair. He moved a little closer, and took out the rifle. There was a telescopic sight: low-powered, but beautifully made, so that looking through it was to feel your vision clarified as well as enlarged. Yes, there she was, and she paused and looked back so that he saw the expression on her face, and he could not understand how anyone so steeped in evil could look so radiant with hope and happiness.

His bewilderment at that made him hesitate, and then the moment was gone, and both children had walked in among the trees and out of sight. Well, they wouldn't go far. He followed them down the stream, moving at a crouch, holding the rifle in one hand, balancing with the other.

He was so close to success now that for the first time he found himself speculating on what he would do afterwards, and whether he would please the kingdom of heaven more by going back to Geneva or staying to evangelize this world. The first thing to do here would be to convince the four-legged creatures, who seemed to have the rudiments of reason, that their habit of riding on wheels was abominable and Satanic, and contrary to the will of God. Break them of that, and salvation would follow.

He reached the foot of the slope, where the trees began, and laid the rifle down silently.

He gazed into the silver-green-gold shadows, and listened, with both hands behind his ears to catch and focus any quiet voices through the insect-chirping and the trickle of the stream. Yes: there they were. They'd stopped.

He bent to pick up the rifle –

And found himself uttering a hoarse and breathless gasp, as something clutched his dæmon and pulled her away from him.

But there was nothing there! Where was she? The pain was atrocious. He heard her crying, and cast about wildly to left and right, looking for her.

"Keep still," said a voice from the air, "and be quiet. I have your dæmon in my hand."

"But – where are you? Who are you?"

"My name is Balthamos," said the voice.

Will and Lyra followed the stream into the wood, walking carefully, saying little, until they were in the very centre.

There was a little clearing in the middle of the grove, which was floored with soft grass and moss-covered rocks. The branches laced across overhead, almost shutting out the sky and letting through little moving spangles and sequins of sunlight, so that everything was dappled with gold and silver.

And it was quiet. Only the trickle of the stream, and the occasional rustle of leaves high up in a little curl of breeze, broke the silence.

Will put down the package of food; Lyra put down her little rucksack. There was no sign of the dæmon-shadows anywhere. They were completely alone.

They took off their shoes and socks and sat down on the mossy rocks at the edge of the stream, dipping their feet in the cold water and feeling the shock of it invigorate their blood.

"I'm hungry," Will said.

"Me too," said Lyra, though she was also feeling more than that, something subdued and pressing and half-happy and half-painful, so that she wasn't quite sure what it was.

They unfolded the cloth and ate some bread and cheese. For some reason their hands were slow and clumsy, and they hardly tasted the food, although the bread was floury and crisp from the hot baking-stones, and the cheese was flaky and salty and very fresh.

Then Lyra took one of those little red fruits. With a fast-beating heart, she turned to him and said, "Will…"

And she lifted the fruit gently to his mouth.

She could see from his eyes that he knew at once what she meant, and that he was too joyful to speak. Her fingers were still at his lips, and he felt them tremble, and he put his own hand up to hold hers there, and then neither of them could look; they were confused; they were brimming with happiness.

Like two moths clumsily bumping together, with no more weight than that, their lips touched. Then before they knew how it happened, they were clinging together, blindly pressing their faces towards each other.

"Like Mary said –" he whispered – "you know straight away when you like someone – when you were asleep, on the mountain, before she took you away, I told Pan –"

"I heard," she whispered, "I was awake and I wanted to tell you the same and now I know what I must have felt all the time: I love you, Will, I love you –"

The word *love* set his nerves ablaze. All his body thrilled with it, and he answered her in the same words, kissing her hot face over and over again, drinking in with adoration the scent of her body and her warm honey-fragrant hair and her sweet moist mouth that tasted of the little red fruit.

Around them there was nothing but silence, as if all the world were holding its breath.

Balthamos was terrified.

He moved up the stream and away from the wood, holding the scratching, stinging, biting insect-dæmon, and trying to conceal himself as much as he could from the man who was stumbling after them.

He mustn't let him catch up. He knew that Father Gomez would kill him in a moment. An angel of his rank was no match for a man, even if that angel was strong and healthy, and Balthamos was neither of those; besides which, he was crippled by grief over Baruch and shame at having deserted Will before. He no longer even had the strength to fly.

"Stop, stop," said Father Gomez. "Please keep still. I can't see you – let's talk, please – don't hurt my dæmon, I beg you –"

In fact the dæmon was hurting Balthamos. The angel could see the little green thing dimly through the backs of his clasped hands, and she was sinking her powerful jaws again and again into his palms. If he opened his hands just for a moment, she would be gone. Balthamos kept them closed.

"This way," he said, "follow me. Come away from the wood. I want to talk to you, and this is the wrong place."

"But who are you? I can't see you. Come closer – how can I tell what you are till I see you? Keep still, don't move so quickly!"

But moving quickly was the only defence Balthamos had. Trying to ignore the stinging dæmon, he picked his way up the little gully where the stream ran, stepping from rock to rock.

Then he made a mistake: trying to look behind him, he slipped and put a foot into the water.

"Ah," came a whisper of satisfaction as Father Gomez saw the splash.

Balthamos withdrew his foot at once and hurried on – but now a wet print appeared on the dry rocks each time he put his foot down. The priest saw it, and leapt forward, and felt the brush of feathers on his hand.

He stopped in astonishment: the word *angel* reverberated in his mind. Balthamos seized the moment to stumble forward again, and the priest felt himself dragged after him, as another brutal pang wrenched his heart.

Balthamos said over his shoulder: "A little further, just to the top of the ridge, and we shall talk, I promise."

"Talk here! Stop where you are, and I swear I shan't touch you!"

The angel didn't reply: it was too hard to concentrate. He had to split his attention three ways: behind him to avoid the man, ahead to see where he was going, and on the furious dæmon tormenting his hands.

As for the priest, his mind was working quickly. A truly dangerous opponent would have killed his dæmon at once, and ended the matter there and then: this antagonist was afraid to strike.

With that in mind, he let himself stumble, and uttered little moans of pain, and pleaded once or twice for the other to stop – all the time watching closely, moving nearer, estimating how big the other was, how quickly he could move, which way he was looking.

"Please," he said brokenly, "you don't know how much this hurts – I can't do you any harm – please can we stop and talk?"

He didn't want to move out of sight of the wood. They were now at the point where the stream began, and he could see the shape of Balthamos's feet very lightly pressing the grass. The priest had watched every inch of the way, and he was sure now where the angel was standing.

Balthamos turned round. The priest raised his eyes to the place where he thought the angel's face would be, and saw him for the first time: just a shimmer in the air, but there was no mistaking it.

He wasn't quite close enough to reach in one movement, though, and in truth the pull on his dæmon had been painful and weakening. Maybe he should take another step or two...

"Sit down," said Balthamos. "Sit down where you are. Not a step closer."

"What do you want?" said Father Gomez, not moving.

"What do I want? I want to kill you, but I haven't got the strength."

"But are you an angel?"

"What does it matter?"

"You might have made a mistake. We might be on the same side."

"No, we're not. I have been following you. I know whose side you're on – no, no, don't move. Stay there."

"It's not too late to repent. Even angels are allowed to do that. Let me hear your confession."

"Oh, Baruch, help me!" cried Balthamos in despair, turning away.

And as he cried out, Father Gomez leapt for him. His shoulder hit the angel's, and knocked Balthamos off balance; and in throwing out a hand to save himself, the angel let go of the insect-dæmon. The beetle flew free at once, and Father Gomez felt a surge of relief and strength. In fact, it was that which killed him, to his great surprise. He hurled himself so hard at the faint form of the angel, and he expected so much more resistance than he met, that he couldn't keep his balance. His foot slipped; his momentum carried him down towards the stream; and Balthamos, thinking of what Baruch would have done, kicked aside the priest's hand as he flung it out for support.

Father Gomez fell hard. His head cracked against a stone, and he fell stunned with his face in the water. The cold shock woke him at once, but as he choked and feebly tried to rise, Balthamos, desperate, ignored the dæmon stinging his face and his eyes and his mouth, and used all the little weight he had to hold the man's head down in the water, and he kept it there, and kept it there, and kept it there.

When the dæmon suddenly vanished, Balthamos let go. The man was dead. As soon as he was sure, Balthamos hauled the body out of the stream and laid it carefully on the grass, folding the priest's hands over his breast and closing his eyes.

Then Balthamos stood up, sick and weary and full of pain.

"Baruch," he said, "oh, Baruch, my dear, I can do no more. Will and the girl are safe, and everything will be well, but this is the end for me, though truly I died when you did, Baruch my beloved."

A moment later, he was gone.

In the beanfield, drowsy in the late afternoon heat, Mary heard Atal's voice, and she couldn't tell excitement from alarm: had another tree fallen? Had the man with the rifle appeared?

Look! Look! Atal was saying, nudging Mary's pocket with her trunk, so Mary took the spyglass and did as her friend said, pointing it up to the sky.

Tell me what it's doing! said Atal. *I can feel it is different, but I can't see.*

The terrible flood of Dust in the sky had stopped flowing. It wasn't still, by any means; Mary scanned the whole sky with the amber lens, seeing a current here, an eddy there, a vortex further off; it was in perpetual movement, but it wasn't flowing away any more. In fact, if anything, it was falling like snowflakes.

She thought of the wheel-trees: the flowers that opened upwards would be drinking in this golden rain. Mary could almost feel them welcoming it in their poor parched throats, which were so perfectly shaped for it, and which had been starved for so long.

The young ones, said Atal.

Mary turned, spyglass in hand, to see Will and Lyra returning. They were some way off; they weren't hurrying. They were holding hands, talking together, heads close, oblivious to everything else; she could see that even from a distance.

She nearly put the spyglass to her eye, but held back, and returned it to her pocket. There was no need for the glass; she knew what she would see; they would seem to be made of living gold. They would seem the true image of what human beings always could be, once they had come into their inheritance.

The Dust pouring down from the stars had found a living home again, and these children-no-longer-children, saturated with love, were the cause of it all.

36

The Broken Arrow

The two dæmons moved through the silent village, in and out of the shadows, padding cat-formed across the moonlit gathering-floor, pausing outside the open door of Mary's house.

Cautiously they looked inside, and saw only the sleeping woman; so they withdrew, and moved through the moonlight again, towards the shelter-tree.

Its long branches trailed their fragrant corkscrew leaves almost down to the ground. Very slowly, very careful not to rustle a leaf or snap a fallen twig, the two shapes slipped in through the leaf-curtain and saw what they were seeking: the boy and the girl, fast asleep in each other's arms.

They moved closer over the grass and touched the sleepers softly with nose, paw, whiskers, bathing in the life-giving warmth they gave off, but being infinitely careful not to wake them.

As they checked their people (gently cleaning Will's fast-healing wound, lifting the lock of hair off Lyra's face) there was a soft sound behind them.

Instantly, in total silence, both dæmons sprang round, becoming wolves: mad light eyes, bare white teeth, menace in every line.

A woman stood there, outlined by the moon. It was not Mary, and when she spoke they heard her clearly, though her voice made no sound.

"Come with me," she said.

Pantalaimon's dæmon-heart leapt within him, but he said nothing until he could greet her away from the sleepers under the tree.

"Serafina Pekkala!" he said, joyful. "Where have you been? Do you know what's happened?"

"Hush. Let's fly to a place where we can talk," she said, mindful of the sleeping villagers.

Her branch of cloud-pine lay by the door of Mary's house, and as she took it up, the two dæmons changed into birds – a nightingale, an owl – and flew with her over the thatched roofs, over the grasslands, over the ridge, and towards the nearest wheel-tree grove, as huge as a castle, its crown looking like curds of silver in the moonlight.

There Serafina Pekkala settled on the highest comfortable branch, among the open flowers drinking in the Dust, and the two birds perched nearby.

"You won't be birds for long," she said. "Very soon now your shapes will settle. Look around and take this sight into your memory."

"What will we be?" said Pantalaimon.

"You'll find out sooner than you think. Listen," said Serafina Pekkala, "and I'll tell you some witch-lore that none but witches know. The reason I can do that is that you are here with me, and your humans are down there, sleeping. Who are the only people for whom that is possible?"

"Witches," said Pantalaimon, "and shamans. So..."

"In leaving you both on the shores of the world of the dead, Lyra and Will did something, without knowing it, that witches have done since the first time there were witches. There's a region of our north-land, a desolate abominable place, where a great catastrophe happened in the childhood of the world, and where nothing has lived since. No dæmons can enter it. To become a witch, a girl must cross it alone and leave her dæmon behind. You know the suffering they must undergo. But having done it, they find that their dæmons were not severed, as in Bolvangar; they are still one whole being; but now they can roam free, and go to far places and see strange things and bring back knowledge.

"And you are not severed, are you?"

"No," said Pantalaimon. "We are still one. But it was so painful, and we were so frightened…"

"Well," said Serafina, "the two of them will not fly like witches, and they will not live as long as we do; but thanks to what they did, you and they are witch in all but that."

The two dæmons considered the strangeness of this knowledge.

"Does that mean we shall be birds, like witches' dæmons?" said Pantalaimon.

"Be patient."

"And how can Will be a witch? I thought all witches were female."

"Those two have changed many things. We are all learning new ways, even witches. But one thing hasn't changed: you must help your humans, not hinder them. You must help them and guide them and encourage them towards wisdom. That's what dæmons are for."

They were silent. Serafina turned to the nightingale and said, "What is your name?"

"I have no name. I didn't know I was born until I was torn away from his heart."

"Then I shall name you Kirjava."

"Kirjava," said Pantalaimon, trying the sound. "What does it mean?"

"Soon you will see what it means. But now," Serafina went on, "you must listen carefully, because I'm going to tell you what you should do."

"No," said Kirjava forcefully.

Serafina said gently, "I can hear from your tone that you know what I'm going to say."

"We don't want to hear it!" said Pantalaimon.

"It's too soon," said the nightingale. "It's much too soon."

Serafina was silent, because she agreed with them, and she felt sorrowful. But still she was the wisest one there, and she had to guide them to what was right; but she let their agitation subside before she went on.

"Where did you go, in your wanderings?" she said.

"Through many worlds," said Pantalaimon. "Everywhere we found a window, we went through. There are more windows than we thought."

"And you saw –"

"Yes," said Kirjava, "we looked closely, and we saw what was happening."

"We saw many other things," said Pantalaimon quickly. "We saw angels, and talked to them. We saw the world where the little people come from, the Gallivespians. There are big people there, too, who try and kill them."

They told the witch more of what they'd seen, and they were trying to distract her, and she knew it; but she let them talk, because of the love they felt for each other's voices.

But eventually they ran out of things to tell her, and they fell silent. The only sound was the gentle endless whisper of the leaves, until Serafina Pekkala said:

"You have been keeping away from Will and Lyra to punish them. I know why you're doing that; my Kaisa did just the same after I came through the desolate barrens. But he came to me eventually, because we loved each other still. And they will need you soon to help them do what has to be done next. Because you have to tell them what you know."

Pantalaimon cried aloud, a pure cold owl-cry, a sound never heard in that world before. In nests and burrows for a long way around, and wherever any small night creature was hunting or grazing or scavenging, a new and unforgettable fear came into being.

Serafina watched from close by, and felt nothing but compassion until she looked at Will's dæmon, Kirjava the nightingale. She remembered talking to the witch Ruta Skadi, who had asked, after seeing Will only once, if Serafina had looked into his eyes; and Serafina had replied that she had not dared to. This little brown bird was radiating an implacable ferocity as palpable as heat, and Serafina was afraid of it.

Finally Pantalaimon's wild screaming died away, and Kirjava said:

"And we have to tell them."

"Yes, you do," said the witch gently.

Gradually the ferocity left the gaze of the little brown bird, and Serafina could look at her again. She saw a desolate sadness in its place.

"There is a ship coming," Serafina said. "I left it to fly here and find you. I came with the gyptians, all the way from our world. They will be here in another day or so."

The two birds sat close, and in a moment they had changed their forms, becoming two doves.

Serafina went on:

"This may be the last time you fly. I can see a little ahead; I can see that you will both be able to climb this high as long as there are trees this size; but I think you will not be birds when your forms settle. Take in all that you can, and remember it well. I know that you and Lyra and Will are going to think hard and painfully, and I know you will make the best choice. But it is yours to make, and no one else's."

They didn't speak. She took her branch of cloud-pine and lifted away from the towering tree-tops, circling high above, feeling on her skin the coolness of the breeze and the tingle of the starlight and the benevolent sifting of that Dust she had never seen.

Serafina flew down to the village once more, and went silently into the woman's house. She knew nothing about Mary, except that she came from the same world as Will, and that her part in the events was crucial. Whether she was fierce or friendly, Serafina had no way of telling; but she had to wake Mary up without startling her, and there was a spell for that.

She sat on the floor at the woman's head and watched through half-closed eyes, breathing in and out in time with her. Presently her half-vision began to show her the pale forms that Mary was seeing in her dreams, and she adjusted her mind to resonate with them, as if she were tuning a string. Then with a further effort Serafina herself stepped in among them. Once she was there, she could speak to Mary, and she did so with the instant easy affection that we sometimes feel for people we meet in dreams.

A moment later they were talking together in a murmured rush of which Mary later remembered nothing, and walking through a silly landscape of reed-beds and electrical transformers. It was time for Serafina to take charge.

"In a few moments," she said, "you'll wake up. Don't be alarmed. You'll find me beside you. I'm waking you like this so you'll know it's quite safe and there's nothing to hurt you. And then we can talk properly."

She withdrew, taking the dream-Mary with her, until she found herself in the house again, cross-legged on the earthen floor, with Mary's eyes glittering as they looked at her.

"You must be the witch," Mary whispered.

"I am. My name is Serafina Pekkala. What are you called?"

"Mary Malone. I've never been woken so quietly. *Am* I awake?"

"Yes. We must talk together, and dream-talk is hard to control, and harder to remember. It's better to talk awake. Do you prefer to stay inside, or will you walk with me in the moonlight?"

"I'll come," said Mary, sitting up and stretching. "Where are Lyra and Will?"

"Asleep under the tree."

They moved out of the house and past the tree with its curtain of all-concealing leaves, and walked down to the river.

Mary watched Serafina Pekkala with a mixture of wariness and admiration: she had never seen a human form so slender and graceful. She seemed younger than Mary herself, though Lyra had said she was hundreds of years old; the only hint of age came in her expression, which was full of a complicated sadness.

They sat on the bank over the silver-black water, and Serafina told her that she had spoken to the children's dæmons.

"They went looking for them today," Mary said, "but something else happened. Will's never seen his dæmon properly, except when they escaped from the battle, and that was only for a second. He didn't know for certain that he had one."

"Well, he has. And so have you."

Mary stared at her.

"If you could see him," Serafina went on, "you would see a black bird with red legs and a bright yellow beak, slightly curved. A bird of the mountains."

"An Alpine chough... How can *you* see him?"

"With my eyes half-closed, I can see him. If we had time, I could teach you to see him too, and to see the dæmons of others in your world. It's strange for us to think you can't see them."

Then she told Mary what she had said to the dæmons, and what it meant.

"And the dæmons will have to tell them?" Mary said.

"I thought of waking them to tell them myself. I thought of telling you and letting you have the responsibility. But I saw their dæmons, and I knew that would be best."

"They're in love."

"I know."

"They've only just discovered it..."

Mary tried to take in all the implications of what Serafina had told her, but it was too hard.

After a minute or so, Mary said, "Can you see Dust?"

"No, I've never seen it. Until the wars began we had never heard of it."

Mary took the spyglass from her pocket and handed it to the witch. Serafina put it to her eye, and gasped.

"*That* is Dust... It's beautiful!"

"Turn to look back at the shelter-tree."

Serafina did, and exclaimed again. "*They* did this?" she said.

"Something happened today, or yesterday, if it's after midnight," Mary said, trying to find the words to explain, and remembering her vision of the Dust-flow as a great river like the Mississippi. "Something tiny but crucial... If you wanted to divert a mighty river into a different course, and all you had was a single pebble, you could do it, as long as you put the pebble in the right place to send the first trickle of water *that* way instead of *this*. Something like that happened yesterday. I don't know what it was. They saw each other differently, or something... Until then, they hadn't felt like that, but suddenly they did. And then the Dust was attracted to them, very powerfully, and it stopped flowing the other way."

"So that was how it was to happen!" said Serafina, marvelling. "And now it's safe, or it will be when the angels fill the great chasm in the underworld."

She told Mary about the abyss, and about how she herself had found out.

"I was flying high," she explained, "looking for a landfall, and I met an angel: a female angel. She was very strange; she was old and young together," she went on, forgetting that that was how she herself appeared to Mary. "Her name was Xaphania. She told me many things... She said that all the history of human life has been a struggle between wisdom and stupidity. She and the rebel angels, the followers of wisdom, have always tried to open minds; the Authority and his churches have always tried to keep them closed. She gave me many examples from my world."

"I can think of many from mine."

"And for most of that time, wisdom has had to work in secret, whispering her words, moving like a spy through the humble places of the world while the courts and palaces are occupied by her enemies."

"Yes," said Mary, "I recognize that too."

"And the struggle isn't over now, though the forces of the kingdom have met a setback. They'll regroup under a new commander and come back strongly, and we must be ready to resist."

"But what happened to Lord Asriel?" said Mary.

"He fought the Regent of heaven, the angel Metatron, and he wrestled him down into the abyss. Metatron is gone for ever. So is Lord Asriel."

Mary caught her breath. "And Mrs Coulter?" she said.

For answer the witch took an arrow from her quiver. She took her time selecting it: the best, the straightest, the most perfectly balanced.

And she broke it in two.

"Once in my world," she said, "I saw that woman torturing a witch, and I swore to myself that I would send that arrow into her throat. Now I shall never do that. She sacrificed herself with Lord Asriel to fight the angel, and make the world safe for Lyra. They could not have done it alone, but together they did it."

Mary, distressed, said, "How can we tell Lyra?"

"Wait until she asks," said Serafina. "And she might not. In any case, she has her symbol-reader; that will tell her anything she wants to know."

They sat in silence for a while, companionably, as the stars slowly wheeled in the sky.

"Can you see ahead, and guess what they'll choose to do?" said Mary.

"No, but if Lyra returns to her own world, then I will be her sister as long as she lives. What will you do?"

"I..." Mary began, and found she hadn't considered that for a moment. "I suppose I belong in my own world. Though

I'll be sorry to leave this one; I've been very happy here. The happiest I've ever been in my life, I think."

"Well, if you do return home, you shall have a sister in another world," said Serafina, "and so shall I. We shall see each other again in a day or so, when the ship arrives, and we'll talk more on the voyage home; and then we'll part for ever. Embrace me now, sister."

Mary did so, and Serafina Pekkala flew away on her cloud-pine branch over the reeds, over the marshes, over the mud-flats and the beach and over the sea, until Mary could see her no more.

At about the same time, one of the large blue lizards came across the body of Father Gomez. Will and Lyra had returned to the village that afternoon by a different route, and hadn't seen it; the priest lay undisturbed where Balthamos had laid him. The lizards were scavengers, but they were mild and harmless creatures, and by an ancient understanding with the mulefa, they were entitled to take any creature left dead after dark.

The lizard dragged the priest's body back to her nest, and her children feasted very well. As for the rifle, it lay in the grass where Father Gomez had laid it down, quietly turning to rust.

37
The Dunes

MY SOUL, DO NOT SEEK ETERNAL LIFE, BUT EXHAUST THE REALM OF THE POSSIBLE·
PINDAR

Next day Will and Lyra went out by themselves again, speaking little, eager to be alone with each other. They looked dazed, as if some happy accident had robbed them of their wits; they moved slowly; their eyes were not focused on what they looked at.

They spent all day on the wide hills, and in the heat of the afternoon they visited their gold-and-silver grove. They talked, they bathed, they ate, they kissed, they lay in a trance of happiness murmuring words whose sound was as confused as their sense, and they felt they were melting with love.

In the evening they shared the meal with Mary and Atal, saying little, and because the air was hot they thought they'd walk down to the sea, where they thought there might be a cool breeze. They wandered along the river until they came to the wide beach, bright under the moon, where the low tide was turning.

They lay down in the soft sand at the foot of the dunes, and then they heard the first bird calling.

They both turned their heads at once, because it was a bird that sounded like no creature that belonged to the world they were in. From somewhere above in the dark came a delicate trilling song, and then another answered it from a different direction. Delighted, Will and Lyra jumped up and tried to see the singers, but all they could make out was a pair of dark skimming shapes that flew low and then darted up again, all the time singing and singing in rich liquid bell-tones an endlessly varied song.

And then, with a flutter of wings that threw up a little fountain of sand in front of him, the first bird landed a few yards away.

Lyra said, "Pan –?"

He was formed like a dove, but his colour was dark and hard to tell in the moonlight; at any rate, he showed up clearly on the white sand. The other bird still circled overhead, still singing, and then she flew down to join him: another dove, but pearl-white, and with a crest of dark red feathers.

And Will knew what it was to see his dæmon. As she flew down to the sand, he felt his heart tighten and release in a way he never forgot. Sixty years and more would go by, and as an old man he would still feel some sensations as bright and fresh as ever: Lyra's fingers putting the fruit between his lips under the gold-and-silver trees; her warm mouth pressing against his; his dæmon being torn from his unsuspecting breast as they entered the world of the dead; and the sweet rightfulness of her coming back to him at the edge of the moonlit dunes.

Lyra made to move towards them, but Pantalaimon spoke.

"Lyra," he said, "Serafina Pekkala came to us last night. She told us all kinds of things. She's gone back to guide the gyptians here. Farder Coram's coming, and Lord Faa, and they'll be here –"

"Pan," she said, distressed, "oh, Pan, you're not happy – what is it? What is it?"

Then he changed, and flowed over the sand to her as a snow-white ermine. The other dæmon changed too – Will felt it happen, like a little grip at his heart – and became a cat.

Before she moved to him, she spoke. She said, "The witch gave me a name. I had no need of one before. She called me Kirjava. But listen, listen to us now..."

"Yes, you must listen," said Pantalaimon. "This is hard to explain."

Between them, the dæmons managed to tell them everything Serafina had told them, beginning with the revelation about the children's own natures: about how, without intending it, they had become like witches in their power to separate and yet still be one being.

"But that's not all," Kirjava said.

And Pantalaimon said, "Oh, Lyra, forgive us, but we have to tell you what we found out..."

Lyra was bewildered. When had Pan ever needed forgiving? She looked at Will, and saw his puzzlement as clear as her own.

"Tell us," he said. "Don't be afraid."

"It's about Dust," said the cat-dæmon, and Will marvelled to hear part of his own nature telling him something he didn't know. "It was all flowing away, all the Dust there was, down into the abyss that you saw. Something's stopped it flowing down there, but –"

"Will, it was that golden light!" Lyra said. "The light that all flowed into the abyss and vanished... And that was Dust? Was it really?"

"Yes. But there's more leaking out all the time," Pantalaimon went on. "And it mustn't. It's vital that it doesn't all leak away. It's got to stay in the world and not vanish, because otherwise everything good will fade away and die."

"But where's the rest leaving from?" said Lyra.

Both dæmons looked at Will, and at the knife.

"Every time we made an opening," said Kirjava, and again Will felt that little thrill: *She's me, and I'm her* – "every time anyone made an opening between the worlds, us or the old Guild men, anyone, the knife cut into the emptiness outside. The same emptiness there is down in the abyss. We never knew. No one knew, because the edge was too fine to see. But it was quite big enough for Dust to leak out of. If they closed it up again at once, there wasn't time for much to leak out, but there were thousands that they never closed up. So all this time, Dust has been leaking out of the worlds and into nothingness."

The understanding was beginning to dawn on Will and Lyra. They fought it, they pushed it away, but it was just like the grey light that seeps into the sky and extinguishes the stars: it crept past every barrier they could put up and under every blind and around the edges of every curtain they could draw against it.

"Every opening," Lyra said in a whisper.

"Every single one – they must all be closed?" said Will.

"Every single one," said Pantalaimon, whispering like Lyra.

"Oh, no," said Lyra. "No, it can't be true –"

"And so we must leave our world to stay in Lyra's," said Kirjava, "or Pan and Lyra must leave theirs and come to stay in ours. There's no other choice."

Then the full bleak daylight struck in.

And Lyra cried aloud. Pantalaimon's owl-cry the night before had frightened every small creature that heard it, but it was nothing to the passionate wail that Lyra uttered now. The dæmons were shocked, and Will, seeing their reaction, understood why: they didn't know the rest of the truth; they didn't know what Will and Lyra themselves had learnt.

Lyra was shaking with anger and grief, striding up and down with clenched fists and turning her tear-streaming face this way and that as if looking for an answer. Will jumped up and seized her shoulders, and felt her tense and trembling.

"Listen," he said, "Lyra, listen: what did my father say?"

"Oh," she cried, tossing her head this way and that, "he said – you know what he said – you were there, Will, you listened too!"

He thought she would die of her grief there and then. She flung herself into his arms and sobbed, clinging passionately to his shoulders, pressing her nails into his back and her face into his neck, and all he could hear was, "No – no – no..."

"Listen," he said again, "Lyra, let's try and remember it exactly. There might be a way through. There might be a loophole."

He disengaged her arms gently and made her sit down. At once Pantalaimon, frightened, flowed up on to her lap, and the cat-dæmon tentatively came close to Will. They hadn't touched yet, but now he put out a hand to her, and she moved her cat-face against his fingers and then stepped delicately on to his lap.

"He said –" Lyra began, gulping – "he said that people could spend a little time in other worlds without being affected. They could. And we have, haven't we? Apart from what we had to do to go into the world of the dead, we're still healthy, aren't we?"

"They can spend a little time, but not a long time," Will said. "My father had been away from his world, my world, for ten years. And he was nearly dying when I found him. Ten years, that's all."

"But what about Lord Boreal? Sir Charles? He was healthy enough, wasn't he?"

"Yes, but remember, he could go back to his own world whenever he liked and get healthy again. That's where you saw him first, after all, in your world. He must have found some secret window that no one else knew about."

"Well, we could do that!"

"We could, except that…"

"All the windows must be closed," said Pantalaimon. "All of them."

"But how do you *know*?" demanded Lyra.

"An angel told us," said Kirjava. "We met an angel. She told us all about that, and other things as well. It's true, Lyra."

"She?" said Lyra passionately, suspicious.

"It was a female angel," said Kirjava.

"I've never heard of one of them. Maybe she was lying."

Will was thinking through another possibility. "Suppose they closed all the other windows," he said, "and we just made one when we needed to, and went through as quickly as we could and closed it up immediately – that would be safe, surely? If we didn't leave much time for Dust to go out?"

"Yes!"

"We'd make it where no one could ever find it," he went on, "and only us two would know –"

"Oh, it would work! I'm sure it would!" she said.

"And we could go from one to the other, and stay healthy –"

But the dæmons were distressed, and Kirjava was murmuring, "No, no," and Pantalaimon said, "The Spectres… She told us about the Spectres, too."

"The Spectres?" said Will. "We saw them during the battle, for the first time. What about them?"

"Well, we found out where they come from," said Kirjava. "And this is the worst thing: they're like the children of the abyss. Every time we open a window with the knife, it makes a Spectre. It's like a little bit of the abyss that floats out and enters the world. That's why the Cittàgazze world was so full of them, because of all the windows they left open there."

"And they grow by feeding on Dust," said Pantalaimon. "And on dæmons. Because Dust and dæmons are sort of similar; grown-up dæmons anyway. And the Spectres get bigger and stronger as they do..."

Will felt a dull horror at his heart, and Kirjava pressed herself against his breast, feeling it too and trying to comfort him.

"So every time *I've* used the knife," he said, "every single time, I've made another Spectre come to life?"

He remembered Iorek Byrnison in the cave where he'd forged the knife again, saying, *What you don't know is what the knife does on its own. Your intentions may be good. The knife has intentions too.*

Lyra's eyes were watching him, wide with anguish.

"Oh, we *can't*, Will!" she said. "We can't do that to people – not let other Spectres out, not now we've seen what they do!"

"All right," he said, getting to his feet, holding his dæmon close to his breast. "Then we'll have to – one of us will have to – I'll come to your world and..."

She knew what he was going to say, and she saw him holding the beautiful healthy dæmon he hadn't even begun to know; and she thought of his mother, and she knew that he was thinking of her too. To abandon her and live with Lyra, even for the few years they'd have together – could he do that? He might be living with Lyra, but she knew he wouldn't be able to live with himself.

"No," she cried, jumping up beside him, and Kirjava

joined Pantalaimon on the sand as boy and girl clung together desperately: "*I'll* do it, Will! We'll come to your world and live there! It doesn't matter if we get ill, me and Pan – we're strong, I bet we last a good long time – and there are probably good doctors in your world – Dr Malone would know! Oh, let's do that!"

He was shaking his head, and she saw the brilliance of tears on his cheeks.

"D'you think I could bear that, Lyra?" he said. "D'you think I could live happily watching you get sick and ill and fade away and then die, while I was getting stronger and more grown-up day by day? Ten years... That's nothing. It'd pass in a flash. We'd be in our twenties. It's not that far ahead. Think of that, Lyra, you and me grown up, just preparing to do all the things we want to do – and then ... it all comes to an end. Do you think I could bear to live on after you died? Oh, Lyra, I'd follow you down to the world of the dead without thinking twice about it, just like you followed Roger; and that would be two lives gone for nothing, my life wasted like yours. No, we should spend our whole lifetimes together, good long busy lives, and if we can't spend them together, we ... we'll have to spend them apart."

Biting her lip, she watched him as he walked up and down in his distracted anguish.

He stopped and turned, and went on: "D'you remember another thing he said, my father? He said we have to build the republic of heaven where we are. He said that for us there isn't any elsewhere. That's what he meant, I can see now. Oh, it's too bitter. I thought he just meant Lord Asriel and his new world, but he meant us, he meant you and me. We have to live in our own worlds..."

"I'm going to ask the alethiometer," Lyra said. "That'll

know. I don't know why I didn't think of it before."

She sat down, wiping her cheeks with the palm of one hand, and reaching for the rucksack with the other. She carried it everywhere: when Will thought of her in later years, it was often with that little bag over her shoulder. She tucked the hair behind her ears in the swift movement he loved and took out the black velvet bundle.

"Can you see?" he said, for although the moon was bright, the symbols around the face were very small.

"I know where they all are," she said, "I got it off by heart. Hush now..."

She crossed her legs, pulling the skirt over them to make a lap. Will lay on one elbow and watched. The bright moonlight, reflected off the white sand, lit up her face with a radiance that seemed to draw out some other radiance from inside her; her eyes glittered, and her expression was so serious and absorbed that Will could have fallen in love with her again if love didn't already possess every fibre of his being.

Lyra took a deep breath and began to turn the wheels. But after only a few moments she stopped and turned the instrument around.

"Wrong place," she said briefly, and tried again.

Will, watching, saw her beloved face clearly. And because he knew it so well, and he'd studied her expression in happiness and despair and hope and sorrow, he could tell that something was wrong; for there was no sign of the clear concentration she used to sink into so quickly. Instead an unhappy bewilderment spread gradually over her: she bit her lower lip, she blinked more and more, and her eyes moved slowly from symbol to symbol, almost at random, instead of darting swiftly and certainly.

"I don't know," she said, shaking her head, "I don't know what's happening... I know it so well, but I can't seem to see what it means..."

She took a deep shuddering breath and turned the instrument around. It looked strange and awkward in her hands. Pantalaimon, mouse-formed, crept into her lap and rested his black paws on the crystal, peering at one symbol after another. Lyra turned one wheel, turned another, turned the whole thing round, and then looked up at Will, stricken.

"Oh, Will," she cried, "I can't do it! It's left me!"

"Hush," he said, "don't fret. It's still there inside you, all that knowledge. Just be calm and let yourself find it. Don't force it. Just sort of float down to touch it..."

She gulped and nodded and angrily brushed her wrist across her eyes, and took several deep breaths; but he could see she was too tense, and he put his hands on her shoulders and then felt her trembling and hugged her tight. She pulled back and tried again. Once more she gazed at the symbols, once more she turned the wheels, but those invisible ladders of meaning down which she'd stepped with such ease and confidence just weren't there. She just didn't know what any of the symbols meant.

She turned away and clung to Will and said desperately:

"It's no good – I can tell – it's gone for ever – it just came when I needed it, for all the things I had to do – for rescuing Roger, and then for us two – and now it's over, now everything's finished, it's just left me... I was afraid of that, because it's been so difficult – I thought I couldn't see it properly, or my fingers were stiff or something, but it wasn't that at all; the power was just leaving me, it was just fading away... Oh, it's gone, Will! I've lost it! It'll never come back!"

She sobbed with desperate abandon. All he could do was

hold her. He didn't know how to comfort her, because it was plain that she was right.

Then both the dæmons bristled, and looked up. Will and Lyra sensed it too, and followed their eyes to the sky. A light was moving towards them: a light with wings.

"It's the angel we saw," said Pantalaimon, guessing.

He guessed correctly. As the boy and the girl and the two dæmons watched her approach, Xaphania spread her wings wider, and glided down to the sand. Will, for all the time he'd spent in the company of Balthamos, wasn't prepared for the strangeness of this encounter. He and Lyra held each other's hands tightly as the angel came towards them, with the light of another world shining on her. She was unclothed, but that meant nothing: what clothes could an angel wear anyway, Lyra thought? It was impossible to tell if she was old or young, but her expression was austere and compassionate, and both Will and Lyra felt as if she knew them to their hearts.

"Will," she said, "I have come to ask your help."

"My help? How can I help you?"

"I want you to show me how to close the openings that the knife makes."

Will swallowed. "I'll show you," he said, "and in return, can you help us?"

"Not in the way you want. I can see what you've been talking about. Your sorrow has left traces in the air. This is no comfort, but believe me, every single being who knows of your dilemma wishes things could be otherwise: but there are fates that even the most powerful have to submit to. There is nothing I can do to help you change the way things are."

"Why —" Lyra began, and found her voice weak and trembling — "why can't I read the alethiometer any more?

Why can't I even do that? That was the one thing I could do really well, and it's just not there any more – it just vanished as if it had never come..."

"You read it by grace," said Xaphania, looking at her, "and you can regain it by work."

"How long will that take?"

"A lifetime."

"That long..."

"But your reading will be even better then, after a lifetime of thought and effort, because it will come from conscious understanding. Grace attained like that is deeper and fuller than grace that comes freely, and furthermore, once you've gained it, it will never leave you."

"You mean a *full* lifetime, don't you?" Lyra whispered. "A whole long life? Not ... not just ... a few years..."

"Yes, I do," said the angel.

"And *must* all the windows be closed?" said Will. "Every single one?"

"Understand this," said Xaphania: "Dust is not a constant. There's not a fixed quantity that has always been the same. Conscious beings make Dust – they renew it all the time, by thinking and feeling and reflecting, by gaining wisdom and passing it on.

"And if you help everyone else in your worlds to do that, by helping them to learn and understand about themselves and each other and the way everything works, and by showing them how to be kind instead of cruel, and patient instead of hasty, and cheerful instead of surly, and above all how to keep their minds open and free and curious... Then they will renew enough to replace what is lost through one window. So there could be one left open."

Will trembled with excitement, and his mind leapt to a

single point: to a new window in the air between his world and Lyra's. And it would be their secret, and they could go through whenever they chose, and live for a while in each other's worlds, not living fully in either, so their dæmons kept their health; and they could grow up together and maybe, much later on, they might have children who would be secret citizens of two worlds; and they could bring all the learning of one world into the other, they could do all kinds of good –

But Lyra was shaking her head.

"No," she said, in a quiet wail, "we can't, Will –"

And he suddenly knew her thought, and in the same anguished tone he said, "No, the dead –"

"We must leave it open for them! We must!"

"Yes, otherwise…"

"And we must make enough Dust for them, Will, and keep the window open –"

She was trembling. She felt very young as he held her to his side.

"And if we do," he said shakily, "if we live our lives properly and think about them as we do, then there'll be something to tell the harpies about, as well. We've got to tell people that, Lyra."

"For the true stories, yes," she said, "the true stories the harpies want to hear in exchange. Yes. So if people live their whole lives and they've got nothing to tell about it when they've finished, then they'll never leave the world of the dead. We've got to tell them that, Will."

"Alone, though…"

"Yes," she said, "alone."

And at the word *alone*, Will felt a great wave of rage and despair moving outwards from a place deep within him, as if his mind were an ocean that some profound convulsion had disturbed. All his life he'd been alone, and now he must be alone again, and this infinitely precious blessing that had come to him must be taken away almost at once. He felt the wave build higher and steeper to darken the sky, he felt the crest tremble and begin to spill, he felt the great mass crashing down with the whole weight of the ocean behind it against the iron-bound coast of what had to be. And he found himself gasping and shaking and crying aloud with more anger and pain than he had ever felt in his life, and he found Lyra just as helpless in his arms. But as the wave expended its force and the waters withdrew, the bleak rocks remained; there was no arguing with fate; neither his despair nor Lyra's had moved them a single inch.

How long his rage lasted, he had no idea. But eventually it had to subside, and the ocean was a little calmer after the convulsion. The waters were still agitated, and perhaps they would never be truly calm again, but the great force had gone.

They turned to the angel, and saw she had understood, and that she felt as sorrowful as they did. But she could see further than they could, and there was a calm hope in her expression too.

Will swallowed hard, and said, "All right. I'll show you how to close a window. But I'll have to open one first, and make another Spectre. I never knew about them, or else I'd have been more careful."

"We shall take care of the Spectres," said Xaphania.

Will took the knife, and faced the sea. To his surprise, his hands were quite steady. He cut a window into his own world, and they found themselves looking at a great factory or chemical plant, where complicated pipework ran between buildings and storage tanks, where lights glowed at every corner, where wisps of steam rose into the air.

"It's strange to think that angels don't know the way to do this," Will said.

"The knife was a human invention."

"And you're going to close them all except one," Will said. "All except the one from the world of the dead."

"Yes, that is a promise. But it is conditional, and you know the condition."

"Yes, we do. Are there many windows to close?"

"Thousands. There is the terrible abyss made by the bomb, and there is the great opening Lord Asriel made out of his own world. They must both be closed, and they will. But there are many smaller openings too, some deep under the earth, some high in the air, which came about in other ways."

"Baruch and Balthamos told me that they used openings like that to travel between the worlds. Will angels no longer be able to do that? Will you be confined to one world as we are?"

"No; we have other ways of travelling."

"The way you have," Lyra said, "is it possible for us to learn?"

"Yes. You could learn to do it, as Will's father did. It uses the faculty of what you call imagination. But that does not mean *making things up*. It is a form of seeing."

"Not *real* travelling, then," said Lyra. "Just pretend..."

"No," said Xaphania, "nothing like pretend. Pretending is easy. This way is hard, but much truer."

"And is it like the alethiometer?" said Will. "Does it take a whole lifetime to learn?"

"It takes long practice, yes. You have to work. Did you think you could snap your fingers, and have it as a gift? What is worth having is worth working for. But you have a friend who has already taken the first steps, and who could help you."

Will had no idea who that could be, and at that moment he wasn't in the mood to ask.

"I see," he said, sighing. "And will we see you again? Will we ever speak to an angel once we go back to our own worlds?"

"I don't know," said Xaphania. "But you should not spend your time waiting."

"And I should break the knife," said Will.

"Yes."

While they had been speaking, the window had been open beside them. The lights were glowing in the factory, the work was going on; machines were turning, chemicals were combining, people were producing goods and earning their livings. That was the world where Will belonged.

"Well, I'll show you what to do," he said.

So he taught the angel how to feel for the edges of the window, just as Giacomo Paradisi had shown him, sensing them at his fingers' ends and pinching them together. Little by little the window closed, and the factory disappeared.

"The openings that *weren't* made by the subtle knife," Will said. "Is it really necessary to close them all? Because surely Dust only escapes through the openings the knife made. The other ones must have been there for thousands of years, and still Dust exists."

The angel said, "We shall close them all, because if you thought that any still remained, you would spend your life searching for one, and that would be a waste of the time you have. You have other work than that to do, much more important and valuable, in your own world. There will be no travel outside it any more."

"What work have I got to do, then?" said Will, but went on at once, "No, on second thoughts, don't tell me. *I* shall decide what I do. If you say my work is fighting, or healing, or exploring, or whatever you might say, I'll always be thinking about it, and if I do end up doing that I'll be resentful because it'll feel as if I didn't have a choice, and if I don't do it, I'll feel guilty because I should. Whatever I do, I will choose it, no one else."

"Then you have already taken the first steps towards wisdom," said Xaphania.

"There's a light out at sea," said Lyra.

"That is the ship bringing your friends to take you home. They will be here tomorrow."

The word *tomorrow* fell like a heavy blow. Lyra had never thought she would be reluctant to see Farder Coram, and John Faa, and Serafina Pekkala.

"I shall go now," said the angel. "I have learned what I needed to know."

She embraced each of them in her light, cool arms, and kissed their foreheads. Then she bent to kiss the dæmons, and they became birds and flew up with her as she spread her wings and rose swiftly into the air. Only a few seconds later, she had vanished.

A few moments after she had gone, Lyra gave a little gasp.

"What is it?" said Will.

"I never asked her about my father and mother – and I can't ask the alethiometer, either, now... I wonder if I'll ever know?"

She sat down slowly, and he sat down beside her.

"Oh, Will," she said, "what can we do? Whatever can we do? I want to live with you for ever. I want to kiss you and lie down with you and wake up with you every day of my life till I die, years and years and years away. I don't want a memory, just a memory..."

"No," he said, "memory's a poor thing to have. It's your own real hair and mouth and arms and eyes and hands I want. I didn't know I could ever love anything so much. Oh, Lyra, I wish this night would never end! If only we could stay here like this, and the world could stop turning, and everyone else could fall into a sleep..."

"Everyone except us! And you and I could live here forever and just love each other."

"I *will* love you for ever, whatever happens. Till I die and after I die, and when I find my way out of the land of the dead I'll drift about for ever, all my atoms, till I find you again..."

"I'll be looking for you, Will, every moment, every single moment. And when we do find each other again we'll cling together so tight that nothing and no one'll ever tear us apart. Every atom of me and every atom of you... We'll live in birds and flowers and dragonflies and pine trees and in clouds and in those little specks of light you see floating in sunbeams... And when they use our atoms to make new lives, they won't just be able to take *one*, they'll have to take two, one of you and one of me, we'll be joined so tight..."

They lay side by side, hand in hand, looking at the sky.

"Do you remember," she whispered, "when you first came into that café in Ci'gazze, and you'd never seen a dæmon?"

"I couldn't understand what he was. But when I saw you I liked you straight away because you were brave."

"No, I liked you first."

"You didn't! You fought me!"

"Well," she said, "yes. But you attacked me."

"I did not! You came charging out and attacked *me*."

"Yes, but I soon stopped."

"Yes, but," he mocked softly.

He felt her tremble, and then under his hands the delicate bones of her back began to rise and fall and he heard her sob quietly. He stroked her warm hair, her tender shoulders, and then he kissed her face again and again, and presently she gave a deep shuddering sigh and fell still.

The dæmons flew back down now, and changed again, and came towards them over the soft sand. Lyra sat up to greet them, and Will marvelled at the way he could instantly tell which dæmon was which, never mind what form they had. Pantalaimon was now an animal whose name he couldn't quite find: like a large and powerful ferret, red-gold in colour, lithe and sinuous and full of grace. Kirjava was a cat again. But she was a cat of no ordinary size, and her fur was lustrous and rich, with a thousand different glints and shades of ink-black, shadow-grey, the blue of a deep lake under a noon sky, mist-lavender-moonlight-fog... To see the meaning of the word *subtlety* you had only to look at her fur.

"A marten," he said, finding the name for Pantalaimon, "a pine-marten."

"Pan," Lyra said as he flowed up on to her lap, "you're not going to change a lot any more, are you?"

"No," he said.

"It's funny," she said, "you remember when we were younger and I didn't want you to stop changing at all... Well, I wouldn't mind so much now. Not if you stay like this."

Will put his hand on hers. A new mood had taken hold of him, and he felt resolute and peaceful. Knowing exactly what he was doing and exactly what it would mean, he moved his hand from Lyra's wrist and stroked the red-gold fur of her dæmon.

Lyra gasped. But her surprise was mixed with a pleasure so like the joy that flooded through her when she had put the fruit to his lips that she couldn't protest, because she was breathless. With a racing heart she responded in the same way: she put her hand on the silky warmth of Will's dæmon, and as her fingers tightened in the fur she knew that Will was feeling exactly what she was.

And she knew too that neither dæmon would change now, having felt a lover's hands on them. These were their shapes for life: they would want no other.

So, wondering whether any lovers before them had made this blissful discovery, they lay together as the earth turned slowly and the moon and stars blazed above them.

38
The Botanic Garden

 *T*he gyptians arrived on the afternoon of the following day. There was no harbour, of course, so they had to anchor the ship some way out, and John Faa, Farder Coram, and the captain came ashore in a launch with Serafina Pekkala as their guide.

Mary had told the mulefa everything she knew, and by the time the gyptians were stepping ashore on to the wide beach, there was a curious crowd waiting to greet them. Each side, of course, was on fire with curiosity about the other, but John Faa had learned plenty of courtesy and patience in his long life, and he was determined that these strangest of all people should receive nothing but grace and friendship from the Lord of the western gyptians.

So he stood in the hot sun for some time while the old zalif, Sattamax, made a speech of welcome, which Mary translated as best she could; and John Faa replied, bringing them greetings from the Fens and the waterways of his homeland.

When they began to move up through the marshes to the village, the mulefa saw how hard it was for Farder Coram to walk, and at once they offered to carry him. He accepted gratefully, and so it was that they came to the gathering-ground, where Will and Lyra came to meet them.

Such an age had gone past since Lyra had seen these dear men! They'd last spoken together in the snows of the Arctic, on their way to rescue the children from the Gobblers. She was almost shy, and she offered her hand to shake, uncertainly; but John Faa caught her up in a tight embrace and kissed both her cheeks, and Farder Coram did the same, gazing at her before folding her tight to his chest.

"She's growed up, John," he said. "Remember that little girl we took to the north-lands? Look at her now, eh! Lyra, my dear, if I had the tongue of an angel, I couldn't tell you how glad I am to set eyes on you again."

But she looks so hurt, he thought, she looks so frail and weary. And neither he nor John Faa could miss the way she stayed close to Will, and how the boy with the straight black eyebrows was aware every second of where she was, and made sure he never strayed far from her.

The old men greeted him respectfully, because Serafina Pekkala had told them something of what Will had done. For Will's part, he admired the massive power of Lord Faa's presence, power tempered by courtesy, and he thought that that would be a good way to behave when he himself was old; John Faa was a shelter and a strong refuge.

"Dr Malone," said John Faa, "we need to take on fresh water, and whatever in the way of food your friends can sell us. Besides, our men have been on board ship for a fair while, and we've had some fighting to do, and it would be a blessing if they could all have a run ashore so they can breathe the air of this land and tell their families at home about the world they voyaged to."

"Lord Faa," said Mary, "the mulefa have asked me to say

they will supply everything you need, and that they would be honoured if you could all join them this evening to share their meal."

"It'll be our great pleasure to accept," said John Faa.

So that evening the people of three worlds sat down together and shared bread and meat and fruit and wine. The gyptians presented their hosts with gifts from all the corners of their world: with crocks of genniver, carvings of walrus ivory, silken tapestries from Turkestan, cups of silver from the mines of Sveden, enamelled dishes from Corea.

The mulefa received them with delight, and in return offered objects of their own workmanship: rare vessels of ancient knot-wood, lengths of the finest rope and cord, lacquered bowls, and fishing nets so strong and light that even the Fen-dwelling gyptians had never seen the like.

Having shared the feast, the captain thanked his hosts and left to supervise the crew as they took on board the stores and water that they needed, because they meant to sail as soon as morning came. While they were doing that, the old zalif said to his guests:

A great change has come over everything. And as a token, we have been granted a responsibility. We would like to show you what this means.

So John Faa, Farder Coram, Mary and Serafina went with them to the place where the land of the dead opened, and where the ghosts were coming out, still in their endless procession. The mulefa were planting a grove around it, because it was a holy place, they said; they would maintain it for ever; it was a source of joy.

"Well, this is a mystery," said Farder Coram, "and I'm glad I lived long enough to see it. To go into the dark of death is a thing we all fear, say what we like, we fear it. But if there's a way out for that part of us that has to go down there, then it makes my heart lighter."

"You're right, Coram," said John Faa. "I've seen a good many folk die; I've sent more than a few men down into the dark myself, though it was always in the anger of battle. To know that after a spell in the dark we'll come out again to a sweet land like this, to be free of the sky like the birds, well, that's the greatest promise anyone could wish for."

"We must talk to Lyra about this," said Farder Coram, "and learn how it came about, and what it means."

Mary found it very hard to say goodbye to Atal and the other mulefa. Before she boarded the ship, they gave her a gift: a lacquer phial containing some of the wheel-tree oil, and most precious of all, a little bag of seeds.

They might not grow in your world, Atal said, *but if not, you have the oil. Don't forget us, Mary.*

Never, Mary said. *Never. If I live as long as the witches and forget everything else, I'll never forget you and the kindness of your people, Atal.*

So the journey home began. The wind was light, the seas were calm, and although they saw the glitter of those great snow-white wings more than once, the birds were wary, and stayed well clear. Will and Lyra spent every hour together, and for them the two weeks of the voyage passed like the blink of an eyelid.

Xaphania had told Serafina Pekkala that when all the openings were closed, then the worlds would all be restored to their proper relations with one another, and Lyra's Oxford and Will's would lie over each other again, like transparent images on two sheets of film being moved closer and closer until they merged; although they would never truly touch.

At the moment, however, they were a long way apart – as far as Lyra had had to travel from her Oxford to Cittàgazze. Will's Oxford was here now, just a knife-cut away. It was evening when they arrived, and as the anchor splashed into the water, the late sun lay warmly on the green hills, the terracotta roofs, that elegant crumbling waterfront and Will and Lyra's little café. A long search through the captain's telescope had shown no signs of life whatsoever, but John Faa planned to take half a dozen armed men ashore just in case. They wouldn't get in the way, but they were there if they were needed.

They ate a last meal together, watching the darkness fall. Will said goodbye to the captain and his officers, and to John Faa and Farder Coram. He had hardly seemed to be aware of them, and they saw him more clearly than he saw them: they saw someone young, but very strong, and deeply stricken.

Finally Will and Lyra and their dæmons, and Mary and Serafina Pekkala, set off through the empty city. And it was empty; the only footfalls and the only shadows were their own. Lyra and Will went ahead, hand in hand, to the place where they had to part, and the women stayed some way behind, talking like sisters.

"Lyra wants to come a little way into my Oxford," Mary said. "She's got something in mind. She'll come straight back afterwards."

"What will you do, Mary?"

"Me – go with Will, of course. We'll go to my flat – my house – tonight, and then tomorrow we'll go and find out where his mother is, and see what we can do to help her get better. There are so many rules and regulations in my world, Serafina; you have to satisfy the authorities and answer a thousand questions; I'll help him with all the legal side of things and the social services and housing and all that, and let him concentrate on his mother. He's a strong boy... But I'll help him. Besides, I *need* him. I haven't got a job any more, and not much money in the bank, and I wouldn't be surprised if the police are after me... He'll be the only person in my whole world that I can talk to about all this."

They walked on through the silent streets, past a square tower with a doorway opening into darkness, past a little café where tables stood on the pavement, and out on to a broad boulevard with a line of palm trees in the centre.

"This is where I came through," said Mary.

The window Will had first seen in the quiet suburban road in Oxford opened here, and on the Oxford side it was guarded by police – or had been when Mary tricked them into letting her through. She saw Will reach the spot and move his hands deftly in the air, and the window vanished.

"That'll surprise them next time they look," she said.

It was Lyra's intention to go into Mary's Oxford and show Will something before returning with Serafina, and obviously they had to be careful where they cut through; so the women followed on behind, through the moonlit streets of Cittàgazze. On their right a wide and graceful parkland led up to a great house with a classical portico as brilliant as icing-sugar under the moon.

"When you told me the shape of my dæmon," Mary said, "you said you could teach me how to see him, if we had time... I wish we had."

"Well, we have had time," Serafina said, "and haven't we been talking? I've taught you some witch-lore, which would be forbidden under the old ways in my world. But you are going back to your world, and the old ways have changed.

And I too have learned much from you. Now then: when you spoke to the Shadows on your computer, you had to hold a special state of mind, didn't you?"

"Yes ... just as Lyra did with the alethiometer. Do you mean if I try that?"

"Not only that, but ordinary seeing at the same time. Try it now."

In Mary's world they had a kind of picture which looked at first like random dots of colour, but which, when you looked at it in a certain way, seemed to advance into three dimensions: and there in front of the paper would be a tree, or a face, or something else surprisingly solid that simply wasn't there before.

What Serafina taught Mary to do now was similar to that. She had to hold on to her normal way of looking while simultaneously slipping into the trance-like open dreaming in which she could see the Shadows. But now she had to hold both ways together, the everyday and the trance, just as you have to look in two directions at once to see the 3D pictures among the dots.

And just as it happens with the dot-pictures, she suddenly got it.

"Ah!" she cried, and reached for Serafina's arm to steady herself, for there on the iron fence around the parkland sat a bird: glossy-black, with red legs and a curved yellow bill: an Alpine chough, just as Serafina had described. It – he – was only a foot or two away, watching her with his head slightly cocked, for all the world as though he was amused.

But she was so surprised that her concentration slipped, and he vanished.

"You've done it once, and next time it will be easier,"

Serafina said. "When you are in your world, you will learn to see the dæmons of other people too, in the same way. They won't see yours or Will's, though, unless you teach them as I've taught you."

"Yes... Oh, this is extraordinary. Yes!"

Mary thought: Lyra talked to her dæmon, didn't she? Would she hear this bird as well as see him? She walked on, glowing with anticipation.

Ahead of them, Will was cutting a window, and he and Lyra waited for the women so that he could close it again.

"D'you know where we are?" Will said.

Mary looked around. The road they were in now, in her world, was quiet and tree-lined, with big Victorian houses in shrub-filled gardens.

"Somewhere in north Oxford," Mary said. "Not far from my flat, as a matter of fact, though I don't know exactly which road this is."

"I want to go to the Botanic Garden," Lyra said.

"All right. I suppose that's about fifteen minutes' walk. This way..."

Mary tried the double-seeing again. She found it easier this time, and there was the chough, with her in her own world, perching on a branch that hung low over the pavement. To see what would happen, she held out her hand, and he stepped on to it without hesitation. She felt the slight weight, the tight grip of the claws on her finger, and gently moved him on to her shoulder. He settled into place as if he'd been there all her life.

Well, he has, she thought, and moved on.

There was not much traffic in the High Street, and when they turned down the steps opposite Magdalen College towards the gate of the Botanic Garden they were completely alone.

There was an ornate gateway, with stone seats inside it, and while Mary and Serafina sat there, Will and Lyra climbed over the iron fence into the garden itself. Their dæmons slipped through the bars, and flowed ahead of them into the garden.

"It's this way," said Lyra, tugging at Will's hand.

She led him past a pool with a fountain under a wide-spreading tree, and then struck off to the left between beds of plants towards a huge many-trunked pine. There was a massive stone wall with a doorway in it, and in the further part of the garden the trees were younger and the planting less formal. Lyra led him almost to the end of the garden, over a little bridge, to a wooden seat under a spreading low-branched tree.

"Yes!" she said. "I hoped so much, and here it is, just the same... Will, I used to come here in *my* Oxford and sit on this exact same bench whenever I wanted to be alone, just me and Pan. What I thought was that if you – maybe just once a year – if we could come here at the same time, just for an hour or something, then we could pretend we were close again – because we *would* be close, if you sat here and I sat just *here* in my world –"

"Yes," he said, "as long as I live, I'll come back. Wherever I am in the world I'll come back here –"

"On Midsummer's Day," she said. "At midday. As long as I live. As long as I live..."

He found himself unable to see, but he let the hot tears flow and just held her close.

"And if we – later on –" she was whispering shakily – "if we meet someone that we like, and if we marry them, then we must be good to them, and not make comparisons all the time and wish we were married to each other instead... But just keep up this coming here once a year, just for an hour, just to be together..."

They held each other tightly. Minutes passed; a water-bird on the river beside them stirred and called; the occasional car moved over Magdalen Bridge.

Finally they drew apart.

"Well," said Lyra softly.

Everything about her in that moment was soft; and that was one of his favourite memories later on – her tense grace made tender by the dimness, her eyes and hands and especially her lips, infinitely soft. He kissed her again and again, and each kiss was nearer to the last one of all.

Heavy and soft with love, they walked back to the gate. Mary and Serafina were waiting.

"Lyra –" Will said, and she said, "Will."

He cut a window into Cittàgazze. They were deep in the parkland around the great house, not far from the edge of the forest. They stepped through for the last time, and looked down over the silent city, the tiled roofs gleaming in the moonlight, the tower above them, the lighted ship waiting out on the still sea.

Will turned to Serafina and said as steadily as he could, "Thank you, Serafina Pekkala, for rescuing us at the belvedere, and for everything else. Please be kind to Lyra for as long as she lives. I love her more than anyone has ever been loved."

In answer the witch-queen kissed him on both cheeks. Lyra had been whispering to Mary, and then they too embraced, and first Mary and then Will stepped through the last window, back into their own world, in the shade of the trees of the Botanic Garden.

Being cheerful starts *now*, Will thought as hard as he

could, but it was like trying to hold a fighting wolf still in his arms when it wanted to claw at his face and tear out his throat; nevertheless he did it, and he thought no one could see the effort it cost him.

And he knew that Lyra was doing the same, and that the tightness and strain in her smile were the sign of it.

Nevertheless, she smiled.

One last kiss, rushed and clumsy so that they banged cheekbones, and a tear from her eye was transferred to his face; their two dæmons kissed farewell, and Pantalaimon flowed over the threshold and up into Lyra's arms; and then Will began to close the window, and then it was done, the way was closed, Lyra was gone.

"Now –" he said, trying to sound matter-of-fact, but having to turn away from Mary all the same – "I've got to break the knife."

He searched the air in the familiar way until he found a gap, and tried to bring to mind just what had happened before. He had been about to cut a way out of the cave, and Mrs Coulter had suddenly and unaccountably reminded him of his mother, and the knife had broken because, he thought, it had at last met something it couldn't cut, and that was his love for her.

So he tried it now, summoning an image of his mother's face as he'd last seen her, fearful and distracted in Mrs Cooper's little hallway.

But it didn't work. The knife cut easily through the air, and opened into a world where they were having a rainstorm: heavy drops hurtled through, startling them both. He closed it again quickly, and stood puzzled for a moment.

His dæmon knew what he should do, and said simply, "Lyra."

Of course. He nodded, and with the knife in his right hand, he pressed with his left the spot where her tear still lay on his cheek.

And this time, with a wrenching crack, the knife shattered and the blade fell in pieces to the ground, to glitter on the stones that were still wet with the rain of another universe.

Will knelt to pick them up carefully, Kirjava with her cat-eyes helping to find them all.

Mary was shouldering her rucksack.

"Well," she said, "well, listen now, Will. We've hardly spoken, you and I... So we're still strangers, largely. But Serafina Pekkala and I made a promise to each other, and I made a promise to Lyra just now, and even if I hadn't made any other promises I'd make a promise to you about the same thing, which is that if you'll let me, I'll be your friend for the rest of our lives. We're both on our own, and I reckon we could both do with that sort of... What I mean to say is, there isn't anyone else we can *talk* to about all this, except each other... And we've both got to get used to living with our dæmons, too... And we're both in trouble, and if *that* doesn't give us something in common I don't know what will."

"You're in trouble?" said Will, looking at her. Her open, friendly, clever face looked back directly.

"Well, I smashed up some property in the lab before I left, and I forged an identity card, and... It's nothing we can't deal with. And your trouble – we can deal with that too. We can find your mother and get her some proper treatment. And if you need somewhere to live, well, if you wouldn't mind living with me, if we can arrange that, then you won't have to go into, whatever they call it, into care. I mean, we'll have to decide on a story and stick to it, but we could do that, couldn't we?"

Mary was a friend. He had a friend. It was true. He'd never thought of that.

"Yes!" he said.

"Well, let's do it. My flat's about half a mile away, and you know what I'd like most of all in the world? I'd like a cup of tea. Come on, let's go and put the kettle on."

Three weeks after the moment Lyra had watched Will's hand closing his world away for ever, she found herself seated once more at that dinner table in Jordan College where she had first fallen under the spell of Mrs Coulter.

This time it was a smaller party: just herself and the Master and Dame Hannah Relf, the head of St Sophia's, one of the women's colleges. Dame Hannah had been at that first dinner, too, and if Lyra was surprised to see her here now, she greeted her politely, and found that her memory was at fault: for this Dame Hannah was much cleverer, and more interesting, and kindlier by far than the dim and frumpy person she remembered.

All kinds of things had happened while Lyra was away – to Jordan College, to England, to the whole world. It seemed that the power of the Church had increased greatly, and that many brutal laws had been passed, but that the power had waned as quickly as it had grown: upheavals in the Magisterium had toppled the zealots and brought more liberal factions into power. The General Oblation Board had been dissolved; the Consistorial Court of Discipline was confused and leaderless.

And the colleges of Oxford, after a brief and turbulent interlude, were settling back into the calm of scholarship and ritual. Some things had gone: the Master's valuable collection of silver had been looted; some college servants had vanished.

The Master's manservant, Cousins, was still in place, however, and Lyra had been ready to meet his hostility with defiance, for they had been enemies as long as she could remember. She was quite taken aback when he greeted her so warmly and shook her hand with both of his: was that affection in his voice? Well, he *had* changed.

During dinner the Master and Dame Hannah talked of what had happened in Lyra's absence, and she listened in dismay, or sorrow, or wonder. When they withdrew to his sitting-room for coffee, the Master said:

"Now, Lyra, we've hardly heard from you. But I know you've seen many things. Are you able to tell us something of what you've experienced?"

"Yes," she said. "But not all at once. I don't understand some of it, and some makes me shudder and cry still; but I will tell you, I promise, as much as I can. Only you have to promise something too."

The Master looked at the grey-haired lady with the marmoset-dæmon in her lap, and a flicker of amusement passed between them.

"What's that?" said Dame Hannah.

"You have to promise to believe me," Lyra said seriously. "I know I haven't always told the truth, and I could only *survive* in some places by telling lies and making up stories. So I know that's what I've been like, and I know you know it, but my true story's too important for me to tell if you're only going to believe half of it. So I promise to tell the truth, if you promise to believe it."

"Well, I promise," said Dame Hannah, and the Master said, "And so do I."

"But you know the thing I wish," Lyra said, "almost – *almost* more than anything else? I wish I hadn't lost the way of reading the alethiometer. Oh, it was so strange, Master, how it came in the first place and then just left! One day I knew it so well – I could move up and down the symbol-meanings and step from one to another and make all the connections – it was like…" She smiled, and went on, "Well, I was like a monkey in the trees, it was so quick. Then suddenly – nothing. None of it made sense; I couldn't even remember anything except just basic meanings like the anchor means hope and the skull means death. All those thousands of meanings… Gone."

"They're not gone, though, Lyra," said Dame Hannah. "The books are still in Bodley's Library. The scholarship to study them is alive and well."

Dame Hannah was sitting opposite the Master in one of the two armchairs beside the fireplace, Lyra on the sofa between them. The lamp by the Master's chair was all the light there was, but it showed the expressions of the two old people clearly. And it was Dame Hannah's face that Lyra found herself studying. Kindly, Lyra thought, and sharp, and wise; but she could no more read what it meant than she could read the alethiometer.

"Well now," the Master went on. "We must think about your future, Lyra."

His words made her shiver. She gathered herself and sat up.

"All the time I was away," Lyra said, "I never thought about that. All I thought about was just the time I was in, just the present. There were plenty of times when I thought I didn't have a future at all. And now… Well, suddenly finding I've got a whole life to live, but no … but no idea what to do with it, well, it's like having the alethiometer but no idea how to read it. I suppose I'll have to work, but I don't know at what. My parents are probably rich but I bet they never thought of putting any money aside for me, and anyway I think they must have used all their money up one way or another by now, so even if I did have a claim on it, there wouldn't be any left. I don't know, Master. I came back to Jordan because this used to be my home, and I didn't have anywhere else to go. I think King Iorek Byrnison would let me live on Svalbard, and I think Serafina Pekkala would let me live with her witch-clan; but I'm not a bear and I'm not a witch, so I wouldn't really fit in there, much as I love them. Maybe the gyptians would take me in... But really I don't know what to do any more. I'm lost, really, now."

They looked at her: her eyes were glittering more than usual, her chin was held high with a look she'd learned from Will without knowing it. She looked defiant as well as lost, Dame Hannah thought, and admired her for it; and the Master saw something else – he saw how the child's unconscious grace had gone, and how she was awkward in her growing body. But he loved the girl dearly, and he felt half proud and half in awe of the beautiful adult she would be, so soon.

He said, "You will never be lost while this college is standing, Lyra. This is your home for as long as you need it. As for money – your father made over an endowment to care for all your needs, and appointed me executor; so you needn't worry about that."

In fact Lord Asriel had done nothing of the sort, but Jordan College was rich, and the Master had money of his own, even after the recent upheavals.

"No," he went on, "I was thinking about learning. You're still very young, and your education until now has depended on... Well, quite frankly, on which of our scholars you intimidated least," he said, but he was smiling. "It's been haphazard. Now it may turn out that in due course your talents will take you in a direction we can't foresee at all. But if you were to make the alethiometer the subject of your life's work, and set out to learn consciously what you could once do by intuition –"

"Yes," said Lyra, definitely.

"– then you could hardly do better than put yourself in the hands of my good friend Dame Hannah. Her scholarship in that field is unmatched."

"Let me make a suggestion," said the lady, "and you needn't respond now. Think about it for a while. Now my college is not as old as Jordan, and you're too young yet to become an undergraduate in any case, but a few years ago we acquired a large house in north Oxford, and we decided to set up a boarding school. I'd like you to come and meet the Headmistress and see whether you'd care to become one of our pupils. You see, one thing you'll need soon, Lyra, is the friendship of other girls of your age. There are things that we learn from one another when we're young, and I don't think that Jordan can provide quite all of them. The Headmistress is a clever young woman, energetic, imaginative, kindly. We're lucky to have her. You can talk to her, and if you like the idea, come and make St Sophia's your school, as Jordan is your home. And if you'd like to begin studying the alethiometer systematically, you and I could meet for some private lessons. But there's time, my dear, there's plenty of time. Don't answer me now. Leave it until you're ready."

"Thank you," said Lyra, "thank you, Dame Hannah, I will."

The Master had given Lyra her own key to the garden door, so she could come and go as she pleased. Later that night, just as the porter was locking the lodge, she and Pantalaimon slipped out and made their way through the dark streets, hearing all the bells of Oxford chiming midnight.

Once they were in the Botanic Garden, Pan ran away over the grass chasing a mouse towards the wall, and then let it go and sprang up into the huge pine tree nearby. It was delightful to see him leaping through the branches so far from her, but they had to be careful not to do it when anyone was looking; their painfully-acquired witch-power of separating had to stay a secret. Once, she would have revelled in showing it off to all her urchin friends, and making them goggle with fear, but Will had taught her the value of silence and discretion.

She sat on the bench and waited for Pan to come to her. He liked to surprise her, but she usually managed to see him before he reached her, and there was his shadowy form, flowing along beside the river-bank. She looked the other way and pretended she hadn't seen him, and then seized him suddenly when he leapt on to the bench.

"I nearly did it," he said.

"You'll have to get better than that. I heard you coming all the way from the gate."

He sat on the back of the bench with his forepaws resting on her shoulder.

"What are we going to tell her?" he said.

"We'll say yes," she said. "It's only to meet this Headmistress, anyway. It's not to go to the school."

"But we will go, won't we?"

"Yes," she said, "probably."

"It might be good."

Lyra wondered about the other pupils. They might be cleverer than she was, or more sophisticated, and they were sure to know a lot more than she did about all the things that were important to girls of their age. And she wouldn't be able to tell them a hundredth of the things that she knew. They'd be bound to think she was simple and ignorant.

"D'you think Dame Hannah can really do the alethiometer?" said Pantalaimon.

"With the books, I'm sure she can. I wonder how many books there are? I bet we could learn them all, and do without. Imagine having to carry a pile of books everywhere... Pan?"

"What?"

"Will you ever tell me what you and Will's dæmon did, when we were apart?"

"One day," he said. "And she'll tell Will, one day. We agreed that we'd know when the time had come, but we wouldn't tell either of you till then."

"All right," she said peaceably.

She had told Pantalaimon everything, but it was right that he should have some secrets from her, after the way she'd abandoned him.

And it was comforting to think that she and Will had another thing in common. She wondered whether there would ever come an hour in her life when she didn't think of him; didn't speak to him in her head, didn't relive every moment they'd been together, didn't long for his voice and his hands and his love. She had never dreamed of what it would feel like to love someone so much; of all the things that had astonished her in her adventures, that was what astonished her the most. She thought the tenderness it left in her heart was like a bruise that would never go away, but she would cherish it for ever.

Pan slipped down to the bench and curled up on her lap. They were safe together in the dark, she and her dæmon and their secrets. Somewhere in this sleeping city were the books that would tell her how to read the alethiometer again, and the kindly and learned woman who was going to teach her, and the girls at the school, who knew so much more than she did.

She thought: they don't know it yet, but they're going to be my friends.

Pantalaimon murmured, "That thing that Will said..."

"When?"

"On the beach, just before you tried the alethiometer. He said there wasn't any elsewhere. It was what his father had told you. But there was something else."

"I remember. He meant the kingdom was over, the kingdom of heaven, it was all finished. We shouldn't live as if it mattered more than this life in this world, because where we are is always the most important place."

"He said we had to build something..."

"That's why we needed our full life, Pan. We *would* have gone with Will and Kirjava, wouldn't we?"

"Yes. Of course! And they would have come with us. But –"

"But then we wouldn't have been able to build it. No one could, if they put themselves first. We have to be all those difficult things like cheerful and kind and curious and brave and patient, and we've got to study and think, and work hard, all of us, in all our different worlds, and then we'll build..."

Her hands were resting on his glossy fur. Somewhere in the garden a nightingale was singing, and a little breeze touched her hair and stirred the leaves overhead. All the different bells of the city chimed, once each, this one high, that one low, some close by, others further off, one cracked and peevish, another grave and sonorous, but agreeing in all their different voices on what the time was, even if some of them got to it a little more slowly than others. In that other Oxford where she and Will had kissed goodbye, the bells would be chiming too, and a nightingale would be singing, and a little breeze would be stirring the leaves in the Botanic Garden.

"And then what?" said her dæmon sleepily. "Build what?"

"The republic of heaven," said Lyra.

Acknowledgements

His Dark Materials could not have come into existence at all without the help and encouragement of friends, family, books and strangers.

I owe these people specific thanks: Liz Cross, for her meticulous and tirelessly cheerful editing of every stage of the work, and for a certain brilliant notion concerning pictures in *The Subtle Knife*; Anne Wallace-Hadrill, for letting me see over her narrow boat; Richard Osgood, of the University of Oxford Archaeological Institute, for telling me how archaeological expeditions are arranged; Michael Malleson, of the Trent Studio Forge, Dorset, for showing me how to forge iron; and Mike Froggatt and Tanaqui Weaver, for bringing me more of the right sort of paper (with two holes in it) when my stock was running low. I must also praise the café at the Oxford Museum of Modern Art. Whenever I was stuck with a problem in the narrative, a cup of their coffee and an hour or so's work in that friendly room would dispel it, apparently without effort on my part. It never failed.

I have stolen ideas from every book I have ever read. My principle in researching for a novel is "Read like a butterfly, write like a bee", and if this story contains any honey, it is entirely because of the quality of the nectar I found in the work of better writers. But there are three debts that need acknowledgement above all the rest. One is to the essay *On the Marionette Theatre* by Heinrich von Kleist, which I first read in a translation by Idris Parry in the *Times Literary Supplement* in 1978. The second is to John Milton's *Paradise Lost*. The third is to the works of William Blake.

Finally, my greatest debts. To David Fickling, and to his inexhaustible faith and encouragement as well as his sure and vivid sense of how stories can be made to work better, I owe much of what success this work has achieved; to Caradoc King I owe more than half a lifetime of unfailing friendship and support; to Enid Jones, the teacher who introduced me so long ago to *Paradise Lost*, I owe the best that education can give, the notion that responsibility and delight can co-exist; to my wife Jude, and to my sons Jamie and Tom, I owe everything else under the sun.

Philip Pullman